PRAISE FOR RICHARD ZIMLER'S

HUNTING MIDNIGHT

"A PAGE-TURNING STORY OF CRUELTY, CONSPIRACY, HUNTING AND ESCAPE, PLOT-DRIVEN IN A WAY THAT MAKES YOU READ MORE GREEDILY, EAGER TO GET TO THE END...BRAVE [AND] INTERESTING...A DELICATE EXPLORATION OF THE WAYS IN WHICH REPRESSED RELIGION AND CULTURE SHAPE EXPERIENCE, IDENTITY AND LOSS."
—SARAH DUNANT, BESTSELLING AUTHOR OF *THE BIRTH OF VENUS*

"AN AMBITIOUS HISTORICAL EPIC...FROM A SUPERBLY TALENTED HISTORICAL NOVELIST, CAPABLE OF COMBINING FASCINATING BROAD-CANVAS GLIMPSES OF HISTORY WITH THE MOST INTIMATE PORTRAITS OF THE HUMAN HEART IN TURMOIL." —*BOOKLIST*

"FROM MIDNIGHT'S FIRST WORDS...THE READER IS CHARMED. [ZIMLER'S] ABILITY TO LAY BARE THE HORROR OF INJUSTICE, TO FIND UNIVERSAL TRUTHS AND POETRY IN EVERYDAY EXISTENCE, AND HIS FAITH IN THE HUMAN SPIRIT, MAKE READING *HUNTING MIDNIGHT* AN UPLIFTING EXPERIENCE."
—*JERUSALEM POST*

"A TALE THAT IS AS FULL OF MEMORABLE CHARAC-TERS AS IT IS OF SPIRITUAL LESSONS...ZIMLER COVERS THE DISTANCE FROM INNOCENCE TO SELF-KNOWLEDGE WITH DEEP INSIGHT, TOLD IN A RICHLY

POETIC STYLE THAT MAKES READING THIS TALE A TRUE LITERARY EXPERIENCE." —*HADASSAH MAGAZINE*

"Mysterious, involving as it does many secrets . . . Midnight, noble and poetic, steals every scene he's in. . . . There's a lot of plot, most of it juicy." —*Detroit Free Press*

"ZIMLER BRINGS TOGETHER DIVERSE ISSUES . . . AND FOLDS THEM INTO [AN] INTENSELY PERSONAL STORY OF LOVE AND BETRAYAL. HIS GRIPPING TALE IS STRONGLY RECOMMENDED." —*LIBRARY JOURNAL*

"FROM THE BOISTEROUS AND COLOURFUL PORTUGUESE CITY MARKETS TO THE LUSH PLANTATIONS OF COLONIAL AMERICA, THIS NOVEL IS A POWERFUL STORY OF LOYALTY AND THE RELATIONSHIPS THAT BINDS ONE TOGETHER." —*JEWISH ADVOCATE*

"The plot races thrillingly along." —*Los Angeles Times*

"Reading *Hunting Midnight* was like discovering a rare gem. Richard Zimler is a brilliant author with a touch of genius." —*Rendezvous*

"A MOVING STORY OF LOSS AND BETRAYAL . . . *HUNTING MIDNIGHT* SHOWS ZIMLER AT THE HEIGHT OF HIS POWERS. . . . ZIMLER IS A NOVELIST OF INNER LIFE, WHO SETS HIS BOOKS FIRMLY IN SOCIAL AND HISTORICAL CONTEXT." —*LONDON MAGAZINE*

"The novel has [a] mythic resonance. . . . An enthralling evocation of childhood . . . The smooth, calm flow of his prose highlights effectively the ferocity of his themes. . . . Zimler describes the world as it is, harsh and cruel. Then he shows us its beauty and how we can change and grow. It's the best sort of political novel, one that is accessible and does not preach." —*Independent* (UK)

"A RIGOROUSLY RESEARCHED work of historical fiction . . . Dramatic." —Andrew Solomon, winner of the National Book Award, 2001

"IN HIS COMPELLING AND DEEPLY MOVING NOVEL, RICHARD ZIMLER WEAVES A GORGEOUS TAPESTRY OF RICH HISTORICAL AND IMAGINATIVE DETAIL, IN WHICH THE HUMAN SPIRIT TRANSCENDS EVEN THE DARKEST ABUSES AND BETRAYALS. THE UNFORGETTABLE CHARACTERS OF *HUNTING MIDNIGHT* WILL BREAK AND MEND YOUR HEART." —ELIZABETH ROSNER, WINNER OF THE RIBALOW JEWISH FICTION AWARD 2002 FOR *THE SPEED OF LIGHT*

"A wonderful novel that spans generations and crosses continents, told with an unforgettable narration. An epic story that—through a quest for personal identity—carries the reader into the mysterious world of the secret ews of portugal in the 19th century. Better than any history text I know, it contains all the ingredients of a bestseller, to the great delight of Zimler's fans—including me!" —Esther Benbassa, professor of Jewish history at the Université de Paris IV, Sorbonne, and director of research at the Centre National de Recherche Scientifique

GUARDIAN
OF THE
DAWN

RICHARD ZIMLER

DELTA TRADE PAPERBACKS

GUARDIAN OF THE DAWN
A Delta Trade Paperback / August 2005

Published by
Bantam Dell
A Division of Random House, Inc.
New York, New York

Book design by Glen Edelstein

Delta is a registered trademark of Random House, Inc., and the colophon is a trademark of Random House, Inc.

Library of Congress Cataloging-in-Publication Data

Zimler, Richard.
Guardian of the dawn / Richard Zimler.
p. cm.
ISBN 0-385-33881-3
1. Fathers and sons—Fiction. 2. Jewish families—Fiction. 3. Jews—India—Fiction. 4. Inquisition—Fiction. 5. Prisoners—Fiction. 6. Young men—Fiction. 7. India—History—1526–1765—Fiction. 8. Historical fiction. 9. Jewish fiction.

PS3576.I464 G83 2005
813/.54 22   2004058240

Printed in the United States of America
Published simultaneously in Canada

www.bantamdell.com

BVG   10 9 8 7 6 5 4 3 2 1

To the many thousands of men, women, and children who were imprisoned by the Inquisition in India.

ACKNOWLEDGMENTS

I am greatly indebted to Kate Miciak for her wonderful (and passionate!) editing, and to Cynthia Cannell for her unwavering support.

Alexandre Quintanilha and Ruth G. Zimler have been kind enough to read early drafts of all my novels and I am once again grateful for their insightful comments. I am also indebted to Joanne Gruber for answering all my questions about grammar.

Personal thanks to two generous literary critics, Michael Eaude and Helena Vasconcelos, and to W.S. for inspiring me (with all he left unexplained!) to embark on this project.

Lastly, I wish to express my admiration for all those extraordinarily courageous people who dared to write about their experiences while prisoners of the Inquisition, particularly Charles Dellon. I could not have written this book without their words.

GUARDIAN OF THE DAWN

PREFACE

What do you think memory is made of?" my father asked me. From the moist tenderness in his downturned eyes and his hand quivering on my shoulder I knew that my mother was caressing his thoughts. Her funeral had been more than two years earlier, and it was a measure of his continuing grief that he put so adult a question to a boy of seven.

"I don't know, Papa," I replied with a shrug, too young to think it worth my while to hazard a guess. But when he withdrew his hand, fear batted its wings at my ears. "Maybe it's made of everything I ever saw," I rushed to add, hoping this was a good enough answer to get him to carry me out to the verandah, where we could watch Indra's great red sun set over the rim of our world.

He considered my reply for a long time, bowing his head and closing his eyes, as though eavesdropping on a distant conversation. At length, he lifted his eyebrows. "But what about the mice who've lived so long in our windows?" he asked.

My gut squeezed into a knot of worry, since I couldn't imagine what he meant, but then he winked at me to let me know that this was only one of his riddles. Amusement radiated from his clear gray eyes and made me feel protected, as though his arms were tight around me.

"Where are the mice? Show me!" I begged, pressing into him with my urgency.

He eased open the wooden shutters, each of which gave a sharp, fugitive squeal. Rubbing at his eyes with make-believe paws, he wrinkled his nose and bent down to me, sniffing greedily at my cheek.

Giggling helplessly, I wriggled away. "You make a good mouse, Papa," I told him.

"I'm glad I'm good for something. Now, what about all that squeaking? And all the voices you've ever heard?" He tapped the top of my head. "They're in there, too, aren't they?" he questioned.

I gave him a big nod and he leaned out the window, breathing in deeply, giving thanks in his silent way for the gold-glowing rice fields and soft, pink clouds. I sometimes think Papa felt most himself when observing the world's colors. We were always alike in that way—drawn out to the world through our eyes.

"It seems our mice have brought the wind from the east this evening," he said contentedly. "And the wind must have asked the forest to send us its scents." He shook his head, astonished by these simple things, and picked up Mama's teakwood hairbrush from the desk behind him. He gripped it in his hands as though it gave him life, and I knew he was about to leave me for his room, where he could sit alone with his memories of her.

"Is something wrong, Papa?" I asked.

"No, it's just . . . Ti, you know I am almost forty-one now. And even so, I can remember all the odors of Constantinople as if I were still living there."

My name was Tiago but everyone in my family called me Ti.

Papa looked beyond me into his boyhood and rubbed the front of his bristly hair, which was already gray. "How I used to love the

mounds of saffron and cloves in the Grand Bazaar," he said dream-
ily. "And the scent of your grandfather's woolen robe when it
rained—all mossy and dark. And the baklava in the bakeries. It
made everything smell like honey, even the light reflecting off the
Golden Horn. How do you think all those different things remain
inside us for years?"

"Maybe they stick to something," I suggested.

He drew his head back in surprise. "So," he replied, frowning
angrily, "you think God coats our souls with glue? Tell me, are my
questions some sort of joke to you?"

Papa glared at me and flung the brush away with an assassin's
force. It whizzed past my head and hit behind me with a thud that
made my heart jump. The next day I noticed a splintered crack on
the left ear of the life-sized, eight-armed statue of Shiva that guarded
our doorway. I'd guess now that damaging the wooden god was
Papa's precise intention; the statue had been Mama's most beloved
part of her dowry.

The nick on Shiva's ear would forever remind me of this quarrel,
and of my mother's enduring place in our lives, but at that moment
I didn't dare look back to see what had happened, because my father's eyes still flashed with rage. I was flooding with tears of misery,
and I must have tried to run off; even now I can feel the urgent ten-
sion between us when he grabbed my wrist, as though a rope were
stretched to its limit.

He kneeled beside me, his eyes sunken.

"Don't hit me!" I pleaded.

He had never laid a hand on me, but since Mama's death I no
longer knew who he was at times.

"What have I done?" he moaned. "Forgive me, Ti." He kissed
me all over, and the tickling of his unshaven cheeks brought my faith
in him back to me. When I was very young, my moods were easily
changed with a diversion, and he cheered me up by simply button-
ing my shirt. By the time he was done, his ink-stained fingers—

moving delicately and quickly against my skin—had returned meaning to my world. "Maybe you're right," he said, taking my hands and swinging them between us like the cord bridge below the waterfall near Ponda when it was rocked by the wind. "God has made our soul sticky, and what stays on it is what we always remember."

He swept me up onto his lap, and for a long time we gazed out the window together, his head over my shoulder, his breathing hot on my ear. He sniffed at my hair like a mouse again, and I squirmed happily inside his embrace.

The first stars soon began to tremble over the tops of the palms, which fanned the just-risen moon with the cool breezes of the descending dusk. I waited for the echo of my father's words to fade completely into the swelling darkness, sensing I would dare to say something new about myself as soon as they were gone. But what? My existence pulsed around me as it never had before, was as present to me as my heartbeat, which was much deeper than normal, as though needing to be heard. I closed my eyes and saw the sun as it had been a few minutes earlier, a red crescent melting over an undulating blanket of hills along the horizon—melting over the endlessly ticking edge of another day of my life, as well. I was Tiago and I was my father's son. Were the world and I separate or the same?

I shuddered. "I feel alone, Papa."

He kissed me and held me tight. I ceded myself to him, along with all I would ever become. As I thought of Mama's hairbrush lying abandoned on the floor, my breaths came heavily, but also with expectation, as if her absence were a golden weight on my chest. I hopped down to retrieve it, then climbed back up onto his lap. He began to comb my hair and said something that I knew would be bound forever to my soul: "You will never be alone, Ti, because I'll always be with you." He moved his hand in an arc to indicate the moonlight that was turning the palms to silver-tipped feathers. "And so will all this."

*   *   *

While confined in my cell in Goa, I often thought of Papa's promise, wondering if he had lied to me on purpose. Or had he meant that my memory of him would outlive his death and always reside inside me? If so, he should have warned me that it would not be enough to save me.

CHAPTER 1

After my arrest in November of 1591, I spoke to no one but my prison guard for nearly eleven months. I was neither informed of the charges against me nor allowed anything to read, and my window, a grudging slit in barren stone, was too high up to allow me a glimpse of the city below. Hope clung to memories of Tejal, and sometimes, too, to the drumming of rain, which reminded me there was a world beyond the control of my jailors. Once, during a storm, I licked a few drops as they scurried down my wall. They tasted of Indra's Millstream and, for a time, my thoughts were splashed with all my childhood freedom, but I often think they betrayed me in the end: I was robbed of God that very night; awoke to find myself more alone than I'd ever been before, banished from the world He'd always watched over. I'd never again feel my toes curl through the red earth of rice fields or learn whether Tejal had given birth to a son or daughter.

Apologizing silently to Papa for not making the better life he'd wished for me, I reached for the treasure made of rust and sharpness I'd hidden at the bottom of my earthenware chamber pot weeks before. Sniffing its holy scent of metallic purpose, counting on defeat as my last friend, I drew it across one arm and then the other. My final portrait would be warm, and designed in my own blood, as it should be.

I knew I was damned when not even my prayers could make the nail dig deeply enough in my life to create the miracle I needed. Still, I bled well, and the river that lies beyond the Sabbath carried me far in its current. Laying my head into the justice of its waters, I dreamed of a horizon of pine and cedar far in the west, on the banks of the Jordan River.

Tejal would be informed of my death; she would now be free to marry another man. That was worth this price I had to pay.

I awoke with a jolt to a sweating priest I'd never seen before knotting rough cords around my arms. I begged him to leave me be, but he continued his work and dumped me with a grunt of disgust onto my cot. I tugged at his rosaries to try to break my fall, sending the beads scurrying over the floor.

"Mulatto bastard!" he shouted at me. "We'll get a confession from you yet!"

No, I thought, in the voice of the child I'd been. *Even though I am not what I was, there's still too much glue on my soul for it to leave me so easily.*

Two guards hunted on all fours for the beads—men turned to groveling boars by the incantation of my contempt. For no reason I could think of I began to paint the stripes of a tiger on my face with blood from my wrists. Later I remembered Wadi's nickname for me and thought: *Yes, I need to become another kind of being, someone ferocious, for if I don't, I shall name others and sentence them to my fate.*

It was my father who had told me that our Dominican and Jesuit masters craved the identities of all those who were like us. Sooner or later, the priests would try to torture the names from me.

I drifted into a feverish slumber. My memories were needles, and all my past was prickly and poisoned—a childhood twisted and finally deadened by fate.

The next morning, just after the bells of prime, guards brought an old, cinnamon-complexioned man with bristling white hair into my cell, undoubtedly hoping that his companionship would keep me from reopening my wounds; the Church would not easily give up the pleasure of deciding how and when I'd be murdered.

The old man's feet were crabs of crusted skin. I turned away; compassion comes through the eyes and I did not want him to know I could still feel such a useless emotion.

He crumpled to the ground when my usual guard—a dim-witted Lisboner with the dull green eyes and fetid breath of a man always sneaking a drink—pulled away his hands from under his shoulders. The prisoner's head fell back at a cockeyed angle and his eyes closed.

O Analfabeto, the Illiterate, as I called my guard, told me that my guest was a Jain accused of sorcery. Torturers had coated his feet with coconut oil and roasted them like meat.

The old man's metallic black eyes opened for a moment and he looked at me as though we shared a damning secret. What it was, I had no idea. Maybe he was only hoping I would be kind to him in his misery.

Striding out of our cell triumphantly, the Illiterate slammed our inner door closed and kneeled down, so that his bulbous face was sectioned by the grille. He showed me a wry smile. "They used coals," he said. "Coals burn much hotter than wood."

Even fire works on their behalf, I thought.

Once the guard had gone, I soaked my shirt in my water jar. I draped it over the Jain's feet, which were hot to my touch. Likely, his very dreams were ablaze. He would never again walk without assistance.

In the night, his breathing was like sand falling into my hands. I slept fitfully. Time panted beside me in my nightmares and became a cyclops with crusted blood on his lips—like my father the last time I'd seen him. He tore the wings off a parrot and pressed the bird's mangled flesh into my hands. I carried it gently, as though it were my own dead child. I pictured Tejal in labor, calling for me to come to her. Was our baby still alive?

Whenever I awoke, mosquitoes buzzed insanely in my ears, whispering that my efforts to help the Jain were pointless.

*   *   *

At dawn, my guest greeted me with a cheerful wave of his hand. Seated on the floor, he was sunken-cheeked and goat-ribbed, and the skin on his chest and belly was pleated old parchment. He looked from the bandages around my wrists to my eyes and smiled gently, inviting me in the way of my homeland to speak. I turned away.

"You should not be so eager for the wings of your next life," he said in Konkani.

I resented his advice. And I didn't trust his voice, which was quick and bright, as though his thoughts were jumping through him. Perhaps it was the pain.

I made no reply, hoping he would assume I did not speak his language and leave me be. Instead, he raised a crooked finger and pointed at my eyes. My mind must have greatly weakened during my confinement, because my heart tumbled at the thought that he might hiss an incantation against me. I backed against the wall.

"There's no need to fear me," he said, pronouncing his words slowly, thinking me a foreigner. "It's just that I've seen your blue eyes before." When I made no reply, he added, "On the butterflies that come to my village every spring."

He raised and lowered his arms as though fluttering his wings, his hands curling out elegantly, like a dancer from Kerala. He smiled, inviting me again to speak.

"Talking to me will only bring you more trouble," I said in Konkani. "I am damned."

"So you *are* from here!" he exclaimed happily, as if we were now on friendly terms. "Then maybe you know which butterflies I mean?

Yes? They are purest black, each one like a moonless night, except that they have blue spots here and here." He touched the sides of his chest. "In my village, they say they are the north wind given form."

I can still feel how I resisted the tug of his musical voice pulling me back toward life. "I am useless to you," I told him, turning aside, wishing I could be as hard and senseless as the prison walls. I felt his curious gaze pressing down on me. Did he want me to vow that I'd never again try to take my own life? I buried my head in my tattered mattress and squeezed my eyes shut, wishing I could vanish. After a time, I thought of confessing to him how I'd murdered Papa, but I believed then that silence had more to offer me than any man.

Only later did I realize what needed to be said first: *I will never speak to you as if you have any authority over me. Only my father had that and I have killed him.* . . .

*   *   *

We were soon given breakfast through the slat in our inner door. My companion hunched his shoulders as he scooped up his rice into his mouth, his meticulous slowness seeming to mock my hunger. As a Jain, he was permitted only vegetables and grains, and I thought of a plan to distance him from me after he held his fried fish up by its tail and nodded at me to take it. The guards must have given it to him as a cruel joke.

"When I was a boy," I said, waving away his offer, "I caught one of those black butterflies you mentioned."

"I knew it!" he said with a sprightly laugh. "You were drawn to it." He touched his chest again to indicate the blue spots. "It was a kind of destiny. Yes, don't you think so?"

"I do not believe in destiny," I replied brusquely. I thought I was speaking the truth. Now I'm not so sure; so much seems to have happened in the only way it could have.

I knew that all life was holy to a Jain—down to the tiniest worm. So it was that I was certain that sooner or later the old man would ask if I'd taken the butterfly's life. When he did, vengeance glowed in my chest like a dark star. "I crushed it in my fingers," I told him, "and I've never regretted it."

Tears welled in his eyes.

"Don't waste your sorrow on a speck of being that has neither soul nor sense," I said. I spoke as though I knew what I was talking about; confinement had given me a grudging, bitter arrogance and a teacherly voice I barely recognized as my own.

Those who claim that people cannot ever really change have never been in prison and learned that miserable walk of confinement that can end only in death.

He pursed his lips tightly together as if unwilling to voice a terrible truth, and I realized what should have been obvious—I was the small, soulless creature he felt sorry for. I laughed for the first time in ages; to be more pitiful than a crushed insect seemed quite an accomplishment.

"If my mind weren't nearly gone, I would find a way to kill us both," I told him.

He gazed up at me, his black eyes sorrowful. I despised his willingness to feel so much for someone he knew nothing about.

"How would you like it if I beat you now?" I said, jumping to my feet. "Would you still care so much about me?" The urge to punish him surged in me with the destructive force of a house collapsing. "I could break your bones and no one here would stop me. They would welcome it."

I made a fist and shook it at him, as though confirming I was the dramatic villain in a play written for me by a secret enemy—the person who'd betrayed me and caused my arrest. The Jain's hands rushed up to protect his face, and in that gesture I saw he'd been beaten as well as burned. When I knocked them away it was as if a rope inside me had snapped, and I was falling freely away from myself. I kept hitting him until I drew blood from his mouth.

Afterward, my fear at what I had become was akin to drowning. I whispered an apology and retreated to my cot, hugging my legs to my chest. I closed my eyes and said nothing for hours, trying to think of what Papa would want me to do, but his voice had disappeared from inside me.

At dusk, I kneeled next to my cellmate. "Kill me," I whispered.

"I can't. It is forbidden to me."

"Please, you don't understand. I couldn't bear being burnt or made to swallow water until I drown. If I'm tortured, I might reveal the names of people who've helped my father and me. If I am dead, the girl I am betrothed to will be able to marry another man." I held his shoulder. "Smother me in the night, while I sleep. I'll give you all I own for that one act of kindness. I'll tell you now where to go when you are free, and you will collect my belongings from my sister and uncle."

He shook his head. I pushed him away.

That night, he crept to me and lay down beside me. He took my hand and gripped it hard.

"Forgive me for failing you," he whispered. "I am very sorry."

I pushed at him, but he held me tight. He was much stronger than I thought. I was sure that his persistence was a sign of madness, but that seemed a blessing; we would be equals during our time together.

We lay in silence. I pictured my sister when she was four years old, her eyes bright with joy; inside the basket I held out to her was a butterfly I'd caught—not the kind the Jain had spoken of, but one that was scarlet and gold. It fluttered to the rim and flexed its wings, glowing in the sunlight like stained glass. My sister giggled as I sniffed at it. When it took wing, she raised her arms and yelped with joy. I stood behind her and put my hands on her shoulders, pressing my love into her, as I'd learned from Nupi, our cook and housekeeper. I was sure we'd always be together.

The Jain caressed my cheek. I knew somehow that he was requesting my thoughts. Or maybe my loneliness over the last year made me want to believe that his every gesture was an invitation to speak of my past.

"The butterfly I caught was not the kind you mentioned," I confessed. "And I didn't kill him. I really only wanted to show him to my sister. And to smell him—though that seems so odd now."

He laughed softly. I turned on my side toward him. His moist breathing was warm against my face. It seemed like the wind of God I'd been missing.

The blackness of our cell made it impossible to see more than the smoke-shapes of my own imagination, but I believed he was looking for something deep inside me. I felt his probing as though it were a stone in my chest. I wanted to embrace him but knew that I'd begin to sob if I did so.

"And what did he smell like?" he asked.

"I thought he'd have the scent of jasmine, since he'd been feeding at the vine climbing up our verandah, and I was too young to know better. But he had the faint smell of the earth."

He was silent for a time, pondering my words. "I shall try to prevent that," he told me.

"Prevent what?"

"Even the smallest animals are observant of our lives," he replied.

I thought he would go on, but he offered no further explanation.

"Keep talking to me," I pleaded. "Say anything you like, only don't let me lie here without your voice." *Our whispers will protect us both,* I thought.

He curled his arm under my head and began to speak of the soothing night sounds we could hear in the city below. I allowed myself to imagine I was with my father and it proved a mistake; terror spread through me. It was centered in my gut, cold, like a stillborn life. I sat up. Who had betrayed Papa to the Inquisition? Aunt Maria? Wadi? Perhaps it had been someone I'd never even met.

"What's wrong?" my companion asked.

"Memories seem to betray me at times. And there is someone I need to find. I have a debt to pay."

"They do not want you to be here," he replied.

"Who?"

"Those memories you speak of. They want you to be free. Don't you think so?"

"If they do," I said skeptically, "then they don't seem to have much of a strategy for helping me."

He uttered a prayer in a language foreign to me. I told him then that we called the butterfly he'd mentioned *trevas azuis* in Portuguese, meaning "blue darkness." He was pleased by the sound of that and said he would call me Trevas Azuis from then on. Feeling the slow rise and fall of his chest beside me, I became aware of our frailty. We had no weapons—no prayers or arguments that would do any good. All we had was each other, and it would never be enough.

He told me his parents had given him the name Ravindra, meaning sun, but everyone had called him Phanishwar—King of the Serpents—since he was a toddler; his father had found him sleeping on their patio one night with a hooded cobra guarding over him. "I cannot remember that particular snake," he said. "But it is true that I have never been afraid of them like other men."

His parents had sent him to apprentice with a snake charmer in Poona when he was ten years old. He was now fifty-seven. "It only occurred to me when I was already a parent myself that my father might have made up the story of the cobra to suit his plans for me," he told me. "That would be just like him. How he worried over us when we were children! My goodness! You see, he wanted to be sure that all of us had a way of earning an honest living. Such a good man he was—always fasting and going to temple. He could never bear how the Hindus and Moslems would kill snakes as if they had no place in the world. 'Phanishwar, you shall show them there is another way,' he used to tell me."

"Is your father still alive?" I asked.

"No, he and my mother are long dead."

"Your burns—they must be very painful."

"Do not worry, Trevas Azuis. I have suffered much physical pain in my life. Pain and I, we are old enemies who know each other's every move. We try to outsmart each other, though he usually wins in the end. I bear him some ill will, it is true, I shall not deny it, but I suppose he is just playing his part and has no choice."

I got up, soaked my shirt in water again, and kneeled beside him. He moaned while I washed his feet, crying silently, thanking me for my kindness. I had not remembered that a man's voice could be so gentle.

When I was done, he patted my head with his hands and blessed me. That first day, Phanishwar seemed to me to represent all that was good about the villagers I grew up with: their delicate manners and quickness to smile; their acceptance of circumstance and certain belief that life was a grand struggle linking everything in the world together; their delight in *we* so much more than *I*.

"Tell me of your life," I said. I wanted to hear a story, to give myself over to the sleep summoned by words whispered in the dark.

He spoke to me about his wife, who had died several years earlier, and his five children; the youngest was twelve and named Rama. His village, Bharat, was on the coast, three days' walk north of Goa. He did not say how the Inquisition had caught him and I did not ask. After a time, he began to sing a soft, golden melody, and I came to see I would not kill myself—just as I now knew that I would confess whatever my masters wanted so as to escape their flames. I would have to stay alive to find the person who had betrayed Papa and me, and take my revenge.

*   *   *

Phanishwar held me through the night, and I could feel his generosity pulsing around us. I had never felt so close to a man other than my father. Our union resembled a dream at times, which is why, I think, when dawn appeared in our window, shaded pink and blue, I found the courage to speak of events I had not believed I'd ever tell anyone.

With him beside me—the King of the Serpents—I knew that

not only my memories but all of nature wanted to free us. I hoped that together they would be strong enough.

I spoke to him first of my childhood, beginning with my mother's illness, which was my earliest full memory.

"I once saw someone cross the bridge back from death toward life," I told him.

CHAPTER 2

For several years after my mother died, I used to sneak on tiptoe across the carpeted silence of my father's library, ease open the bottommost drawer of his desk, and slip out the leather case in which he kept his drawings of her. Eager to study her face and compare it with my own, I would carry the sketches to the mirror hanging in my room and press them, one after another, against the glass. Sometimes I imagined she was my reflection—that we were the same person.

Once, when my father was away in Goa, I tore up one of my favorite portraits of her. I must have been eight or nine. I don't remember my cramped reasoning—I know only that I was so angry that I felt compelled to destroy something beautiful and valuable. It may have been my own way of trying to consign her death to a safe place in my mind—or even of restoring her to life through a flash of wicked magic.

Dizzy with shame, I raced out of the house and tossed my sinful bits of evidence into the waters of Indra's Millstream, a lazy branch of the Zuari River that slipped through the slender valley of banana groves and palms at the eastern edge of our property. My guilt afterward was so heavy that my gut ached as though I'd swallowed sand. I confessed my mischief to Papa on his return the next day, certain that he would hate me. Instead, he lifted me up and twirled me around.

"One old drawing is nothing compared to being home with you," he told me.

I could not understand why he didn't punish me. I wanted him to. I think I wished to be sure—for one stinging moment—that I had all of his attention, and that Mama's ghost would not lead him away from me. Maybe, too, I wanted to be reassured there was justice in the world, even if it meant a reddened backside.

"But it was a beautiful thing," I told him. "And you made it so we could keep it." Confessions must have a way of following one another, because I added, "I go into your bottom drawer every few days and take out your pictures of Mama."

Papa gave a quick laugh of surprise, then shut his right eye tight, as he often did when I was up to no good—making believe he was afraid to see all I'd done. He put me down. "Listen to me, Ti. There's nothing wrong in keeping some things secret from me. You need to have your own life. But you must promise me something. When you feel like tearing up more drawings, or doing some other permanent damage, you will come to me first so we can talk."

As I gave him my word, I shivered with renewed guilt. He noticed my discomfort and added, "Look, son, your mother's death makes me as angry as it does you. There are times when I want to tear up every memory I have of her."

*   *   *

As I grew, I began to see that I'd inherited my mother's curving lips and the soft depth in her eyes, though mine were blue and hers had been light brown—the color of almonds, my father used to say.

"More than anything else you've inherited all your mother's mischief," Papa used to tell me, groaning comically, as if I made his head throb. He'd chase me around the house afterward, growling, trying to banish our sadness with his clowning, which became his way of keeping her absence from destroying us. Sometimes he'd dance an improvised jig with me or yip like one of the barking deer who were always eating the roses in our garden. Then we'd collapse together onto the pillows of golden silk that had been part of Mama's dowry and snooze in the sun pouring in through the windows. Our helpless laughter probably saved our sanity, and yet maybe I ought to have told him that it only left me sad in the end, as though we'd betrayed our own true feelings. But I could never have put such complex thoughts into words at that age. And I would never have willingly hurt him.

In my favorite of his drawings, which Papa hung over my bed, Mama's long black hair was swept under the moonstone-white head scarf that my sister, Sofia, would later inherit. My mother's hands were slender and graceful, and were gesturing toward the Archangel Gabriel as though they were dancing for him. Gabriel has wings of burgundy and yellow, the same colors as in my mother's sari. To me, it always seemed as though Mama and the angel might be one and the same being in different form.

Sometimes I would sneak my mother's scarf away from Sofia. Holding it as I looked up at the portrait, I would wonder about the mystery of time—because here I was growing up and Mama would never know me.

The drawing of my mother with the Archangel Gabriel was a study for a Koran my father had made for the Sultan of Bijapur. The Sultan had invited Papa to India a decade before I was born and paid him an annual stipend for his illuminated Korans and prayer books. My mother, whom Papa met and courted seven years after his arrival, became the model for Khadija, wife of the Prophet Mohammed. I never saw her pose for Papa, but in my dreams I have seen him sketching her. And though they are not even touching, it seems as if they are making love through their eyes—perhaps even conceiving me.

After I met Tejal, when I was eighteen, in our moments of inti-macy I used to remember Mama's warm, protective scent. The odd thing is, whenever I breathed in the memory of her, it was as though she were a presentiment of something in my future rather than my distant past. Maybe love cannot help but look ahead.

*   *   *

Mama became ill with trembling fevers and chills in early June of 1576, when I was four and a half years old. It scared me the way her teeth chattered and how she would fall asleep with her eyes wide open. Even in the moist summer heat, Papa had to cover her with heavy woolen blankets and move her bed next to the hearth, which he kept blazing day and night. Her breathing was often desperate, as though she were starved for air, and much of the time she was too frail even to whisper.

Papa hung a vellum talisman around her neck with the Jewish angels Sanoi, Sansanoi, and Samnaglof painted as long-robed wise men holding lion-headed staffs; the three angels were said to be able to protect women from Lilith, the Queen of the Demons, and all of her bloodthirsty helpers.

Watching Mama from the foot of her bed, listening to the un-forgiving monsoon rains outside, I felt as though we were being swept away. The curtains of rain over our windows were so thick that we could see no life beyond them. The whole world was water, and the urgent drumming on our roof was so loud that there were times at night when I would screech like a parrot and hear my voice only as a distant scratching. The monsoon became a living thing that summer—malevolent, damning, endlessly greedy. Occasionally—at its own whim—it would retreat for half a day, backing away slowly, turning around now and again to gloat in eerie silence over the dam-age it had done. During these reprieves, we'd see that our garden had become a pond fringed with weeds and tiny ferns. The sudden magic of reborn sunlight would turn their drenched leaves to crystal.

I spent my days by Mama's sickbed, playing on the floor with my shadow puppets and animal dolls. I only left the house to sit on the verandah when Papa insisted on our taking advantage of a break in the storms. If Nupi tried to lead me away, even to wash my face, I'd flail my arms and holler. She called me far too stubborn for my own good, but I could tell from the hard look in her eyes that she respected my determination. We moved my parents' bed into the sitting room so that Papa and I could sleep together near my mother. He would curl up behind me and rub my hair to get me to fall asleep.

Mama was able to sit up sometimes, especially in the morning. Papa would spoon tea into her mouth and coax her to eat some rice. Her lips were gray and cracked, and trying to smile made them bleed. Years later, my father showed me a drawing he'd done of her during her illness and I told him it didn't look like her. But it did; I just didn't want to believe that the hollow-eyed, ashen-faced woman was really her.

I was sitting with Mama one afternoon at the end of that terrible June, drawing monkey faces on a piece of paper. Nupi had made her drink a tea of crushed night-jasmine leaves and gingerroot to put her to sleep, and though it had worked, her breathing still came with difficulty. It was as if her lungs were flecked with rust.

When I noticed that her wheezing had stopped, I stood up. Her chest was still to my touch, and her glassy eyes were not looking at anything in our world. The room was turning slowly around me, as if I were at the center of a wheel. Far away, I could hear my father talking to Kiran—the wet nurse—while she fed my baby sister, who had been born seven months before, in December of 1575.

Nupi was scraping coconut in the kitchen; that persistent, clawing sound would forever remind me of death.

I shook my mother and called softly to try to wake her. Then I ran off for Papa.

Nothing he did could rouse her. He kissed Mama on the lips, then brushed her eyes closed and kneeled by her side with his head bowed. The rains beat down on us as he sobbed, and I was thinking that we were all more fragile than I had ever guessed, my father most of all. Did I see in the fatal curve of his back that my mother's death would break him? If she hadn't died, would he still have asked me for the poison so many years later?

Nupi was holding me while I stood nearby, her bony knees against my back and her strong hands on my shoulders. They pressed down on me to keep me from launching myself into Papa's arms. I remember the feeling that a shadow—maybe mine, though I wasn't sure—was tiptoeing away from us and would never return.

Kissing Mama's hands, Papa finally called me to him. He placed her fingertips over my eyes, then his own, whispering the Kaddish prayer in Hebrew.

Sometimes I can feel the weight of my mother's touch on my eyelids. It is usually a comforting memory, but it can scare me, too, as if it meant the dead would always have too much power over me.

*   *   *

When Papa went with Nupi to fetch my sister from Kiran, I climbed up onto the bed and pulled Mama's limp arm around my waist, hoping for her to wake up. At length, a tremor shook me, and I could no longer hear the din of the rain, though the shutters were open a crack and it was flooding everything in sight. The silence was one of expectancy, as if my head were concealed inside a glass jar that was about to shatter. The light dimmed around me.

"Don't worry, Berekiah," my mother suddenly whispered, using my father's name. "Ti and Sofia have each other."

When I snapped my head around to look at her, I clearly saw her lips sculpt the last two words. Or had I drifted to sleep for a moment and only dreamed it? Her eyes were still closed, after all.

I leaned over her face and touched her cool cheek. I was not frightened. I expected her to open her eyes any moment. "Mama," I whispered, "it's me. Wake up."

My father came back into the room, cradling my sister, and I rushed up to him to tell him what had happened.

"That's impossible," he said, frowning dismissively.

Shame slithered through me and I dashed away, managing to break free of Nupi's grip at the doorway. Papa called into the garden after me, his voice fraying with desperation, but I would not return. He searched around the wet hydrangea and hibiscus bushes, letting himself be soaked, his face twisted with fear. I watched him from the edge of a rice field, shivering, my bare feet buried in the mud, the water up to my knees. I told myself I hated him.

That evening, he apologized for not believing me and begged me never to run off again.

"If I lost you or your sister now, I couldn't go on," he confessed.

Before he covered his eyes with his hand, I caught a chilling glimpse of his lost look, so I came to him and pressed myself into his legs.

My father was tall and strong, with large, gentle hands. When he picked me up, I held his ears. It was a game we played, his cue to give an elephant honk through his make-believe trunk. That day, however, he sat me in his lap without a sound. He told me that Jews like us, and Hindus like Nupi and Kiran, believed that the soul of a dead person could cross a bridge back to life for a brief time—if there had been something left unsaid or undone. That was what I had seen Mama do. "Do you understand?" he asked.

I said I did, but the dark, musty odor of his distress made me feel threatened, and having his arms around me was all I cared about. He pressed his lips to my brow and asked me again what Mama had said. After I told him, he stood and pondered my reply.

"Whenever we'd go for a walk, she always had to rush back to get something she'd forgotten," he reasoned. "This time, she needed to come back to reassure us." He smiled at me gratefully. "It was lucky you were here with her and heard what she wanted to say, Ti. It must have comforted her."

Why do children who've lost a parent always seem to believe they must take on responsibility for the living? I didn't tell Papa what I was thinking: that he was wrong and that Mama meant for me to take care of my little sister from now on. She meant that even if she had spoken to me in a dream.

CHAPTER 3

Sofia's deep-set eyes were dark green and moist, like shadows on a deep lake, and from very near the moment she was born my sister would gaze at everything around her as if surprised by all existence. Nupi said her look of wonder was really secret vigilance, and after forty days, when it was safe for my sister to leave our house according to Jewish tradition, the old cook brought her to Jaidev, the holy man who cleaned wax from the inside of your ears with a thin wire, to find out who she'd been in a previous life.

I adored Jaidev because he had imploded cheeks and coils of matted hair falling to his waist. He was sitting like a Buddha when we approached, his sun-baked hands cupped on his bony knees. He was covered in hard white dust, since he rolled around in dry earth like an elephant to clean himself.

When his eyes opened through all that crust, they were alive with a secret black fire. "Nupi comes with Master Ti!" he exclaimed, holding out his hands to greet us.

"And who's this little chapatti?" he asked, sticking out his tongue at the baby, which made her kick her arms and legs.

Knowing what was wanted of him, he accepted our coins, then spread Sofia's fingers out like a starfish. Powder shook from his hair as he gave us a startled look. "A Brahmin!" he exclaimed.

Leaning down for a closer look, then disappearing into a trance, he discovered that she'd been a Hindu princess kidnapped by a Moslem caliph more than five hundred years before. "She was beautiful and very clever, and she was able to make her way home in the end," he told us. Holding up his hand in a pose of teaching, he added, "But that is why your little Sofia is always looking around."

Nupi was pleased with this verdict and handed him an extra copper coin.

"And everyone loved her," he called after us.

*   *   *

My father snorted when Nupi told him about Jaidev's finding. He told our cook that the little girl looked around all the time because she was learning about everything outside herself—about big things like her need for sleep and cuddling, and tiny things, too, like the stickiness of rice squeezed in her fingers and the "odd beliefs of certain members of our household."

Nupi huffed when he directed that last remark her way, and over the years to come she made ironic reference to her "odd beliefs" whenever she was proved right about some important matter or even a trifle. But I could tell that Papa's criticism secretly pleased her, because it meant that he considered her part of our family.

*   *   *

What is outside of me is everything, and yet it comes right inside me when I look at it or touch it.

That's what I guessed Sofia was thinking when she stared at the world, because that's what *I* was thinking when I watched her, and I didn't yet know the difference between her and me—not in any adult way, with clear borders around myself.

Sometimes she'd squeal with joy at seeing a finch take wing from the wooden railing on our verandah, or a thread-legged beetle skate over a puddle in the garden, and Papa said I'd been the same way. I loved my being like her, and I hugged that knowledge to me as tight as I could when I was lonely. Both of us were children of Mama and Papa and could never be anything else.

About eighteen months after Mama died, when Sofia was two, her interest shifted, and everything she saw and heard she wanted to put in her mouth.

One balmy evening while Papa was teaching me the constellations, I told her the stars were delicious and made believe I was eating them. She reached out just like me and folded them—the captured stars—into her mouth.

The eager pleasure of being imitated for the first time made me tingle, but I also felt unsure of myself, as though I did not yet know what to do with my power over my sister and perhaps would never know. Nupi surprised me by encouraging me to play this game with her. "At least I won't have to hunt for anything but starlight to come squeezing out her little behind." She laughed.

*   *   *

So many things I made for Sofia as she grew—twigs fashioned with string into stilt houses, stones piled high into ancient fortresses that she could send crashing down, papier-mâché crowns, swords, and hats. Shadow puppets of animals became my specialty, and I was very good at cutting them out from paper by the time I was seven. I wanted her to be strong and quick—and I probably wanted her to be a boy, too. I began tossing my leather ball to her before she could even walk, and once—with Papa's dyes and sable brushes—I painted her face blue, like Krishna's. I thought Nupi would be overjoyed, but she told me she'd prepare me as vindaloo if I ever did such a half-witted thing again. Nupi had the most intimidating eyes of anyone I'd ever met. The rest of her looked frail, and she only had two rickety yellow teeth on the bottom and another three on top, but I'm sure she cultivated a crippled, withered look to surprise her victims.

Her fingers may have had knobs at the joints that put her in agony when it rained, but her hands were like vises. No one dared cross her except Papa.

I learned all my local proverbs from Nupi. *"Bhaanshira zari aayla"*—"the rag has suddenly got a strand of silk"—she'd say in Konkani if Sofia or I got too big for our britches. "Every grain of sand on a beach has its place," she'd tell us whenever I dared to question the value of a seemingly meaningless chore. Or if she gave us a good piece of news, she would add, "Though we all know that Kali will have her day," since she was of the opinion that good times only tempted the Goddess of Destruction to gather up her sword. My favorite of her expressions, however, was "The guardians of the dawn know the night better than anyone." Nupi used it whenever my family faced hardship, and it generally meant that hope made us feel times of darkness more deeply. In that respect, it was very much like *Only those who know sadness also know joy*. . . . Yet as I grew older, I also began to understand that she could use it to mean that people who protected others often faced the most danger.

Her great enemy was constipation, and she was always eating fennel seeds to make up for what she called her "demonic" bowels. She could talk about her discomfort for hours, describing in rigorous detail her efforts to produce a satisfying result. Sofia and I learned to deflect her by begging her to tell us stories about the *gandharvas* and *apsaras,* the Hindu sprites of the forest and rivers.

In the time of Rama, a sprite was born who could see into the future, and his name was Tiago. . . .

Nupi always put Sofia and me in her winding tales. When I was much older, I realized it was because she wanted to make sure that we survived my mother's death intact, that our lives—and stories— would continue into the future. I was devoted to her, and I adored listening to her delicate storytelling voice, but I secretly used to fear how she kept her vigilant eyes on me.

"We seem to overlook love when it comes to us from the most obvious places," Papa once told me when I was irritated with Nupi, but I didn't really understand what he meant until I was nearly an adult.

*   *   *

Unbeknownst to Nupi and my father, I used to carry my sister up the staircase from our courtyard onto our roof after a rainstorm, and we'd look across the rice fields—liquid mirrors in an emerald valley—being worked by women and children from Ramnath, the village nearest our house. We used to make believe we could see the ocean, twelve miles to the west. I'd talk to her about how Papa had taken a sailing ship from Constantinople to India before we were born. And before that, how his family had fled Portugal because King Manuel and other bad men didn't want them to live freely as Jews.

Sofia and I often slept together, and I would fold her into my belly as though she'd been given to me as a present. When Papa was feeling sad, he would carry us into his bed, growling that he was the caliph who had kidnapped her in a previous life and we were now his prisoners once again.

*   *   *

Our worst times were when my sister would shriek in the middle of the night out of hunger. She could be very fidgety and stubborn, so Papa and the wet nurse, Kiran, had to sometimes walk her around the house for over an hour to get her to take some milk. I took over from them sometimes and—imitating what I'd seen them do—would put the tip of my thumb to her lips every few minutes to see if she was ready.

Kiran's face would fill with gentle purpose whenever she clutched Sofia to her breast. The youthful wet nurse seemed to have the power of a goddess—over fire, earth, air, and water; over life and death. She'd spread her black tresses like a curtain over the little girl so the two of them could make a world unto themselves. Kiran had big round eyes and a long, looping neck. She wore silver bangles on her feet and bracelets on her arms, so she tinkled like festival bells wherever she went. I was awed by her beauty and separateness from my family, and when I was older Papa told me that I was always asking her if I could feel the V-shaped scar on her forehead that her father had made with a knife when he was drunk.

Kiran swore to Durga Devi that she'd never go home to him and, in the end, she kept her word; she left us when my sister was two and a half, and, with a reference letter addressed to the Sultan from my father, made her way to Bijapur, all her possessions—including two silk saris that had been my mother's—wrapped in a single shawl. We never saw her again.

I was always jealous of the unity Kiran made with my sister and would often watch them from their doorway, thinking hard about life and death. If I could have fed my sister from my own body, I would have. And I'd have thought her better off with milk from her brother. Who else would ever love her as much as I did?

Perhaps this made me a strange child, and I can see now why Papa's European friends and especially my aunt Maria occasionally had fun at my expense, holding golden filigree hearts up to my ears and wondering aloud if I might not have been happier to have been born a girl. I hated their nasty cleverness and laughter, and I sometimes fought with their children. Though I was small for my age, I was very determined, and a skinned knuckle or scraped knee only served to make me punch that much harder. Papa would punish me for fighting by shutting me up in my room, but I was always unrepentant.

"I'll only stop if you make them be quiet about me and Sofia!" I used to shout at him from inside my room.

Sometimes my fury made Papa so upset that he'd sit with his head in his hands and say nothing for hours, not even if I came to him and snuggled into his arms. In this way, I slowly learned to be gentler with him.

It is a terrible turning point when we understand that we can damage our parents badly, and I sometimes wish I'd learned it a little later in life.

Our Hindu neighbors and my little playmates from Ramnath never once teased me about my fervent loyalty to my sister, which is one reason, I think, why I've always felt more at ease with Indians than Europeans. They did not believe that tenderness for her made me less of a boy. Nor did they think that oddity was a curse or something to fear, as Christians and Jews sometimes did. They saw my unusual devotion to her as a blessing—one that could not necessarily be understood but which had its place in the garden-universe lorded over by Vishnu.

*   *   *

After Kiran left, our house suddenly became too large and cold for me. All its comforting corners seemed to harden, and its doors seemed to be forever waiting for a visitor who would never come. For weeks at a time I trudged around from room to room thinking I was now an intruder. I even hated my bed, and the down pillows that had made a rocky coastline when I played at naval battles on my sheets, and the shady alcove on the north side of Papa's library where I read my books when everywhere else was too hot. I got it into my head that I wanted a staircase and a second floor added to the house. I no longer remember why. Maybe I needed a new place to start over.

One afternoon, after Papa refused to build a staircase for me once again, Nupi led me crying into her kitchen. When I explained what was wrong, she ordered me to sit.

"What for?" I asked.

"Will you ever just do what I say without making a fuss?"

She'd made a batch of steaming dal for herself and spooned some with her old iron ladle onto a banana leaf for me, then gave herself a smaller portion. She moved her ancient wooden stool up to the table we'd recently given a new coat of bright yellow paint and instructed me to do the same with the cane chair behind her broom.

"You want me to eat with you?" I asked.

She looked around, then peered over my shoulder. She even up-turned her large cauldron, which had a wedge of black soap hiding underneath. "I don't see anyone else here," she said, "so you're my only choice."

For the first time in our lives we ate together. A white hibiscus flower from our garden peeked over the rim of the cracked earthen-ware jar between us.

"Flowers are good," she announced to me when I touched it. I came to learn that this was an essential postulate in her guidebook to life. "And your mother would want to know you're eating well," she added.

As we ate our dal, Nupi kicked my bare foot now and again to make me look up, since I tended to get lost in thought of late. She told me I mustn't leave over a single lentil or she'd report me to my father, which was an attempt at humor, since she was always saying Papa was too easy on me. When I didn't smile, she gave me a serious look and said I was to eat with her in the kitchen whenever I was feeling bad.

"You mean it?" I asked.

"I never joke about food," she replied, which was true enough.

I sometimes think that Nupi's simple offer that day saved my life, because I did eat with her—and often—over the coming years. And I have always associated the taste of her dal on that first occa-sion with the kind of love that never fails to act in time of need. Sofia told me much later that she did, too, and I would guess that Nupi invited my sister to eat with her on occasions I don't even know about.

I wish I had done something in return for our old cook that day—had collected a basket of the violet-colored orchids we called cat's whiskers for her shrine to Ganesha or simply hugged her. I didn't yet realize that all she really prayed for—and what she most wanted in life—was that my sister and I would not die young. But that, of course, was a guarantee—and gift—that no one could give her.

*   *   *

Throughout my childhood, my happiest times were in the morning. Nupi would rise at dawn to make us chapatti, which I ate with shredded coconut and palm sugar, and in winter she'd fry up some moong beans with garlic and basil leaves. My father and I would sit around the great limestone table in our courtyard, washing our meal down with dark tea, and he would show me the drawings he was working on for the Sultan. Nupi sometimes peered over our shoulders at them, too, though she had the irritating habit of sucking loudly on a betel nut, which made Papa think up endless errands to keep her away. After that, he and I would read together from the Torah and I would have my drawing lesson, which could go on until noon, since I was to be a manuscript illuminator, like him, when I grew older.

In the sketches I made of Papa from this time, he has tired and worried eyes. It's astonishing that I never realized that his concern was focused on the tiny artist drawing him so carefully. How much confidence in God's watchful eye he must have lost after burying Mama.

In a vague way, I also began to understand that it was drawing that would restore the world to the way it had been before my mother's illness; when I had a reed pen in my hand I felt I was not powerless and that the world had been made for me. Naiveté is a boy's prerogative, of course, but I wonder—if I could travel back in time—if I would warn myself against such eager optimism. In any case, I doubt I'd have listened to my older self, since—despite my having witnessed Mama's death and being forced to bid a tearful farewell to Sofia's nurse, Kiran—it was not then in my nature to doubt the goodness of the world.

Sometimes, when he was feeling lonely, Papa would ask me to walk him around the house, and I'd put my little hand in his and we'd peek in on Sofia. If she was sleeping, we'd kiss her cheek or pat her fluffy blond hair. Then we'd head to the courtyard, cross past Nupi's basil patch, and end in the kitchen. We'd watch her stoking her coals or peeling tamarind pods to make her famous custard, and ask her what she had planned for our midday meal. Finally, we'd go to Papa's library, where he had his work desk. We scarcely conversed on these little household journeys, but once we were seated together he might pick up a leather-bound volume of Portuguese poetry and read to me while I sat on his lap.

He'd also recite poetry to me after he tucked me under my covers at night, reading by the light of a single candle always kept in a little white ceramic cup by my bedside. No light was ever like that one. It was softer and rounder, and it made anything said to me in my room so much more secretly my own.

*   *   *

Once a year, on the sacred evening before Yom Kippur, our Day of Atonement, Papa would allow me to look at a sumptuously illuminated manuscript written some sixty years earlier by my renowned great-grandfather, Berekiah Zarco, a powerful kabbalist from Lisbon who had been forcibly converted to Christianity in 1497. We kept this priceless treasure, which was entitled "The Bleeding Mirror," in a secret drawer at the back of Papa's wardrobe, wrapped in a black velvet pouch embroidered with the initials *BZ* in silver thread. I used to love to pass my fingertip over the magnificent cover illustration— a peacock shamelessly fanning his iridescent green, purple, and blue tail feathers across the title, which was in such highly polished gold leaf that I could see my own reflection peering back at me.

"It was my grandfather's intent that everyone who picks up this book should see himself in it," my father told me on more than one occasion, and I used to believe that our illustrious ancestor must have been so magical a kabbalist that he was gazing at me right at that moment from inside his manuscript.

"The Bleeding Mirror" was an account of a massacre in Lisbon in 1506 in which two thousand converted Jews—so-called New Christians—were murdered by a Church-inspired mob and burnt in the city's main square. Papa had been named after Berekiah, which he regarded as having given him a special obligation, I think, because after he would read his grandfather's description of the pogrom to me, he would always say, "And that is why Portugal must forever remain in our past. You are never to set even a single toe in that country, Ti." As though to gratify my love of secrets, he would sometimes raise a finger to his lips and say: "And you are not, under any circumstances—even if you are threatened with death—to tell anyone outside our family that we own a copy of this manuscript."

*   *   *

One winter morning, I discovered Papa crying in bed, naked, shivering in the cold, his shutters wide open. It made me desperate when he would cry. I suppose I knew somehow that his tears were nothing I could really soothe. They seemed to threaten my very existence because they reminded me that we moved in different worlds, and though I could visit his adult universe, I could never stay there. This time, he told me he'd dreamed of my mother locked out of our house and calling to him. He folded me in his arms as though we were both shipwrecked. Would he have been happier in Bijapur or Bombay, where he might have found companionship? He always told me he didn't want to have to start over again in another place, but it was Nupi who finally told me the truth. One day, after I'd repeated to her what Papa had told me, she looked up from the wooden spoons she was lining up on her table and fixed me with an astonished expression. "Don't you know he doesn't want to take you and Sofia from this house, where your mother is still present?"

*   *   *

Once, after helping Papa dig out a rotting peepul stump at the back of our garden, I saw him squint up toward the blazing afternoon sun. He said, "Ti, you often ask me about the things your mother loved, and I never remember to say the most obvious. Your mother opened like a flower when sunlight reached her. Your sister has inherited that from her."

I understood then the drawing that Papa made of Mama after her death and which he kept over his bed. In it, she is kneeling inside a cavern of dark cloud, golden rays shining forth from her, as if she were the sun awakening.

CHAPTER 4

Papa's younger brother, Isaac, lived only a day's ride away in the Portuguese city of Goa. The capital of a colony of the same name, it was founded on land the invading Europeans had won in battle from the Sultan of Bijapur nearly a hundred years before. Once every few months Isaac and his wife would visit us for several days, or, if Papa felt equal to a journey, we would brave the muddy roads and insolent inspections of the border guards to travel to their home. They lived just off the Rua Direita, in a two-story stone house with lace curtains in the windows. It was only a short walk from there to the river, where the forest of tall-masted sailing ships would inevitably get Papa and me talking about what life was like in far-off Istanbul and Lisbon. A large cross was carved in relief on the lintel above their front door; Isaac, who'd followed my father to India, had been baptized on deciding to live in Goa, since Jews were not allowed to reside permanently inside Portuguese territories. I did not yet think to ask if my uncle practiced his former beliefs in secret, but surely such delicate information would never have been entrusted to me at so young an age.

Closing my eyes, I can still feel today how ill at ease the city used to make me, as if I would forever be too puny to match the grandeur of the stone churches and too inexperienced to decipher the intricate patchwork of its streets. As for the tens of thousands of Portuguese residents, they looked like feudal lords and ladies in their endless layers of gauzy and frilly clothing. The men wore feathers in their caps, too, which I thought idiotic. Their scent of olive oil made my nostrils itch and I cowered in the presence of their African slaves. I hated the women's penciled eyebrows, which looked to me like bat wings.

Uncle Isaac always had surprise gifts for Sofia and me, and even if it was just some heart-shaped sweets made of milk, sugar, and cumin, we climbed all over him to snatch them from his hands. We loved his wild merriness, the twinkle of youth in his eyes, and his long brown hair. Papa opened his arms with such radiant joy when they greeted each other—as if he'd spent weeks in darkness just for the pleasure of seeing him—that I knew the brothers had played together as children. And so many of their gestures were alike, too—how they rolled their eyes when they heard us say something nonsensical, for instance, or panted with their tongues out like puppies when Nupi carried supper to our table. They often made each other laugh without anyone else knowing why. Maybe it was my father's having known Isaac for many years before meeting my mother, so that he—more than anyone else—could remain separate from her death.

Uncle Isaac couldn't live closer to us because his business in exporting Indian cloth and dyes to Lisbon meant he had to live by a port. This seemed a silly reason to me when I was little and I often told him so.

Aunt Maria was Christian by birth. She came from an aristocratic Portuguese family that had lost much of its wealth in the shifting fortunes of the spice trade. Even so, she maintained a distant, haughty bearing in public and had her personal slave shade her from the tropical sun with a parasol of crimson silk wherever she went. She was extremely proud of her pale skin and always said it was something not even a fortune in gold could buy. She also hired Indian bearers to carry her in a palanquin to Mass on Sunday, like many of the Portuguese, though this was frowned upon by my uncle, who would walk alongside her. Maria wore cascading silk gowns even in the moist heat of a summer afternoon and always had a pink lace handkerchief ready to wipe away the rivulets of perspiration running down her cheeks and neck. Once, she escorted my father and I to the river with her hair pulled tightly back and coiled inside a black velvet cone with a small crown of pearls at the top. I couldn't help asking if it hurt.

"Discomfort in clothing and coiffure," she told me in her highly ornamented accent, "is a sign of good breeding." Turning to my father, she added distastefully, "Though none of these Hindus, not even the Brahmins, understand that."

I thought she was very odd because she ate her papaya with salt and crossed herself whenever a dog or cat ran past. Sometimes, for reasons I could never fathom, she even traced a cross on my forehead, which always seemed to make my skin itch.

To my great frustration, I could never seem to do anything right in my aunt's eyes. I was too doting on Sofia or too boisterous with my Hindu playmates. My soiled feet rankled her in particular. I was sure she hated boys, and the slanting looks she often gave Uncle Isaac convinced me she didn't much care for grown men either. I desperately tried to become invisible whenever I was in her presence. I didn't think Papa ever noticed my discomfort, but one day he asked me to try to forgive her for being so rude, since she was an unhappy woman.

"Unhappy about what?" I demanded. This was after a particularly unpleasant stay at their home.

"She and Isaac are childless," he replied.

"But she doesn't like children!"

"She wishes you were hers," he said, to my great surprise. "And it makes her angry that you aren't."

My heart tumbled, dragging me deep inside a feeling of dread. "You'd never give me to her, would you?" I asked hesitantly.

"Give you to her!" my father exclaimed in horror, and then he began to laugh. After a brief negotiation, we agreed that I'd never have to stay with my aunt for more than six days in a row. "The Lord took six days to create the world and then rested," Papa said, "so we should be allowed the same blessing."

*   *   *

Uncle Isaac and Aunt Maria were not to remain childless for long. In December of 1577, when I was almost six and Sofia just two, they adopted an orphan almost exactly my age. Why they didn't take in an infant, I never found out, but I once overheard a disgusted Nupi explaining to Papa in her broken Portuguese, "That sister-in-law of yours . . . she wants a boy that comes already housebroken!"

My new cousin had been named Wadi by his Moslem parents, who had been murdered by Portuguese soldiers raiding an Arab ship off the Malabar coast, but the nuns who cared for him decided he ought to have a Christian name and called him Guilherme. By an unfortunate coincidence, my aunt's Indian cook already had that name, however. Recognizing this as an opportunity to win praise for herself as a pious soul, Maria resolved to call the boy Francisco Xavier, after the Jesuit Missionary who had converted tens of thousands of Hindus in Goa several decades earlier. Nevertheless, neighbors usually referred to him as the *pequeno mouro*—Little Moor—which made her hazel eyes go beady with anger, since she always avoided mentioning his having been adopted, even with people who knew. Out of range of adults, Sofia and I always called him Wadi, since we considered it a very nice name, and exotic to our ears—and since he seemed to prefer it. After a time, Papa did, too. He told us that the original Francisco Xavier had petitioned the Pope to establish the Inquisition in Goa, and that as a result converted Jews like Isaac, and former Hindus, too, had to carve crosses over their doorways to reassure the Church that they had not slipped back into their outlawed ways. *Conversos,* as they were sometimes called, even risked being burnt alive in a special place by the river if some treacherous soul seeking the Church's blessing were to accuse them of still practicing their old beliefs. Several unfortunates died in flames nearly every year. "No child, not even one in your aunt's pious care, should have to begin life with so poorly chosen a name," Papa told us.

"Or spend more than six days with her," I reminded him.

*   *   *

At first I found Wadi infuriating, since he would not even answer the simplest of questions.

"Are you hungry?" my father would ask him, or "Do you want to draw pictures with me and Ti?" and all he would do was tighten his lips, afraid to make a peep.

The first time I met him I asked if he wanted to help me weed Nupi's basil patch. Basil was a plant considered holy by Hindus, so this was an honor I'd had to beg our cook to grant us, but Wadi just jerked his head away as if I'd slapped him.

After he and his parents had left, I confessed to Papa how enraged he made me and accused him of regarding himself as too good for us.

"But he's still just learning Portuguese!" Papa exclaimed, horrified by my lack of common sense.

"Oh, I didn't think of that," I said, feeling like a complete fool.

Regarding myself as very magnanimous, I resolved to give him another chance the next time he visited.

Wadi was a few inches taller than me and as slender as a wire. He had olive skin and stunning green eyes that were rimmed in black, and long delicate lashes that made him look pensive when he was quiet. My aunt and uncle thought he was quite handsome, which was true enough. They were also convinced that everything he did was charming, which was far less true. In the presence of adults, for instance, his walk became a soldierly march, and even I was vaguely aware that it was not a good sign, though I did not yet guess the obvious—that it meant he was ill at ease in his new home. At the time, in fact, it only made me want to hit him. His mother used to make him soldier-step around the room for strangers, who always agreed—while cooing—that he was an enchanting little darling.

On his second visit to our home, which gave us our first real chance to be alone, he refused to climb a mimosa tree along the banks of Indra's Millstream with me. Insulted, I told him I'd never invite him to do anything with me ever again, which made him race away with tears falling down his cheeks. Unfortunately, he told his mother—still sobbing—of my rudeness. When she informed Papa, he went off like gunpowder.

"Ti!" he shouted from the sitting room, as soon as he heard me coming up the steps of our verandah. "Get in here *now*!" I slunk in holding the mangoes I'd gathered for Nupi, juice sluicing down my sticky hands. Papa stood over me like the God of the Torah. "Put that damn fruit down!" he bellowed.

As I did so, I stole a look at Aunt Maria, leaning back luxuriously on Papa's velvet armchair, fanning herself, showing me an expression of regal contempt, as though I were a rotten egg. Nupi must have crept out of the house as quick and silent as a mongoose and slipped around to the verandah, because she was gazing in at us through the window there, her face crinkled with worry.

"Do you mind giving us a little privacy?" Papa told our cook, banging the shutters closed without waiting for a reply. The stiff whack of the wood did not sound promising. Sweat poured from me; I could not think of what I'd done. I wiped mango juice from my palms onto a fold in my dhoti, staining it yellow.

"Are you trying to make Wadi unhappy?" Papa demanded. "Or is it simply that you're completely unable to see things from his point of view?"

"I—I don't know what you mean," I stammered.

"Oh, no?"

My father rolled his eyes as though it were only too obvious I was lying and recapitulated what Aunt Maria had told him. I dared not look at her, but I felt her satisfaction eating at me like acid.

"Papa, I only said what I was thinking."

"Not all your thoughts are made of gold, you know. Ti, that poor boy has yet to learn to trust us. Wadi needs time."

"I tried to show him turtles and dragonflies and things," I pleaded. "And it was like he didn't care. And then I wanted us to climb a tree so we could see across the rice fields to the top of the Hindu temple, and . . . and . . ."

"I know," he interrupted in a softened voice. "But you could learn a little patience. Kindness without patience is nothing." Seeing I didn't know what he meant, he added, "Other people aren't always ready for the nice things we do for them, so you must wait for them to catch up and help them along."

Papa took my shoulders. "Ti, other people are as real as you are. They do not just exist inside your head." He placed the tip of his forefinger in the center of my forehead and pushed to make his point. "We are all of us fragile creatures who sit at the center of our own universe."

"You're saying that it's my fault Wadi doesn't want to do anything with me," I stated for the record.

"No, I'm only saying that your cousin deserves your love and friendship."

That reply took me aback, since I didn't understand why Wadi deserved *anything*. When Papa dismissed me, I darted away, unwilling to show Aunt Maria my tears.

*   *   *

On Wadi's next visit I was bathing Sofia in the courtyard when he appeared in the doorway. Determined to win Papa's good graces, I invited him over with a friendly wave, but he just stood there like a clay statue, so I then asked him to join me in my clearest Portuguese. He made no reply. How was I to solve this three-foot-tall, gawking riddle? On sudden inspiration, I stepped up to him and put Sofia in his arms, showing him how to dry her with my towel. He was nervous at first and tried to hand her back, but I insisted he keep her. We even powdered her bottom together and combed her soft wisps of hair. From that moment on, whenever Wadi was in our home, he would follow my sister as though she were his one link to the rest of humanity. He loved to sit her in his lap and talk to her in a tiny, squeaky voice that made her laugh; he'd entertain her with the shadow puppets we cut out together. To help her walk on her bowed and uncertain legs, he stood behind her and held her hands high above her head, telling her she was the cleverest girl he ever saw. When we were away from our parents he sometimes whispered to her in Arabic, though as the years passed he stopped doing that and claimed he'd forgotten all the words he once knew. Through Sofia, he learned to trust me, Nupi, and Papa. And maybe his father and mother, as well.

Over the next months, I managed to coax Wadi into joining me on many adventures in the nearby villages. Boys don't need many reasons to like each other or to want to spend time together, and it was enough for me that he was a very fast runner and had impossibly large feet, like a giant rabbit—and that he could holler louder than anyone I knew. We could talk endlessly about the silliest topics— like what the golden-bearded monkeys were eating when they picked at each other's fur or the purpose of a belly button. He also became very dutiful when helping at our house—at gathering cat's whiskers for the shrine that Nupi kept in her room, for instance. Whenever I would sketch him, he would sit patiently, keeping still for longer than seemed possible, nearly always pleased with the results, which he would carry back with him to his home and hang on the wall over his bed. He had affectionate nicknames for everyone. Sofia was the Flying Squirrel, since she was small and quick, and Nupi was Senhora Fennel-Seed, since she was always eating them to prod her bowels. He called me Tiger. It was a play on my name and on how ferocious I could become when irritated. Whenever he sensed me getting furious, he'd cross himself and look heavenward as if he were seeking divine help, which made me like him a great deal, since it was a kind of backwards acknowledgment of my power.

Wadi could get so helplessly weak when he was really laughing that he could not stand up, and when he cried it was as if he were melting. Sometimes I think that he felt his emotions more deeply than other people and that was why he later learned to hide them so well. Is it possible that he was the most sensitive person I ever met?

*   *   *

When Wadi and I were in Goa together we got in the habit of slipping away into the rickety Hindu neighborhoods, which were as dirty and noisy as a divine underworld, and therefore of great interest to us. We liked to be jostled by the swarming crowds, especially at the markets. Everything and everyone reeked of coconut oil and turmeric, and a thousand other odors more difficult to trace, and I'm sure we were drunk at times on the very air.

Sometimes we would encounter a scene of suffering so great that I felt my vision go dim and my breathing falter. I particularly remember an armless and legless beggar of indefinite age whom we used to see inching crablike through the streets, his stumps wrapped in blackened old banana leaves and his hair so matted that it looked like fraying rope. It was said that his limbs had been chopped off at birth by his father so that he could better earn his living.

Once, we saw two Indian scaffold makers kicking the beggar away from the house they were working on as though he were a leather ball. When I asked them why they hated him, they replied that they didn't, but that he was an Untouchable who had no right to bother good people. I worked up my courage to approach him that day and gave him some copper coins, which he took in his mouth.

I remember, too, the time the palm-leaf roof of a teahouse collapsed on Wadi and me, which put us in a fit of hysterics as we crawled under the tables toward the door, until a fire started in the kitchen. Then we had to rush out for our lives, and forever afterward this made a terrific story to tell. We sometimes said that we had saved two babies from the flames, so that people would think we were heroes.

On another occasion at this same teahouse, Wadi found a big brown beetle with ferocious mandibles at the bottom of his cup, dazed but not yet dead. When he held it up with its legs wiggling for the owner to see, the smiling man—who was little more than a stick with a turban at the top—put his hands together in a position of prayer and exclaimed, "Another winner!" He handed Wadi a withered necklace of frangipani blossoms as a prize. If I had not been there, I would never have believed it.

My cousin gave me the garland as a gift, and I kept it by my bedside for weeks. After the flowers had dried to a brittle yellow, it disappeared one night. Nupi denied having taken it while I was sleeping, but I figured she'd had enough of its sour smell and had thrown it out. Two years later, I found out the truth, and in the process learned something about my sister I'd never suspected.

*   *   *

It became obvious after a time that Sofia and I were Wadi's refuge. He never marched like a soldier when he was alone with us, and he spoke Portuguese more fluently, too, since his mother wasn't around to make him nervous. To avoid Aunt Maria's punishments, he also quickly began to reveal an advanced talent for stealth. He would leave a clean set of clothes in a reed basket under our verandah, for instance, or at the bread shop next to his home in Goa, so that even after our most mud-splotched escapades he could greet his parents looking like a Portuguese prince.

Unfortunately for me, my cousin's cleverness had the unforeseen effect of confirming to my aunt that I was a bad influence, since by comparison—with twigs in my hair and streaks of dirt across my face—I generally looked like a low-caste ditchdigger. To my great displeasure, Wadi never made any attempt to convince his mother otherwise, explaining to me that he could hardly disagree with her without giving away his secret. "Besides, Uncle Berekiah never punishes you," he used to say. "He'd rather lie on a bed of broken glass than wallop you."

Hearing jealousy in Wadi's voice, I always forgave him, but as we grew up, I began to suspect that it was very convenient for him to have a designated villain so close at hand.

*   *   *

Only a few months after his adoption Wadi suffered a seizure. Hearing him thrashing, Aunt Maria ran to his room, secured him in her arms, and shouted for help. Uncle Isaac was working at his warehouse, so her servants and neighbors came running, which only made my aunt more anxious, since now everyone could see that her son was not only a Moor but afflicted by a frightful illness that might even be contagious. When his convulsions ended, a Portuguese physician made Wadi inhale the vapors of kerosene and a burning cotton rag. The poor boy was exhausted and scared, and covered in a patina of sweat. "He looked like he'd fallen in a well and drowned," Uncle Isaac told us after we'd rushed to Goa. I remember how my uncle's eyes were rimmed red with worry, and that he seemed short of breath. "Ti," he said to me, "I'm sorry to say that I don't think that Wadi is going to have an easy life."

I was gratified that he spoke to me as if I was an adult, and when I swore to him I would help, he smiled and patted my head absently, thinking—I was sure—that a little boy could do nothing against such a terrible fate.

*   *   *

On this same trip to Goa, I remember that my father and Aunt Maria had a rancorous quarrel. We had gone with my aunt to see an old friend of hers who had given birth to twins two weeks earlier. The young woman was still weak from the ordeal, and she kept a painted statuette of the Virgin Mary on her pillow as a talisman. All her visitors bent down to kiss it upon entering the room, as was the Portuguese Christian custom. My father, however, refused, even when my aunt nudged him. "Maria, my dear, the only virgin I've ever kissed was my bride," he told her, not without a touch of humor. "And kissing another one fashioned out of a tree branch and painted so incompetently is of no interest to me."

My aunt let out a gasp and looked as though she would strangle him, since Papa had spoken in the presence of her friend's physician and two Indian servants, but it was only outside on the street that she gave him a vicious tongue-lashing, the gist of which was that he was a miser in matters of the heart. My father heard her out without interrupting, his arms crossed defensively over his chest, his expression one of resolute patience. When she at last concluded, it was with a patronizing shake of her head, as though he were beyond even her charitable efforts, which was probably why he gave her a reply that kept her quiet the rest of the afternoon: "Maria, has it never occurred to you that tolerating your silly opinions and satanic tirades without ever once insulting you might be an act of generosity on my part? And that I am able to do so only out of love for my brother and respect for the choices he has made in his life, whether I agree with them or not?"

*   *   *

Wadi confided in me that he never remembered his seizures afterward, but he always knew when they were about to strike. "It's like a lightning storm is building inside me," he said. "I can see flashes, and I smell the air burning—like caramel."

Wadi's voice would change a few years later, but at the time it had a quaver in it, as though a little pebble were stuck at the back of his throat. Hearing it always made me feel protective of him.

After his second seizure in the presence of his mother, Aunt Maria begged him not to ever frighten her like that again. With one hand over her heart and the other gripping his arm as though she might never let him go if he didn't bend his will to hers, she told him, "I don't know if I'd survive another, so you must never do it again—do you hear me?"

Wadi imitated his mother nearly perfectly, so I know exactly how desperately she had pleaded. He never said what he'd replied to her, but I'm sure he must have pinched his lips together and kept to silence. After all, he suspected by then that no amount of willpower—and no number of Ave Marias—could stave off his attacks, which Aunt Maria began to call his *desvios,* detours, so that people who might overhear their conversations wouldn't have any idea what they were referring to. Maybe he decided then and there that deception would give him his only chance at happiness, because he soon told me—swearing me to silence—that whenever he saw flashes in the air he would run as fast as he could down into the root cellar and close the door behind him, so that no one could see or hear what was happening to him.

*   *   *

I saw one of Wadi's "detours" for the first time when I was eight and a half, and it was to deepen my affection for him—and even for my aunt—in a way I could never have predicted. Today, it seems a moment around which my whole life turned.

We were on our verandah, plucking the feathers from a butchered guinea fowl that Nupi was going to prepare for our supper. "Here it comes," Wadi moaned.

"What is?" I asked, but by the time I finished my question his eyes were so filled with fear that I knew what was about to happen. I have only seen such a gaping, terrified expression one other time in my life, and on that occasion it was beyond my power to offer any help at all.

"I've got to hide!" he whisper-screamed. "Tiger, help me!" He reached out for me, looking as though he were slipping over the edge of a cliff.

Before I could take his hand, his eyes glazed over and his head fell back, thudding on the wooden floor. He gave a heavy grunt, as if he'd been punched in his gut, and his arms and chest began to spasm. He was like a rag doll in the clutches of a djinn. A stain of wetness spread across the front of his trousers.

Lifting up his head onto my lap, I shouted for Papa. Blood was dripping from Wadi's mouth; he must have bitten his cheek or tongue. Deep underneath my terror, one thought kept drumming: *His blood will join us together forever.*

Papa and Uncle Isaac soon came running out to us. Aunt Maria was at the marketplace in Ponda with the maidservant who always accompanied her from Goa.

The seizure lasted a few minutes. Papa kept telling me that Wadi would be just fine, but I had my doubts and started to cry, fearing for his life. When his shaking ended, the boy lay unconscious in his father's arms. I ran off for water from our well, and Nupi washed his face and arms, which were drenched with sweat. Finally, he awoke, but he remembered nothing of what had happened and was unable to speak. He drank as though he'd been in the desert, and spit out more blood, but luckily, he'd only nipped the inside of his lip. When he found the strength to lift his arms, he did not reach out for his father, as I thought he would, but instead extended his hand to me. It may seem odd to say so, but I took it as if chosen by God Himself. I refused to loosen my grip on him even when Uncle Isaac carried him across our house to his bed. After all, who would ever voluntarily let go of God's hand?

*   *   *

When Wadi was safely asleep, I asked Papa if we could say a prayer for him. He thought that a very good idea. "Which one do you want?" he asked.

"I don't know. I'm not sure I know one that fits."

My father's eyes shone with amused affection. "All prayer spoken in truth *fits,* as you put it, Ti," he laughed.

I had always liked Hanukkah, the Jewish Festival of Lights, so I led us in the prayer that Papa had taught me the year before: *Baruch atah Adonai, Eloheynu Melech ha'olam, asher kidshanu bemitzvotav, vetzivanu, lehadleek ner, shel chanukah.* "Blessed are you, O Lord, who sanctifies us by giving us a way of life directed by holy commandments and who has commanded us to light the lights of Hanukkah."

That night, Papa set his flint to a beeswax taper and let me bestow its flame on each of the seven candles of our menorah. This we placed on a table by Wadi's bed, so that if he woke in the night he would not find himself in darkness.

*   *   *

After his seizure, Aunt Maria was very kind to both her son and me; she did not leave his bedside all that day and night, and the next morning she came out to the verandah where I was watching the sunrise and thanked me for helping him.

Rubbing a weary hand back through her hair, which she hadn't brushed, she gripped the string of pearls around her neck as if just barely holding on to her sanity. "I'm so sorry for how I look," she murmured, and she went on to call herself an embarrassment, but I thought she was beautiful. Her eyes seemed pure and honest—and so terribly sad. I felt as if I were seeing her for the first time.

"Sometimes I wonder where I am," my aunt confessed to me. "And how I got here. Do you ever feel that way?"

"I'm not sure."

"I'll tell you a secret," she whispered. "I get frightened when I feel this way—as though I might do anything to change my life, even take a ship back to Portugal." She took my chin in her hand. "Tiago, you and I got off to a bad start," she said. "Do you think we might try again from the beginning?"

The ornamental frills had vanished from her accent, and I sensed I'd never hear this simple voice of hers again unless I said yes. For that reason more than any other, I agreed, but even as I gave my assent I could feel a part of me leaning away from her. After all her jibes I knew I'd never trust her completely. Even so, when she brought Wadi some soup and bread for breakfast, kneeling beside him to help him eat, I saw clearly that I had underestimated her love for him—and with it, the depth of her suffering.

Aunt Maria sat embroidering in a chair by Wadi's bedside after he dozed off again, and as I watched her quick, sure hands I thought of my mother. Jealousy stirred deep inside me, surprising me. I felt as though I'd been abandoned and was tempted to try to say something clever or pleasing to her, but the right words wouldn't come to me and I slunk away.

Back in my room, I thought of something new: my aunt simply could not help saying wrong things all the time. It was because she'd been so unhappy before Wadi came into her life. That was what Papa had been trying to tell me.

*   *   *

Papa told me a few days later that Uncle Isaac and Aunt Maria had asked the nuns who'd cared for Wadi why they'd failed to say anything about his attacks, but the sisters swore they'd never known about them. My father suspected they were lying and that the boy must have been previously turned down for adoption for this very reason.

Now, nearly four decades later, I can see that maybe it was the nuns—and not Aunt Maria, as I've always thought—who gave Wadi the idea of writing a new past for himself. Given his circumstances, it may even have seemed natural and right to him.

*   *   *

The part Wadi wished me to play in his life—at least when our adventures overlapped with the universe of adults—became absolutely clear to me one blustery spring day when we were nine. He invited me that afternoon to come with him to visit the Safa Mosque on the road to Ponda. It was a place forbidden to him, since Aunt Maria said all Moslems were either thieves or pirates, but when I raised that objection, Wadi sneered at me and declared he would go alone if I hadn't the courage to join him. Though his parents had never spoken to him about his capture aboard an Arab ship, he had overheard more than three years of gossip by then about his origins: he wanted to hear Moslem prayers for himself.

From inside a nearby thicket of palms, making believe we were spies for the Portuguese Crown, we watched the worshipers file inside. Wadi laughed in a forced, malicious way at the long robes worn by some of the men, and at the droning chants of the muezzin. From that, I guessed that he was considering his own life and the path he had been forced to take. *Maybe I'm not anywhere near where I was meant to be.* That must have been what he had begun thinking that day, in the itchy way that insights of an adult nature sometimes come to children.

Squatting next to him in the shadows, I felt the danger in him, and it was as though he were not with me at all, but inside a cavern of secret thoughts. I even believed I could smell the darkness around him. It seemed to be waiting to envelop me too, and I trembled with an urgent feeling of dread and expectation.

Once the service had begun, we came out into the open and sat on the rim of the stone fountain that centered the orange grove in front of the mosque, listening to the muffled voices inside. It began to drizzle, and while I was swirling my hand through the dappling water in the fountain, Wadi threw a stick through one of the windows. To my horror, a man inside was hit. He screamed loudly, and before I could say anything, Wadi raced off, shouting that Moslems were heathens. I took off behind him.

We ran so fast through the woods that he slipped and tumbled down a sharp ravine of ferns and weeds, scraping his arm badly. I ripped a strip of cloth from my dhoti and wrapped it around the wound. He cursed himself for being so careless.

"My mother is going to kill me," he moaned.

"No, we'll get fresh clothes from the basket under the verandah and give the soiled ones to Nupi to wash. We'll make believe that nothing happened. No one will ever know."

At home, Nupi agreed to help us, though she scolded that we had gone too far this time and mumbled to herself about Portuguese children being pampered and spoiled. All went well that day, but Uncle Isaac noticed Wadi's bruises the next morning when he roused him for the long trip home. My cousin said he'd stumbled while dashing out of the way of a palanquin carrying a *pandito,* an Indian physician, who was rushing to a patient's bedside. Uncle Isaac knew, however, that in the countryside doctors went about on foot or, at most, in an oxcart. Threatened with a spanking, Wadi told the truth about visiting the mosque—except that he added that I'd bullied him into going and had even made him run home though the rain! He said nothing, of course, about his having made fun of the Moslem worshipers or having thrown the stick through a window.

My father called me in to his library that morning and confronted me with Wadi's account of my treachery, shushing me up each time I attempted to interrupt. As he raged on, it seemed clear to me that my cousin must have known Uncle Isaac would never believe his explanation about a rushing palanquin. He had wanted his father to accept his second description of events without question, and the best way to do that was to be "caught" at telling a lie, then "forced" to give the real explanation. After all, Isaac would believe that his son would never dare to lie twice in a row.

Couldn't he simply have told his father that he'd had a seizure and had fallen on some stones? That would have satisfied everyone, I thought—at least until my father finished his tirade and was looking at me as if this was my sole opportunity to explain myself. Then it occurred to me that Wadi didn't dare bring any additional attention to his affliction, already considered a curse by his mother.

Was this need to conceal his suffering the cause of so much he would later do?

I was not sure what to say to Papa. I was furious, but I knew, too, that had Wadi told the truth, his mother would have realized that he was curious about his Moslem origins, and that would have surely led to an explosion. My cousin would also have been given a severe lecture by his father, who'd have feared any undue attention drawn to the religious beliefs of his family. It hadn't occurred to me yet that Aunt Maria's refusal to talk openly about her son's adoption was a farce that could only lead to deeper lies, but maybe Wadi already felt it drawing him toward a danger he couldn't escape. Maybe he couldn't tell the truth.

Only many years later did it occur to me that my cousin might have been badly confused about his own feelings; perhaps he even secretly wanted his parents to know he'd visited a mosque so that his previous life could finally be acknowledged.

Before I could say something—anything—about all my knotted thoughts, my father's face softened. He called me to him and kissed me.

"I can't bear being angry at you," he whispered. "And that silence of yours, like I'm an ogre . . . Ti, sometimes I just don't know what to do with you."

"I'm sorry, Papa."

"If you'll agree not to visit any mosque with Wadi again, then we'll forget this ever happened."

I gave my word and was not given any punishment. Even so, I never considered this a happy ending; I'd let my father believe a lie about me, and I knew I'd never fully trust my cousin again.

CHAPTER 5

My life with my sister, Sofia—like my relationship with my cousin, Wadi—soon began to develop in not altogether pleasant ways.

With her honey-colored hair and her fair skin, all the residents of Ramnath, the nearest village, knew her by name by the time she was five. The gnarled old women selling fish in the marketplace and even the coconut tappers high up in the crowns of palms used to smile like proud relatives and whisper to one another when we'd pass. It took me a long time to realize that my sister misunderstood so completely everyone's delight in her. By then nothing I could say could make her believe that her mixture of European and Indian features shouldn't embarrass her.

"Everyone stares at me!" she once told me with hollow despair when she was seven. "My hair is too light. I look all wrong."

"You're crazy. They're not thinking bad things. They just—"

"What's different is *ugly*!" she shouted as though she were fighting for her life. "People say that about—"

Sofia was about to say *you,* since I, too, was a mixture of European and Indian, and my blue eyes never allowed me to pass unnoticed. Clapping her hands over her mouth, she apologized. She even rushed to me and kissed my cheek. I pretended she hadn't hurt my feelings, but it was as if she'd slit my belly open with a razor and put her own terror inside me.

*   *   *

I sometimes heard Papa whispering to Nupi about how unexpected it was that such an eager baby had turned into so reticent a girl, and Sofia's shyness in public, when it didn't vanish with the passage of time, soon began to worry him. He confided in me that she always seemed to be listening for the sound of an invisible intruder tiptoe-ing toward her.

Other boys and girls only made her fidgety and unhappy. Cow-ering behind Papa or me, she'd pull a veil of hair in front of her face, exactly as her nurse, Kiran, had done when Sofia was an infant. Wadi was the one person near her own age with whom she felt at ease, and the eager loyalty he displayed to her as a baby continued throughout her childhood. What he liked most was to show her new wonders he'd found; it was a way, I think, not just of encouraging her but also of revealing his deeper emotions—feelings that could never emerge in front of his mother. I remember, for instance, that he and I once discovered thousands of baby frogs in the valley below Ramnath where Indra's Millstream plunged into a clear pool. The tiny pop-ping balls of green splashed at the lapping edge of the water and hopped through the tall grasses and lotus blossoms onto our feet and legs. There were so many that we could scoop up handfuls simply by reaching down. We dropped them in each other's hair and inspected their little white bellies and made croaking sounds while puffing out our cheeks. We walked in our bare feet like herons not to step on any.

"We've got to show them to Sofia!" Wadi exclaimed, and with that he was racing back to our house.

It was about this time that I began to believe that the darting en-ergy he always showed when he was with me was his way of keeping away his detours—as if he was determined to run so fast through life that his affliction wouldn't be able to catch up with him.

Sofia loved the frog babies so much that we carried jarfuls back and spread them all over our garden. Then we lay ourselves down on the grass and let them jump and play all over our chests and bellies, and it was as if the world itself were tickling us.

For the next few years we had so many frogs around our farm that they sometimes ended up clumped in Nupi's basil garden, much to her grumpy irritation. Neighbors who worked in the surrounding paddies complained that they attracted cobras and vipers, which was a more serious problem, as death by snakebite was not uncommon. The little monsters even found their way under our pillows and into our clothing chests. Once, waking in the middle of the night, Papa began to slip on his silken slippers and shrieked in horror at the slimy reception his toes received. For years afterward, he would imitate how he'd hopped around on one foot, screaming my name and Sofia's in rage.

*   *   *

Taking my cue from Papa, I tried to use humor to put my sister at ease whenever we had to meet someone outside the family, but after a time, I stopped even that, since she'd only accuse me of teasing her and "being like everyone else." I begged her to tell me what that meant, but she always refused to explain. Her stubborn reticence was a mountain that even I could not scale.

Once, when she was particularly furious at me, however, she let on more of what she was thinking. "Everyone wants me to be different than I am!" she yelled.

It was true enough that I wanted her to be less timid, so, feeling a pang of guilt, I apologized, whereupon she whispered, "Ti, I get all shivery sometimes—I'm so uncomfortable that it's like I need to wriggle out of my skin and become someone else."

*   *   *

With time, I began to think of my sister as two people—a girl of easy smiles and radiant eagerness when with Papa, Wadi, Nupi, and me, and another of furtive, doubtful glances and awkward stances when with neighbors, family friends, and strangers. What pleased her most by the age of eight or nine was to be left alone to practice her calligraphy at her small fold-out desk on the north side of the sitting room, below the window shutters Papa painted her favorite shade of blue. Sofia would hunch for hours over her paper, sitting on her cane stool as compact as a secret, her hair tied back with Mama's head scarf. She could spend weeks creating intricate designs out of ant-sized Hebrew letters—a technique she picked up all by herself after sitting next to me during one of my lessons and which was called micrography. To shape her tiny letters—little more than dots to the naked eye—she used a reed calamus that Papa kept needle-sharp just for her. She checked her progress through a round, ivory-handled magnifying glass that he'd commissioned from the Sultan's mirror maker in Bijapur and had given her as a gift.

Even today, whenever I see Sofia in dreams, she is generally seated at her little desk, and it is as if the blue of the shutters, the spangled dust in the room, and the time between then and now were telling me: *Beware of this memory, because it shows that everything might have come to pass differently. . . .*

I cannot say whether Sofia's temperament molded itself around this exacting work or whether, to the contrary, micrography fit precisely into her character, but we soon realized that it pleased her like nothing else. Even so, Papa gave her lessons only when she asked for them: he soon realized, the hard way, with screams and stamping, that she liked to be full owner of this part of her life. She surprised me when she was only ten by asking me to teach her to make her own inks, and I happily did so based on Papa's recipes. I later realized what ought to have been obvious: this knowledge would give her even greater independence.

Seeing Sofia so content inside her own secure world did a great deal to loosen my knots of worry about her. Even so, I would still stare at her sometimes with overly keen, big-brotherly attention, which would make her lift up her magnifying glass in such a way that her eyes looked as large and sweet as a camel's. As I grew up, I realized that this was a comic form of armor—that being adored can also be a burden—and I learned to give her complete privacy when she worked. Papa predicted a glorious future for her as a calligrapher to the Sultan.

It was at this time that she drew a tiny micrographic lotus flower at the corner of the head scarf she'd inherited from our mother. When she wore it, she hid the flower from view. The petals spelled out our names: Sofia, Tiago, Berekiah, and Chana, which was what Papa always called Mama, though her real name was Chandara.

Given my nature, it's no surprise that, at times, I grew cramped with envy of my sister's talent and otherworldly patience. Papa must have sensed this. When I was fourteen and Sofia ten, he asked us to work together for the first time. He was making a prayer book as a gift for the Jewish school in Cochin. At first, my sister and I quarreled like wasps, but after we'd finished half a dozen pages, my ambivalence toward her eased. Not only did I feel that we made more beautiful illuminations than I ever could have expected, but I realized that we were impassioned by different things and would therefore not get in each other's way over the coming years. I loved to give form to what was wildly colorful and ornamented—orchids and sunrises, or the clattering flight of a cloud of parrots—and Sofia adored what was most exact and small.

And perhaps hidden, too...

One Sunday evening, after a long afternoon of Torah study, while trying to find a Turkish copper coin that Papa had given me as a good-luck charm, I discovered a nest of objects at the bottom of my sister's clothing chest. Half of what was there we'd known nothing about and the other half had gone hopelessly missing over the past few years: a string of my mother's coral beads, a wax doll from Portugal, tortoiseshell buttons, a pouch of rose-colored seashells, a drawing of my father that I'd done when I was eight (and that I'd spent days trying to hunt down more than a year earlier), and—most astonishing of all—the frangipani necklace given to Wadi as a prize for his finding a bug in his tea. I was too shocked to be angry, and too flattered by her thinking enough of my drawing to steal it, so I never mentioned to Sofia that I'd found her cache. And I never told Papa, though I suppose it's possible he already knew about it.

But when I next saw my sister, it almost seemed as if I could see her treasure chest in her eyes. So many things were hidden inside that girl. . . .

*   *   *

Working together on our illustrations brought Sofia and me together in one other valuable way, for we soon began to talk more often about important things. Sitting in the shade of the Persian acacia in our garden, our toes curling through the carpet of pink, thread-like flowers in the coarse grass, I learned, for instance, that she day-dreamed about going one day to Venice, London, and the other great cities of Europe.

"I might even live in Portugal," she confided in me one day.

"You'd better not tell Papa that."

"Not now, silly! I mean when I'm older."

"They hate us there. Remember how it says in our great-grandfather's book that the Jews will always haunt the dreams of the kings of Europe?"

"But that was sixty years ago!"

"Still, Papa wouldn't approve of you going to Lisbon even if you were an adult."

"What if I went there without his approval?"

Sofia took my breath away speaking like that. On another occasion she even asked if I thought Jesus Christ was like Jaidev, the *sadhu* who had told us she had been a Hindu princess in a previous life.

"You mean, did Jesus have matted hair down to his waist and a face covered with powdery earth?" I asked, acting stupid because we were on dangerous territory. I could even feel the statue of Shiva listening in on our conversation from the doorway.

"No, you know what I mean—holy."

"That's what the Christians say," I replied, saying with my tone that I had no idea if it was true.

"He was the Son of God, you know."

"Who told you that?"

"Aunt Maria. And Wadi."

"I think if you have questions about Jesus you ought to talk to Papa."

She rolled her eyes. "Did God love His mother?"

"Whose mother?"

"The mother of Jesus, silly."

"You mean Mary?"

"Yes. Did God love her?"

"It's written in the Torah that the Lord loves us all."

"You're really irritating sometimes." She sighed.

"Why?"

"You always make believe you don't understand what I mean." She folded her arms over her chest. "Did God love Mary like Papa loved Mama?"

How could I have answered that?

I said I wasn't sure and told her I needed to go inside to study Torah. That night, after she was in bed, I told my father about our conversation, and though he didn't speak about it with Sofia, I know he asked Aunt Maria not to proselytize to her. The girl suspected something was amiss, however, and soon told me that our father didn't like it that she knew about Jesus being holy.

"How do you know that?" I asked.

"Because he's always steering me away from churches when we're in Goa. He doesn't think I know, but I do!"

I learned in this way that Sofia was far more observant than either Papa or I had guessed.

*   *   *

My sister was only allowed to leave the immediate vicinity of our property if Papa, Nupi, or I accompanied her, even if it was only to bathe in Indra's Millstream. Our vigilance increased her heavy sense of isolation, but Papa would have it no other way, since he'd heard stories about girls who were kidnapped and forced to marry Hindu widowers five times their age. She used to complain to me sometimes that I was a spy and our father her jailer, although she didn't dare voice aloud her resentment to Papa. Celebrations always seemed to accentuate this resentment of hers, and I remember that just after a trip to Ponda to celebrate her eleventh birthday she burst into tears on coming back home and reaching her room. When she finally allowed me inside, she told me more about the depth of her unhappiness.

"I'm all alone!" she sniffled.

"You've had me and Papa and Nupi since you were born," I said, believing at the time that we should have been enough for her.

"But I want friends!"

"You have your calligraphy. You love that."

She glared at me as though I were a demon. "You're not listening to me," she said. "You never listen!"

"There's Wadi," I pointed out. "He's devoted to you."

"But he lives so far away. I hardly ever see him. And he's older than me, anyway. I don't know if we could be *real* friends."

"Sofia, whenever we go to Ramnath or Ponda you never seem to enjoy it. Other girls think you don't like them."

She looked shocked.

"It's true," I added. "They think that you don't talk to them and you pull your hair over your face because you feel superior."

That just made her cry harder.

"Have you felt this way for a long time?" I asked, fearing her reply.

She nodded hesitantly, as though I might punish her for the truth.

I do not believe I'd ever realized just how deeply she felt her otherness until she looked up with bruised eyes, as if she'd been battered by life. Do older siblings always believe their brothers and sisters are happy even if presented with ample evidence to the contrary?

*   *   *

As a result of this conversation, I worked hard to get Papa's permission for us to visit our aunt and uncle in Goa more often, thinking that it would be a good idea for my little sister to see all different kinds of people of mixed European and Indian heritage. I also reasoned that if Sofia could become the constant friend of one person outside our immediate family—of Wadi—she would begin to open herself up to everyone. Thus I suppose I have only myself to blame for what was to take place between them.

CHAPTER 6

I spoke of my childhood to my cellmate Phanishwar as a way, I think, of weaving those times long gone into a pattern that made sense to me. After all, life seems to have very little interest in assembling itself into a design that can help us understand how we've reached the present tense; we must do most—if not all—of that work ourselves.

I'd avoided questioning the old Jain about how he'd come to be in prison, but on our third evening together, after awakening from a nap, he waved me over to his cot and said, "It was a terrible mistake, you know."

"What was?"

"My coming to be arrested."

"How did it happen?"

He moved his striped coverlet behind our backs as a cushion and replied, "One day, I received an invitation to visit Goa from a Portuguese Brahmin. And then, when—"

"The Portuguese do not divide themselves into castes," I interrupted. "There are no Brahmins."

He took a sharp intake of breath, as though pained. "Please, you are not understanding me," he said, his lips twisted with frustration. "The man wore an emerald as big as a soursop seed on the end of his beads."

"His what?"

"He had a long string of beads tied at his waist."

"His rosary. It's for counting prayers."

"But the emerald . . . What else could the man have been but a Brahmin, my Blue Darkness?"

Phanishwar gazed at me as though I were ruining his story; he clearly believed a large gemstone trumped any facts I might put forward.

It was dusk and our double iron doors were bolted closed for the night. A timid wind crept through our window occasionally, carrying the mossy scent of the storm-drenched city. Time seemed to be moving slowly around us, like a tiptoeing ghost.

"If only the Portuguese Brahmin would come to me now," Phanishwar moaned. "Rama and my other children must be drowning in such a sea of worries! Oh, what to do . . . ?" He held his head in his hands as if a great buzzing were shaking it apart. "You must tell me what I must do to leave here."

"I don't know. Maybe if you confess your sins to the priests they will let you go free."

"What sins do you mean?"

"Did you ever speak contemptuously of Christianity? If someone overheard you, that would be enough to—"

"Christianity is the religion of the people of Goa—is that right?" he interrupted.

"Yes."

"But I would never speak contemptuously of another religion," he said indignantly.

"Maybe you inadvertently said something about Jesus that they didn't like."

"Who is Jesus?"

"He's like Krishna—an incarnation of the Christian God. He lived fifteen hundred years ago in a faraway country."

The Jain shrugged as if these were unnecessary details. "I swear that I pray every day and fast during each cycle of the moon," he told me. "And I have never willfully injured a living thing. I am not celibate, it is true, but I am also not a monk." His black eyes opened wide with surprise. "Do you think they want me to be celibate—is that it? At my age, perhaps I ought to be, but I like women...." His face shone with naughty delight. "I like them too much, I fear."

"I don't know what they want even from *me,* let alone you," I retorted. "Listen, when you were first arrested, did you tell them clearly that you'd received an invitation from a Portuguese nobleman?"

"I tried to, but the soldiers were deaf to me." He shook his head in despair and held up four fingers. "It has been four months since I was taken prisoner. Please, you tell them for me that I wish to leave. You speak Portuguese very well, don't you?"

I nodded.

"And anyone can see you are an educated young man. You can read and write, can you not?"

"Yes."

"I knew it!" He smiled endearingly. "Then you will make them understand."

"But they know I'm a Jew."

"A Jew?" He made a beseeching gesture by clasping his hands together and lifting them high. "Please, you say so many things I do not understand. Explain to me."

I told him about our belief in one God and that our holy book had been written by a prophet named Moses. "The Christian rulers of Goa think that Jews are wicked," I added.

"Their Jesus did not like your Moses—is that it?"

"Jesus *did* like Moses—it's the Portuguese people who follow Jesus' beliefs who don't."

"It sounds too complicated. In any case, it does not matter," he declared. "Anyone who sees your blue eyes wants to help you."

I shook my head at his innocence. "Tell me how you got an invitation from a nobleman to visit Goa."

"I was dancing with Dharanendra in front of the Parsi fire temple and the Portuguese Brahmin came to talk with me. He wore so many layers of clothing. In my foolishness, I thought he looked silly, but he was so—"

"Who is Dharanendra?" I interrupted.

He gave me a boyish laugh. "My cobra—and also a great prince," he replied.

"I don't understand."

"Do you know who Parsva is?" he asked. When I answered no, he rubbed the gray stubble on his cheeks while considering his words. "Parsva is the twenty-third of our Jain saints—very holy and very courageous. Once, in a previous lifetime, many centuries ago, he came upon an evil Hindu Brahmin about to throw a snake into his sacrificial fire. Oh, what to do, what to do? Running fast, he snatched the terrified creature away from the Hindu and smacked the man on the head with his staff." Phanishwar clapped his hands together. "Later, when he was reincarnated as Parsva, the same evil Brahmin appeared to him as a demon hurling lightning bolts, but you know what?"

"What?"

"The snake he'd saved in his previous incarnation had also been reborn as a cobra prince named Dharanendra. Wasn't that a good thing! And very helpful that he should be around when Parsva needed him, because he spread his hood over our saint and saved his life. Even today, on some cobras, you can see Dharanendra's crown shining on the back of his hood if you look closely. That is the proof that he has a princely soul, my Blue Darkness."

Phanishwar spoke triumphantly and made a solemn bow toward me, as if I'd been the hero of his story. For a moment, he seemed much more than an uneducated snake charmer. I began to wonder if he wasn't a holy man in disguise; I'd heard of Indian *sadhus* traveling in disguise around the countryside, to better observe the world.

"You think snakes have a soul?" I asked him.

He showed me a puzzled look. "You will excuse me, but for an educated young man you do not always make much sense. If snakes had no soul, how could they be alive?"

"Phanishwar, I have no answers for questions like that."

"Even plants and trees have a soul, of course," he said, as if I had provoked him on purpose and this could not have been more obvious. His expression hardened. "Tell me honestly and do not spare my feelings. Are the Portuguese like the Hindus? Do they sacrifice animals?"

"No."

"You are not keeping even a particle of the truth from me?"

When I shook my head, grateful tears filled his eyes. "Then Dharanendra will dance with me again!" he exclaimed. Flashing a relieved smile, he added, "Have you ever seen a Hindu charmer?"

"In Ponda, many times. He played a gourd flute and his cobra always swayed in his basket, like it was drunk."

He wrinkled his nose in disgust. "Anyone can charm a snake sitting in a basket. There is little danger. A cobra cannot strike so quickly if his tail is below the rim. The most terrible thing," he whispered, "is that the Hindu charmers pull out the fangs of their snakes. One day, my master ordered me to do that for him—to a cobra we had just caught. I had apprenticed with him for three years and he considered it an honor for me to do this for him. An honor to hurt a cobra? Such a silly man he was! I refused, so he chased me from his home with a broom. Can you believe it? I was only thirteen. How sad a young boy alone can become! And how lonely is the world to him! I started walking back to my village and after two days I came upon a Hindu festival where priests were sacrificing snakes—tossing them into a pyre. It seemed an omen of something evil, and I wanted to be heroic like Parsva, but I was so very small and frightened. So I asked one of the elders if he would release the poor creatures if I could make one of them dance on my belly."

"Had you ever done that before?"

"No, but I had to create something wonderful, and it was all I could think of. When the Hindu agreed to my challenge, I looked into their snake pit, and I saw a beautiful large cobra, six feet long, curled around a tiny one, trying to keep it hidden and safe. The little creature was a baby and I could see that his mother wanted it to live more than anything, so I lifted her up and whispered my plan to her. I was quaking with fear, but what could I do? I lay down on my back and, pinching her head delicately between my thumb and forefinger, lowered her slowly onto my belly. The villagers made a circle around me, watching with their eyes nearly jumping out of their heads. So many people were standing around me, and all of them were afraid to move or even breathe! The silence made by snakes can be very loud, my Blue Darkness. The whole world holds its breath in front of a cobra." He covered his right ear with one hand and his eyes with the other, leaving a crack to peek at me. "Some people couldn't listen or look."

"So what happened?"

"The mother cobra sat quietly for a time, then raised her head and lifted her hood as though to strike. People screamed, but I looked at her sweetly so she would be certain that my intentions were good." Phanishwar showed me a benevolent smile, then raised his hands slowly over his head. "I caressed the air back and forth like this.... 'Now, to save your child, you must dance with me,' I told her."

Phanishwar's eyes were bright with mischief.

"So she danced?"

"No, the hateful monster bit me as hard as she could!" he yelled with glee. "Right here." He leaned his head to the side and showed me a scar on his neck. "Feel it."

I traced my fingertip over the raised skin, laughing with him.

"You like it?" he asked with a hopeful smile.

"Very impressive."

"My skin turned blue and yellow and got all puffy," he added excitedly. "Such an attraction I was! Men and women and children came from twenty miles around to see me—the Jain boy with a neck painted by a cobra's fangs. All because that hateful monster tried to kill me!"

He shook with good humor. I felt happiness filling my body for the first time in months.

"I have been bitten eleven times," he said with pride. He named each of the villages where a snake had struck him and counted them off on his fingertips, but they only added up to ten. His exaggerated look of befuddlement made me laugh again. He was clowning for me, just as my father had, and though I was grateful, I also felt despair waiting for me underneath all he said.

"Oh, yes, in Bastora, the little beast caught me on my foot!" he recalled in a burst. He showed me the mangled toenail the snake had left him with. "That first time, the mother cobra left me on Indra's holy mountain for two days and one night," he said merrily. "And when I awoke I was feverish for another two days." He made his face sad. "The poor villagers all thought I was going to die and prayed to Devi to help me. 'Oh, what shall we do to save the little Jain boy?' So they sacrificed the mother snake, the poor thing. It was a terrible thing to do. But you know what? When I was well, they gave me the baby snake for having demonstrated such courage, as well as two coconuts for my journey to my village, and a jackfruit, too, and some incense for my prayers. The children placed flowers around my neck and told me I was their Serpent King. I named my snake Dharanendra."

"You were very brave. But maybe just a tiny bit foolish for trying to get the mother to dance on your belly."

"No, you are wrong, my Blue Darkness. For I soon succeeded! You should see Dharanendra dance with me now."

"You still have him? Can snakes really live that long?"

"Do you know the Jain story of the man who painted more than a hundred temples, and all of them blue?"

"No, but does he have anything to do with Dharanendra?"

"You shall decide that for me. You see, when anyone asked the painter why he didn't use yellow, red, or green, he always replied, 'I have found the color I need, and which pleases me, so it would be foolish and disloyal to use another!'" Phanishwar bowed toward me again.

"So your snakes are all Dharanendras?"

"Every one. I came to Goa with Dharanendra the Ninth."

"And you've been able to teach all of them how to dance?"

"Of course. The secret is that you must pretend you are the cobra." He linked his thumbs and placed his hands, palm forward, behind his head to form a hood. "If you become just like him, he dances like he's done nothing else his whole life. I can even get him to twirl and, if he does not have too much food in his belly, to make a kind of hop." I must have given him a skeptical look, because he said, "I swear it! You will see for yourself as soon as we leave here."

"If that ever happens."

"It *will* happen, because you will tell them we are here by mistake." He jiggled two fingers in the air, then snapped them toward my chin like an attacking viper. "And you must ask after Dharanendra." He grimaced. "I do hope he has not bitten anyone. He gets angry when I am away."

"You still haven't told me about the Portuguese nobleman."

"Because you make me get ahead of myself," he declared.

"Me?"

"Yes, you are too . . . too inquisitive." He winked, and I could see he was teasing me again.

The friendship deepening between us worried me all of a sudden—as if it might lead me far from myself.

"What is it?" he asked, patting my knee. "Please, I hope I have not offended you."

"No, it's just . . . it's just that emotions come to me unexpectedly. Sometimes I seem completely lost."

He kissed my forehead. "You are a fine and handsome boy, my Blue Darkness," he said. "And all will be well for you. I can see that."

I was about to speak of my feelings, but he held his finger to his lips, as if it was dangerous to say more. *Who is this man?* I thought, and for the first time in my life I sensed I was in the presence of a being much wiser than I could ever be—the incarnation of a very great soul.

"Who—who are you really?" I stammered.

His eyes twinkled. "We are all a great many people. Even you. Now, I will tell you something few people know," he said very seriously. He seemed to be relishing the chance to talk to me of important matters. "But first you must tell me if you know why snakes are so terrifying to almost everyone."

"Because they bite. And they can kill."

"Exactly true, but that is not the only reason. With their venom, snakes can not only kill us but also put us in a trance, where we can sit with Indra on his throne. I have heard it said that cobras are the blade of a sword that can set us free from our chains or end our life. Their mouths feed on the creatures of the earth and their tails rise high up to heaven, so that when you become a snake you are in both worlds at once. Remember when your mother took the bridge from death to life to say one last goodbye to you?" he asked, scratching the stubble on his cheeks again. "Snakes can carry us onto that very same bridge."

Before I could reply, he draped his arm over my shoulder and pulled me closer to him.

"Now," he said, "as I was telling you before you interrupted me...I was dancing with Dharanendra, and when we finished, the Portuguese Brahmin came to me and said he would like me to visit him in Goa. He assured me he would pay me handsomely to entertain the guests at his wedding."

"Did this nobleman tell you his name?"

"Yes, and he had four of them. Isn't that a wonderful thing? He called himself Father Carlos Miguel Fonseca. Magnificent names, don't you think? They slide across my tongue every time I say them."

"How was he dressed?"

"He wore dark robes, and there were two jeweled pieces of metal joined together around his neck. Like this." Phanishwar crossed his index fingers. "He told me the name of it as if it were a very powerful thing, but I've forgotten."

"It's a crucifix—a Christian symbol. Were there other men with him?"

"Five others, and they treated him with such reverence that I knew he was very important. Such a nice man, too. He must have been faithful and kind in his previous life to have been born so well. And he was always smiling, as if he were hiding a very fine joke under his tongue."

He was hiding one, and it was on you! I thought. "Phanishwar, he was not a Brahmin or even a nobleman," I said roughly. "What he was enjoying was a chance to fool you."

"No, you're wrong. He might even have been royalty. Like Dharanendra! I wondered about that. A king . . . Perhaps I met the King of the Portuguese. Do you think so? Would you know the King's face if I described it to you?"

"He's a priest."

"No, no, no—that's impossible. He was dressed in so many layers of clothing. Only a great lord could—"

"He was a Dominican or Jesuit priest. Priests rule the Inquisition here. Don't you see? That first name you heard—Father—it means he is a member of the Christian Church. He tricked you."

"But he invited me to dance with Dharanendra at his wedding. No one would lie about such a holy day."

"Christian priests cannot marry!"

"Is that truly so?" My cellmate's face darkened as he pondered the consequences of this new information, but then a smile crossed his lips. "I understand now! We were speaking through an interpreter and that silly man must have made a mistake. It was his *son's* wedding!" he declared with renewed vigor.

"Phanishwar, I really believe that he . . ."

My affection for him was so strong by now, and he so desperately wanted good news, that I did not finish my objection. I let the truth slip away from us, may God forgive me. "So you journeyed to Goa for this marriage ceremony?" I said instead.

"Yes, we—Dharanendra and I—came three days early. We crossed into Goa on a very nice boat, but soldiers peered in my sack and discovered him sleeping. Such a fuss they made—hollering and shrieking! I laughed till my belly hurt because they were jumping like toads and would not go near the sack. You'd think that my Dharanendra was a crocodile! I knew that Father Carlos Miguel Fonseca was going to laugh, too, and I explained to these men about my invitation from him. I'm quite sure a monkey could have understood me, but those Portuguese..." He jiggled his hand in front of his face and made his eyes go blank. "No matter how slowly I talked, they looked at me without a particle of understanding. They were very unkind and put me in irons. And they brought me here." He shook a fist. "I'm sure that if Father Carlos Miguel Fonseca knew where I was now, he'd be so very angry with them. I'm sure I've already missed his son's wedding. When he finds out, he will punish those wicked men. Then you and I will be invited to his palace."

He spoke with such certainty that I nearly began to believe that this priest had meant well, after all.

"I will tell the guard your story," I assured him, patting his shoulder. "I'll ask him to summon the Portuguese Brahmin you met."

"And you will please make sure Dharanendra is well." Phanishwar tapped my foot to make sure he had my attention and wiggled his finger across the air between us. "If you want, I shall even teach you to make him dance on your belly. Then you will always be able to make an honest living, my Blue Darkness, no matter where you go. And maybe you will sit with Indra from time to time in heaven. Those are very nice gifts to give someone you love, are they not?"

CHAPTER 7

At dawn I taught Phanishwar the Jewish morning prayers, and he showed me how to begin the day as a Jain. First we intoned the word *nisihi,* which meant "abandonment," he said, and which signified our moving into a sacred space. He then had me walk clockwise three times around the center of our cell, where his wooden carving of Parsva climbing up a coiled serpent toward heaven would have been had it not been confiscated by Portuguese soldiers. Together we sprinkled water onto the invisible saint. Soon it came time for us to offer rice, sweets, and fruit.

"Oh, dear, what shall we do?" Phanishwar moaned. "I'm so confused in here that I did not remember to save anything from my supper for him."

He thought for a long time in silence, his hands clamped over his face like a child hiding his eyes, then sprang to life and asked me to pull out four hairs from my head.

"But why?" I asked.

"Do it, do it, do it!" he said hurriedly, flapping his hands as though shooing away bees. "You have such thick hair. You can spare four strands without putting up a fight."

The outer door to our cell creaked open at that moment and our breakfasts were eased in the slot by the Illiterate, who stank, as usual, of palm liquor. I begged him to tell Father Carlos Miguel Fonseca that Phanishwar was here. "This man is a famous snake dancer that Father Carlos once met," I explained, pointing to the Jain.

The Illiterate merely grunted but my companion showed me a grateful smile. "Now we shall have justice," he said, satisfaction in his eyes.

He tied my hairs together and spread their ends out to form a flower, which he placed at Parsva's feet. "It has four petals," he said. "One each for human beings, animals, gods, and demons."

We designed a crescent of breakfast rice next to the blossom. As I repeated Phanishwar's prayers, I knew that Papa would have been furious with me for addressing an idol—even an invisible one conjured up from the imagination of a good and honest man. But I also knew that my father was dead now and that my life had to move in directions neither of us could ever have foreseen.

*   *   *

For another month, we heard nothing about our request to see Father Carlos. Phanishwar and I established a playful sense of camaraderie, and—true to the great Indian sun of optimism nearly always shining inside him—my fellow prisoner remained convinced that he and I would both be set free the moment his priestly friend learned of our suffering.

"Such an important man is probably on a great voyage of learning," the Jain said. "As soon as he returns he will come to see us!"

*   *   *

As the weeks passed, I grew grateful that Phanishwar respected my moods. Sometimes I could not help crying like an abandoned child, and he would hold me in his strong arms, speaking to me in his soothing voice about his family, so that I soon felt I would recognize each of his children if I met them in the street. At other times, it took all my willpower to keep from shrieking, and I would pace mile after mile in my cell, my thoughts as potent with danger as monsoon clouds. He learned to not even try to address me at such times.

Without my even being aware of it, the Jain slowly brought me back into a world watched by God; because of him, I began to believe that I would see my family again before too long and that, somehow, we would start our lives over.

One afternoon, our double doors opened and a gray-haired, portly priest stepped inside our cell. I knew who he was right away from the cabochon emerald dangling from his rosary. Phanishwar, who had been napping, bolted straight up.

Father Carlos rested his hands on his generous belly and, after a quick sigh, smiled at the Jain as though relieved to have found him after an arduous search. The Illiterate and another guard stood stiffly behind him.

"There you are!" the priest exclaimed in Portuguese.

Phanishwar drew his hands together, bowing low to our guest. "Thank you for coming to see me, your lordship," he said in Konkani.

"Do you speak his language?" the priest asked me.

"Yes," I replied, and translated what the Jain had just told him.

"I'm the one who should thank you for coming to see me," Father Carlos said in a sweet voice.

"I'm sorry that I cannot stand up to greet you, your lordship," the Jain told him. "Please, I mean no offense. You must believe me."

"None taken," he answered with a smile.

Blessed be the surprises of life, I thought. *Phanishwar was right about this man!*

"And I am so very sorry I missed the wedding you invited me to," my friend said, "but I have been here for many months and the guards would not let me go."

Father Carlos looked at me hard and long as I repeated the Jain's words in Portuguese. When I was done, the priest grinned as if he were proud of me, and reached out to brush my arm. I had to resist the urge to fall to my knees and beg him to release me. There was a heavy sickness in my gut, as if all the hope that had been buried there were about to betray me. I could hear Papa saying, *Stay calm and you will make it home to Tejal. You will raise my grandchild and—*

"If only I'd known, I'd have come here immediately!" Father Carlos told Phanishwar. He had a beautiful voice—as though deepened by years of patient study. I'd forgotten that the sound of Portuguese could be so moving.

"You'll be safe with me now," he said to Phanishwar. Addressing the guards, he said, "Pick this man up and take him with us. Be careful with him."

Obeying, they carried Phanishwar as though he were seated in a sedan chair. He grimaced, embarrassed by all the attention.

"Oh, dear, such a fuss I'm causing," he said to Father Carlos as he passed me. "Please forgive me."

Terrified that he would forget me, I said in Konkani, "Phanishwar, I will give you everything I own if you can set me free."

"Have no fear, my Blue Darkness. I will be back for you before sunset." He fluttered his arms. "Who else but you could fly me home to my village by the light of the moon?"

*   *   *

I saw nothing of Phanishwar for the next two days, but my rekindled hope spun intricate daydreams. I imagined us walking arm in arm to his village and greeting Rama and the rest of his children. I invited them all to our farm. Nupi prepared chicken koorma for our feast. Such thanks we gave to the Lord of the Torah and the Jain saints that day!

With my fingertips, I traced the scars I'd cut into my wrists, overjoyed to have them now, for they were proof that I had survived the worst. I asked the Illiterate about Phanishwar's whereabouts that first evening and the next morning, of course, but our guard merely frowned, plainly regarding me as a nuisance.

On the third day, just before supper, the door swung open to reveal the Illiterate cradling Phanishwar—unconscious and limp—in his arms. The guard dumped him onto his cot with a resentful grunt.

"Indian fool weighs more than you'd think," he declared. He rubbed his hands together as though to rid them of a nasty stain.

I saw no marks or burns on my friend's body, but blood was crusted at the corners of his mouth.

"You hurt him again, you son of a bitch!" I yelled.

"Keep quiet, Jew!"

When I spit at him, he shouted, "I ought to beat some sense into you!"

"Try!" I shouted defiantly, but I didn't give him a chance. Ramming into him, I pinned him against the wall, breaking at least one of his ribs with a glorious crack. He gasped and shouted for help, but I managed to grip him by the throat. How good it was to have him in my power. I would have killed the vicious lout—and without regret—but another guard came running and pulled me off of him.

"You're dead, Jew!" the new man shouted at me, raising his truncheon above his head.

*　　*　　*

I awoke in darkness. My head was throbbing. Somewhere beyond my door, Nupi was talking to my father about a trip we were about to make to her village.

"The sun will keep us safe," she told my father.

"But the sun cannot see through stone," he replied.

Then the world receded from me. I was floating. I thought I could smell the night—like burning cinnamon. The moon was above me, creating silver spirals of light around my head and a pulsing glow in the grove of bamboo below me. I wondered if this was death. I hoped so.

When next I awoke, it was as though I'd been dropped from a great height. My whole body ached. I tried to lick my lips, but the pain was unbearable. The second guard must have kicked me in my face and broken my jaw. I pressed my finger into my temple and it felt as though a nail were being driven into the bone.

*   *   *

The next morning, I informed Phanishwar with hand gestures that I could not speak. He brushed his cracked lips against my swollen jaw, then sat with his back to me, staring at the wall. He would not touch his breakfast or turn to face me, no matter how I tugged at him. I did not yet know that he could not lift his arms to take his food.

Hours later, he began to howl. It was an ungodly sound and I crouched like a beggar at his feet to have him explain, but he just shook his head. That evening, however, as the last shadows of sunset fled up our walls, he came to me, sat by my cot, and told me what had happened.

Upon leaving our cell nearly four days before, he'd been carried to a room with hundreds of books in shelves along the walls. Father Carlos took down a large black volume and read from it at his desk by the light of a golden candlestick as tall as a man. A small Indian with a crucifix around his neck interpreted for them.

"What the priest read was all about me—I could not believe it," the Jain told me in a puzzled voice. "He described how I'd charmed Dharanendra on the day we met. There was even a tiny drawing of me that he'd done. Why would a Portuguese Brahmin sketch me? It seemed very odd. I asked him about that, and he replied, 'I am recording the customs of India because they will soon be gone. All traces of sorcery and superstition will be as dust. I have come here to record them for posterity.'"

Phanishwar told him he did not see how the customs of India would soon disappear, since they had been practiced for thousands of years.

"All your gods are dead," the priest explained with an eager smile. "We have destroyed them with this." He held out the cross around his neck.

When Phanishwar asked how Indra, the King of the Gods, could die, Father Carlos replied in a grave and ominous voice that he had been killed by Christ's compassion, as all infidels and heathens would be. "He is already buried," the priest said, "only you do not know it yet."

"That made no sense, my Blue Darkness," the Jain told me now. "Even if Indra were murdered by a great demon who could assume the shape of a cross, he would be reborn immediately. Burying Him would change nothing. Even tiny children know that." His eyes opened wide with supplication. "Tell me, am I not right?"

"You must be," I mouthed, by way of reply.

Phanishwar said that Father Carlos next opened his book to a blank page and dipped his pen into black ink. "Now tell me all you can about snakes and how you train them," he said.

"But it could take hours," the Jain had protested. "I would only bore you."

His host laughed sweetly. "I'm in no rush. And I want to know everything."

My friend told him all the stories about snakes that he could re-member, and how he tried to enter into Dharanendra when they danced. He even spoke of how the venom of a cobra contains both heaven and earth, although he did so in a whisper, since it was teach-ing of power and not for everyone's ears. The priest scribbled away without interruption until he learned that serpents had immortal souls subject to the same cosmic laws as those of men. Hearing that, he made his guest pause and asked him many questions about the soul's size, shape, and constitution, which led Phanishwar along a twisting path to other esoteric subjects that he knew little about. He was unwilling to displease his host, however, and made up his an-swers as best he could, although he took care to add that it would be best if Father Carlos consulted a Jain priest.

By now, Phanishwar had begun to enjoy the warmth of the

Jesuit's presence and his eager questioning. Father Carlos smiled as if all truth made him happy, and the Jain was very proud to be listened to by a Portuguese Brahmin—though a bit ashamed, too, since he was only a snake dancer from a tiny village, and he could neither read nor write. He kept apologizing for being from such a low and insignificant caste, and for missing the wedding to which he'd been so generously invited. He swore he would perform for the priest at his convenience—and he would never accept a single piece of silver or even copper from him!

He then risked a question. "Does your lordship know anything about my snake—about Dharanendra?" he enquired.

"Of course I do! I shall bring him to you when we're finished."

Phanishwar blessed and praised Father Carlos, and even insisted on kneeling next to him and kissing his feet. It had been at least three hours since they'd started talking, so the Jain thought it best to mention me now. Crawling back to his chair, he told the priest, "The blue-eyed young man in my cell is here by mistake as well. He says he is a Jew and that he believes in only a single God, but I do not know if it is Vishnu or Shiva or Devi, or one worshiped by only the Portuguese, or if the Jewish God, too, has been killed by the compassion of your Christ."

The priest laughed till he cried for no reason that Phanishwar could fathom, then asked to hear more about snakes. After another hour or so, the Jain had spoken of all he was at liberty to say, and his host set down his pen. "You have been extremely helpful, Phanishwar, and I give you my thanks," he said.

He patted the Jain's hand as if they had become great friends, then went to the door and summoned an assistant. Their brisk conversation was not translated for Phanishwar, yet the priest's confident nod toward him made him certain that he was about to be released. A rush of excitement left him dizzy. He began to speak of me again, but the Indian interpreter interrupted him.

"His Excellency wishes to ask if you will confess now to the charge of sorcery. If you will, then he will arrange an audience right away with the Grand Inquisitor."

Phanishwar gave the reply he'd practiced in our prison cell: "It is true, your lordship, that I have not been celibate. I did not think it necessary, since I am not a monk. I confess this willingly and I offer my humblest apologies." He smiled hopefully, thinking he'd spoken well.

"But what about all your years of practicing sorcery?" Father Carlos asked. His tone had hardened.

"To my knowledge I have never injured anyone with a word or thought," Phanishwar replied, since this was his definition of sorcery.

"I have just written twenty pages about nothing else!" the priest shouted. "Do you think I don't know why you came to Goa? Do you think I am an idiot?"

"Dharanendra and I...we...we came for your wedding," Phanishwar stammered.

"If you don't make a full and honest confession, then you have come to Goa for your own funeral!" the other man thundered.

The Jain was silent, wondering how to win his host back to his side. The Portuguese Brahmin seemed to be two men, and the second was not at all friendly.

"Would you deny Christ the truth about your evil ways?" Father Carlos demanded.

Falling to his knees again and speaking slowly, so there could be no errors of translation, Phanishwar replied, "Please, your lordship, summon the boy from my cell. He will explain everything to you in Portuguese, just as you would like."

The furious priest spoke no more to his guest, but instead summoned two guards. When they took hold of Phanishwar, the Jain begged not to be burnt again and cried out that he would be celibate from now on.

"I'm afraid that you have no other choice while you are Christ's prisoner," Father Carlos informed him.

*   *   *

He was carried down several flights of stairs to the dungeon where his feet had been singed over coals. The odor of rotting flesh there made him grow faint with dread, and when men in long capes tied his hands behind his back with ropes that smelled of the sea, he was unable to put up a fight. He could whisper only that it was all a mistake. They attached his bindings to an iron pulley near the ceiling and secured a reed basket filled with stones to his feet. Three times he was hoisted fifteen feet into the air and then dropped to inches above the ground. His screams were so piercing and his prayers so endless that an iron bit was forced in his mouth and fastened with leather straps around his head. After his shoulders were torn from their sockets, he was left to dangle all the rest of that day and night. At least, that is how he remembered it; he soon lost hold of the passage of time.

At some point, an iron poker was jabbed into his ribs and questions were asked of him, but what they were or what he replied, or for how long the torture went on, he could not say. A putrid snake crawling with maggots was tied around his neck before one of the worst sessions. He did not think it was Dharanendra, although he was told it was.

"I no longer cared if it was my beautiful friend," Phanishwar told me, sobbing. "Do you see what has happened, my Blue Darkness? I'm no longer the man I was. I'm no longer a man at all." His eyes were rimmed red with hopelessness. "I cannot lift my arms or walk. What will happen to my young son? What will happen to Rama?"

*   *   *

I cannot say what Phanishwar felt over the next few days, since he spoke not a word to me and even neglected his morning prayers to Parsva, but rage twisted through my gut like a living thing, making me throb with the need to destroy our prison. But kicking at our cell door brought no one and only made me despise my helplessness.

The black pain in my jaw cleaved to every breath and my self-hatred came in crushing waves. When exhaustion overcame me, my dreams were tales of revenge cobbled together from old Torah stories that I no longer believed in. I tasted my father's blood when I awoke in the night, as I had when I'd visited him in this same prison.

I told Phanishwar in a frail, agonized whisper that overpowering our guard was our only way out, and I begged for his opinion on my plan, but he refused to answer me.

On the day when I was to be taken to have my hair cut, I worked myself up into a state of mad fury. When our new guard—a small man with red, flaking skin on his cheeks—stepped into the cell to escort me out, I leapt at him. I was still strong enough to wrestle him to his knees, but when he twisted inside my arms, his elbow knocked into my jaw. All fight was gone from me in an instant. Howling in agony, I crawled away while he threatened to beat me senseless.

Phanishwar cursed him and said he would be reborn in hell.

The new man understood Konkani and laughed. "Reincarnation is only for *arroz preto*," which was what some of the Portuguese called Indians to try to humiliate them. It was the coarse black rice eaten by peasants.

Under my breath, I swore on my father's memory that I'd attempt escape again, but secretly I surrendered all I was and would ever be to my captors. How could I go on fighting? My ribs had become rungs in a rickety ladder, and I bled whenever my shin brushed my cot. My knobby fingers were those of a skeleton.

Whose eyes had I now? Surely not my mother's or any living being's. It was a good thing I had no mirror.

A man's will is nothing compared to physical pain, which made a desert of all my plans but one: to kill whoever had denounced my father and me and brought us to this foul hell.

I found what solace I could in feeding Phanishwar from my hands and washing him every day. Even trying to lift his arms made the poor man shudder with agony. He moaned through most of the night. I would creep to his cot and put his head in my lap, swatting the mosquitoes away from his face so he might sleep without inter-ruption. I learned the feel of his tears on my hands. Sometimes they seemed to be seeping out of my fingertips.

If men and women cried from their hands, maybe compassion would come to us more easily, I began to think, and it is a thought that has never left me in the years since.

Holding Phanishwar, I often slept sitting up, dreaming of death. It was a ship with black and red sails that would carry us far away, with the salt wind of Shiva's breath behind us. Many mornings I saw Tejal standing before me, naked, holding out flame-tree blossoms in the reed basket I'd always used to collect flowers for Nupi. I refused to take the blooms. I couldn't. *If only I had succeeded in killing myself, then you would be free,* I told the girl.

The darkness of our cell at night became the memory of Tejal's softness, and she even kissed me on the lips one morning to wake me.

It was my abject hunger, I think, that created these visions.

Mama wore her white head scarf whenever she appeared to me. She cradled me in her arms, just as I cradled Phanishwar, and when I looked down at my hands I saw hers. It was as if we'd become the same person. She told me she would be waiting for me when I came home. I thanked her for her promise, but even in my dreams I knew she shouldn't make such a vow. How could she escape from the prison cell she shared with me?

One night, just before dawn, Wadi reached out to me, his fingers straining.

"The air is burning!" my cousin shouted.

I pulled him to safety. I felt as though I had saved us both.

I suppose we are all prisoners of our past friendships—even when we have grown to regret them.

*   *   *

An Indian doctor was finally sent to us after three weeks. He maneu-vered Phanishwar's shoulders into their sockets while the Jain wept. I could see from the physician's coolness of demeanor that he had done this many times before. Before he took his leave, I kneeled in front of him.

"Give us poison," I mouthed.

I was not sure if I'd use the poison on myself or save it for Phanishwar, but it would be good to have; a Jew, I think, should always be ready—and willing—to kill himself.

The doctor pushed me away, but I clung to his legs until the guard pried me off of him.

*　　*　　*

Even though Phanishwar's physical pain was easing, I still could not get him to tell me what he was thinking. He asked that I leave him be. When I came to him in the night, he would push me away, saying, "Parsva is dead and buried."

With hand gestures I asked him to say both our Jewish and Jain prayers, but he refused. In the debased world to which he had descended, snake princes could no longer protect Jain saints, and men could not make cobras dance.

After four weeks, I was able to open my mouth wide enough to swallow small handfuls of rice and even chew some morsels of fried fish. I could speak in a whisper without being unmanned by the pain.

I told Phanishwar that Father Carlos had lied about Indra's death to trick a confession of sorcery from him. "You've beaten him by not giving him that," I said.

"You're the one who is tricking me!" he replied angrily, his eyes flashing violently. "My own ignorance of the world has ruined me. What a fool I was to believe I understood the ways of men!"

"You will see—Parsva and Dharanendra will one day shatter the crosses of all the Christians in India."

The old Jain laughed at me, then mumbled incomprehensibly in a voice I no longer knew.

A few days later he stopped eating again. He snapped his eyes shut whenever I approached him, and feigned deafness.

One night, however, he called out to his son Rama in his sleep.

"I can't go on like this," he whispered when I woke him.

"You must eat and get your strength back," I told him.

"No, I must die as quickly as I can so that I can come back as a murderer. Then I shall kill them all."

*   *   *

A few days later, a rose-ringed parakeet appeared in our window and looked down at us from the sill. Phanishwar's beliefs must have sculpted the shape of my madness, because I recognized my father in the bird's glowing eyes. *He's returned to save me,* I thought. *He will let me catch him so I can tie a note to his foot.*

I tried to coax the parakeet down, but he would not come. Jumping up, I made a swipe, but he flew off with only my curses to take back to his nest.

What would I have written if I could have used my blood as ink? And to whom? Not even my uncle would have been able to help us in our prison. If that were possible, then he would already have come to visit me.

Phanishwar was growing frail from lack of food. I feared he would succeed in ending his own life. We hardly ever spoke, and he lay all day and night on his cot. The sores on his back became bloody and infected, and he stank from his own filth.

Hoping to save him—and to encourage myself—I told him that the parakeet had been sent by Parsva. "He was the reincarnation of your Dharanendra. He flew here to make certain we are still alive."

The Jain closed his eyes as though considering my words very seriously, then replied as if it were obvious, "Ah, but I do not think we *are* alive, my Blue Darkness."

*   *   *

Phanishwar and I were moving in opposite directions, and as I grew stronger his suicidal resolve made me mean-spirited with him. I told the old man I despised him for not fighting against our enemies, which was not even half true. Then I fell before him and sobbed, because I knew I might say anything to get out of this prison—even confirm to the priests that he was a sorcerer or name my aunt and uncle as secret Jews.

When I confessed to him that I might betray him, the Jain fixed me with a look of compassion that I will always remember. It was as though his eyes contained all the great and small things of my life—the sun and moon, the scent of jasmine on our verandah, Nupi singing a lullaby about Ganesha . . .

"I want to die," he told me. "So what you tell our jailors will not make a particle of difference. In my next life, I will have my revenge for what they've done to Indra and Dharanendra."

"But your hatred for them won't be reborn," I protested. "You will be someone else—a baby, with no memory of what has taken place in this life."

He held his hands over his ears and would make no reply.

*   *   *

Two days later, the warden entered our cell and told me that my audience with the Grand Inquisitor, which I'd been requesting for over a year, had finally been granted. I would be taken to him in twenty-four hours. After the warden locked our door again, Phanishwar held my gaze for the first time in weeks. He was all brittle bones and sagging flesh, yet I saw a flicker of hope and friendship in his glassy black eyes, moist now with tenderness for me. Was he not so resigned to death after all? Did he want me to tell him I'd make an appeal to Church officials on his behalf?

I knew that this alone might revive his spirit, but speaking of him to our jailors would undoubtedly prejudice my case. I turned away from his gaze and lay facedown on my mattress, trying to smother my guilt, but that night I curled up behind him on his cot. The warm touch of his hand on mine changed my plans.

"I will tell them that you are ready to confess," I said.

"No," he whispered.

I sat up. "Listen to me, Phanishwar. You must tell them you have practiced sorcery in the past, but that you now renounce all your former beliefs and accept Christ as your savior—as God. Do you understand me? Otherwise you *will* die—and not of starvation. Before that blessing comes to you they will torture you again."

"I cannot turn around and go back toward life. I cannot be what I once was. All that is gone now."

"I don't believe that," I told him. I squeezed his hand. "This . . . this may sound silly," I said hesitatingly, "but I sometimes think you may be someone greater than I could ever imagine. Someone who has come down to this world from Indra's mountain."

"I'm not," he said. "I'm just a Jain snake dancer. Do not fool yourself."

"Would you tell me if you were—someone great and powerful, I mean?"

"How can I know that? I have never had any power."

"Maybe you don't even know your true nature. Isn't that possible?"

"You are confusing me. My Blue Darkness, it would not matter even if I were Vishnu or Shiva. I am here now. I am a prisoner. That is all you need know."

"Phanishwar, it would be a monstrous crime for you to die here, at the hands of such worthless men," I said in desperation. "It would be unforgivable. You must think of Rama."

He began to cry softly. I gripped his shoulder so he could feel my resolve; I told him again that he had to admit to sorcery.

"I'm not sure . . . I can't think of what to do. . . ."

Papa always told Sofia and me that love had been used by God during the six days of Creation to fashion the world, but holding Phanishwar as he sobbed, I stopped believing that. Later, he reminded me that Hindus and Jains had a name for our era of cruelty: they called it the Age of Kali, a period of debasement and ever-deepening spiritual darkness against which all our struggles were useless.

*   *   *

A silky dawn light was falling across my legs, and I was seated on the floor of our cell. Phanishwar lay on his cot behind me, combing my hair with his fingers. On waking that morning, he'd agreed that I could make a plea on his behalf.

Hearing the warden approach and knowing it was almost time for me to leave for my audience with the Grand Inquisitor, I kneeled before my friend. He smiled, fighting back tears. The outer door to our cell clanged open. My pulse began racing.

"They're here for me," I said, rising up. "Phanishwar, I don't know what I'll say if they torture me. . . . I may not find the courage to speak of you. Forgive me if you can."

"Don't worry. Go now." He waved me off like an elder gesturing to a young man.

"I'll try to save us both," I promised.

He held a finger to his lips—as he did whenever he believed it was too dangerous to speak of the future. Did he sense an irreversible change coming in our lives? Sometimes even today, his suffering wakes me in the early morning and I wonder who he really was and what he was trying to tell me. I picture his black eyes as if they might create new life in me—or change the past to something I can more easily live with. But maybe my impression of his greatness was only an illusion conjured up by confinement.

*   *   *

I might have been able to walk steadily and securely behind the warden to my audience if I had not been forced to leave Phanishwar behind. As it was, I stumbled ahead, doubting the solidity of my steps. For the first time I dared to admit to myself that I desperately wanted Tejal to wait for me. If I gained my freedom but lost her, what would any of this mean?

We walked through dank corridors until we came to a high-ceilinged hall, its walls hung with blue silk tapestries with brilliant yellow stripes. The warden stopped at the doorway and, making a bow to two small figures seated at a table inside, murmured that I was to proceed forward alone.

I had long imagined Father Tómas Pinto, the Grand Inquisitor of India, as an ogre with a face disfigured by cruelty, but he was merely a gaunt man in long dark robes and a four-cornered hat that would have struck me as comical under other circumstances. He looked no more than forty—too young to be condemning men and women to death, I reasoned rather naively at the time. There was an austere and knowing look in his eyes, as if we were old enemies—but it occurs to me now he had been through this a thousand times before, and was most probably deeply bored at having to listen to yet one more Jew or Hindu needing to learn of Christ's mercy.

He sat at one end of a table about five paces in length that had been raised on a foot-high wooden platform and covered in an elegant green and scarlet brocade, with an interspersed design of golden crosses. A slanting light shone in through the windows, their curtains not quite closed.

He wants to sit up higher than the men he judges, I realized. *And he wants to display the wealth that the Church confiscates from the people it imprisons.*

Such a fool I still was to think that understandings such as these would give me an advantage. After all I'd been through, I didn't yet see that the Inquisition had its own logic and castes, and that nothing I valued meant anything in this place. To these men, my thoughts were those of an Untouchable, as valueless as dust.

At the far end of the room, against the wall, hung a life-sized crucifix. Blood crusted on Christ's hands and feet. If he had been Phanishwar's Parsva, I would have bowed to him. As it was, I silently prayed that He and His followers would be swallowed up by the ancient soil of India—that even their footprints and shadows would be forgotten.

A squat olive-skinned man sat at this end of the table, holding a feather pen. He had tightly pursed lips and was looking at me as though puzzled by something. Maybe he was surprised that a young man who had broken the rib of a guard had so withered a face and such stringy flesh on his bones. I was suddenly aware of the odor of filth on me, and all the wasted time that had turned to dirt and hopelessness. I smelled as my father had on my last visit to his cell— like a crushed animal left to rot in the sun. I looked down at my hands and saw my overgrown fingernails, like those of a beggar of seventy. How could I have not seen what I'd become until now?

I prayed to the Lord that they would not question me about murdering Papa; if I were to admit that, I would never leave this place alive.

On the table in front of my judge was set a foot-high flag of Saint Dominic, the founder of the Inquisition, carrying a sword and an olive branch, bearing the embroidered motto *Misericordia et Justitia,* "Mercy and Justice." The way the Inquisitor began caressing this flag in his hand, as though stroking my fear, swept all thought from my mind. My heart seemed to be beating outside my body. When I closed my eyes, my own dread seemed to be swaying me from side to side.

"Approach the table," said the secretary.

His voice came like the breaking of a seal; terror flooded me.

I do not know how I walked forward; my feet felt made of brittle bone. Stopping three paces away from the Inquisitor, I began to cry, for no reason other than being able to face the man who could set me free. I felt like I had run for an entire year, across every minute of every day, and I had at last reached my destination.

"I confess all my crimes," I moaned. I fell to my knees.

My voice sounded pitifully toneless, but that was good—he would surely see that I was not trying to challenge him. My vision seemed to be failing, too; the room had grown very dark.

The mind races in frenzied directions when cowed by circumstance—I trembled at the thought that I was about to be blinded by the Lord for bowing down to this evil man.

The secretary instructed me to sit on a bench by the Inquisitor.

My pulse thumped in my ears as I shuffled there, and I could not look up. I sat as erect as I could and faced the doorway out—my gateway home.

"Put your hand on the Missal in front of you and swear to declare the truth and preserve the holy secrecy of the Inquisition," the secretary told me.

After I'd spoken this oath, Tomás Pinto asked, "Do you know the cause of your imprisonment and are you ready to confess your crimes?"

His voice seemed to fill up every inch of me. At first, I could not form an answer.

Over a year earlier, upon being arrested, I had feigned innocence; now I told the damning truth: "I am a Jew, and I have often practiced the rituals of my people with my father. I am ready to sign a confession to that effect."

My words came out as though they'd been clinging to me since birth. Looking up, I wondered if I was at all different from the poisoned light, the stale air, the cemetery smell of wax and dust. I felt as though I were ready for my shroud. And for the soil of burial to spill over me.

"It is good that you have become your own accuser," the Inquisitor told me, "but in the name of our Lord Jesus Christ, you must confess all that you know so that you may experience the mercy this tribunal is ready to offer all those who truly wish to make amends for their offenses. Now, are you a Jew or a New Christian?"

"I am a Jew," I declared, and my voice echoed against the walls and ceiling like an accusation of the foulest sin imaginable. I would never have guessed that the word *Jew* could sound so damning.

"Yet the dead say you are something else," the Inquisitor told me.

"The dead?"

"Your father was a New Christian," he said sternly.

I didn't understand what he meant and reasoned that he was making the first move in a game meant to ensnare me in lies. He was trying to confuse me.

"If he was, then . . . then I was not aware of it," I stammered.

"And his father and grandfather, what were they?"

"They were Jewish, too."

The Inquisitor patted moisture from his cheeks with a handkerchief and frowned with discomfort.

May the heat of my homeland chase all the Christians from India, I thought.

"Yet a witness has told us your great-grandfather converted to Christianity," he said.

It was true enough that Papa's illustrious grandfather Berekiah—along with all the Jews of Portugal—had been forced to convert to Christianity in 1497, but only someone in my family could have given this information to the Inquisition.

"Who is your witness?" I asked the priest.

"I'm afraid that is precisely what you must tell *me*," he replied in a pleased voice. He took a sip of water.

"But how can I?"

"If you practiced your Jewish rituals," he said, wiping his lips, "then you must know who was with you—or who saw you."

I couldn't think of what to reply. "Don't take me back to my cell!" I begged. "I'll tell you everything you want, but I can't wait months again for another audience. I'll never make it."

"Then tell me about your great-grandfather."

I sensed the truth would never be enough, but that was all I had: "His name was Berekiah Zarco, and he was converted in 1497, in the city of Lisbon. He was a renowned kabbalist and he moved his family to Constantinople in 1507. I know the names of his brothers and his younger sister. They were Mordecai and Judah and Cinfa."

"A kabbalist? Then you must have studied such magical practices in your family." Keen interest quickened the Grand Inquisitor's speech.

If I admitted this, I'd be accused of sorcery—just like Phanishwar. Yet if I denied it, and if Wadi or my aunt and uncle had testified secretly against me, then my judge would know I was lying.

"Kabbalah is never taught to anyone under forty," I answered, telling a partial truth, since many advanced practices were withheld from initiates.

"Are you certain of that?"

Here I believed I could outsmart him. "No, in point of fact I'm not certain of anything regarding kabbalah. My father was only a simple manuscript illuminator."

Admiration for me flashed in the Dominican's eyes, but for only an instant, and then he was on the attack again. "Having a great-grandfather who was a convert to Christianity made your father a Christian as well, did it not?"

This had never occurred to me. Now I understood how the Inquisition had been granted so much power over Papa.

"I did not know that was the case, Your Excellency."

"I expect you now wish to amend the confession you made earlier?"

"Yes . . . I am a New Christian. I see that now."

I was too dazed and panic-stricken to realize I had just lost any hope of freedom; I had admitted to being a lapsed Christian—the worst crime possible in their eyes, and one for which I could be burnt at the stake.

"Yet you've never been baptized, have you?" he enquired.

"Not to my knowledge."

"Are you ready to be baptized?"

"I am."

"First you must tell me what Jewish crimes you committed when visiting Goa."

"We never practiced Judaism in Goa. We knew it was forbidden and might cause trouble for my aunt and uncle, who are good Christians."

"Yet we have witnesses who tell us a different story, and to convince us of your sincere repentance, you must tell us of your crimes and give us the names of the people who saw you commit them."

I was sure that anyone I named would be arrested immediately.

"I have many relatives in Turkey," I replied, trying to wriggle free. "A few of them, including my grandfather, once visited us at our farm. I was very small, but I remember they took part in the Jewish Passover service at my home."

"But who here in India knew you had fallen back into your Jewish ways?"

"I did. And my father."

A shadow of displeasure crossed his face. "Please, don't try to be clever," he advised me brusquely. "It will only make your position a worse one."

I saw perverse amusement in his eyes. *He's toying with me,* I thought, and I realized then, for the first time, that he might very well have moved Phanishwar into my cell not to keep my spirits up, but to destroy my will. *That* was what I sensed hiding in the Jain. Maybe the old man's injuries had even been faked. The Inquisitor had used him to weaken me.

"What about your cousin, Francisco Xavier? You have not mentioned him and I find that odd."

"He is also a good Christian soul," I answered firmly.

"You're very sure of that, are you?"

The cat-and-mouse expression on his face confused me. Had he taken Wadi prisoner as well? I almost wished this were so, for that would have meant that my cousin could not have been responsible for my father's imprisonment.

"I'm quite sure," I said.

"Do you still maintain that you have never practiced Judaism in Goa?"

"I do."

"You mean to say you never uttered a single blasphemy against the Church?" There was disbelief in his eyes.

"Never, Your Excellency."

Pinto stared at me with his lips sealed tight, waiting for me to recant, but Papa and I had never so much as said a blessing over our wine when inside Portuguese territory. We'd been very cautious.

"I'm told there are six hundred and thirteen duties that each Jew has in life," the priest said in a quick, businesslike voice, "and that the first of these duties is to believe in a single God."

"That's true. We call them *mitzvot*."

"I've also been told that half of these duties are negative injunctions—acts which must not be performed. Tell me, do you think that Christianity is less rigorous than Judaism? Or less demanding of its believers?"

"I would not think so, but ... but I have no way of knowing."

He scowled. "The witnesses against you say you are an intelligent young man, but apparently they're wrong."

"May I sign my confession?" I asked, since I'd heard that prisoners were made to do so before being publicly humiliated in an Act of Faith and then sentenced to serve time in a civil jail.

"Shut up, you stubborn fool!" the Inquisitor shouted. He picked up a silver bell, gazing at me hard, his jaw set with rage, making it clear my life was in his hands.

"I beg you not to kill me," I moaned. "I will do anything you ask."

The smile of the victorious crossed his lips, and I understood that I'd begged at just the right moment. He put his bell down. "What do you say to a little riddle that may help you understand your predicament? If you answer it correctly, I'll allow you to sign your confession. That's quite fair, I think."

"More than fair, Your Excellency."

In a tone of challenge, he gave me his riddle: "I speak to you on my journey—*and only to you*—from my departure point to the very end. And though I always die in the same place, you can hear me speaking from my closed grave if you pay close attention. Who am I?"

Nothing would come to me; it was as though my mind were hurtling in a hundred different directions at once.

The Inquisitor stared at me impatiently. "Well?" he demanded.

"I ... I don't know. Might it have something to do with a ghost?"

The ringing of his bell seemed to explode inside me and I

jumped up. When I saw the warden coming back in the room to lead me away, I felt a rush of air through me, as though my soul were fleeing through my body.

*   *   *

When I awakened in my cell, Phanishwar was gone. Was he being tortured and killed as a sorcerer?

Odd how the bruised mind desires a safe object for its contempt; as I sat alone on my cot, I thought it likely that the Jain's mission to break me had been accomplished. The traitor had been granted permission to return to his village.

CHAPTER 8

Papa and I were in his library when I first broached the subject of Sofia spending more time with Wadi and his parents. He was seated at his desk, fingering a four-sided top—a *dreidl*— that he'd made for me when I was small. He expressed doubts about my plan, and I argued until he thrust up his hand like a shield. "Ti, if you'll excuse a small criticism, you tend to think too doggedly about your sister." He opened the volume of Abraham Abulafia's philosophy he'd been reading before I'd come in.

"What exactly are you trying to say?" I said, unable to keep the hurt I felt out of my voice.

"What I mean, Ti," he said sternly and without looking up, "is that it's probably best if we just leave things as they are for the time being." He traced his finger down the edge of a page, looking for the citation he wanted, as though I didn't exist.

Rather than start a quarrel I was sure to lose, I rushed away, cursing his rudeness. At supper we glared at each other like enemies, and I snapped at Sofia to mind her own business when she asked me if we'd had a disagreement, which only made my father say the inevitable: "I'll thank you not to speak like that to your sister!"

At bedtime, however, I heard Papa padding his way slowly to my doorway in his old slippers. I knew he was coming to apologize. Bare-chested because of the wilting heat, he panted in my doorway with his tongue out, trying to get me to smile. But it was my turn to make believe he was invisible, and I kept my gaze on my book.

"Ti, I take back what I said before. I'm sorry."

He touched his fingertip to his closed lips, his way of asking if I forgave him—a gesture carried over from when I was tiny.

I wanted to make him plead, but the frail candlelight was making sagging crescents of skin under his eyes. It startled me to realize that he had grown older without my noticing it. Had we already completed most of our journey together?

"I'm sorry, too," I said.

Papa came inside and struck a flint to a second taper on my side table, telling me that my room was not a cave and I, as far as he knew, was not a bat. He dropped down on the end of my bed as if he'd crossed the Arabian desert to reach me. I sat up and closed my book.

"Your father is an old elephant, isn't he?" he said glumly.

"A bit hard to understand sometimes, but I don't mind," I replied.

His expression grew serious. "What you propose is sound, Ti. Please understand that I'm just worried your aunt will try to make your sister into a Christian if she spends more time there—behind all our backs. That's what made me so rude to you before."

"Would a sermon now and then from Aunt Maria be such a high price to pay if Wadi could help Sofia find her place in the world?"

"Without Judaism I don't think Sofia could ever find her place."

"Papa, she's not about to convert. She's seen how cruelly the Christians treat the Hindus in Goa—and how they keep slaves from Africa. And she loves her Hebrew micrography. She wouldn't be able to keep working at that if she were baptized. It would be considered a sin."

"I hadn't thought of that." He smiled, giving me a cagey wink. "You know, Ti, sometimes I think you're even cleverer than your mother!"

I told him then that Sofia had once confessed to me that she felt so uncomfortable with herself that she wanted to wriggle out of her skin. He stared out my window, searching, it seemed, for a strategy. Seeing his somber profile, I had the feeling that he wanted my mother to make this decision. Likely he felt sometimes that the wrong parent had survived.

I think the great lesson I learned from my father at moments like this was that people are more fragile than we think—and that we never get over some deaths.

"Thank you for letting us stay here after Mama died," I told him. "It was very generous of you."

"What do you mean?" he asked.

"After she died, we didn't move. You wanted me and Sofia to be able to stay where we'd always lived."

"Nupi told you that, didn't she?" When I nodded, he said, "Listen, Ti, it was no sacrifice—I wanted to stay here. I'll always love this house." He grinned. "Where else could I find frogs living in my underwear? And a cook who meddles in everything we do?"

We laughed together. "Papa," I said, "there's things I'd like to tell you—about myself."

In hindsight, I can see that the possibility that he would die young—just like my mother—produced a steady drumbeat of dread beneath everything I did and thought throughout my childhood and adolescence.

"Go ahead," Papa replied, giving me a concerned look.

"It's nothing bad," I assured him. "It's just that sometimes . . . sometimes I think I've never said the most important things to you. I don't want you to . . . to leave without my saying them."

"To leave?"

I could not say the word I meant.

He patted my feet, then squeezed them tight. "When you were a baby, your feet were so tiny and soft—each of the toes like little fern tendrils. Ti, I know you are growing up. And that means you're thinking new thoughts—the kind that young men have. As for me, I'm turning into an old man. But that's how it should be. That's the way this life works. Have no regrets. I know you, and you know me, and anything you haven't said I see with my eyes each time I look at you."

As we stared at each other, the intimacy between us became too deep—as though we might both fall inside and never find our way out. It's odd how life must be lived on the surface of things. Otherwise, we would grow too cognizant of the little farewells and deaths we live every day.

Papa broke our silence to talk more about Sofia. Maybe it was only the special mood of transcendence around me, but he seemed to listen to me more carefully and fully than he ever had before. *What luck to still have Papa with me,* I was thinking the whole time we talked. *And what good fortune Sofia and I have had in our lives.* This was—just as Papa had observed—a thought that was new to me; even at the best of times, I'd previously believed that we'd had lonely childhoods.

In the end, my father agreed that it was a good idea for Sofia to spend more time in a big city where people with her mixture of European and Indian features were everywhere. "But listen," he added, "we must never leave your sister alone with your aunt." Explaining that Moslem, Hindu, and Jewish children were sometimes forcibly baptized when away from their parents, he added, "And we must not let her ever enter a church without one of us present."

"You make Aunt Maria sound like a witch," I said.

"Your aunt has a good woman inside her, Ti, but we both know she is concealed far below that vain creature we usually see. To someone as vulnerable as your sister, *that* woman is far more dangerous than a witch."

*   *   *

I decided to speak frankly to Wadi about my concerns for Sofia and enlist his aid. He and I were fifteen now, and he was five and a half feet in height—as tall as his father. His shoulders had broadened and his face had gained an adult angularity. He kept his black hair cropped short, which I thought very dashing, and there was often bristle on his chin. He was fast becoming a man. As for me, I looked like a pink-cheeked cherub standing next to him, though, to his credit, he never made fun of me or tried to bully me. His concern for my feelings did a great deal to win back my trust in him—the trust I'd lost when he'd lied about my having prompted him to visit the mosque near Ponda. Yet I was only too aware that he still hid his emotions and thoughts when they didn't fit his mother's expectations, and when he feared being ridiculed because of his affliction. The older he got, the less spontaneous this made him, and he sometimes spoke and acted as though he were involved in a cautious game of chess. I think there was always a danger that, like Aunt Maria, he would bury all that was best in him so far down that it would become unreachable, even to himself. I did not then realize that I had assigned myself the goal of keeping these qualities available to us all. In a way I was being selfish: knowing there was so much more to him made me feel special—like a sorcerer able to see what is invisible to others.

True to form, Wadi easily dismissed Sofia's shyness and self-loathing as products of her youth that would soon disappear.

"I hope you're right," I told him, "but when we visit Goa, I'd really appreciate it if you'd introduce her to your friends and take her around the city. I'll make up excuses for not coming along. She needs to go places without me or our father."

"Maybe," he said, tilting his head doubtfully, afraid perhaps to tell me what he really thought. When I pressed him, he said, "I think she's going to get bored—or annoyed with me."

"But why? She thinks you're wonderful!"

"Sofia's only eleven, Tiger, and my friends are all our age. And there's Sarah, too."

"Who's Sarah?"

"A girl I met."

I was pleased for him, but this was the moment when I first realized that the friendship that had begun the day I'd handed him my baby sister to dry would likely become a shadow of what it had been. Wadi, sensing my mix of emotions, crossed himself. When I frowned, he looked around to make sure no one could see us, then touched himself suggestively. "You could easily find a girl yourself, you know. It would be good for you."

"Maybe."

"Don't be jealous," he said.

"Why would I be?"

"I don't know. So if it's not that, then what's wrong?"

"Nothing," I lied. "It's just that I'm still thinking about Sofia. I want you to help her meet other girls. You can be her bridge to the world. Like we were for you when you were little."

"It frightens me to think that I won't be able to help her like you want me to," he said, in the the true voice he tended to use only with Sofia and me. "I wonder sometimes if I can live up to what you want me to be."

"What do I want you to be?" I asked, puzzled.

"Ever since we were little, I could feel something in you tugging at me. I feel it right now. It's like . . . like you're always telling me something even when you're not saying a thing. Like your voice is in my head." He shrugged. "I don't really mind it. It's just weird. Maybe I even like it." He laughed. "You must think I'm crazy."

"No. I sometimes hear you talking to me, too—when everything is quiet. It's because we grew up together. It makes everything different. It's like when your father was carrying you in his arms and you took my hand. That kind of thing changes people."

The moment I said this I wished I could have taken it back; Wadi had an unwritten rule that intimacies between Sofia, me, and him were not to be spoken about. I must have very badly wanted to keep our lives the way they were. "So will you help me?" I hurried to ask.

"Do I have any other choice?" he said, punching my shoulder.

"No," I answered. I didn't hit him back because if I did, he'd have thought that I was defending my having broken his rule.

He twisted his lips into an exaggerated frown. "Why do I get the feeling *you're* getting *me* into trouble this time?" he said. "And on purpose!"

*   *   *

Over the next two years, we visited my aunt and uncle as frequently as possible. Although Sofia was reticent at first to go out without Papa or me, Wadi lived up to his vow. He charmed her with his gallantry and bright-eyed eagerness to show her his city, and as he moved closer to adulthood he grew bolder about drawing her out with affectionate clowning whenever her stubbornness seemed to have him defeated. It sometimes seemed as if his newfound maturity left him freer to act like a little boy with her.

Many years later I learned that some of the students at the Jesuit school Wadi attended were forbidden by their parents even to talk to him. Like so much else, my cousin kept this to himself, and I can see now what courage he displayed in going everywhere around the city with Sofia.

From my room upstairs, I'd often watch Wadi and her leave the house. And though loneliness perched beside me on the sill, I felt strangely good about remaining by myself—as though freed from an obligation. In such moments during my youth, I came slowly to accept my solitary nature.

On the few occasions that I accompanied Wadi and his friends to the river or a teahouse in one of the Hindu neighborhoods, I noticed that Sofia had learned to laugh without veiling her face with her hair. And though she tended to attach herself to him or me like a leaf in a storm, the girls would sometimes pry her away to tell her a giggling secret. After a time, they adopted her as their protégée and showed her the proper way to walk in a flowing Portuguese dress and fancy leather shoes, and how to hold a parasol, which she never tired of demonstrating to me, Nupi, and Papa. I'll always remember when she returned to our uncle's house one afternoon with her tresses braided with silver and blue ribbon. Papa and I congratulated her, but I feared how beautiful and adult she looked, and from his sideways glance at me, I knew he did, too.

*   *   *

Sofia was awed by her new friends and spoke of them as though they were visitors from a far-off land of greater knowledge. Her dress and manner became more Portuguese under their tutelage, although when we returned to our farm, she always put on a sari.

"Mama wouldn't recognize me otherwise," she explained to me one afternoon as we were planting potato tubers in our garden. It was a vegetable that had just reached our district for the first time and Nupi, delighted with their taste, had enlisted our aid in her kitchen plot.

Sometimes we are able to sense a fulcral moment in someone else's life. "Don't be absurd," I told her. "Mama would know you in total darkness. And she wouldn't care if you looked more Portuguese than Indian."

Sofia burst into tears when I said that. Holding her as she shook, I couldn't remember ever feeling closer to her.

*   *   *

"My friends think she's the cutest thing in the world," Wadi confirmed to me one morning after she'd stayed out late with him the night before at the grand fair in Goa held in honor of St. John.

When I heard that, it was as if a gate in me opened; I could walk into my future without having to look back for my sister. Until that moment, I hadn't even realized my *own* freedom had been held hostage by her unhappiness. I knew suddenly that I hadn't felt envious of Sofia's active social life because—somewhere inside me— I'd always known it was necessary to forsake these new friendships to win back my destiny. So blind to my own motivations was I at times.

*   *   *

Sofia and Sarah—the young woman whom Wadi was courting—became particularly fond of each other. I remember Sarah from that time as a thin, dark-haired girl in clothing that always seemed too frilly for her. She tended to smile as if she were fighting sadness, which made Sofia and me try all sorts of silly antics to make her laugh. She particularly liked my sister's imitation of a turtle eating a cabbage leaf—a comic routine she'd picked up from Papa, of course.

Sarah's mother had died of smallpox when she was very young, and she was being raised by her father, which made us feel a special kinship with her. This knowledge also gave deeper meaning to the quick, possessive way she took my sister's hand each time they were together. Sofia told me many secrets about Sarah, swearing me to silence. Sarah became the first girl whose inner world I ever got to know in any depth.

Laying her head on my lap, Sofia would tell me about how one of the boys had fallen in the river while showing off his balance, or how Sarah had found the coin that was always hidden inside a loaf of *bolo rei* and given it to her as a present. Once she came to my room after a boat trip with Wadi and his parents and lay down beside me in the dark. "Thank you for being my brother," she whispered.

*   *   *

It was obvious from the surreptitious way that Wadi always made sure he knew where Sarah was—and the gentlemanly manner he adopted when speaking to her—that he was hopelessly in love with her. What Sarah felt for him was harder to say. I suspect she was afraid of the range of jagged emotions he roused in her, because she always seemed on guard in his presence—and jittery, as if ready to flee. It didn't help her confidence any that Aunt Maria told her that her family was not good enough for my aunt and uncle to accept a supper invitation. I wasn't there when she said this, but Sofia was, and she told me that the poor girl looked as if she'd been forced to swallow dirt, her eyes filling with humiliated tears. I wished I could have been there to assure her that my aunt would have despised *anyone* her beloved son had chosen.

When I asked Wadi about this, he first denied it had ever happened, then exploded in curses at his mother's betrayal. This only succeeded in bringing on a bad convulsive fit that left him weak for two full days, during which time I chastised myself for insisting he always be honest with me. Why couldn't I leave him be, if that made his life easier?

For the first time I had an inkling of how unfair I could be with others. No wonder Sofia had once called me a spy!

As for my own feelings for Sarah, I never mentioned to anyone that I felt confused by them. Once, when I was mentally punishing myself with thoughts of my puniness in comparison to Wadi, Papa sat down on the verandah next to me and said, "Your time will come. And when you feel that passion for a girl inside you, this won't seem like very much."

I was grateful for his protective arm over my shoulder, but I also hotly resented his implication that my aching desperation was insignificant.

*   *   *

I think Sofia learned a great deal from Sarah that might have otherwise been taught to my sister by our mother—not the least of which was how to understand that womanhood was beginning to transform her body. By her thirteenth birthday, she'd gained a fullness of form that changed the way she did everything, even how she sat at her desk doing her micrography. That hunched little knot of shyness and diligence was replaced by a tall-postured young lady who sometimes opened the shutters simply to feel the breeze blowing through her unbound hair and over her shoulders. Once, when the sun was pouring in, she even let her gold-edged crimson sari glide down her hips and fall onto the floor. I caught a glimpse of her as I was passing the doorway, and I instantly remembered Papa telling me that Mama, too, had opened like a flower in the sunshine.

Buttons, bird feathers, and drawings no longer went missing around the house now that our little girl of hidden sorrows was gone. I even discovered my withered frangipani necklace one day on the table next to my bed.

"I was throwing out some old clothing," Sofia told me, "and discovered it jumbled inside a dress. I can't imagine how it got in with my things."

*   *   *

Sofia was becoming ever more attached to her life in the city and could gab on endlessly about her new friends over supper. So it was that at the beginning of December of 1589, just a few days after her fourteenth birthday, Papa gave her permission to stay at Uncle Isaac's house for three weeks, on the condition that she promise to never enter a church with Aunt Maria. On the morning of her departure, Sofia sobbed against my chest and said she was being abandoned.

"You're impossible! You're the one who wanted to go."

"But now I don't want to."

With Sofia it was always important to keep a door unlocked and a candle burning in a window, so I said, "If you're unhappy, just send word to us here and I'll come for you."

She regained her resolve after another brief cry and went off with an escort of kind Hindu neighbors who were on their way to Goa. Days later I remembered our old rule about not staying at my aunt's home for more than six days at a time, but in Sofia's letters, she wrote only of the exciting adventures she was having.

It was at this time that she got in the habit of writing secret messages for me in micrography. Using her magnifying glass, I would decipher her words. Usually it was just some silliness. But in her last letter to me on this particular stay, she wrote, *I've wriggled completely out of my skin and found something better underneath.*

CHAPTER 9

In late January of 1590, after a weeklong visit that Wadi and his parents spent with us in honor of my eighteenth birthday, Sofia and I went down to Indra's Millstream to escape the scalding heat wave that had turned our home into an oven. She said she wanted to tell me something important, but could only do so when we were far away from our house.

We sat on a rock with our feet splashing in the water. Sofia told me that the day before, while I'd been studying Torah, Wadi had gone with her to gather bead-tree leaves, which Nupi wanted for curing a rash on my father's elbow. Once they were out of view of our house, he dangled a red silk handkerchief from his hand that he must have stolen from his mother's clothes chest. Pretending it was a bell, he shook it by his ear. "I'm taking you off for a surprise," he'd said, his expression one of wily mirth.

"What are you plotting?" Sofia asked him, cautious, suspecting a boyish escapade meant to try her patience.

"I've got something in mind you're sure to like," he answered, "but I'm going to have to blindfold you." When Sofia turned around toward our house, looking back to see if she'd been followed, he added in an ominous voice, "No, no one can see us. We're all alone, you and I."

"Wadi, I'll need to see where I'm going—I might fall," my sister had replied. She spoke very gravely, though pride and defiance made her give him a false laugh a moment later, as though he were asking nothing of her.

"It was like he was threatening me," she told me now. "And I wanted to convince him I wasn't afraid, even though I was. It was like he was going to hurt me in some way that could never be healed. Wasn't I being silly?"

I wanted to tell her that no, her instincts seemed right to me, since I could already see where this was leading, but I merely asked her what Wadi had answered.

"He showed me a hurt face and said, 'You don't trust me?' Imagine him saying that," she said to me, astonished. "I mean, who in his right senses could fully trust an eighteen-year-old like Wadi, with all that mischief in his face. And all that energy!"

Sofia crossed her eyes and let her tongue curl out, and the moment she did that—to give her story less importance than it had—I knew the truth. From that moment on, I felt fear watching me from behind.

Sofia told me then that she would have instructed Wadi to keep his blindfold and surprises to himself were she not determined to be the equal of him and his friends. Folding her arms over her chest, she had retorted, "If you are to be my eyes, Wadi, then you must promise to keep me far from anything that looks dangerous."

He gave her a resentful look, but as she would not relent in her request for a promise, he spoke aloud his vow. Her pulse skipped as he fastened his handkerchief over her eyes. There was no going back now.

A leaden sky was pressing low upon the fields and forests,

threatening a rainstorm, so they walked swiftly, Wadi tugging her by the hand up a footpath of packed dirt bordered by ferns and small palms.

"Wadi, please, you are about to snap my arm from my shoulder!" she'd exclaimed. In truth, however, his tight grip on her hand as they navigated up whatever hill they were climbing made her tingle across her shoulders and at the back of her neck. Furthermore, she adored being disagreeable with him. It made her feel as though she were floating, and more herself than ever before—though how she might have both such impressions at once, she couldn't imagine.

In their entwined fingers, she felt his pulse as golden and powerful. So easy it was to make him happy, she realized; all that was required was a small ceding of her will to his devotion.

She attempted to blindly orient herself, but Wadi spun her round to foil such efforts. In the end, giggling and wobbling, she had to admit she was bested by his cleverness—and utterly lost. She scented rotting leaves and moist earth, and the far-off odor of smoke. *I am walking through a dream that both Wadi and I are having,* she thought. *And in the end we might even wake together.*

To her questions about their whereabouts, he would reply only that they were coming closer to their destination.

With his arm around her waist, he guided her up a steep pathway, then over a fallen tree trunk. Finally, they crossed two rows of puffy bushes that brushed against her legs, and she was reminded of the soft and hidden nature of all the pleasures she had ever known, most particularly the micrographic prayers she scripted alone. After a few more steps, he gripped her shoulders and asked her to stand perfectly still. A thin drizzle had begun to fall. She could smell his breath, warm and exultant, on her face. Her spirit rose when she realized she did indeed trust this young man—this boy with callused hands and sharp green eyes who had always been her brother's best friend. More than that, she believed he was the most beautiful creature she had ever seen.

This was the moment that she felt her heart opening.

She imagined Wadi had brought her to a hidden garden belonging to a Brahmin family—there'd be coral-colored hibiscus flowers and a pearl-white jasmine cascading to her feet... There'd be a statue of Shiva beneath a mimosa tree.

Freeing the knot at the back of her head, he pulled his handkerchief away.

"Oh, God!"

A cliff face rose up toward her, jagged with menace. Sofia's spirit tumbled. Teetering two hundred feet above a ravine, with the sky wheeling round her, she reached out with her hand and found nothing at all. She stumbled backward, the land seeming to fold over her.

This was the sand-colored cliff we used to call Hanuman's Head, because from a particular angle it resembled a flat-nosed monkey in profile.

Wadi reached out to keep her from falling and called her name, panic tightening his voice. Doubled over to catch her breath, she waved away his worried questions.

Straightening up and patting down her sari, she pushed away his hands—so coarse and meddlesome—and took a few more deep breaths. "Idiot!" she yelled at him. Her eyes were daggers aimed at his center, where he had conceived of this plan now gone so badly wrong.

Trembling with fury, she then clouted him on the arm and ran off back down the pathway, crying freely. The rain was pounding at her. She felt as if she were still that awkward little girl she had never wanted to be, and it made her want to hurt herself.

"It's my favorite lookout," he called to her. "From here, you can see the whole valley...."

He ran after her. When at last he caught her, he begged her to explain her rage.

"Wadi, one slip and I'd have fallen all the way to the bottom! I'd be nothing but mangled bones and hair. Not everyone likes looking upon certain death, you know! And what if you'd had one of your detours, tell me that?"

"Sofia, when I'm standing there, with nothing between me and the world, I . . . I never feel so alive. I wanted to make you feel alive, too. That's all I wanted. Really, that's all. . . . I'm sorry! I wasn't thinking."

The rain was soaking into the folds of her sari and seeping into her sandals, filling her with a remorse so tangible that she began to ache. She hated the moist stench of the weeds around them, hated being so full of jumbling emotions beyond her control. She would have given anything to let herself go again—to stand before Wadi as that helpless spirit of dark and mysterious feelings she had been while blindfolded.

He pleaded with her to sit with him on the ruins of an ancient temple wall. She was unsure she could forgive someone who had not yet learned—after all these years—that she was very different from him. She dropped down, turning away from his needful, supplicating glance, and hid her head in her hands.

How is it that sometimes, lacking words, one can find the exact—and perhaps the only—way back toward salvation?

Without her asking, Wadi took her tresses in his hands and began to braid. She had begged him to do this for her on numerous occasions, and even shown him how, but he'd always refused, regarding it as a woman's activity.

Who am I becoming? he began to wonder. *Who is this boy I am, who likes braiding a girl's hair in the rain and who doesn't care who sees?*

I know that's what he was thinking because he told me so later, during a lapse in the tight-fisted grip he normally held over intimacy. Falling in love must have set him far off his usual course for a time.

As for Sofia, she confided to me that his touch created such a tussle of desires inside her that she longed to run off again and scream for Papa and me. Instead, she sobbed. She became the rain sliding down her back and the movement of his hands. And she stayed with him. *This,* she thought, *is the true test of my bravery.*

*   *   *

Long before my sister reached her quiet epiphany, I'd remembered each time Wadi had betrayed me as though we had always been heading straight toward this moment. The three of us were facing a dark woodland ahead, and all I could think of to say was that she had to proceed very slowly. That only made her laugh, as from her point of view her love was already fully formed—and polished by all the daydreams of romantic adventure she'd been having for a year or more.

Rendered fragile by her revelation and wanting to be alone to think, I said that if we didn't get back soon, we'd be devoured by mosquitoes. Sofia gazed down shamefully and wouldn't look up.

"What is it?" I asked.

"Something...something I've been meaning to tell you for a long time," my sister replied. "When I was little, Papa and I were in the marketplace in Goa, and I overheard two Portuguese children and their mother talking about how ugly I was. I felt like I was standing there naked and the whole world was laughing at me. I felt...I felt like I was nothing but shame."

"Did you tell Papa?"

"How could I? I was so embarrassed."

"But you could have told me."

"Ti, after I stopped shuddering, I turned to stone. I couldn't speak. I stayed that way for six years. Do you understand? And I started collecting all those things in my clothes chest. I know you found them. I thought I'd need a dowry. And what had Papa given me from Mama? Hardly anything. An ugly girl like me—I'd need as much as I could get." She smiled through her tears. "But now Wadi has changed everything. I know I'm only fourteen, and I know you think it's not the right thing to do, but it is."

*   *   *

I decided not to tell Papa about Sofia's revelations, since I could too easily imagine him forbidding her from leaving our house for giving her heart at so young an age to a Christian boy—even one related to us by adoption. Secretly, too, I didn't want my father to hold me responsible for this 180-degree turn in destiny. Of course, so few Jews lived near us that he must have been expecting—and dreading— such an attachment for many years. Or had he intended to send Sofia to his family in Constantinople when the time came? Later, he told me so in prison, but I think now that it must have been an afterthought formed by all his regrets.

On our next trip to Goa, I stuck very close to Sofia, and I was wedged uncomfortably between Wadi and my sister most of the time. In front of our parents he did his best to appear composed, but when it was just the three of us, his eyes were locked on her. I cornered him one morning in his room and asked what had happened with Sarah. He told me that she'd been forbidden from seeing him months earlier because he'd had a bad detour while walking with her at the *baratilha,* the flea market set up by Indians in the evenings. A great crowd had gathered.

"I'm sorry," I said, and meant it.

"Don't be. I was tired of her anyway."

The way he spoke so casually of Sarah made me indignant. I suppose I was fearful for my own relationship with him.

"I want you to tell me exactly what you feel for my sister," I demanded. I felt an imminence gripping us both, as if his coming words were sure to be an incantation able to alter all our futures.

"Just what I've always felt," he insisted.

"And what exactly is that?" I asked.

"We're friends—we've always been friends. What do you take me for?" He walked to his desk and picked up his quiver and bow. We were always practicing archery of late, because he was trying to become his school's champion and I was trying to hit anywhere within ten feet of the target.

"Wadi, I can see what's going on. And I promise I won't betray you. But you'd better be more careful than you ever imagined possible. If my father finds out about your interest in Sofia, there's no telling what he might do." *Or what I might do to you if you hurt her,* I probably should have added, because I felt as though I were bracing for one of the bloody-knuckled fights I used to have as a boy. I wanted to clout him just then. He was stronger than me, but I had pent-up rage on my side.

"Your father will be happy for us," he announced with a smile.

"If you think that, you don't know him. You're a Christian. And he's sure to think that you're taking advantage of her being so young."

"But Tiger, she kissed me first!"

"She *kissed* you?"

"It wasn't what you're thinking. It was just a kiss between friends."

"Wadi, do you see any Sanskrit writing on my forehead?"

"What?"

"Or maybe something written in Arabic across my nose? Somewhere it must be written that I've got the brains of a lizard, because that's what you're treating me like!"

"All right. We kissed, but it was just once. That's all we did."

"That better be all."

"Or what?" he retorted, defiant.

His eyes were threatening, but I was clenched with rage. "Or I'll see to it that she never sees you again. Not in Goa, not on our farm, not even in your dreams!"

*   *   *

I rushed off to see Sarah later that day; a door had unexpectedly opened before me and I had to run through it before it snapped closed again. We talked in the tearoom of her small home, a platter of Indian milk sweets scented with cardamom sitting untouched between us. She spoke in glum monosyllables and twirled a lock of hair by her ear around her finger. My heart drummed the whole time, my life balanced on the point of a needle.

I never told her what I felt, but she read it in my silences. And she said nothing to give me hope. At the door, she handed me silver earrings shaped like bells and kissed me on both cheeks. "Give these back to Wadi," she told me.

*   *   *

What is memory? my papa asked me when I was seven. Was it a palace in the soul, thoughts entwined into a chain, a bridge between all we have been and ever will be? Where does September of 1590 reside inside me that I can remember so clearly how it changed our lives?

I was eighteen and a half now—taller than Papa, but still given to boyish swings in mood. I was awkward in my new body and unsure of my new standing in the world, so joy flared up in my chest like a dark fire whenever I was treated like the man I wanted to be—when my cheeks and chin were shaved by Kahi, the barber in Ramnath, for instance. Sitting on his yellow stool in the marketplace, the scratch of his razor across my skin came as confirmation of my having reached a better stage in life. Advaki, Iraaj, and the other Hindu elders who'd known me since I was a baby would gather around to make sure Kahi didn't so much as nick me, chewing betel-nuts and spitting like proud uncles.

I wore my hair long, with bangs twisting over my brow, hoping I looked like Rama in a temple spectacle. I daydreamed of sexual escapades even when I ought to have been studying Torah, and though I had embarked on secret trysts with girls on occasion, I had yet to feel any real stirrings of love since Sarah. Happily, I was not a virgin, but I had only just barely fallen across that border. Wadi had tricked me into going to a house of prostitution in Goa two years before. He'd told me that it was a Turkish *hamam,* but I soon discovered I'd be getting neither a bath nor a massage; when the door to my dressing room opened, a young woman with thick rings of kohl around her eyes and wearing only silver anklets reached out for me. By then I was wearing only a towel, and I was in no position—or disposition—to find Wadi and start a quarrel.

Papa and I had embarked on a new form of friendship of late, and he particularly adored strolling arm in arm with me in the temple gardens in Ponda, showing me off to one and all. I had become his companion as well as his son.

Nupi was now a foot shorter than me and would squint up at me in front of her Hindu friends, telling them she mistook me each morning for a minaret, which made everyone fall into merry laughter. I'm sure she picked up this habit of repeating comic scenes from my father—as we all did, I suppose.

Sofia's face was round and full, colored with all her new discoveries about herself, and her sari now fell in gentle folds across her chest and hips. Though she was not yet fifteen, she was adult in profile, and when she wore our mother's moonstone-white head scarf—which she now kept with her always—she looked to be seventeen or more. She was pleased about that—and proud, too.

Now I can see that Sofia may even yet have wished to be someone different from who she was.

Wadi had become a handsome young man, nearly six feet in height, with a powerful and confident bearing. Neighbors still called him the Little Moor, but now it was in good-natured jest. He'd proved himself a fine student at St. Paul's, the Jesuit school in Goa, and was unrivaled at Latin. He'd also achieved his goal of school archery champion, for which he received a handsome copy of a New Testament printed in Lisbon in 1542. As a reward, Uncle Isaac had begun to take him on trips all over India to look for new sources of fabric. By comparison, I was leading a provincial life, and when Wadi told me about the marvels of Bombay or Madras, I greatly resented my limited life.

He and Sofia had wisely decided to keep their love a secret and had both become accomplished actors. They believed everyone was fooled and were confident that after another year and three months, when Sofia celebrated her sixteenth birthday, they could tell the truth without too many fireworks going off. How far they'd ventured into the landscape of physical love I dared not ask.

At the beginning of that fateful month, my father called Sofia and me into the sitting room and told us that he had to take a trip to Bijapur to make sketches of the Sultan and a new mosque he'd recently erected. He would be gone for an entire month. He kept rubbing his hands together nervously and apologizing, saying that his absence would be difficult for us all, but he had refused the invitation of his benefactor twice over the previous two years and could not say no again.

We knew we'd be fine alone with Nupi, but Papa explained the complication that was worrying him: toward the end of his stay in Bijapur, our cook was going to have to return to Benali, the village of her birth, for the last three days of the festival of Ganesh Chaturthi, in honor of the Hindu God of Wisdom. I was sure we were old enough to stay alone, but Papa wouldn't hear of it. He intended to ask Nupi if we could accompany her, but first he wanted our agreement. He informed Sofia and me that we could not stay with our aunt and uncle in Goa because Uncle Isaac was taking Wadi to Diu, the small Portuguese colony northwest of Bombay. At the time, I didn't know that Isaac had asked to take me along as well. Papa never told me that because he would never have considered leaving Sofia alone, and it was just as well that I only learned of my uncle's generous offer much later—I'd have been furious at having to give up this opportunity to travel. And I'd have missed taking the next step on the path to myself. . . .

That evening, behind the closed door to his study, I overheard Papa propose his plan to Nupi. She interrupted him right away, which was very uncharacteristic, protesting that she could offer us nothing like the comfort we were used to. Shame made her voice quiver. I knew that she was cringing, her hands shaking in her lap.

"The floors of my family house are of cow dung," she moaned in Konkani. "The walls and roof are made of palm leaves." She then switched to her halting Portuguese to make sure Papa understood her despair. "It's no good—superstition everywhere. Everyone sleep on jute mats . . . thick smoke from the kitchen. No windows, no windows at all. Hens run in and hens run out and . . . and . . ." Nupi lost her way and began to weep.

Papa reassured her that we were not silk dolls and would be happy in Benali. Very likely he was kneeling next to her and holding her hand.

"It's impossible!" she shouted. She always believed that if she spoke loud enough she could win any quarrel with my father. "People in my village believe in magic!" she hollered. "Oh, so much superstition. Ti and Sofia will be asked to make offerings to the gods. It's no good—no good at all! Everyone will tell them what Ganesha can do for them."

"Such as?"

"Good fortune—a pretty wife who knows how to cook for Ti. A handsome high-caste husband for Sofia."

"She is hardly of a marriageable age quite yet," Papa pointed out.

"She's fourteen. In some villages, girls are married for two or three years by that age. No good—no good at all!"

"Then I'll have to send them to my sister-in-law in Goa. My brother will be away during their stay, but if that's my only choice . . ."

Nupi adored Uncle Isaac, but she thought Aunt Maria was useless. This, then, was Papa's trump card.

"Aunt Maria? No, no, no! That woman cannot even boil rice!" Nupi spoke as if it were a sin worse than murder.

"No, but the children will probably get all the sweets they want. If they have no chicken koorma worth eating for three days, it won't kill them." Koorma was Nupi's specialty, although we could not eat it very often because she made it so hot it took the skin off the inside of our mouths.

"But without Uncle Isaac there, she might serve cow meat! What then? Tell me, what then?"

Out of deference to Nupi and our Hindu neighbors, Papa had always forbidden us from eating beef, even when we were away from home.

"She would never prepare an entire cow, just pieces," he replied, no doubt hoping to make things worse. He was probably fighting hard not to grin.

"What pieces?" the old cook shrieked.

"The legs. And they say the ribs are delicious. And then there are the ears..."

"Ears! Oh, no, no, no, it cannot be! Tell Aunt Maria to keep her cow pieces! Nupi will take the children."

CHAPTER 10

Benali was on the coast about thirteen miles from our farm. It would take almost a whole day for us to get there. It was within the Portuguese province of Goa, ten miles southwest of the city itself, so before leaving for Bijapur, Papa made us promise to be careful about never reciting Jewish prayers, even to ourselves. He gave Sofia and me wooden crosses and told us to slip them on should any Catholic priest or missionary come stumbling into the village in search of trouble.

Papa had arranged for us to ride on donkeys borrowed from neighbors, but after only a few hours our sore bottoms cried out so insistently for leniency that we made more than half the journey on foot. Nupi swore she'd been permanently damaged and said she would not be surprised if she were constipated for an entire year. "That smelly, nasty creature has broken my bottom," she told every person we passed, pointing at the poor shaggy culprit as though it were a demon.

Nupi told Sofia and me that Benali was where the entire province of Goa had been created by Shri Parasurama, an incarnation of

Vishnu, when he'd shot an arrow into the sea and ordered its waters to recede. Before the Portuguese occupation, many villagers had kept a shrine to Parasurama in their homes.

A few miles from Benali, the rainstorms of previous days had made a giant muddy hole in the road. A buffalo had fallen in the afternoon before and had to be hauled out by men with ropes. A noisy marketplace had grown around the scene of this accident, since the hundreds of travelers that passed each day were practically obliged to chatter about the poor creature and the inconvenience of it all—which made it the perfect spot for selling everything from bananas and sweet limes to monkeys and birds, as well as for drying chilies and fish, and separating the pulp of coconuts from their husks. Stalls made of palm fronds woven through bamboo poles were quickly erected, and musicians, dancers, and tattoo artists came along, trailing a scattering of dusty cats and packs of filthy dogs that smelled as bad as fishing nets. A ragged family of dark-skinned Madrasi farmers was there as well, fleeing the drought in the south and begging food in their indecipherable language. My arms were thicker than the men's legs and the children were mantis-creatures with distended bellies and huge mud-colored eyes. Some local men shooed them away like jackals, which was hard to bear. After a brief family conference, Nupi left us and purchased butter, a large sack of chickpea flour, and a jackfruit for them with coins Papa had given us for an emergency. The Madrasi blessed her tearfully, the women falling at her feet. Nupi also bought an earthenware jar of *feni,* the local palm liquor, for her sister and her husband. As an afternoon meal, we ate moong beans and rice served on plantain leaves. For a sweet, we sucked on bright yellow mangoes in the shade of a tamarind tree to the drumming of a Bengali tabla player whose wife's hair was crowned with marigold flowers. She took a liking to Sofia, who allowed her to weave some blossoms in her tresses. Even a year ago, my sister would not have consented to this.

Just before we reached the coast, we took a rough path through a tangled forest of teak and bamboo. The cool winds coming off the

ocean in the distance shook the treetops, sending fuzzy yellow cater-
pillars raining down on us. Their bristles stung like pellets of fire. I
covered Nupi with a cape from my pack and pulled her ahead while
Sofia came up behind with the three donkeys. Barking deer yapped
angrily at us as we reached the beach.

"Don't worry—they're always here," Nupi said. "They guard this
route to the sea. We're not far now."

The sun, low in the sky, was turning the endless ocean to a sheet
of gold. The air smelled fresh and cool. Nupi whispered a prayer to
Devi, her protectress.

Blessed be the Lord for bringing me here, I thought. I felt as if I had
always wanted to come to a place like this—where the sea was light
made visible.

When we finally arrived at Benali an hour later, sweating like
foot soldiers, my sister and I created quite a sensation. Mop-haired
children with curious eyes gathered around us, shrieking with glee.
The older villagers—most of them Nupi's kinfolk—made our acquaintance with good-natured pats and satisfied smiles. "For so
many years we've heard about you!" they kept saying, and they told
us stories from our childhoods, including the time a frog curled up
in my father's slipper. That left me stunned, since I had had no no-
tion of Nupi's pride in us until that moment.

One elderly man with a face as wrinkled as ancient leather stayed
apart from the others and scowled, spitting out betel nut juice like
blood. I paid him little attention, since four girls standing in a giggling knot behind him wore only cotton skirts tied around their
waists. Another girl soon drew my attention, however, because of the
unlikelihood of what she was doing in this out-of-the-way hamlet.
She was sitting on a palm stump, curled over a book, avidly getting
in a last hour of reading before sundown. She was tall and slender,
and she wore the simple Portuguese dress and white blouse of a
schoolgirl, but her feet were bare. Her skin was the color of sandalwood, and she had that graceful way of resting her chin on her hand
that only Indian girls have. Her long dark hair was braided tightly

and tied at the end with a ribbon of gold-threaded violet silk that I wanted very much to undo. When she noticed me staring, she stuck out her tongue and went back to her book.

*   *   *

Benali was about thirty palm-leaf huts set in a grove of tassel-crowned tamarisks and peepul trees. In front of each home was a baked-mud courtyard polished with cow dung, with a low rim of rough bricks to keep out the fine white sand of the beach. We put our bags in one that had a small silver cross dangling from a leaf above the door and a pile of earthenware plates drying out front. This dwelling belonged to Nupi's younger sister, Ajira, and her husband, Bharat. We would not be meeting him or their son, Kintan, because they had moved into a Hindu temple just across the border from Portuguese territory for the duration of the festival. They were there to fast and pray for the health of Bharat's father, who was gravely ill. In fact, as we soon discovered, Nupi had to come home this year precisely because Ajira was so lonely. We liked Nupi's sister immediately—the quick way she smiled and took our hands, as though she had been waiting all her life to greet us. Ajira had a softer way of speaking than her older sister and a very sweet way of laughing, as if she were made out of tinkling bells. She would have been pretty still, but smallpox scars cratered her cheeks. She asked us many questions right away. Were my eyes a darker color when I was small? Was our father from the far north of India? She simply could not fathom that there was a land called Europe four thousand miles west of Goa where people didn't believe in Vishnu and Shiva, and where no one even considered that they might have had past lives. She said I was telling tales. When I added that Europeans never cooked with coconut milk, she threw up her hands. "No, no, no, it's impossible!" she said, the urgency of her disbelief making us laugh.

Ajira had decorated the entranceway to her home with arabesques of rice flour, which was the tradition here. We complimented her on her designs, which we stepped around like herons. Over ginger tea and hot chapatti, sitting in a circle with the others, I summoned my courage and asked her the only question that mattered to me: "Who was that girl I saw reading a book?"

"It must have been Tejal," she replied, examining the coals that she was going to add to her fire.

"Does she live here?"

"Yes and no."

"Enough of that," Nupi snapped. She gave me one of her iron-willed glares.

I stuck out my tongue at her, which I'd never done before. She drew back her head like a startled hen.

"You're growing up too fast for your own good," she told me tartly, and then she asked Sofia and me to finish our tea right away and gather flowers for her before the descent of dusk. She handed us a reed basket, but I refused to go until my question was answered.

"Tejal is from the village," Nupi said with a grudging frown. "She is our cousin Shanti's daughter. But she no longer lives here."

"Where does she live?"

"Ti, must you be such a pest? Tejal lives in the city. Now please get me some flowers and then we'll talk all you want."

As we left, Nupi and Ajira burst out laughing. Later she told me that they had agreed that I looked like a duck standing in the monsoon rain with its beak open. Apparently it was a village expression for boys suffering the pangs of love.

A dozen children followed us into a valley of wildflowers just beyond the village jute and chickpea fields. They were sun-darkened and completely naked, and some of them were filthy, but they were as sweetly insistent and as beautiful as whizzing dragonflies. They begged us in eager voices to lift them into the air and whirl them around, so Sofia and I made believe we were millwheels until we were dizzy. They wanted more, but we said we had work to do, so they helped us gather flowers, running this way and that, whooping and shrieking, dropping blossoms in our basket and racing off again when I told them we needed still more.

When Sofia and I returned with a full basket so quickly, Nupi glared at us like we'd been practicing black magic.

Sofia grinned. "We had *gandharvas* and *apsaras* helping us." They were the Hindu sprites that Nupi had told us stories about when we were little.

Nupi laid our pink, white, and yellow wildflowers in the sandy soil by the trunk of a tall coconut palm behind her sister's home. With her gnarled old hands, she carefully spread them in a crescent. When they were just as she wanted them, she closed her eyes and began to tremble.

"What's wrong?" I asked.

She shushed me and had us kneel down with her. Our long shadows climbed up the sandy hill ahead of us. After she'd whispered prayers, she said, "I planted this palm for my son when he died."

"You had a son?" I exclaimed. "Why didn't you ever tell us about him?"

She chewed her gums while she thought about that. "Ti, it took me several years to be happy you were not him." She squeezed my hand. "When you get a little older, you will learn that many things become secrets without you wanting them to."

"It must have been a long time ago," Sofia said.

"Many years before you were born—you and Ti both."

For me, this was a moment of awakening. Until then, I hadn't seen Nupi as a woman with a life—and a past—fully independent of that of my family.

*   *   *

That night the village held a banquet in Ganesha's honor, and we were instructed by Nupi not to look up into the sky—it was considered bad luck to even get a slanting glimpse of the moon during this holiday because it had once had the bad manners to laugh at the God of Wisdom.

A dozen people sat between me and Tejal, who wore a stunning, violet-colored sari and sky-blue shawl. Nupi had told me that she was studying at a convent school in the city of Goa and that she was fifteen. Tejal would not even turn to face me, which filled me with frustration. I felt as though my future were hiding inside her black eyes.

By the time our meal ended, I'd eaten so many prawns and coconut cakes that Nupi said I looked four months pregnant, which she thought hysterically funny. I drank *feni* instead of water to spite her, since she kept trying to take the jug away from me. The dancing and drumming afterward left my vision spinning. I went to rest in the sand near the water's edge, and in my half-dreams I was standing on a chair to peek through the shutters to see who was coming up our verandah stairs. When I looked up, Tejal was looming above me. She carried an earthenware cup in both her hands, as if a ceremonial offering.

"Excuse me, but Ajira asked me to bring you some ginger tea," she said softly.

Startled, I sat up and thanked her. Holding the steaming cup against my temple and closing my eyes, I sensed my mother's presence. I realized she was the person who had been about to come up the stairs. I could see her carrying my baby sister in her arms.

"Are you all right?" Tejal asked.

"I'll never drink *feni* again as long as I live," I replied, groaning for comic effect. "All of me feels swollen."

She showed me a fleeting smile, which had the effect of quickening my pulse, then turned to walk away.

"What were you reading when my sister and I arrived here?" I called after her.

"A book," she said matter-of-factly.

"I know, but which one?"

"It is called *The Golden Legend*," she replied, speaking Portuguese for the first time. She pronounced each word as though it had its own very precise place. I liked that.

"Is it good?" I persisted.

"It's a holy book," she declared, as if its quality were irrelevant. "It is about Jesus Christ and the saints."

Her beautiful hands gestured in circles as she spoke. They seemed to put me into a trance.

"I've never read about him," I said.

"Never?" Her eyes widened in astonishment. Her dark skin was so radiant in the moonlight that it seemed as if she'd descended out of the night to be with me.

"Jews don't often read the New Testament," I explained.

"If you will permit me to say so, the nuns say that the Jews are very stubborn for not believing in the divinity of our Lord."

"I happily permit you," I said with a small bow of my head, enjoying her formal way of speaking. "But what do *you* say about the Jews?"

She started. Maybe it was the first time anyone had asked for her opinion on this matter. "I . . . I do not know," she said hesitatingly. "I've never met any."

"I'm afraid you have now."

She knew from my silly way of smiling that I was asking for her general opinion of me. She gave me a serious look. "Please, drink your tea and you will feel better," she said in a controlled, mature tone, as though I'd been a problem to her many times before. I can't say how, but at that exact moment I realized she was very intelligent.

"I will if you sit with me," I said.

She looked back nervously at the village, tethered to it by traditions that must have forbidden her from sitting alone with a stranger. A great pyre was burning now, and the music was ever more frantic.

"I guess the nuns would not like it," I said, challenging her to be her own person.

"The nuns are far away. It is my father I am worried about," she answered darkly.

"Just sit. You can tell him you were only being hospitable to Nupi's godson."

"Is that what you are?"

"I don't know. I think sometimes she became a kind of god-mother to me the day she saved my life." I said that to be mysterious, but after I'd spoken I realized it was true.

"Nupi saved your life?"

"I'll tell you all about it, but first..." I patted the sand next to me.

Tejal narrowed her eyes, assessing the danger ahead. When she sat down, she covered her legs with the fringe of her sari. I took a sip of tea and offered her some, and she dared to accept, which I took as a very good sign. As she drank, I felt a release in my chest—as if a hinge had popped free.

I was able to talk of intimate feelings then, of the period after my mother had died, when Nupi had invited me to eat with her any time I was feeling lonely. "And I did," I told Tejal, as if it were the moral of the story, "until the house became all mine again."

We talked for a time about how my mother's death had changed Papa and me, and I was moved by how carefully she listened. Yet both of us were keenly aware that we were avoiding trickier topics more close at hand. After an awkward silence, I asked how she had come to attend school in Goa.

"Ajira and Nupi were kind enough to do that for me," she replied. "I ought not to tell you this, but my mother says that I taught myself to read when I was little—by looking at an old scroll my father kept by our shrine."

"Why shouldn't you say that?"

"Because no one knows for sure how I did it. My mother says that Ganesha must have come to me in my dreams and given me lessons. Everyone found out, of course, and Ajira told my parents she'd find a way to pay for my schooling in Goa, if they would permit it. My father thought that a girl with an education was a very bad idea and yelled at her to mind her own business. Such a commotion we had! But Nupi came home to Benali for a brief stay when I was seven years old and wore him down. My father finds Nupi very intimidating."

"He's not alone," I said, laughing.

"The whole village now contributes to my education. The elders have decreed it. They now think it is an honor to have a village girl studying with Christian nuns. And if you will excuse my saying so, they also believe it may give them merit in the eyes of our Portuguese rulers. And afford them a special leniency, as well."

"What will you do when you're finished with your schooling?"

"I want to work in the Royal Hospital. And when I have learned enough, I will return here to Benali."

"I would think it a shame if you became a nun."

She looked away, unsure how to reply, then wiped the sand off her legs with a brisk wave of her hand and stood up. "Permit me to say that I must go back now," she said.

I reached up for her hand, but she shook her head and ran off.

*   *   *

That night, Nupi, Sofia, and I carried our jute mats onto the patio to sleep under the stars like the other villagers. For a time, we listened to the rise and fall of the ocean without speaking. Then our old cook explained to us that when she was just nineteen, her husband and son died of dysentery caused by poisoned well water. Nine adults and twelve children were buried that summer. Ekath, her son, had been only three years and four months old. Two weeks after the funeral, she walked out of the village one dawn. When she passed the final border of peepul trees, she felt as if the world itself—the sea wind and last stars of night, even the leaves beneath her feet—had chosen her path. "I was alive and my loved ones were dead. It was a terrible thing. I could not understand why or how. But I knew it was my fault. I kept myself apart from the world for twenty years, until your mother and father found me."

"They found you?"

"I was living at the temple in Ponda. I had only a bowl for rice—nothing more. Your parents took me in, though I insisted I was not worthy. You see, your mother would not take no for an answer." Nupi was sitting up now and touched her chest. "I don't know how, but she understood the night that was in here."

*   *   *

Tejal's parents must have questioned her about her conversation with me, because the next morning everyone began to refer to us as Nupi's godchildren. We were treated with merry affection by everyone but the old man I'd seen on first arriving at Benali. Just after breakfast, he spotted me as I stepped out of Ajira's hut and scowled at me as though I'd stolen a treasure from him. When I asked about him, Nupi merely told me he felt cheated by the world for reasons that were held under lock and key in the distant past. Stupidly, I made fun of his leathery skin as a way of dismissing him, but she rebuked me sternly, saying, "You don't know where his heart has been, so leave him be!"

*   *   *

I wanted to apologize to Tejal for having chased her off the evening before with my insistent behavior, but she was already working in rice fields half a mile east with her younger sister. I couldn't go to her because Nupi had made Sofia and me promise to help paint the plaster heads of Ganesha that would be worn during the final night of festivities.

The villagers hid these giant hollow likenesses in several different homes in case a Catholic priest or Portuguese official were to come for an inspection. The ears, trunk, and face fit cleverly together using pegs, and two elders—twins named Darpak and Harmut—were able to assemble them in the smokehouse in a matter of minutes. The two old men reeked of *feni* so badly that Sofia and I held our noses behind their backs, which—once they'd seen us—

only made them burst out laughing. Their long white hair was shimmering like salt crystals from a dousing with coconut oil and their hollow-cheeked resemblance to each other made the pair look like they'd stepped out of some ancient myth. Despite their woozy state, they used their goat-hair brushes with swallowlike quickness. Obeying their instructions, we gave the largest Ganesha a blue face and the other two more lifelike brownish tones. All three were painted with luscious, wine-colored lips and black-rimmed golden eyes. We were finally finished near noon, at which time the two old artists placed the largest one on my head and the middle one on Sofia, balancing the masks on our shoulders and lacing them cleverly around our chests to keep them from jiggling. When we told them the eyeholes were positioned well and that we could see ahead without difficulty, Harmut draped crimson capes over us in such a way that the cords around our chests were hidden, then tied them at the waist with black sashes. Darpak brought us an ancient, rusted mirror. I discovered I adored being an elephant.

Harmut slipped away for a moment and came back with a slender, doe-eyed young boy named Arjuna, who was soon fitted with the smallest head. Within seconds, he'd become a baby elephant, his platter-sized ears sticking out comically. I realized then what ought to have been obvious—that we were embodying Ganesha at different ages.

The men had us link hands—with Arjuna in the middle—and step around the room to test our balance. It was cavernous inside the god's head, and sound was deeply muffled. Poor Arjuna began to cry, and after we took his head off, Sofia cheered him up by saying that if he did his best to play an elephant then Ganesha just might let him come back as the biggest one in all of India.

Then we discovered the villagers had tricked us.

"Tomorrow," Darpak said, holding up a finger of instruction, "you will be so kind as to put your costumes on as we finish eating. I know what you are thinking, but do not fear—we will bring you necklaces and flower garlands so that you are properly attired. Then, as soon as we give you the signal, you will walk out of the smoke-house toward the banquet, where the people will dance for you. You just follow us. All will be wonderful and all will be magnificent!"

"And you will bring great praise to us from the gods!" Harmut exclaimed.

"What are you saying?" Sofia asked.

"Nupi's godchildren are playing Ganesha," Darpak replied, giv-ing a little jump of delight. "You will be the God of Wisdom him-self!"

*　　*　　*

As soon as we could get away without offending the two old men, Sofia and I ran to our cook, who was sitting behind a naked toddler on our patio, combing her silken hair.

"It wasn't my idea," she said the moment she saw our faces. She held up her hands and shrank back. "The elders decided it would honor us to have you play Ganesha."

"But we might ruin everything," Sofia protested hotly.

"It's not hard playing a god. Just be appreciative of what the vil-lagers say and do. And tell them they will have a wonderful year. By the way, this is Matri," Nupi said, obviously wanting to change the subject. "She's my cousin Radrani's granddaughter."

"I think it's a bad idea," I replied. "Papa won't like us being idols. It's a sin in Judaism."

"You're not idols! Nobody really believes you're Ganesha. You're only him in Benali. And only now." She tugged at the end of Matri's hair so that the infant would turn around. "Can my Portuguese chil-dren really think Hindus are that stupid?"

Not knowing what the old woman wanted, Matri simply giggled and drooled.

"Of course I don't," I replied. "But some people might pray to us."

"Not to you, to what you represent! And what you represent is God! Did you never listen to *any* of the stories I told you as a boy?"

Nupi clapped her hands together, which meant she was nearing the end of her patience. "Besides," she winked, "A certain *menina*—young lady—will be most impressed."

I still wasn't certain it was the right thing to do, but after hearing that, I shushed up my sister's continued objections, earning myself a smack on the top of my head for my efforts.

*   *   *

A short while later, Sofia and I took a long walk out to some scruffy hills in the southeast, where we found the charred ruins of two Hindu temples that had been burnt to the ground by the Portuguese a few years earlier. A wooden carving of the monkey god Hanuman was poking out of the crystalline white crust of an abandoned salt pond nearby, his long tail grasping a papaya still bright with yellow paint. After I cleaned it off, my sister said she wanted it. She made such a fuss when I hesitated that we had a quarrel, but I gave it to her in the end.

When we returned to the village, Tejal and her younger sister Idika were standing in the ocean up to their hips, cooling off after their morning of labor. I was not sure I could go to them without drawing attention to my excitement, but Sofia understood by now what was in my head and began to drag me forward.

"You are not wasting this chance!" she declared.

I fought back, but when she threw sand at me, I chased her into the water. Idika came to talk with us, but not Tejal. When I dared to approach her, she faced away from me, as though afraid even to breathe. I said I hoped I hadn't created problems for her. She nodded, accepting my apology, then walked immediately back to the village, the water dripping off her shoulders and hips. Even the sun seemed to follow her back to the huts.

*   *   *

In the afternoon, I saw Tejal reading on her palm stump again, but I'd vowed to make myself wait for her invitation this time. She knew

I was there, but didn't look up. After a time, she began to fidget with the beads of her amber necklace, seemingly on the verge of tears. I hid behind a peepul tree until she rushed back to her home.

That evening, at our banquet, Sofia volunteered to exchange places with Tejal, but the girl was not permitted to leave her parents. I ate my food glumly, angry with everyone, and during the festivities afterward I refused to sing a lullaby about Rama freeing Sita from the king of the demons, that Nupi had taught me when I was tiny and which everyone was clamoring to hear. Ajira came to me later and whispered that even though I hadn't meant to, I'd insulted Nupi in front of her family and friends. Feeling shamed, I raced away far down the strand, wondering in my hopeless, adolescent way why—despite my best intentions—everything was always going wrong.

*   *   *

In the morning, I apologized to Nupi, who told me that she understood.

"Be careful, Ti," was all she added, and by the look she gave me I could see she wanted to discourage me from pursuing Tejal.

Three scruffy fishermen with large coarse hands summoned me away from our breakfast. They said they had a special treat for me, and I soon discovered it meant sitting on our heels under a grove of palms and watching for fish in the water, while half a dozen of their colleagues sat in two village boats about fifty yards from shore, clutching their woven nets. It seemed like an excuse for the men to quiz me about my family until one of them jumped up hollering. He told me to bang the brass gong they'd hung from a palm trunk.

At my signal, the boatmen rowed swiftly to a spot pointed to by my shouting colleagues and dropped their nets. One man dove out of each of the boats and drew them together. We ran down the beach to join them as they sloshed out of the surf. Men and boys soon came running from the village, and together we hauled in the heavy nets, swollen with hundreds of jumping silver-black fish a man's hand in length.

I was very excited, astonished by our catch, and when I turned to look back at the village, Sofia and the other women and girls were watching us with proud eyes. Among them, nearly hidden at the back, stood Tejal. She was the only one who wasn't smiling or chattering. She looked like a shadow of the others.

I ruined everything by saying I was Jewish, I thought.

*   *   *

"Are you going to be all right?" Sofia asked Arjuna.

We were standing together in the smokehouse.

"What?" he replied in a muffled squeak.

"Juna, can you see me?" his nervous mother questioned, holding up her oil lamp.

He nodded his elephant head, his tiny hands clutching his gold-tipped earlobes. "My nose itches," he declared, and we thought he meant his own, but he began to scratch Ganesha's trunk, which made us all laugh.

We were reeking with coconut oil that Harmut had rubbed all over our elephant heads, and the air smelled of grilling fish. I was now wearing a papier-mâché crown, painted purple and pink, and inlaid with pearls. We had necklaces of white hibiscus and fire-colored marigolds around our necks. Little Arjuna gripped a sword in one hand and a staff in the other.

Sofia and I cradled more than seventy garlands of flowers in our arms. These we were to hand out to each of the villagers, even the babies.

It was a sunset of russet and gold, and the sea was extraordinarily calm, like a mirror. Arjuna went out first, Darpak holding his hand, then came Sofia, and finally me. I'll never forget the gasps of the villagers, and their eyes, wide and radiant; three thousand years of history and myth had just become real for them. They looked at us, hands to their mouths, as if we were made of rubies shining with the depth of their own secret dreams.

A hush came over the banquet. I was nervous, but I was determined to do well in order to make things up to Nupi. The villagers touched their foreheads as a mark of respect to us as we passed. When the drumming started, they began dancing before us, led by a young boy and girl leaping and prancing, and making ferocious animal faces.

Darpak led Arjuna to the very center of the celebration, where he stood the boy on his shoulders and began swaying to the rhythm of the music. So young a god being held by such a gentle old man . . . I can't say how, but it became the meaning of the whole festival for me—it was about time and how we age, and the need for God to work through us. After all, if we do not carry Him, who will?

A man-sized wooden sculpture of Ganesha standing inside the Wheel of Life—villagers had saved it from a nearby temple destroyed by the Portuguese—was carried from its hiding place at the back of the smokehouse and placed in the sand at the ocean's edge. We stood beside him, and the people came to us one by one, mothers with babies, brothers and sisters, old widowers and widows, and as we told them what a glorious year they would have, each bowed down to have us place a flower garland around his or her neck. How lucky for Sofia and me to be given this chance to crown them with happiness!

A broken old woman cradled in her son's arms asked me to bless her. When I did, she gave me a glorious, toothless smile and kissed my trunk.

Nupi approached us, and I took her hands and thanked her.

"Ssshhhh," she hissed. "Don't forget who you are."

"Keep still, woman!" I bellowed. "Cannot Ganesha express gratitude to one of his servants?"

Nupi's eyes flashed with anger, but then she understood me and grinned. I asked the musicians to stop playing for a moment, and then I sang the lullaby they'd been wanting. I strayed from the tune once or twice, but even so, Nupi stood taller than I'd seen her in years.

Arjuna, Sofia, and I were then seated at the head of a long mat

and given offerings of fruit and flowers. I'd just gotten a very big coconut when I heard a great crack above me.

The next thing I remember was seeing Nupi's face as though
through gauze. She was crying and my head was throbbing.

"Ti . . . Ti . . ."

Sofia was behind her, calling my name. She held our mother's
head scarf in her fist.

I tried to stand but was too weak.

"Where's Papa?" I asked. I was very worried that he had not
come home yet from Bijapur. I wanted him to carry me to my bed.

I must have passed out again for a time. When I woke, Tejal was
holding a cup of ginger tea to my lips. I took a sip and looked at the
dark horizon behind her. The whole world was shivering in the cool
moonlight.

I realized I was lying on Ajira's patio and that I was very cold. I
sat up, frightened. Someone draped a blanket over my shoulders.

"What happened?" I asked Tejal.

"There . . . there was an accident," she replied nervously.

"What kind of accident? Sofia's not hurt, is she?"

"No, I'm right here," my sister said, dropping down next to
me, leaning into my chest like a cat and hugging me. "Are you all
right, Ti?"

"I think so. Arjuna—did the accident happen to him?"

"No, he's fine," Sofia assured me.

Nupi pushed away the small crowd around me with insistent
hands and crouched next to me.

"Can you see me?" the old woman demanded. She leaned closer.
I could smell the pungent scent of betel nut on her breath.

"Of course."

"Did you tell him?" she asked Sofia, who shook her head.

"Listen, Ti, someone hit you," Nupi said. "With a sword. It's
lucky for you that Ganesha has such a very hard head. And that the
blade was rusty. Otherwise . . ." Her hands, which had been clasped

tightly together, broke open like my head might have. "You have a gash on your forehead, but thanks to Ganesha it's not deep. We've put medicine on it. You may have a small scar, but you will be fine."

"Who hit me?"

The old woman bit her lip. "My father-in-law," she replied.

CHAPTER 11

Nupi and Sofia sat beside me. The old cook gripped my hand and prayed to Devi for my health. I told her and my sister to go back to the celebration, but they insisted on staying with me.

Nupi told us that her father-in-law, Madesh, was the leathery old man always spitting betel-nut juice. He'd never forgiven her for what he called *killing* his son and grandson.

"It was my job to fetch the well water for my family, so maybe he was right," she told us glumly.

"That's impossible," my sister exclaimed. "You must have drunk the water, too. You couldn't have known it was bad!"

"The water made people die, not you," I added.

Nupi rested her hand on my chest. "It's so long ago, and so many things have come to pass in my life, yet it seems like yesterday."

"Why did Madesh try to kill Ti?" Sofia asked her.

"He didn't think it fair that I should have a godson. So angry, so angry... He was trying to take Ti from me, because he believes I took his son and grandson from him. Life has taught him this."

"Where is he now?"

"In his hut. The elders will decide tonight what is to be done with him."

"What do you want them to do?" I asked.

"He has to live with his shame now. Maybe that's enough. Unless . . . unless you would like further punishment. You're the one he injured, Ti. The elders will do what you ask."

I knew what I wanted, but I didn't say it yet for fear that Nupi would just shush me up.

*   *   *

The next day, we learned that the elders had decided Madesh would spend a year exiled from Benali. It was our last morning there, and it took a long time to pack our bags because two of Ajira's silver bangles had gone missing. We turned the whole hut upside down to find them and failed. Nupi took me aside and whispered that Ajira had probably hidden them herself because we were about to leave her all alone. "She wants to keep us here," she said sadly.

Ajira hugged me tight as we said goodbye and made me promise to return for the festival the following year. Before setting off, I asked to be able to face Madesh. Darpak and Harmut brought him to me.

"I do not regret what I did," the old man snarled as I met him outside Ajira's hut. He stood with his hands folded over his chest, making a show of his fury, as if he'd waited all his life for this moment. The entire village clustered around us. "I wish I'd sliced you right in half!"

I was not angry—only glad to be alive. And confused that someone who didn't know me could hate me so much.

"It makes no difference to me what you feel," I told him with bravado, though I was lying. Thinking of what Nupi would want me to do, unwilling to embarrass her, I added, "I've heard about what happened to your son and grandson, so I do not want to see you punished any more than you already have been."

"You have no right to come here as you did," he declared,

scowling. "Or even to speak of my family! This is our village, not yours." He spoke to everyone. "He's not even a Hindu!"

Some villagers yelled out that Madesh was a coward. I heard Ajira's voice among them.

Turning to Darpak and Harmut, I said, "May I ask him to do one thing for me as a token of repentance?"

"Yes," the twins replied.

"Madesh, I want you to apologize to Nupi—in front of everyone. If you do that, then I will ask that you be allowed to remain in Benali."

He spit betel juice on my sandaled foot, which I could not pull back in time. Hearing his demented laugh, the ache in my gut turned quickly to rage, but Nupi began cursing him before I could damn him. Held back by her sister, she stopped screaming only when Sofia kneeled down to clean my foot with her hand, which made my skin go cold all over. Then my sister did something even more courageous: she walked right up to Nupi's father-in-law and wiped her filthy palm on his arm.

What bravery that young girl showed! I respected her as I never had before.

Madesh gasped. I can still hear his sharp intake of breath, as though he'd been cut with a knife. He wanted to hit Sofia, but he didn't dare.

Sofia was so clenched with anger that she was trembling. It was chilling—I'd never seen her like that. Then she burst into tears and doubled over as though about to faint.

I wrapped my arms around her and drew her away.

*   *   *

I'd hoped that Tejal would speak to me before our departure, but I didn't even catch a glimpse of her. Our trip home was gloomy at first, and for two hours Nupi said nothing to me or Sofia. I was sure it was the pain of leaving her sister and all her relatives, but when she finally spoke, it was of other concerns.

"I do not know how I am going to explain the gash on your head to your father," she told me. "He will never forgive me for letting this happen. I knew we shouldn't have come. It was all wrong... all wrong from the very beginning. Such mistakes one makes over and over... everything repeated endlessly..."

Nupi hid her face in her hands. Sofia and I looked at each other helplessly.

"I'll just tell Papa that a wave knocked me over while I was swimming," I said with false cheer. "He'll believe that."

When Nupi looked at me, the kohl her sister had painted around her eyes was smudged and she was dripping black tears. "Oh, no," she whispered. "I would never lie to your father. I could not live with your family if I did. I would have to leave your home as I left my village."

"I don't understand—nothing terrible happened," Sofia insisted.

"But it could have," Nupi replied. "Ti could be dead now. We could be living in a world without him." She looked away, pensive. "It is an omen. It is very bad. And your father will never trust me again."

"I will tell him the truth," I said. "And I will make him understand that it was not your fault."

"You will not succeed," she replied despairingly.

"So you don't trust me!" I was furious.

"How can you say that to me? It's just that I am... I am not worthy of your help in this—"

"Listen to me!" I interrupted roughly. "*I* was the one who was hurt. My father and you will both have to respect my wishes. It's no omen—it's just something an angry old man did because he has suffered too much."

I cannot say what gave me such confidence, especially since my father was sure to be upset that Sofia and I had played the part of idols. Nupi wiped her eyes as if standing before a mirage. "I don't know how I could not have seen before that you've become a man," she said.

*   *   *

The second half of our journey was friendly and easy, and Nupi even consented to ride her donkey for a few miles. When we reached home, Papa was there to meet us, though he had told us he would arrive the following afternoon. He noticed my wound right away and inspected it by candlelight while I explained that Madesh had snuck up on me and whacked me for not being his grandson. I said nothing about our having played Ganesha, since Sofia and I agreed we were too exhausted from the trip for a lecture on the evils of idolatry. We would say nothing until the gash healed; then I'd tell Papa the whole truth.

He had commissioned a neighbor woman to prepare a feast of chicken stew, which we ate under the welcoming stars of home. Before bed, Nupi pushed into my hand a letter—written on three dried peepul leaves—that she had been instructed to give to me only upon our arrival.

Dear Ti—

Thank you for the little statue of Hanuman. How did you know that He was my favorite god? It was a lovely surprise, and I appreciate your care for my feelings (and my father's vigilance!) in sending it to me with your dear sister. I will not bring it to school (the nuns would only confiscate it, thinking it—and me!—terribly wicked), but I shall keep it always.

Madesh was evil to have tried to hurt you, but I am glad of one thing: when I stood over you and thought of your eyes never opening again, the prospect of never getting to know you became unbearable to me (imagine being given a beautiful leather-bound book and not being permitted to ever read even a single page!). So I would like to continue writing to you, if you don't mind. I cannot promise anything clever in what I tell you, however. But if you feel like it, you may write to me at the convent school, although you must never mention anything about being Jewish, as the nuns read all our letters. When next you come to Goa to visit your aunt and uncle, perhaps we can meet again.

Yours truly,
Tejal

P.S. Please excuse how I behaved when we first met, but I sensed you were about to change my life. That frightened me, but it no longer does. (Perhaps the mischief of Hanuman is behind all I feel and that cannot be described. It would be just like Him!)

Sofia was already in her bed, lying in the soft moonlight, when I came in carrying the leaves from Tejal in my hand. "It's just me," I whispered. All of me was tingling. I felt transformed by her note—as though I were walking across a tightrope while holding my dreams.

In a slumber-filled voice, my sister whispered, "Me who?"

I lay down beside her and moved my hand over her hair like an elephant's trunk searching for a sweet. "Guess," I breathed.

I was hoping she'd say "Ganesha," but she simply curled back into me and pulled my arm tight around her shoulder, which was even better. I lay awake for hours beside her, creating a new life out of my desires while she and the rest of India slept.

*   *   *

After another week my scab was nearly gone and it seemed pointless to provide my father with further details about how I'd been hurt. For breaking my promise to tell him the whole story, Nupi was snappish with me, but in the end she simply tucked some more fennel seeds under her lip, fixed me with a disappointed look, and recited one of her favorite local expressions: "Calling for the sun to return at dusk never does any good."

Tejal and I began to write long letters to each other once a week, and seeing her handwriting after days of waiting made me feel as if I were about to race across a bridge to my true home. She sent them care of the kindhearted peasant woman who supplied bread to the convent, and advised me to do the same after discovering that several pages I had written had been confiscated.

I often ran to my room after getting a letter, and once I bumped into Mama's statue of Shiva, sending it crashing to the ground. I chipped a finger on one of his eight hands, which made Nupi shake her head as though I were doomed by too fervent a love. Papa used to say the history of our family was written in Shiva's scratches and scars.

It was a very bad idea to send me on even a minor errand during this period of lovesickness. I remember that Nupi once asked me to go to town for eggs and I brought back a cabbage!

After that, Papa developed a new comic routine, and when we would all go to the market in Ramnath together he used to imitate me reading a letter and putting stones into my basket.

I was glad now to see both Portugal and India in my face when I looked in my mirror. I felt I had journeyed home to myself.

*   *   *

Tejal wrote mainly about her reading, and of her fondness for Sister Ana, a tiny, beak-faced nun from Lisbon who gave her books taken from a secret cabinet in the library and who brushed her hair with an ivory comb before bed. Hindus in Goa guessed at the wishes of their gods from the way petals fell from their shrines, and Tejal was sure that the gentle-hearted nun had been put in her life by Hanuman because a hibiscus petal had dropped off his brow and fallen right into her hands as she had prayed in her parents' home for Sister Ana's health.

So it was through her letters that I learned of her adoration for her favorite teacher, and of her fascination for the frightening stories she told her, particularly if they described a demonic possession, which all the nuns believed in and feared more than any other affliction. Tejal never tired of reading about the martyrdom of saints, since their blood-soaked faith made her bury her head with the most delicious terror into her pillow at night and wonder about loyalty, good and evil, the afterlife, and all those other important matters that tend to invade our sleep as we change into adults. She would often write to me about the lives of these holy men and women, from birth through epiphany to martyrdom, and in this way I learned the little I was to know of Christian lore. I presumed Tejal had become a believing Catholic, but when I asked in one of my letters, she replied, "No, I am still a Hindu, but when Sister Ana talks about Christ as if she really were married to Him it seems the most beautiful thing in the world to me, as if she has sacrificed more than anyone else could ever understand."

Tejal scarcely mentioned her schoolmates, and when I asked why, she wrote me that all but a few of them ridiculed her, not so much because she was Indian but because she came from a faraway village of poor fishermen. The other girls taunted her by calling her *carapau*—mackerel—and would flap their hands at their necks like gills when their teachers weren't looking. She had on one occasion been bloodied by kicks from a gang of four of her enemies. In consequence, I began to worry for her safety, and to understand, as well, that her shyness veiled a great deal of emotion. When I wrote to her of my concerns, however, she answered that the taunting didn't bother her. I didn't believe her bravado: it sounded precisely like what Sofia and I would have said in similar circumstances.

*   *   *

In one of my first letters, I asked Tejal if she'd have preferred to still be living in her village.

"Sometimes I would," she wrote, "but it's the sacrifice I must make, so you must not tell Nupi or anyone else of my difficulties with the other girls. Everyone in Benali must believe that I'm happy. I must not appear ungrateful to them."

Her confession left me upset and frightened because I had found someone who could shift the course of my entire life, and yet I had less influence than the wind over what she had to endure. When I wrote that I was more worried than ever about her, she replied: "Sister Ana is looking out for me, and behind her are all the saints, and sitting above them at the top of his peepul tree, a papaya in his tail, is Hanuman."

It took me a long time to realize that this was no mere show of optimism, but that she really did believe in the magical protection of her Hindu gods. Since I didn't, however, it did me precious little good when I'd wake in the middle of the night picturing her weeping in her cot.

*   *   *

Too embarrassed to reveal the depth of my feelings, I began to write mainly of my studies, which had now climbed up the long staircase of Torah into the twilight world of kabbalah, many teachings of which had been passed down in my family for centuries. I suppose I was aiming to impress Tejal, as well, since this meant that I was being trusted by my father with hermetic practices that could be dangerous in the wrong hands. I felt certain that any girl with faith in her gods had to respect that, and she did ask me many questions, though I was at liberty to answer only a few of them.

Papa and I now spent our mornings practicing our breathing exercises and talking about God's hidden life, which he explained was present in every corner of the universe—but most of all in the human body. We took long walks together to study how the *sephirot*— the ten primal attributes of the Lord—gave each animal and plant its form and determined its progress through life.

One cool dawn, he took me to Salim Lake, and we practiced permuting the letters from prayers while on jute mats spread in a small clearing guarded by a grove of giant bamboo, each stalk as thick as a man's wrist and many as tall as the cathedral towers in Goa. He told me that India was especially dear to the Lord because there was no more fertile place on earth.

"India knows in its soil and sky and waters that God is in everything and everyone, and it's why I will never leave here."

Papa spoke with the relief of a voyager who has reached home after years of arduous travel, but now, when I close my eyes, I hear him as though he were pronouncing his own death sentence.

*   *   *

On our first trip to Goa after our stay in Nupi's village, Tejal was able to obtain permission to meet me for an afternoon at my uncle's house. She shuddered like a drenched kitten when she stepped inside in her white school dress, gripping a bouquet of pink oleander blossoms in one hand and a leather-bound book in the other as if they contained all her strength and certainty. Her just-washed hair was shimmering down her back.

The look she gave me—her soft dark eyes appealing for help—made me want to embrace her and take her away. She and I kissed cheeks in the Portuguese manner, and I introduced her to my aunt and uncle with careful formality. Isaac stood behind me and, sensing my state, gripped my shoulders.

"We're very glad to have this chance to meet you," he told Tejal.

"If you will permit me to give you a gift, I've brought you these flowers," she said, handing her bouquet to my aunt. "I hope you like them."

"They're lovely!" Aunt Maria exclaimed, her voice so genuine that I was lulled into a sense of safety.

"They're very beautiful," my uncle agreed when his wife held them up for us to admire.

"I see you have a book with you, too," my aunt said cheerfully, adding, "It must have a great many pretty pictures in it—I mean, so a girl like you could appreciate it."

A girl like you meant Indian, of course.

"I'm sorry, but it doesn't have any pictures at all," Tejal replied, failing completely to grasp the cruelty of Aunt Maria's implication.

"You can't mean that you're able to read!" my aunt huffed with theatrical astonishment, lifting a hand to her cheek to accentuate her surprise.

Tejal was biting her lip, unsure of how to reply.

"I can see what you're up to," I told my aunt, "and I want you to stop."

"What's wrong with my asking Tejal a question?" she asked, feigning puzzlement. When I frowned, she looked at me down the length of her nose as if I were an affront to her dignity, and I realized that we had never stopped being enemies. To her husband she added innocently, "Have I said something wrong?" She gave him a squinting look meant to say: *If you don't support me in this, there'll be trouble. . . .*

"It's just that voicing assumptions aloud can often get us into trouble, Maria," Isaac replied. "Look, why don't you and I let the children talk alone for a while?"

"Tejal and I will go out into the garden," I said. "Come on," I told her eagerly, "it'll be nice out there." But when I reached for her arm, she shivered. Her skin was very cold.

"Please don't leave us so soon," Aunt Maria said, sensing, no doubt, an opportunity to do real damage. "So is it true that you can read?" She smiled with false benevolence.

"Of course she can," I snapped. "I've told you she's in a convent school."

"It's . . . it's true, Senhora Zarco," Tejal said in a shamed whisper, afraid now to look up, as if literacy in an Indian girl were a crime.

"You ought to be very proud of yourself," Uncle Isaac told her.

"I am the first girl in my village who has had the benefits of education," she said, apologizing with her tone.

"The very first—how wonderful for you!" Aunt Maria exclaimed, and she looked at me as though she'd won a bet between us.

"What book do you have, Tejal?" my uncle asked, eager to change the subject.

"The New Testament," she replied nervously. Probably thinking my aunt might next accuse her of robbery, she added, "One of my teachers was kind enough to give it to me."

"Were you born a Christian?" Aunt Maria asked. "Or were you forced to believe in all those animals when you were small?"

"What animals, Senhora Zarco?" Tejal began biting her lip again.

"That horrible one with the elephant head, for instance."

"Ganesha," I snarled. "Don't you even know that? How long have you lived in India?"

"Who would like some cashew-fruit punch?" Uncle Isaac asked before she could reply. "I made it myself, Tejal. It's good, I think, but I'd like your opinion. You can take it out to the garden with you. I'll go get it from the kitchen. How about coming with me, Maria?"

"No, I think I'll stay here."

"As you wish," he said, and, giving her a warning with his eyes, he started away.

"Tiago, the name of an elephant in India can hardly matter to the one true God," my aunt announced in a condescending voice.

My uncle stopped in the doorway and gave her a displeased look, but she nodded haughtily at him, and then at me and Tejal, as if she had just bestowed her wisdom on all of us.

"I'm sure you're right, Senhora Zarco," Tejal said, making a deferential little bow. "I have yet to learn many things."

"I just think it must be very confusing to have all those *hundreds* of gods and goddesses. Tell me something—how can you pray to a statue of a monkey without laughing?"

"Maria!" Uncle Isaac exclaimed hotly. He returned to her and put his arm around her waist, but she pushed his hand away.

"Just a minute," she said.

Tejal's eyes had moistened, and her lips were squeezed together as though she might never speak again.

In my desperation, I told my aunt, "Hindus worship Hanuman because He symbolizes all that's playful in the world. He is all that can't be predicted."

She shook her head. "That's philosophical rubbish you must

have learned from your father. Even the Hindus who are educated don't believe that."

"Whatever they believe, at least they don't go around forcing everyone to convert, like all your horrible Catholic priests!"

"That's . . . that's blasphemy, Tiago Zarco!"

"Will both of you please, for the love of God, be quiet!" Uncle Isaac shouted. "Maria, you and I are going to the sitting room to let Tiago and Tejal be alone for a while." He placed his hand at his wife's back and pressed her forward.

"I shall want to talk to you later about Christianity, my dear," my aunt threatened, turning back to us.

"There won't be time," I said with controlled fury.

"There's always time for God," she declared, as though she'd trumped me.

Looking at her self-satisfied grin, it was as if she'd taken off her mask, and it struck me that this had nothing to do with religion. She was venting her fury because Tejal was young and beautiful—and at me because I was in love with the girl. Was it possible that my aunt had never felt any deep affection for anyone, even Uncle Isaac? Had I even been wrong about her devotion to Wadi?

Her barren life is what this is about, I realized.

As she and my uncle walked away, I felt that this knowledge gave me power.

"Aunt Maria, you ought to be more careful what you say," I called after her. "Your motives may not be as unknown to me as they seem."

She whipped around. "Tiago, are you threatening me?"

"Yes, I think I am."

"Tiago," my uncle intervened harshly, "I'll thank you to see to Tejal's comfort. You are being a very bad host."

While he pushed his wife out of the room, I escorted Tejal through the house and down the back steps into the garden. "You'll feel better outside," I told her. Her face was pale. I could see she wanted to burst into tears, but that her pride wouldn't let her.

It takes all her strength to fight them, I thought, and by *them* I meant all those who wanted to diminish her.

We sat together on the wooden bench under the tamarind tree that centered the garden. I clasped her hands in mine to warm them and explained that Aunt Maria was just jealous of her. I apologized for our quarrel, but I felt the triumph of giving up on my aunt; I knew I would never try to win her approval or affection ever again.

"I ought never to have come," Tejal said sadly.

As I was wondering how to turn this defeat around, I heard tapping above us. Papa was leaning out his window and motioning for us with wheeling hands to come upstairs. In my mind, I could hear him saying, *Have confidence in your old father. . . .* But confidence was the one thing I did not have, since I knew he'd always intended for me to marry a Jewish girl.

"Papa wants to meet you," I said, trying to sound cheerful.

She grimaced and pressed her hands together to summon her resolve. "Please, not until I've had a chance to become myself again," she told me.

After signaling up to my father to wait a few minutes, I offered to bring Tejal a cup of Uncle Isaac's punch. She said she just needed to sit quietly for a few minutes. "It happens to me sometimes," she added.

"What does?"

"It will just sound odd to you."

"It won't—I promise."

"My life seems unreal to me at moments like this—as if I will wake up soon and discover I am not a girl and not in India—that I am not anything that I am."

Before I could reply, she closed her eyes. I felt as if the world were revolving slowly around me. *Everything is coming to a stop,* I thought. *Soon I, too, will find I am no longer who I thought I was.*

I dared to caress her cheek. *Let this girl at least know that I mean her no harm,* I thought.

She kept her eyes closed.

"It will make no sense to you," I whispered, "but when we're together I remember how soft my mother's skin was. All the years of separation between us disappear. You do that for me. No one else ever has."

She squeezed my hand, but kept her eyes shut tight.

How easy it was for me to believe at that moment that we could overcome all the obstacles before us, but maybe that is as it should be for a young boy looking across the length and breadth of love. When she could talk again, we conversed for a time about my mother, and how I sometimes discovered Papa drawing her from memory in the early morning. I told Tejal how much it pleased me that he would always let me watch him sketch. It was how I'd always known he trusted me.

I asked again if we might go up and see my father.

"Yes, I think we'd better," Tejal said.

As we stood up, I said in Konkani, "I want you to know that nothing and no one could ever make me betray you."

I had written to her of my difficulties with Wadi and hoped she understood that for me this was more important even than the many declarations of love I had written to her.

*   *   *

Papa slept in his brother's library when we were in Goa, and Tejal gasped when she looked across the hundreds of volumes on his shelves.

"It's nice living inside a jungle of books, isn't it?" my father said with a welcoming smile.

"I think I could spend years here, Senhor Zarco."

That reply pleased Papa. He kissed her on both cheeks, and in the way he stood taller afterward, I saw that he was quite fond of her already.

He motioned for Tejal and me to sit in the chairs he'd pulled in front of Uncle Isaac's desk, then combed his hair back with his hand.

He was very nervous. I realized I'd forgotten that my father was not so different from most men and that he might want to make a good impression on a beautiful girl.

Tejal and I sat together facing him, both undoubtedly fearing his judgment. We were three travelers setting off for a new land. I sometimes wish we had closed our eyes at that moment and given thanks for all we were about to leave behind.

Papa asked her a few questions about her school, but she gave no more than the briefest answers. She later told me her heart was beating in her ears.

Sensing this was the wrong way forward and wishing to win her trust, Papa offered her a vellum manuscript of two ancient Jewish folktales that he had translated from Hebrew into Portuguese for her. They were about the wicked plottings of Lilith and Asmodeus, the Queen and King of the Jewish Demons, since those were the kind of stories that I'd told him she adored.

I hadn't any idea how carefully he'd prepared for this meeting until she opened the manuscripts and we saw the magnificent illustrations he'd drawn for her in the most brilliant blues, pinks, and oranges. I particularly remember Lilith flying over Jerusalem, her tresses on fire and her mouth dripping blood, and a hawk-winged, yellow-eyed Asmodeus standing atop a mountain of skulls in Gehenna, the Jewish hell, about to toss the head of Goliath into a boiling ocean. Papa had never before illuminated a book for any of my friends.

Tejal stared at the images with rapt eyes, a hand over her heart, in the way Indian girls often acknowledge deep emotion.

"You . . . you made these for me, Senhor Zarco?" she stammered.

"Yes. These two stories were my favorites when I was a boy. Lilith used to keep me up at night all the time. My mother would hang a talisman around my neck to protect me from her."

When I told him how touched I was by his kindness, he flapped his hand at me and said it was nothing. He picked up a thin book and handed it to me. "This is for both of you," he said.

It was a Spanish adventure story called *Lazarillo de Tormes*. I showed the title page to Tejal.

"It's more interesting than it might at first seem," Papa said. He hunched his shoulders and looked around conspiratorially for comic effect. "Don't tell Aunt Maria or Uncle Isaac I gave it to you." He circled his hands around his neck and grimaced as though he were being strangled. "That would only cause me complications.

"I must say it's nice to keep secrets with young people," he continued, grinning as though he'd sown mischief in the world. He then bolted over to the window and called us over, pointing down to the tamarind tree. I hadn't seen him behave so youthfully in years.

"It was my Ti who planted that broad giant when he was tiny," he told Tejal. "It was just six inches high, with a few scruffy leaves."

"Papa, please," I said, thinking he was about to embarrass me with stories from my childhood.

"Shush," he said, tapping my head with his fist. "I didn't want you to plant it. You didn't know that, did you?"

"No."

"See, he thinks he knows everything, but he doesn't," he told Tejal in triumph, and his pride in me was so clear in his radiant eyes that she laughed with him.

"But why didn't you want me to plant it?" I asked.

"I was angry at your mother's death, and irritated at your aunt Maria for telling me that God had His reasons for taking her. I didn't want anything to grow here. I wanted revenge."

I didn't understand the point of his story until he added, "But you were right to plant it, and all these years later that tamarind tree is beautiful. Ti, all I mean to say in my awkward way is that you sometimes know better than I do."

Holding his right hand over Tejal's head, he whispered a Hebrew blessing.

I was very happy, of course, but I still could not imagine how he was going to permit me to marry a non-Jewish girl. Maybe he saw that unspoken question in my face, because as I left him that day, he whispered, "There are some tricks you haven't learned yet, my son. So just have some faith in your old father for now."

*　　*　　*

Tejal and I returned to the garden and began reading *Lazarillo de Tormes* as soon as we left Papa. She didn't understand Spanish well enough to read it herself, so I translated it aloud to her into Konkani. Looking into her eager eyes, I again felt like travelers embarking on a journey together, but this time there was added a sense of her dependency on me. How greatly I wanted to be needed by her!

That warm afternoon under the tamarind, as Lázaro—the book's hero—told of his adventures as a morally dubious servant to a blind and paupered nobleman, it began to seem as if he'd always been meant to accompany our explorations into love. When it was time for me to walk her back to her convent, Tejal asked me to keep the book for her, along with the folktales, since the nuns would confiscate them if they found them. Before leaving my aunt and uncle's house that day, we kissed as we never had before, as though we were attempting to enter each other, and in the darkness behind my eyes I found myself somewhere I had only glimpsed in my most astonishing dreams.

*　　*　　*

The growing intimacy of our correspondence served to make Tejal and me more sure with each other when we met at my uncle's home, and we now held hands even in front of my father, though the first time we did so with him looking on I nearly fainted.

"You need never be embarrassed in front of me," he told me later. "I know I haven't done so bad a job as your father when I see you able to give love so well and so freely."

Soon, Papa began clowning for her at my aunt and uncle's supper table, starting with his imitation of me at the marketplace and ending with his old favorite, a frog in his slipper. Today, when I think of those days of togetherness, of my eager dreams and our secret glances, it seems as if they are all framed by that easy humor—as though my father's way of being were a kind of metaphor for all that would now be possible for me. Yet I can also see what I didn't even then suspect—that I had no real comprehension of who Tejal was and what she needed. I only thought I did because we were glowing with expectance. I mistook that haloed light for knowledge, and probably she did, too. Maybe we were meant to—for after all she was just fifteen, and I only eighteen. We were venturing forth from out of the mystery of ourselves, groping as best we could.

*   *   *

The thought of being one day able to sleep side-by-side with her in the same bed now frequently overwhelmed me at night. I began to consult a Bengali copy of the Kama Sutra—that Papa believed he'd successfully hidden from everyone—whenever he left the house. Sitting on my bed, a chair propped under my door handle for protection against Nupi, who was prone to walking in on me without knocking or even calling my name, I turned the drawings this way and that in order to figure out what exactly would be required of me.

I finished *Lazarillo de Tormes* on my own, and though the story made me laugh aloud, I was left troubled by God's total absence from the narration. Life happened, and much of it was bad, though quite a bit of it was comic and wonderful. And that was all there was—no pattern, no meaning, no revelation. When I told my father my conclusions, he said, "Read it in another ten years and you might feel differently."

"Papa," I replied, irritated with his dismissive tone, "it's very unlikely that the sentences in the book are going to rearrange themselves into a different order over the next decade."

He smiled. "No, but you will. And next time you read it you might find that the Lord is not so absent as you think. In fact, you might find Him in the place you least expect Him."

*   *   *

Everything might have been good and calm in my life at this time, but Sofia and Wadi were growing ever more resentful that they had to keep their relationship a secret. Soon they began to take their frustration out on me.

"Boys get everything," my sister snarled at me while we sat together working on a Koran for the Sultan's chief physician. "If only I'd been born one."

"If you'd been born a boy, you wouldn't be in love with Wadi," I replied in a whisper, since I was not sure where Papa was and didn't wish to betray her secret.

"Who knows, maybe I still would be," she retorted, smiling cagily.

I wasn't sure what she meant by that. When I asked, she stuck out her tongue at me, picked up her reed pen and magnifying glass, and made believe I'd disappeared. Some silent force inside her seemed bent on hurting me.

"Sofia, I'll go with you to see Papa if you want," I said later that day. "We'll tell him how you feel."

She shrugged as though it was pointless.

"I think I can convince him to accept Wadi," I added. "He's feeling so happy right now. It could be the perfect time."

"Ti, the very last thing I need is your help," she declared.

In point of fact, that wasn't true, since she often asked me to lie to Papa when she wanted to be alone with Wadi—to say I'd been with them at a fair or the marketplace. I felt corrupted by this subterfuge, but could not refuse her.

Given both their natures, I see now that Wadi and Sofia may have preferred leading a double life—and of involving me in it against my will. Likely this pretense seemed both less risky and more exciting to them. And I'd learned from my cousin not to underestimate the gratification he took from deception.

*   *   *

One afternoon in February of 1591, Papa called me into his library. I could tell from his clenched jaw that he was furious. I noticed a letter sitting on top of the desk, its red wax seal in pieces, as though crushed by a fist.

"Has something bad happened?" I asked.

"You might say that. I found out how you got that scar on your forehead."

"But I already told you—Nupi's father-in-law hit me."

He shook the letter at me. "But you conveniently forgot to tell me how you provoked him." Papa glared at me, daring me to disagree.

"Provoked him? I . . . I didn't do anything."

"You and Sofia played Ganesha at the festival in Benali."

"Oh, that," I said matter-of-factly. "It wasn't much—we just walked around and handed out flowers while wearing elephant heads. It was just like playing with shadow puppets."

"Didn't you think I'd find out? Do you think I am a fool?" Papa slammed his fist down.

"It just didn't seem so important," I lied, but with desperate conviction in my voice.

"Oh, so you held the truth back because it wasn't important."

"No, not exactly. It was because I didn't want you getting angry at me."

"Did it never occur to you that Madesh might not like you being the center of the attention of the whole village? That it would only make him think more desperately about his dead son and grandson?"

"No, it—"

"Can you see how for him you were flaunting your good health and happiness?"

"I'm sorry if he felt that, Papa, but the village elders asked us to be Ganesha. It would've been wrong to turn down their hospitality. The Torah teaches us that we are—"

"The Torah!" he thundered, shaking with outrage. "Does it also teach you to receive offerings while pretending to be an idol? To accept hospitality when it means renouncing your religion?"

"We didn't renounce Judaism! And we weren't idols. We were

playing a Hindu god for the villagers. They knew who was inside the elephant heads. Papa, it was symbolic. Can't you understand that?"

"Ti, I assure you that I don't need lessons from you in the symbolic meaning of ritual."

"Did Nupi tell you what happened?"

"No, though she should have. Isaac wrote me about it."

I realized then what had happened: Sofia had entrusted Wadi with all the details I'd held back from our father, and he must have let something slip to Uncle Isaac or Aunt Maria. He'd gotten the better of me again.

"So what do you want me to do now?" I asked, hoping to get my punishment over with quickly.

"Find Nupi and your sister and bring them here."

"It wasn't their fault. They had nothing to do with it."

Papa sat down and folded his hands together on top of his desk in an attempt to regain some measure of composure.

"So you're saying that Nupi had nothing to do with what her father-in-law did?" he asked.

"That's right."

"Ti, did you hear what I said? Get Nupi and Sofia now."

I found them hanging the washing behind our house. When I hastily explained what had just happened, the old woman looked longingly to the west, toward Benali, as if she were about to run away from her life a second time. Sofia, sensing that possibility, linked arms with her. We walked together into Papa's study, feeling shipwrecked.

Nupi took one look at his rigid face and burst into tears, gripping Sofia with both of her gnarled hands as if holding on to the receding edge of the world. We helped her sit down in the armchair in front of Papa's desk. Seeing her face peeled open to misery, I became furious at how he just sat there frowning.

"Sofia," he began, "I realize that you are younger than your brother, but I thought you would show better sense than to play at idolatry."

"I'm sorry," she replied glumly.

"Nupi, I trusted you with the children. And you know how I feel about offerings to gods. Why do I have to hear about this from my brother?"

The old cook fell to her knees before my father, her hands clasped in prayer.

"Please don't do that," he begged, rising.

Her words became sobs. He turned his back to her and made believe he was looking for a book on his shelves as she crawled to him and prostrated herself. It was a scene of terrible cruelty. Sofia bent down to try to lift Nupi back to her feet, but the old woman batted her away roughly, then hid her head in her hands. She wept as if her soul were spilling out of her.

"Papa, please do something," I pleaded. "You're being a tyrant."

He jerked around, his face twisted with contempt. "I'm tired of being lied to by you—by the three people I love most in this world. Don't you see how disrespectful it is? And how it can poison all that is good in our family?"

"We didn't mean to lie," I protested. "It just happened."

"Nothing just happens. Have you listened to anything I've said about the ways God works in our lives? Ti, get out of here. Get out of here *now*! I want to talk to your sister and Nupi."

"No," I replied. I felt my future as a man turning around this moment.

"What did you say?"

"I may have done some very wrong things, and I may have acted thoughtlessly, but I won't go until you help Nupi up and apologize to her."

Papa leaned toward me threateningly. "You'll do what I say. This is still my home."

"I won't," I replied defiantly. "Nupi did nothing wrong. She protected Sofia and me, just as she always has. Sofia and I accepted offerings as idols and you may punish us for that if you want to. But it gives you no right to be so mean to Nupi. She's a Hindu. She believes in Ganesha. The villagers do, too. We made them happy. What's wrong with making people happy?" I was shouting now, carried away by the desperation I sensed all around me, aware that I was also fighting for Tejal and my love for her, since she, too, was a Hindu. "You are being disrespectful to Nupi's gods and all they stand for. That can't be in the Torah."

In Papa's horror-struck face, I read instantly that I'd gone too far.

"Get out of my house!" His voice seemed to rip the air between us. "And don't you dare come back until you're ready to apologize."

"I was born here and it's my house, too," I stated for the record. "And it always will be."

I whipped around and ran out of the room. Sofia came racing after me.

"Don't leave," she implored me. "He doesn't mean it, Ti, but you gave him no other choice. You have to go back and say you're sorry."

"Saying that would just mean telling another lie. And I'm finished with lies forever."

I didn't need to add, *Even for you and Wadi;* I could tell from her somber nod that she understood my message.

We could hear Nupi moaning inside. It seemed to prove how powerless and weak we were.

"I can't stand it," Sofia said, tugging at her hair. "I'll do anything if she'll only stop. I don't know how Papa can bear it."

"Did you have to tell Wadi everything?" I asked.

"Ti, I didn't think that anything bad could happen. It was all just an accident."

No, he wanted to get me into trouble, and maybe you, too, I thought.

*   *   *

The only conclusion I came to while stomping through the rice fields around our home—cursing the mud and stink of decay and everything else—was that my friendship with Wadi had just been split right in half. This was the end of us.

It would never have occurred to me that you could feel fondness and loathing for a person at one and the same time, and I saw now what I'd never wanted to acknowledge—that my faith in my cousin had always been more important than even my affection for him, precisely because it was the more fragile of the two.

*   *   *

Papa refused to look up at me when I passed his library door two hours later, and he took his supper alone in his bedroom. Nupi sat in her kitchen hunched over her table, her eyes barren, her fingers picking at the wiry hairs on her chin. She packed a flour sack that night with her few possessions, stuffing her favorite cooking spoons inside as if they were daggers stabbing into all her regrets. From her absent look, I could see her thoughts were with her dead husband and son. She said she'd leave at first light and return to her village, but Sofia and I emptied everything from her sack and told her we'd never let her go. We put her to bed and sat with her while she wept, spending most of the night by her side. By the light of a single candle, my sister gazed at me with fondness for the first time in weeks and I was grateful, at least, for that.

None of us got much sleep that night. Papa had deep pouches of sadness under his eyes in the morning. I still believed he ought to be the one to make peace, but the gravity of misery inside me was pulling me ever closer to an apology.

Nupi did not join us for breakfast and stayed alone in her kitchen. No one spoke until I said, "Papa, I'm sorry for offending you, but I won't lie to you again, so I can't say I regret what I told you. But I didn't mean to hurt you. I don't believe I ever have. I think that ought to be enough."

As he gazed down, considering his options, Sofia burst into tears and hugged him as if she were breaking apart. Her despair shattered the spell of madness between us. Papa kissed her. "Don't you see," he told us desperately, "I worry about the two of you constantly. You can't imagine the nightmares I had in Bijapur. Now listen closely...."

You must be very careful when I'm not with you. You have to think things through. Nupi must, too. I have to demand that of her, even if it seems cruel to you. It is my responsibility as your father. I owe it to your mother, if nothing else."

Later that morning, Papa went to Nupi in her basil garden and asked if he could weed it with her. As they squatted together, he explained himself to her calmly, and very soon they were talking about what to have for supper. When he began clowning for her, her exhaustion and relief made her break into giddy laughter, her hands clamped over her eyes like a little girl.

*   *   *

On Wadi's next visit to our home, I confronted him about his betrayal. He and Sofia were in our garden, and he was showing her how to hold a bow, standing behind her with his hands over hers. He'd erected a shadow puppet of a mongoose on an iron poker as their target.

"Did you have to tell your parents that we played Ganesha at the village festival?" I asked him.

"I didn't," he replied, without looking at me. To Sofia, he said, "Line it up with the mongoose. Higher . . . a bit higher . . . that's it!"

"Then how did he find out?"

"I'm not sure. Maybe my mother overheard Sofia telling me."

Wadi obviously thought this was a very unimportant topic and pulled the cord back in preparation for letting the arrow fly. My sister was licking her lips with anticipation.

"You helped cause a lot of grief in our home—especially to Nupi, which I find very hard to forgive," I persisted. "The least you could do is tell us you're sorry. And apologize to Nupi."

Ping. The arrow shot off in too low an arc and fell ten feet short of the target. Their laughter seemed like a slap across my face. Sofia ran off for the arrow.

"Answer me," I warned Wadi.

"What?" he asked, raising his eyebrows theatrically, pretending he hadn't heard me.

"I want to know why you did it."

"I told you I didn't."

"Ti, leave him alone," Sofia said threateningly. As she walked by me, she shoved me to the side.

"Don't tell me what to do," I snapped back.

She frowned condescendingly. "Go study Torah and leave us alone."

"Sofia, I'll only give you this advice once: do not always trust everyone you love." I looked directly at Wadi.

"You're just jealous!" she shouted as I turned to leave.

"Of Wadi? I can see you're never going to hit any target if your aim is that far off."

"Not him, *me*! You don't like it that Wadi loves me and not you! You've never liked it. You've always wanted him for yourself."

All movement came to a halt around me. Thoughts would not form. Wadi lifted up his bow slowly, and targeted an arrow toward my eyes, his jaw set as though ready to kill me, but at that moment, I would not have flinched even if he had let it fly.

I turned on my heel to leave, wondering if she was right. It had never occurred to me before that a life with him was even conceivable. Would we have been damned forever if we'd given free rein— even once—to our affection? Was that what I'd wanted?

Something hit me hard on the back. Looking down, I saw a gray stone, and by the perverse way Wadi and Sofia were smiling at me I could see they were glad to have wounded me, and that their passion was going to make them do even worse if I let them.

"I'm no longer going to lie to Papa about your whereabouts," I declared to them. "You've gone too far now."

Wadi imitated my way of speaking, which I interpreted as his nasty way of agreeing that our friendship had died, and I could see from Sofia's haughty, ruthless gaze that I was now her enemy.

Seeing only impatient contempt for me in their eyes, I began to tremble. Were my own shameful desires really behind every moment of easy laughter and affection I'd shared with my cousin?

I fought off tears when I was with them but could not help breaking down in my room. *I'll have to go far away if they tell anyone,* I thought.

*   *   *

I spent the rest of that day gripped so tightly by a dark sense of dread that I thought I might run away and never return. My breathing itself seemed constrained by impending disaster, as if the ground were about to open up and swallow me.

I discovered during these first hours of anxious distress that one's past can be torn apart by a single instant in the present. None of what I'd lived seemed as I'd intended now. I'd been misperceived by my sister, Wadi, and probably everyone else all along.

Was this what Aunt Maria meant when she'd held an earring up to my ear and made fun of me for wanting to care for my sister?

Denying that I'd ever had such feelings for my cousin could not help me now, since Wadi and Sofia believed I did and might be able to convince even my father. And how *could* I deny them, since I didn't even know myself how far I'd have gone to make our bond even deeper? Do two boys who grow up together ever know where their intimacy will lead them and how it will end? If they say they do, if they say that sin could never have found them as they sat on a riverbank watching the fall of the sun or ran through a forest in the rain, then I do not think they've lived anything like the life I have had.

*   *   *

I awoke with a start well after midnight. Someone had just sat down at the foot of my bed. My shutters were closed and the room was black.

"Papa?" I said to the dark form, sitting up in a panic.

"It's me," Wadi said.

"What are you doing here?"

"I was just wondering if I should strangle you while you slept." His voice was cool and decisive, as though he were tightrope-walking over any emotion he might have been feeling.

Before I could swing my feet over the side of the bed, his hands closed around my neck. I tried to pry them away but failed. I fought him, but I couldn't breathe.

Then he released me with a dry, mocking laugh. I fell over onto the floor, gasping, desperate to fill my lungs. Standing, he walked out of my room and eased the door closed.

CHAPTER 12

The possibility that my father would find out about Sofia and Wadi's accusation of me erected an invisible barrier between Papa and me. Sometimes he asked me what was wrong, but I would always lie. I could not have borne his shame along with my own. After a time, to explain my withdrawn moods, I invented stomach ailments for which Nupi was always preparing me ginger tea.

I might have begged Wadi and Sofia not to reveal anything, but I suspected that my supplications would only tempt their further cruelty. *My weakness will confirm to them they were right, and end any chance I may still have at happiness with Tejal.*

So it was that I began to avoid them both, scuttling away like a crab at the approach of their footsteps. Over the next few months Sofia and I never talked once as brother and sister.

I thought all the time, of course, of the boyhood adventures I'd had with Wadi, but hindsight is an effortless liar. How could I be certain about my past feelings when they were veiled by years of distance and all the experiences I'd had since then? I saw only one thing clearly: the secrecy and stealth Wadi and I would have had to employ in order to conceal any physical bond between us would have undone me. I'd never have voluntarily given him the means to cause my destruction—and to create so much shame for my father. So he would have had to overpower me.

Had he ever considered bending me to his will when we were alone at Indra's Millstream? Was *that* the animal-like danger I sometimes scented on him?

How close had we been to leading a double life?

*   *   *

At the center of the ever-expanding world of sin and doubt around me was a single memory: Wadi giving me a leering smile and reaching for his sex when he first spoke of Sarah. He'd told me not to be jealous. I hadn't understood that he'd meant *of Sarah*—just as I hadn't understood Sofia's accusation at first. The connection couldn't be accidental. Maybe Wadi had given me signals for years that he wanted our relationship to move along a different path.

Did Sofia yet suspect that her accusation of jealousy ought to have been made to him, not me?

How frustrated he must have been that I didn't understand his desires, though maybe he believed that I sensed them easily enough and denied him on purpose. If so, then he must have convinced Sofia to accuse me in order to exact revenge. Wadi hadn't needed to shoot an arrow at me that day in our garden: Sofia had done it for him. And she had very good aim, after all.

Or was I inventing his motivations now in order to comprehend a final betrayal I could not otherwise explain, to write the end of our friendship as a story where I was the victim? Did Wadi's nature still elude me completely?

*   *   *

Papa summoned me into his study one day in late March to say how troubled he was by my disintegrating relationship with Sofia, but I couldn't even begin to explain what had taken place between us without revealing the nature of her feelings for Wadi. My fear of what she could do to me certainly made up the greater part of my silence, but I also wanted to show her that the brother she persecuted was still morally her superior.

"We're growing older and growing apart" was what I said instead, which was true enough. "But I think we will come back together in the end."

With a resigned look, Papa accepted my reply, which—at the time—I half believed myself, since I was unable to imagine that all our years of caring could come to nothing. In fact, as I uttered my prediction, I realized that Wadi would undoubtedly soon reveal a secret of hers, or commit some other treason, forcing her to wake at last from her romantic daydreams. It seemed the only possible outcome of a friendship with him.

I only hoped she wouldn't be too wounded by him, in part because I'd undoubtedly have to be the one to care for her in the months of loneliness to follow.

As I reached the door, Papa stilled my hand. Panic swept through me: I sensed he was about to ask me about what had happened between me and Wadi.

"Ti, I didn't want to have to speak about certain things with you, but now that your relationship with your sister has deteriorated... How strongly does Sofia love your cousin?"

"For how long have you known about them?" I asked, relieved that I didn't have to talk about myself.

"Since the time Sofia asked to stay in Goa for a few weeks. But I was sure only when you began your own life in earnest—without worrying so much about her."

"She loves him deeply," I said.

Deeply enough to let herself be convinced that she had to choose between us, I wanted to add.

"And does he love her?"

"I think so." *Unless,* I thought, *he has taken up with her just for the pleasure of destroying our family's harmony.*

"I'll have to have a serious talk with Isaac about this very soon."
Papa heaved a great sigh.

"Maybe not."

"Why?"

"I have my doubts that it will last."

"Go on."

I could not speak of Wadi's betrayals of me without damning
him in my father's eyes—and risking my cousin's revenge against
me. So I referred instead to how quickly he'd tired of Sarah.

"Do you think it will be a good thing for him to fall out of love
with Sofia?" Papa asked.

"Neither good nor bad," I answered, feeling that all the important things in life were beyond our control. "Just the way it will be."

*   *   *

Tejal was able to get permission to visit us during the Easter holidays
because Nupi was her great-aunt and had promised her parents she'd
look after her. One night, after everyone had gone to sleep, she and I
sat on the verandah. It was the kind of perfect evening that India
weaves out of a whispering breeze, with every star in place and all the
sounds of the forest seeming to come out of an age long past. Yet I
was restless. I felt as though the Lord of the Old Testament might
appear at any moment and force me to fight Wadi to win back my
identity.

I hadn't the courage to explain to Tejal why I was no longer on
friendly terms with my cousin and my sister—and why I'd been so
quiet during her visit. A wall—built of my deep fear of being re-
jected by her—had grown up between us.

I was watching her rereading Papa's folktales, the comforting
weight of her head on my shoulder, when the moon, freeing itself
from a cloud, lit up her face and hair, giving me the strange impression that she was an eternal being—and would be with me for only
a very short time unless I acted decisively. It was one of those mo-

ments when we believe in revelations and fortune. I sensed that we were destined to be married and that she'd give me invincible strength if we were. My mind took off on fantasies after that, most of them silly, but in one of them I realized that declaring our engagement would solve all my problems. I could then laugh off any accusations of shameful desires. Our love made this the ideal solution. If only I could convince Papa that a Hindu girl could be my bride.

"I want to marry you," I said.

Did I change into a being of careful strategies as I spoke these words or had I simply never seen my own tactics so clearly before?

"What did you say?" Tejal asked, sitting up, her face showing alarm.

"I suppose we might need a year or so to prepare everything. I'll have to talk to your parents, though I have no idea what will be expected of me. And somehow we'll have to convince Papa that—"

Her face twisted with distress and she dropped her manuscript.

"What's wrong? I thought you'd be happy."

"Oh, Ti, I cannot leave the convent school just because you want me to. The whole village has contributed to my education. They are counting on me. It is impossible—so impossible that I cannot even think of how to reply to you."

I leaned down to pick up her folktales. "But I want you to finish your studies and to work at the Royal Hospital. I'll move to Goa. I'm sure my uncle will hire me."

"Ti, my father is only a fisherman. We own nothing of value. If you found a Brahmin girl, you would—"

"Why are you trying to insult me?" I interrupted. I spoke more harshly than I needed to; I wanted to prove I was not hiding any ulterior motives.

"Insult you?" she questioned despairingly.

"By implying that I want a Brahmin bride. I am happy your father and mother are from Benali. I love it there."

"You do?"

"I was Ganesha there, remember? Anything can happen in your village."

She flung her arms around me. In my naiveté, I hadn't realized how our different backgrounds had caused her constant worry since we'd met. Now, the caste system seemed cruel to me in a way it never had before. It was as though it symbolized all the traps the world set for us.

Wriggling free of my kisses of reassurance, she jumped up and announced she wanted a wedding by the seaside—with only our parents and close relatives in attendance. I insisted instead on grand festivities—sitar and tabla players, dancers from Kerala, and so many flowers that we'd attract clouds of bees and honeybirds.

Announcing our love as loudly as possible will be useful, I thought, and I felt my strategy—like a mill wheel—giving its first complete turn.

She bit her thumbnail, afraid to agree. "Do you think we could?" she asked, kneeling next to me.

It delighted me the way her gestures were so graceful and child-like at the same time. I felt giddy having such a girl want me and pressed my lips to hers, holding her face between my hands. It was a kiss of desires openly declared, and after a time she pushed me away.

"Ti, no," she protested. She jumped up, angry, brushing off her sari as though it had become soiled.

"Is it wrong to want to be with someone you love?" I asked. After I stood up, I showed her what I meant by lifting a fold in my dhoti.

"Ti, stop!" She turned away. "This is not like you at all. If my father knew . . ."

I gave a small laugh to make light of what I'd done and tucked myself back in.

"You can turn back now," I said. "See, all gone!"

I whirled my hands around like a fakir making his mouse disappear, but Tejal didn't smile. Indeed, she looked close to tears.

"The villagers will expect a big wedding since they contributed to your education," I argued, eager now to change the subject. "I wouldn't want to disappoint them."

She stared at me without replying, her face adult and serious. Then she reached out and touched the straining outline of my sex.

I gave a little moan. When she squeezed, I felt all of me flowing out toward her. I stepped closer. Her breathing was warm on my chest.

"Don't be afraid," I said. "I promise I'll never hurt you."

I felt I was winning myself back by swearing that.

I kissed both her cheeks and licked her ear playfully, which made her shiver.

"I love you," I whispered, "so don't be scared."

She reached under my dhoti and ran her hand slowly up and down my hardness as though testing the length and breadth of her own will. I suspect she was also confirming that she could own me through so simple a gesture; dark triumph slowly lit up her eyes.

Imagining the warm moistness of her, my heart seemed to tumble. When she took her hand away, I pressed myself into her hip insistently.

"No more, Ti," she said gently.

She slipped out of my embrace and sat down. When she reached up for my hand, I gave it to her. She brought it to her lips. Then, smiling enigmatically, she stared off into her thoughts as though she'd forgotten me. I was unsure of what to do.

"Maybe we can get Sofia and Arjuna to play Ganesha like they did at the festival," she said, turning back to me with a hopeful look.

I kissed her lips, but gently this time.

You've proved what you had to, I was thinking, *so don't risk pushing her away . . .*

"I don't think anyone will be able to play Ganesha at our wedding," I said.

"Why?" she asked, clasping my hand between both of hers, which was a gesture she made when she was unsure of how to proceed.

"We both know that Papa adores you, but you're a Hindu."

"I cannot believe it will bother him so much."

"By Mosaic law, the children of a Hindu woman cannot be Jewish, even if the father is. Papa will want you to convert. Just as my mother did."

We spoke for a time about what that would involve, and Tejal said she didn't think she could swear that there was only one God, which is the very first *mitzvah*—commandment—of Judaism. "Hanuman has always protected me, Ti. I do not think it would be right to deny Him in favor of another God." Seeing my distraught face, she caressed my cheek. "Don't worry, I will have a long talk with your father about us," she said in a voice that seemed surer than I'd ever heard from her. "I know I can convince him to help us."

What gave her such confidence? Maybe she'd been waiting for me to ask her to marry me since that first evening in Benali.

Biting her lip, as though rising to a challenge inside herself, she reached under my dhoti and played with me again. "If your father lives with Lord Shiva guarding his doorway," she whispered conspiratorially, leaning into my ear as though we were talking about forbidden lovemaking and not a powerful god, "then he is more willing to make compromises with a Hindu girl than you think."

She gripped my stiffness and jiggled it in her hand as though testing its weight.

She is getting used to the feel of me, I thought, knowing that this was what I'd wanted for many years.

*   *   *

The next morning, Tejal told Papa that she wished to speak to him before I started my lessons with him. He agreed, and I accompanied the two of them to the library, where she put her hand on my chest and shook her head. "No, Ti, let us talk alone for a time."

When the door was closed behind them, I thought, *She'll have to be very agile to avoid his traps.*

I kneeled down with my ear to the keyhole, but after only a few moments the door swung open. My father stood there grinning in triumph, his hands on his hips, leaning back like a pasha.

"Did you lose something on the floor, young man?" he asked.

I heard Tejal's laughter behind him.

"Very well, I'll go," I said in defeat. "But please just listen to what she has to say. And remember that you're not obliged to think up every possible objection."

As I turned to leave, I saw Nupi peeking in on us from a window in the sitting room. She saw the request in my eyes and gave me a signal with her hand.

"Negotiations with Tejal will begin when I see that you have gone out to the garden," Papa bellowed. "And don't bother to ask Nupi to come around here snooping for you," he added, loud enough for her to hear. He lifted his nose in the air like a happy puppy. "I can smell her fennel seeds a mile away."

*   *   *

A half-hour later, Tejal came out to the garden, gazing down despondently, her steps unsure. I reached out to steady myself but found only air.

"Oh, Ti, nothing is wrong. I was only acting. I'm such a silly girl sometimes!" She embraced me so hard—her head pressed against my bare chest—that it seemed as though she wanted to enter inside me. "I'm sorry, so sorry! You must forgive me."

"I don't understand," I said, breathing in the reassuring scent of her.

"Your father and I thought we would make it even better for you by making believe things went wrong. But when I saw you go all pale, I just couldn't do it."

"Then they haven't?" I asked, sensing for the first time that Papa's comic instincts and Tejal's acting talents were about to become a dangerous combination for me.

"No, your father and I have agreed on everything. He will give me lessons in Judaism and we will read the Torah together. If, after that, I still choose not to convert, I will not have to."

"He's agreed to abide by whatever decision you make?" I asked in disbelief.

When Tejal nodded, relief spread through me like a warming ocean; Wadi and Sofia would no longer have any power over me. Through Tejal and my father, God had granted my prayers. Everything would go well now.

"Your father also told me something about *Lazarillo de Tormes*," Tejal said, holding herself apart from me and grinning girlishly. "He says the hero of the book is Hanuman!"

"Tejal, I have no idea what you are talking about."

"A mischief-making god isn't only a Hindu tradition," she said emphatically. "That's the secret of the book, he told me. Lazarillo is a trickster. I will be permitted to believe that Hanuman is a part of the Lord if I decide to convert. In fact, I must believe it!"

She tugged me to the verandah so that she could explain herself while we sat together.

"Your father told me that all the birds and trees and snakes we see, and everything we feel and even dream . . . it's all a reflection of God. Devi and Lakshmi and even Vishnu are aspects of the Lord of the Torah. His different forms are called the *sephirot* in Judaism, he said. The Creator who appeared to Moses has wings and an elephant head and a papaya in his tail and everything else we can imagine. So I can continue to believe that Hanuman watches over me. In fact, your father said that it's a secret, but that Hanuman helps to protect each of us from the moment we are born and even before that. Because we all have a trickster inside us. And it's a good thing that we do!"

I knew then what Papa had meant about God being in the most obvious place in the book.

"He never told me anything like that," I said, a bit resentful.

"Maybe he will when you are old enough to understand it," she said, laughing.

Something so astonishing occurred to me then that I remember feeling as though Tejal and I were being watched by the trees and bushes, by the blue sky and distant horizon: I suddenly knew Papa must have been aware of Wadi and Sofia's threats against me. He was more observant than I'd ever guessed and was telling me I had to meet their treachery with equal cleverness. That was why he had given us *Lazarillo*.

The window to his library squealed open at that moment and he looked up to the heavens, his head bowed as though he'd been crushed by fate. This was for our benefit, of course, and was to become another of his comic routines in the months ahead. "May the Lord forgive me," he said, his voice quivering with mock fear, "but I can refuse that girl nothing she wants."

*   *   *

I was sure that all would be happy and calm from then on, but Papa's agreement with Tejal made Sofia even more resentful. One morning after Tejal had gone back to Goa, while I was having my hair cut in Ramnath, my sister swept into Papa's bedroom as he was dressing and stated that she could take no more.

Seeing the weight of trouble in his daughter's eyes, he came around his bed to her and reached up to cup her chin, but she refused to let him touch her.

"No more of what?" he asked.

Standing back as if her life depended on distance, stiff as a soldier, she announced, "I'm in love with Wadi and I intend to marry him." Then she turned her back on Papa and rushed out of the room.

This was later recounted to me by Nupi.

Papa caught up with her as she was sobbing into her pillows. Months of bitter frustration were spilling out of her. She moaned that she felt like a leper in her own home.

"Sofia, it breaks my heart to see you like this," Papa told her.

"Then . . . then I can marry him?" she asked hopefully, sitting up and wiping her reddened face with our mother's head scarf.

"I'm glad you are in love, but I won't lie to you—I do not believe Wadi is right for you."

"Just because he's a Christian?"

"If it were only that..."

"Then what? Papa, please, it can't be anything else. It just can't be!"

Papa explained that Wadi was too much like Aunt Maria for his liking and that he'd known all along that my cousin had betrayed me many times when we were boys. He told Sofia he would have intervened all those years ago, but he believed that some things were best left to children to work out for themselves. "I think Wadi is intelligent and passionate, and capable of wonderful kindness, but he is not trustworthy," he concluded. "He lives life behind a curtain. I fear he will hurt you in the end. I admit, too, I've always wanted you to marry a Jewish boy, and Aunt Maria will never let him convert."

He prepared himself for another flood of tears, but instead her body tensed up and her eyes opened wide, as they did whenever she was ready for a fight.

"Papa, does Wadi have to remain friends with Ti for me to marry him? Is that it?"

He sat on the end of her bed and rubbed her feet, hoping to avoid a quarrel that would only end in harsh words from both of them. "Of course not. That's not what I was saying. This isn't about Ti."

"It's his fault, too, you know. Ti is always wanting things from people—things they can't give him. Or shouldn't give him."

Papa jerked his head back in surprise. "What is that supposed to mean?"

Sofia spoke her charges against me in the little-girl voice that usually won concessions from our father and me. "He always wanted Wadi to be different than he is—and me, too. I think he was even in love with Wadi. He hates Wadi now for choosing me instead of him!"

Our father stood up and looked away as though listening to two voices at once—mine and my sister's, perhaps. At length, he said,

"Sofia, don't you think I know my own son's heart? I know how he felt about Wadi, and I am far more aware than you will ever be of what boys sometimes do with each other before they grow up into men. But Ti is not *in love* with his cousin now. If you think that, you're wrong." He walked to the door. "I must tell you," he added coldly, "I would never have expected you to feel such contempt for your brother's feelings."

When Nupi told me these things, she pulled me down to her height and whispered one of her sayings in my ear: "The sky embraces the moon no matter what shape it takes."

So that I could have no doubts about her exact meaning, she kissed me on the cheek and said, "No matter what shape *you* are or have ever been."

"But what about me, Papa?" Sofia demanded of our father, and the hurt in her voice pleaded for him to reconsider.

"Time will show us what Wadi really feels for you," he replied. "Let's talk about this again in another year. If you are still in love with him then, and he with you, then I'll be happy to reconsider."

"You don't love me—you never have!" she shouted. "Not like you love Ti."

At that, Papa choked back the terror he had always had—that he had been inadequate to help his only daughter at her most difficult times and that the wrong parent had died.

Chapter 13

Returning from my audience with the Inquisitor, I was relieved to find Phanishwar gone from our cell; I cursed him as a traitor who'd been obeying the secret commandments of my jailors. The old man had no doubt been selected for his storytelling talents and his simple warmth, both of which made good weapons in what I regarded now as an all-encompassing plot against me; everyone I'd ever met was in this conspiracy, and their contempt for me had become the stone and iron of my prison.

Now, decades later, I can see how useful it was for me to believe this fantasy, since my anger kept despair at bay. After a couple of months, however, the slow grind of time began to erode my absurd faith in hidden enemies lurking in every corner of my past, and the windless heat produced an aching loneliness in each of my breaths. Whether the Jain had betrayed me or not, I hoped he was safely back in his village. This wasn't generosity on my part; it was knowing that I—in his place—would have done the same.

Many times over the coming months, as I lay in the dark, I'd hear him again telling me about his youngest son, Rama. Through an alchemy of the mind I'm unable to explain, the hope and courage in his voice came to mean that our destinies could never be separated—no matter what happened to me from now on. One morning, I summoned the courage to ask the Illiterate what had become of my old cellmate.

"Oh, he was buried months ago!" the guard replied insolently, as though I should've known. He made a slicing motion with his hand across his throat and grinned, but who could trust the word of a drunkard who relished keeping men in cages?

*   *   *

The song of Rama that I sang for the villagers of Benali . . . naked, sun-darkened coconut tappers calling down their greetings to Sofia and me . . . Mama's lips sculpting my name for the last time . . . Papa handing me the *dreidl* he'd carved for me . . .

I searched through thousands of memories for an understanding of how I could be here when everything I knew was outside, but even the simplest ideas became too much for me to fathom. Inside and outside, falsity and truth, compassion and cruelty—all were dyes that had run together in the recesses of my mind and would never now be completely separated again.

I thought constantly of the Inquisitor's riddle, but I knew I'd never find the answer; by now, I believed that the things I most wanted would forever be denied me.

Sometimes I imagined my mother under my cot, the size of a doll, lying there with her eyes closed. She seemed to be waiting. But for what?

I've spoken to many other long-term prisoners in years since and have learned that we lose our reasoning for a time. We come to believe that we can hear the thoughts of distant lovers or speak with animals. Maybe madness is the mind's last protection against suicide.

Or maybe madness has no purpose at all. And nothing does. Life is made only of stone and iron and rope.

*   *   *

And yet revelations come to us . . .

One particularly warm evening, as I lay in my cell sliding away into dream, I discovered why the Inquisitor had mentioned to me the six hundred and thirteen duties each Jew must perform—the *mitzvot*. The next morning I told the Illiterate I was ready to admit everything.

"I will name the witnesses against me," I said, swallowing hard on my betrayal, but knowing it was the only way I'd ever be free.

It was nearing the end of October of 1593 by my reckoning. I'd been in prison for twenty-three months.

I'd been told once by the warden that a public Act of Faith—*auto-da-fé*—for all those prisoners either to be burned at the stake or freed from the Holy Office generally took place once a year, on the first Sunday of Advent, which I knew to be a month or so before Christmas. If the Illiterate did not pass on my message soon, I'd be spending a third year in my cell.

Three weeks and two days passed, and I prayed for help to both the Lord of the Torah and Parsva, whose imaginary statue I placed at the head of my bed, as my saintly protector against all that had come from Europe to my homeland. It was during this time that I began to think of myself as Indian and not Portuguese. I wondered why it had taken me so long to see this truth. *Blue eyes do not make you one of them,* I whispered to myself in Phanishwar's voice.

After breakfast on the twenty-fourth day, which I counted with grains of rice left like secret wishes under my mattress, the warden came to my cell and led me to the great hall, where I was once again summoned to sit with Father Tómas Pinto, the Grand Inquisitor.

"I'm told you have a confession to make," he said, leaning back in his chair and folding his arms over his chest in a skeptical manner. "Have you guessed my riddle yet?"

"No," I said. "But I know now why you spoke to me about the *mitzvot*."

"You do?" he said with an amused smile. "I suppose we can consider that a good start, under the circumstances."

I found that I wanted to please him—like a schoolboy sitting before his lord and master. I'd have juggled stones for him or declaimed ancient poetry—or slit my wrists again and given my death to this man as a present. After all, what better gift could there be than blood for a priest who wants to own the souls of his victims?

Sitting across from a human being who possessed the power to murder me, I learned that it is a great relief to surrender—to allow oneself to be debased if that is all that's left.

"One day," I began, speaking carefully the words I'd practiced, "when we were here in Goa, my aunt asked us to accompany her to the home of a friend of hers who had just given birth to twins...."

I went on to explain how my father had refused to kiss the young mother's statuette of the Virgin Mary, and how I'd also turned away from it.

"We failed to honor the mother of our Lord," I concluded. "It wasn't what we did, it was what we *didn't* do. We made errors of omission—the same kind of errors that Jews can make who fail to obey a *mitzvah*."

It seems pathetic to admit it now, but pride in my cleverness made me smile like a little child.

"And who witnessed this crime?" the Inquisitor asked.

"My aunt and the young woman's physician. And her two Indian servants." To protect them from persecution, I added, "Aunt Maria was furious afterward and quarreled bitterly with my father. She kissed the statuette, of course—on entering the room and on leaving. The Indian servants kissed it, too."

My sister had been there as well; I prayed that my interrogator didn't know that.

"And was that the only time you failed to show respect toward our Lord?"

"No, there were many other instances." As though digging up long-buried treasures, I told him we had passed in front of the cathedral on dozens of occasions without ever going inside to pray, and had refused to say a Christian grace over our meals when my aunt and uncle did so. "We even neglected to say 'if God wills it' when speaking of the future in casual conversations," I told him.

I testified against myself for over an hour. Self-betrayal took on its own exhilarating rhythm, like a frenetic dance over a grave. I hoped to become the most loathsome Jew he'd ever prosecuted and thereby win his favor. *Burrow down into the earth as far as you can,* I kept thinking.

When my throat became so dry that I could no longer speak clearly, the secretary poured me a glass of water.

"And what about your affront against the Bishop?" the Inquisitor demanded as I gulped some down.

"I . . . I don't remember ever even speaking of him. But if you say I said something offensive, then I must be mistaken. I apologize."

"On one of your visits to Goa, the Bishop arrived from Lisbon." He showed me his cat-and-mouse smile, delighting in this new move in our game.

I gazed down into memory but could find nothing. The priest allowed the silence to damn me, his face contemptuous. With a swipe, he reached for his silver bell.

"Please have mercy on me," I pleaded. I brought my hands together as I had seen Christians do, and I silently prayed to their Lord for the first time in my life: *Blessed be the Son of God, who can make the hand of an evil man wither. . . .*

The ringing of his bell made my heart collapse. Hearing the footsteps of the warden behind me, I jumped up in panic.

"Sit down!" the Inquisitor ordered.

I obeyed, hugging my arms around myself.

"You are a wretch!" he told me, licking his lips as though he wanted to spit at me.

"I can't remember the Bishop's arrival," I moaned. "Is ignorance my crime? Is that what you want?"

A light of recognition flashed in his eyes, as if he'd caught me in his claws. "Now you are beginning to understand the depth of your heresy," he said in a damning voice, and he held up his hand, palm forward, for the warden to keep his distance.

"You were aware of the arrival of someone else on the Bishop's ship," he said more calmly. He spoke as though taking me by the hand and leading me forward.

There was only one possibility I could think of. "Once, I heard a rumor that an Angolan king was aboard a ship in the harbor. It was said that he was a giant."

"And who heard you express your desire to see him?"

"My uncle and aunt. My father, too, and Francisco Xavier, my cousin. But they didn't want to go see him. They said an African king was not worth our while. I remember that clearly. I was the only one who wished to get a look at him."

"One other person was there."

As soon as he said that, I knew that someone in my family had testified against me in great detail—and against my father as well. How else could he know about my sister being there?

"Who was with you?" he demanded.

My heart was throbbing. I knew this could mean that even my debasement was pointless; if the Holy Office imprisoned Sofia I would never be able to live my life, even if given my freedom. It no longer mattered what she had done to hurt me. Our past was beyond salvation, but I could protect her present and future.

"I cannot recall anyone else," I lied. "Unless...maybe...maybe a servant of my aunt's was with us."

"It was someone in your family!" he persisted.

"No, no one."

"I have been lenient until now," he said threateningly. "But I remind you that fire and water are with me in this battle for your soul, just as they were in the battle for your father's."

"I could not bear being burnt."

"You will bear whatever Christ decrees!"

"My sister," I moaned. "My sister was there. It's true. But she was a young girl. She told me that Africans ought to stay in their homeland. She is innocent."

"She sounds like a clever girl. Did your father permit her to kiss the Virgin?"

"No, but she did it anyway," I lied. "My sister has always been very strong-willed."

"I see," he replied, smiling as though he'd won a competition against me. I sensed he knew I was lying, and yet he made no further accusation.

"And what of the dead?" he questioned.

"I don't understand."

"For you New Christians," he said with a smile, "dead thorns can be even sharper than live ones."

"Does that have to do with the answer to your riddle?" I asked.

"It might."

He took a manuscript that had been hidden on his lap and placed it on the table between us. I recognized the cover immediately: a peacock fanning his emerald, blue, and purple tail across a title in golden Hebrew letters.

I reached out for it without thinking, as I'd have reached to save a loved one from the hands of the Angel of Death, but he drew it away from me. We looked long into each other's eyes, and I saw how pleased he was that he'd been able to prove to me in this way that a member of my family had purposely betrayed my father and me.

"Yes," he said, nodding. "Your great-grandfather's manuscript is ours now. No Jew will ever see it again. Or even know of its existence."

I was drenched in sweat and it was hard to breathe. Aunt Maria, Uncle Isaac, or Wadi must have stolen the manuscript; they were the only people who knew of its hiding place at the bottom of Papa's wardrobe.

"Now, Tiago Zarco, think of our riddle," the priest said seductively, as though inviting me to take a step with him toward redemption. "I speak on my journey to you—*and only to you*—from my departure point to the very end. And though I always die in the same place, you can hear me speaking from my closed grave if you pay close attention. Who am I?"

He held my great-grandfather's manuscript up to his ear as though listening to what was inside.

"*A book,*" I whispered, and I realized I should have guessed.

He grinned. "Good boy."

"A book speaks to each reader and always ends in the same place," I said. "When we close the cover for the last time, the journey is over and it goes to its grave, but we can still hear it speaking to us."

"We could have saved much suffering if you were cleverer, you know."

"I'm sorry," I apologized. I knew it was absurd, but I couldn't stop myself from behaving as though he were the one who'd been hurt.

"How could you be ignorant of your identity when your great-grandfather was telling you your whole life that you were a New Christian? Every year your father would read to you about his conversion. It's astonishing you could be so foolish."

"I see that now. It is unforgivable."

"Every sin is forgivable if it is honestly confessed to our Lord. And if we pray with a devout heart to be worthy of Him."

His voice had turned gentle; he was pleased with this outcome. My ignorance and desolation offered him an opportunity to show mercy. Maybe no one wants to regard what they do as evil, I have thought in years since; even the demons of hell likely think they are doing good and necessary work.

"And are you ready to make a full confession of your crimes?" Pinto continued.

"I am."

Over the next hour, the secretary took down my deposition. The Inquisitor then summoned the warden, who ordered the Illiterate to lock irons around my ankles and wrists.

After I was tugged outside, a tiny Castilian priest joined us. Having been kept out of daylight for so long, the sun against my face felt like burning metal, and I had to nearly shut my eyes to keep them from pouring with tears. The Illiterate held my chain as though it were a leash and summoned me forward by jerking it. The wounds made by the irons soon began to sting, but the pain was a help to me; it kept me from dwelling on more troubling thoughts. People stared and pointed. One merchant, laughing, called out that he'd pay for me to take a bath and threw a copper coin at me.

A bare-chested Portuguese laborer, trying to be clever, lifted up his hands in mock devotion and said, *"Jai Shri Dalit,"* meaning "Praise Lord Untouchable." Several coarse-looking men jeered at me.

"Where are we going?" I asked as we trudged over the cobbles through the stifling heat, but neither the priest nor the Illiterate would answer me.

We reached the Dominican church. A gaunt-faced Indian flower seller whom I recognized from my long vigil in front of the Holy Office was sitting by the door, pink frangipani woven into her gray hair. She wore a wooden cross around her neck and as I approached, she kissed it, then reached out a hibiscus blossom to me. But when I tried to take the white flower the Illiterate pulled on my chain, so that I tumbled over.

By the time I looked up, my guard had already slapped her across the face, knocking her to the ground.

I've thought a great deal about the spontaneous goodness of that woman many times since that day. More than anything else, the Illiterate's brutality to her was why I attempted, years later, to ruin his life—and why I hope with all my soul today that I succeeded.

Inside a small side chapel, holy water was sprinkled over my forehead as the priest intoned in Latin: "In the name of the Father, the Son, and the Holy Ghost..."

Then we were walking back toward the prison. Its façade seemed to rise over me like a phantom from its grave, and I pulled back on my irons, in such a state of dread that I wet myself. I appealed for help to the onlookers gawking around me, provoking the Illiterate to circle my neck with his meaty arm and choke me. Gagging, I fell to my knees. He tugged me forward relentlessly, so I was forced to crawl on all fours over the filthy stones of the square.

"He may be baptized, but he still insists on walking like a Jew," he told the priest, and they had themselves a good laugh.

*   *   *

Two days later, a document listing my crimes was read out to me in the Grand Hall by a priest I'd never seen before. I signed it with a hesitant hand; the Inquisitor refused to tell me if this meant death or life for me. All he'd say was that it was the only way toward Christ.

He then made me swear that I'd never reveal anything of what befell me while under the jurisdiction of the Holy Office. Afterward, I fell to my knees and again begged him to tell me what would happen to me.

"You will wait," the priest replied indifferently.

The following Saturday, the Indian servant who took my sheet once a week to be washed failed to appear. Immediately following the chiming of vespers at the cathedral, the bells sounded a second time. I wondered if some special ceremony was under way.

I'd been asleep for a couple of hours when the bolts in my doors ground open, startling me awake. The warden stepped briskly inside and handed me dark garments and an earthenware oil lamp. He instructed me to dress quickly and said he'd be back for me soon.

"If I'm to die, please tell me," I implored him. "I need to prepare."

"I'm not permitted to tell you anything of what awaits you."

I put on my long-sleeved jacket and trousers—both black with white stripes—as if dressing for the last time, shivering like a lost child. All of my body's sensations seemed prickly and alive. It was as though the world itself, at this last possible moment, were trying to tell me something I needed to learn—to reveal its deepest mystery— through the breeze across my face, the scent of moist grasses in the air, the soft touch of my fingertips on my cracked lips. . . . I told my-self that I'd be returning to God, but the truth was that I was living in a world without higher meaning. I knew I'd be dying alone after too brief a life. I felt cheated. I'd never learn who had betrayed my father and me—I'd never be able to take revenge. *Such a worthless and senseless journey I've been on,* I thought in utter misery.

The condemned may evidently make silly, puerile gestures in or-der to keep from losing their resolve at the last minute, and after I thanked Phanishwar for my few days of happiness in prison, I lifted up his imaginary statue of Parsva and made believe I was embracing a child—the child Tejal and I had made together. Then I began my final prayers to a Lord I no longer believed in.

*　　*　　*

When the warden returned, he escorted me into a gloomy, low-ceilinged chamber where dozens of prisoners were lined up with their backs to the wall, motionless, no doubt afraid even to breathe deeply, lest they sabotage their fragile chances for freedom. Most gazed glumly down at their bare feet; some sobbed with hands over their eyes and mouths. At least two had fainted and were lying on the ground, being given water by priests. I looked for Phanishwar but couldn't find him.

I took my place at the back, trying to keep my footsteps from making any sound, and every few minutes another unfortunate would shuffle in. I found myself with so many men, all of whom had suffered just like me. And yet there was no comfort in it; I felt dis-tant from them and exiled from myself.

A lit taper was given to each of the prisoners, and it seemed fit-ting that we began to cast distorted shadows of our gaunt faces along the walls, as though the stone should know and record what we had endured. Staring at my flame, my strength seemed to give out.

"God help me," I whispered, wiping away the tears as they came to my eyes.

Priests distributed a robe to each man. Like most prisoners, I was made to wear a yellow one with a large red X painted on both the front and back—later I was told this was a cross of Saint Andrew, and that these *sambenitos* were given to those who had committed heresy or other crimes against the Church. About twenty other men, mostly Indians, were instructed to put on gray robes on which their likenesses were depicted inside burning firebrands, with winged, barbtailed devils flying away from the flames. These were prisoners who'd been made to confess to sorcery. If Phanishwar were still a prisoner, he ought to have been among them, but he was not. I prayed to Parsva that he and his young son, Rama, were together again.

After conical hats painted with flames and devils were placed on the heads of seven of the Hindus condemned for practicing the worst black magic, we were all ordered to sit on the floor. Servants handed out warm rolls, dried figs, and rice, and we were given water to drink. I knew I couldn't eat even a crumb, but the tiny, darting priest who seemed to be in charge told me to put at least a crust of bread in my trouser pocket since the ceremony would go on for many hours and I was sure to be hungry when it was completed.

"I'll be allowed to eat when it is all over?" I whispered.

"Yes, but you'll be given nothing more until breakfast," he replied.

He must have thought my weeping was in thanks for his kind counsel, but in truth it was because he had told me, without meaning to, that I was not to be set aflame.

*   *   *

The bells of the cathedral began ringing again at daybreak and we were summoned one by one to the Great Hall, where the secretary of the Inquisition gave each of us an escort to accompany us through the Act of Faith. A captain of the Portuguese fleet in Goa, a man by the name of Jácome Morais, was selected for me. A rotund individual with pendulous jowls, smelling of olive oil and leather polish, he shook my hand and then tried to hide how he wiped his palm on his trouser leg.

Morais conducted me out into the warm air of the square, where a procession led by a dozen Dominican friars was marching behind a giant embroidered banner depicting their founder, St. Dominic, garlanded by the motto *Mercy and Justice.* A hundred prisoners walked ahead of me, a dozen of whom were women being led on separately from the men. Wire-tailed swallows were performing acrobatic arcs in the sky above us, twittering madly, and a stunning purplish light was rising far in the east. All around us were the crowds. I'll never forget a little boy in a feathered cap, sitting on his father's shoulders, pointing gleefully at me, and behind him his mother, holding an infant in her arms. Hoping to see someone I knew, I looked into each countenance, but then I realized—struck by how clouded my mind must have been—that coming here would be dangerous for anyone in my family.

Maybe my aunt and Wadi also stayed away because they were worried I'd accuse one or both of them of betrayal, but I wouldn't have made a scene; I hadn't the strength for it. I was made only of apprehension and the desire to get this over with.

For an hour or more we were paraded through the streets, and I'd never seen such tangled masses of people scrambling and shouting. The more eager amongst them pawed for a clearer view of our wretchedness. My feet began to bleed, and I fought to keep from limping so as not to draw further attention to myself.

When we arrived at the Church of St. Francis, we found the central door festooned with palm fronds. Entering with bowed heads, we sat down in the pews, next to our escorts. The moist air was sweet with incense from censers bellowing out their smoke. The dreadful solemnity of the occasion was like a yoke on my shoulders. I'm sure the other prisoners felt it, too, for we all sat there as though trying to shrink to nothingness. Thrones in gold and green brocade framed each side of the central altar, which was draped in black, with tall silver candlesticks on top. A youthful priest carried a life-sized crucifix through the main doorway. He was followed by three men, one of whom was a cripple being held up by two escorts, and a woman with protruding eyes and a shaved head. Behind them were five crudely painted, life-sized wooden figures held on poles—three men and two women. Indian porters carried an equal number of leather-bound chests on their heads.

I later learned that the statues represented those who had been charged with crimes against the Church after their deaths; the chests contained their bones, stolen from their tombs. I also didn't know it then, but the crucifix facing away from them meant that they were beyond hope.

And then my heart began to race. Though his thick white hair had been clipped short and his face was hideously bruised and swollen, I recognized the penultimate prisoner—the crippled man—as Phanishwar. Like his neighbors, he wore a gray *sambenito* bearing his crude portrait, with bright yellow flames licking upward toward animal-headed demons, and a conical hat with the same figurations. Below his crudely executed likeness was his name in great black letters, and underneath it the nature of his crime: **FEITIÇO,** sorcery, and what would be written on his tombstone, **MORREU QUEIMADO**—he died by burning.

His face was weary, and his cheeks were so swollen that he looked like an old man who'd drowned. Was he so far gone that he didn't realize what they were going to do to him?

I cannot say how, but I knew in my heart that he was the most important man in the room—the incarnation of a great and godly soul. It would be a crime against all of nature to fail to help him. I found myself standing up.

"Sit, you fool!" my escort whispered, tugging me roughly back down.

My goal was now to get Phanishwar's attention, but the old Jain would not look at me as he walked to his seat in one of the last pews.

After that, I could no longer see him; there were too many prisoners between us.

Only one thought remained: *Whom can I appeal to for help?*

As the Grand Inquisitor took his place on the throne to the right of the altar, I dared to speak to the Captain.

"Are the people at the back going to be burnt?" I whispered.

He nodded.

"And is there nothing that you can do to save them? One of them is a great man—maybe even the reincarnation of a Hindu god."

He gave me such a look of hate that I shivered.

The Portuguese Viceroy of India, dressed in blue silk robes, sat down now on the left throne, and the life-sized crucifix was laid atop the center of the altar. An elderly priest with a prancing gait then made his way up to the pulpit and presented a sermon in his high-pitched nasal voice for what seemed an eternity. I cannot say what he lectured us on; my desperation was beating in my ears and the only voice in my head was my own. I must have descended into madness again; I believed that if I concentrated hard enough I could send my thoughts to Phanishwar. Over and over I told him, *If you confess, it may not be too late....*

Two laymen dressed in blue silk robes soon came to the pulpit and began to read aloud the accusations against each man. When a prisoner's name was called, he was escorted by the warden to the middle aisle, and then to a second altar near the entrance doors. There, after kneeling, he was ordered to lay his hands atop a Missal and listen to his sentence.

A hollow-eyed boy with a shaved head, not a whisker on his pink cheeks, peed down his trouser leg as he shuffled to the altar. Some onlookers laughed mockingly. Soon, several other prisoners, including one old woman, had made worse messes of themselves.

When my name was called, I shuffled back through the nave, turning to face Phanishwar when I came close to him. The room seemed very dark. At one point, he was only three paces away. I could've reached out for him. I ought to have, though it might have cost me my life.

As I was walking past him, Phanishwar looked up at me. His eyes opened wide.

You must confess in order to be able to return to your Rama, I tried to tell him with my eyes, but his gaze became hard; he looked at me as though I were one of his jailors.

Then I was past him, nearing the altar. When the warden pressed down on my shoulder, I knelt with my hand on a Missal. Feeling my life turning around this moment, I learned first that I was excommunicated and that all my earthly possessions were forfeited in favor of the Crown, though I owned not so much as a single grain of saffron in Goa. So far so good, and I felt my breathing easing, as though I were nearly a free man, but then I was told that I was banished from Portuguese India and sentenced to four years in a Lisbon prison known as the Galé.

My son or daughter will be five by then and Tejal will have surely given me up for dead, I thought with despair.

Stumbling back to my seat, unable to trust my feet, I again mutely begged Phanishwar to confess. He turned away from me as though he despised me. I cursed him as a fool, but as I sat down next to the Captain again it occurred to me that the Jain was probably suffering from the same delusion that had plagued me for weeks: he was thinking that, from the beginning, I'd been part of a conspiracy against him.

Led by the Grand Inquisitor, some twenty priests assembled at the center of the nave; each carried a small wooden pointer. One of them was Father Carlos, the man who'd fooled Phanishwar into coming to Goa and whom I recognized from his visit to our cell. I gazed down to hide my face from him; if he spotted me, I believed he'd move me to the group of those beyond hope.

Dispersing into the pews, the priests tapped each of the prisoners on the shoulder with the tips of their pointers and pronounced an incantation in Latin that had the effect of withdrawing the order of excommunication and reinstating us as Roman Catholics. *These Christians obviously hate only sorcery that isn't their own,* I was thinking.

Unfortunately, their magic wands did nothing to dispel my four-year prison sentence.

"We are brothers now in the Mother Church," Captain Morais exclaimed, smiling like a proud father, as soon as I'd been tapped by a priest. Offering me congratulations for what he called my good fortune, he made a show of embracing me, taking from his pocket several small custard tarts wrapped in a white cotton cloth that his wife had baked for whomever he'd been chosen to escort. This time, he did not wipe his hands on his trousers; evidently, the stain of Jewishness had been magically removed from me as well.

The Grand Inquisitor, having returned to his throne, then received each of the men and women to be burned at the stake for the greater glory of Christ, as well as the five statues and their bone cases. Later I was told that this was no farce, as it first appeared to me, but instead a catastrophe for their families: this meant that all their worldly possessions would be immediately confiscated.

The proceedings were read against these unfortunates, even those who were dead, and in this way I learned that three of the effigies had been New Christians found guilty of heresy. I also discovered that one of the dark-skinned men was not a convert who'd lapsed into his old Hindu beliefs, as I'd presumed, but a Thomasite Christian accused of sorcery for believing in a different liturgy. St. Thomas himself had converted his ancestors to Christianity fifteen hundred years before, but that didn't stop these tyrants from pronouncing judgment on him.

Phanishwar stumbled forward, led by the warden and an escort, who propped him up. He would not have understood anything of what was being said to him in Portuguese, and he met the judgment of death—read to him in a cool, contemptuous voice—with an expression of trancelike impassivity. Maybe all his training with Dharanendra had prepared him for this one moment of confronting the Angel of Death. I prayed that he was safe with Parsva.

Phanishwar and the other condemned prisoners were tapped on the chest by the warden to signify that they were beyond hope, then conducted out through the doors by bailiffs of the Portuguese Crown. We other prisoners were marched behind them, in the direction of the river, still accompanied by our escorts, and made to stand in observance. On the bank, nine tall stakes had been driven into the ground, each surrounded by a great pile of logs. The night smells of India reminded me that the forest was nearby, and the half moon seemed about to fall into the dark waters.

An executioner in a hood cut with eyeholes used thick rope to bind each of the prisoners, even the effigies. When it was Phanishwar's turn, I dared to speak to the Captain again.

"Please stop this," I begged.

"It's too late," he told me.

"I've got to get closer," I told him.

He grabbed my arm. "Don't be a fool!"

I jerked free and pushed to the front of the crowd. The Jain was now tied with his hands behind his back, gazing up into the sky as though searching the constellations for something long forgotten. His trance had been broken and he was twisting with discomfort. He seemed confused, almost drugged.

Two of the men and the lone woman begged for—and were granted—the mercy of dying as Christians. A hooded executioner placed a rusted iron collar over their necks and tightened it with a winch. Their limbs shook horribly as they fought for air, and their eyes seemed as though they might pop from their sockets, but it was over in less than a minute for each of them. They hung limp in their bindings as though caught in a net.

A great cheer rose up from the crowd after each execution, but we prisoners made not a noise.

Phanishwar and the Thomasite Christian refused to become Roman Catholics. Their logs were set ablaze.

If You are present in our world, make this stop, I prayed to the Lord, but the flames caught right away on Phanishwar's trousers. All too soon, billows of smoke were engulfing him. He began to howl in agony, pulling at his bindings, his face clenched. He knew now he was about to die in agony.

"Parsva, help me!" he shouted.

The terrible smell of charring skin reached us now. Two prisoners in front of me fell to their knees, praying aloud for Christ's mercy. Others began to vomit.

"Help me!" Phanishwar shouted in Konkani.

The Thomasite Christian was also screaming.

"Phanishwar!" I called to him, then a second time, louder, and he spotted me. His eyes flashed with recognition.

"Help me!" he called again. He strained with his arms, trying to reach out to me.

I reached a hand over my head and made it into a fist, but there was no time to think of what to say. Stupidly, perhaps, I shouted, "I never betrayed you! And I see what they're doing to you." I could not bear him leaving this world believing I was a traitor.

Yet what good could my allegiance do him now? And how could my acting as a witness help anyone?

They must have treated his prison clothes with oil; Phanishwar flared up like a torch before I could shout anything more.

I made myself watch his face crackle and blacken, sensing that the utter destruction of this gentle man was the key to the world I'd been born into.

A human being melts more quickly than you'd think possible. And burns with greater fury. The stench is unbearable. It is what hell must smell like.

I said nothing more until he was just a lump of charred skin and bone.

"Parsva cannot be killed," I whispered then, speaking to my own hopelessness.

And I vowed: *If you are reborn as a murderer, then come to me and I will help you.*

*   *   *

I refused to leave when the prisoners were summoned away. I was insane with terror and grief, and I wanted to stay where I was as a protest, but I was dragged away by my escort, who slapped my face so hard that I feared my jaw had been broken again. He and two other men took me to my cell, where I cried until I fell into the merciful darkness of sleep. At dawn, when I awoke, it all seemed a dream until I picked up my clothes from the floor and smelled the smoke of Phanishwar's blackened flesh in them.

*   *   *

Two years were added to my sentence for my outburst at the Act of Faith. The Grand Inquisitor gave me this news himself after a furious lecture on my shocking behavior. Then his voice softened. "I've already forgotten there ever was a Jain sorcerer in our midst, and you should, too," he told me. "Think now only of Christ and the sacrifice He made for you."

He handed me a document describing my religious duties over the next six years: to make confession once a month, attend Mass every Sunday, repeat the Lord's Prayer and the Ave Maria five times a day, and form no friendships with heretics. Once again, he ordered me to never reveal anything of what I'd seen or heard while imprisoned by the Holy Office. Disobeying him has been my only triumph in this life, I believe.

As I trudged back to my prison cell for the last time, the Inquisitor's advice about keeping Christ's sacrifice in my thoughts turned my mind back to the night before, and I seemed now to understand everything. It was like a bolt of lightning piercing total blackness and turning my mind the white of bone: *These priests tied Phanishwar to a stake and set him ablaze because they don't really believe that Jesus had the strength of will to let Himself be killed for His beliefs. They needed to see their Savior's final moments enacted for them—to see that a man could bear such agony. They made us witness their spectacle because they cannot admit that anyone else might possess greater faith than they do. Christ has to be murdered anew each year to fill up their hollow souls.*

CHAPTER 14

Now that Sofia had revealed her love for Wadi, she behaved as if there was no turning back. Though she didn't dare confront Papa directly for his opposition to their marriage, she criticized him incessantly for his smallest failings. Once, she even accused him of being an embarrassment to her because a group of ragged village boys in Ramnath had coaxed him into taking off his sandals and trying to capture them in a game of *kabbadi* on a fallow chickpea field behind the marketplace. I saw the wound in our father's eyes as he wiped the red clay from his feet afterward, and I wanted to yell at her, but he gave me a dark look that told me I was to stay out of it.

Papa suffered her humiliations with good-natured patience, telling her on more than one occasion that he didn't think God would judge him too harshly for obliging a fifteen-year-old girl to wait a year before marrying. Sofia next decided to refrain from eating breakfast with us. On the fourth morning of her protest, hoping for a truce, he carried warm chapatti to her room.

"How can I be hungry when I'm a prisoner?" she told him.

He did not tell me what he replied, but he never again brought food to her room.

Two days later, he purchased a necklace of coral beads for her in Ponda, but she refused to put it on for him. Later that week he failed to convince her to accept a vial of jasmine perfume that had come all the way from Ceylon.

All his gifts proved useless, but I can't blame him for his errors in judgment, or for how he groped forward in seeming darkness; his beloved Sofia was as defiant as she was unhappy, and the fragile compass he'd always had in his heart could no longer find his daughter's center.

As for the frigid reception my sister gave to all his efforts, she'd decided—perhaps honorably—that if she couldn't get what she most desired, she wouldn't take anything from him. To me, she seemed very little changed from the girl who'd refused to play with other children or meet strangers. Now that I was older I realized how very forceful she was—more powerful in her own stubborn way than any of us. Despite all the friendships she'd formed in recent years, she'd never learned that a gesture of conciliation—one as small as a kiss—might accomplish more than a blockade.

One night at bedtime she started a brutal quarrel with Papa over his having given her wet nurse, Kiran, two of our mother's saris instead of saving them for her dowry. Their argument left Papa in tears, and he confessed to her in a voice of desert sand that he was exhausted. "I dreamt a few nights ago that you and I were drowning," he told my sister. "I could see the minarets of Constantinople in the distance, but we couldn't reach them. So if this is the only way to save ourselves..."

He told her in a grave and hesitant voice that he would allow the marriage to take place six months hence if Wadi demonstrated nothing but loyalty and affection for her over that time. "And if he'll agree to allow you to remain Jewish, at least in secret," he added solemnly. "I'm going against my own better judgment in not asking for you to wait at least a year."

I overheard him offer this concession from my room and wanted to reassure him by running in to him and hugging him, but her reply stopped me in my tracks.

"I won't wait," she declared.

She must have given him a look of defiant finality because Papa, without another word, left the house. I jumped out my window to avoid having to speak to Sofia and rushed after him as he sloshed across our storm-drenched garden, but he told me to go back home. Out of breath, desolate, he said, "Ti, I know you want to help, but in the state I'm in I feel unable to talk to anyone but the dead."

I'll never forget having to leave him there, his legs splattered with mud, abandoned to all that he believed he'd done wrong in his life.

Maybe it is inevitable for each of us to face our regrets alone, but I wanted so much to help him then that I ached with uselessness. How much real good can any of us do for our loved ones at their most difficult times?

My sister's easy dismissal of such a just compromise puzzled me for several days until, one night, while drifting to sleep, a new possibility jabbed me in the gut: she was pregnant! If that was true, then I understood why the marriage had to take place now.

I tiptoed into her room and called her name.

"Ti?" she whispered back. "Is that you?" Her voice sounded so friendly that I gave a little laugh of relief.

"Yes, did I wake you? I'm sorry."

"No, I was up."

I sat at the foot of her bed and explained my suspicions, adding that I wouldn't say anything to Papa until she gave me her permission.

"We'll find a way out of this trap together," I assured her in a brotherly voice.

She sat up. In the harsh light from my candle, she looked like a shadow puppet of some vengeful deity; her fingers were blades and her eyes seemed bent on my destruction. She'd become someone I didn't know at all.

"Wadi was right about you!" she snapped.

"What are you saying?" I asked.

"You want to think I'm evil. You've always wanted to be the good one. I was a stubborn little girl and now I'm a monster. How could you even ask me such a wicked thing?"

*   *   *

During the first few days of warfare between Papa and Sofia, Nupi had hidden in the kitchen with her hands over her ears whenever my sister raised her voice, singing prayers to Lakshmi and Devi in her toneless voice to drown out the madness. We'd eaten many meals together on her cracked little table, doing our best to converse about trifles.

"Sofia stretched her netting too far and is now surprised that it's ripped," Nupi now told me.

The old cook was of the opinion that girls had to obey their fathers until they were married, at which time dominion over them was transferred to their husbands. "But since everything now is in such a terrible tangle," she added, shaking her head morosely, "your father may have no choice but to accept the marriage without delay."

I asked her to tell him that.

"Me? No." She shooed me away as if I were being a nuisance.

"But he respects your opinion."

"Maybe I'll say something when the time is right, but that time has not yet come."

"And when will that be?"

"When I have no other choice."

So it was that Nupi kept her lips sealed tight and learned to go about her work without being noticed. She even began to neglect her sacred basil garden. She'd stand with her hands on her hips while looking over the withering plants, her jaw set hard, as though it was only right for them to suffer along with the rest of us.

*   *   *

I recognized, of course, that from Sofia's point of view her love was being trampled and that I was being favored unjustly, so after about ten days of suffering the deathly silence now pervading our house I went to her again. My sister was wiping cobwebs from the corners of her room, wielding her broom like a sword. From her doorway, I told her that I planned to ask Papa if Wadi could come for an extended visit. That way, he could prove how much he loved her. I'd go away for most of his stay so that she and our cousin could have all of Papa's attention.

"It's impossible," Sofia told me coolly.

"But why?"

She scraped her broom across the ceiling. "Wadi has forbidden it."

"Forbidden what?"

"You from helping."

"I don't understand."

She frowned at me as if I was being obtuse. "You heard me, Ti—Wadi doesn't want your help."

"Judging from your tone, you don't, either," I observed.

"No."

"Sofia, please stop all that horrible swatting for a minute. And take a good look at how you're behaving toward Papa before it's too late. Don't you see how unfair you're being?"

She jabbed into a tangled web at the corner of her windowsill and made no reply.

"Are you going to let Wadi determine everything you do?" I questioned, a sneer in my tone.

"Now that you aren't friends, Wadi said he has the right to keep you out of his life."

"I was your brother before I was anything to him."

She turned and lowered the broom, bristles down, balancing her chin on the handle. I couldn't help looking to see if her belly had grown over the past week. I didn't think so.

"I love him, Ti," she said softly. "I love him so much that I have no choice in what I do or say. Do you understand? I'm sorry, but that's the way it is."

"So what does that mean for me and you?"

Her eyes targeted me as if I'd said the worst thing possible. "It means that I'll do whatever he asks me," she declared.

I said nothing. Beneath all my mean-spirited thoughts I was wishing that things weren't the way they were, but more than that I was gripped by an odd feeling of arrival that I didn't understand at the time. Later, I realized that my sister was giving me the rules of our new relationship, and that I was grateful to know where I stood with her. *Ti, this is how it will be with me from now on. . . .*

*   *   *

When I told Papa that maybe Wadi ought to come for a long stay with us, and that I'd stay in Goa while he was here, he rolled his eyes.

"Ti, don't you think he should be the one to suggest a visit? He has been courting your sister for months."

"Maybe he's frightened of you."

"If his fear of me is stronger than his love for Sofia, then what does that say about their future together? Should I let her marry a coward?"

I hesitated a moment but decided not to hold anything back. "Yes, Papa, I think maybe you should let them marry. We've no way of knowing who he really is—he's too hidden for that. In any case, you can't prevent her from making mistakes anymore."

"If that's true, then neither can you," he announced, expecting to startle me, and maybe even hurt me—just as he'd been hurt. But I knew that in my bones by now and simply nodded.

*   *   *

Early the next morning I came to Papa as he was seated on the veran-dah steps, drinking his tea, and unburdened myself of a fear that had gnawed at me all night. "Sofia may simply run off with Wadi one of these days and we'll never see her again. If you want to have an influence over what she does, then you've got to agree to her marriage right away."

Papa said he'd thought of that possibility, too, but had been too afraid to even whisper it. "I couldn't go on if I never saw her again," he confessed.

Thinking of what Nupi had told me, I said, "Then you have no other choice."

That evening, he informed Sofia and me he had something special to tell us over supper. After we sat down, he slipped off the gold band his parents had given him when he left Constantinople for India and handed it to Sofia. "For you," he said. He closed her fist around it and kissed her brow. Once, a long time earlier, he had told me that I would have the ring on my twenty-first birthday, so I was shocked.

Sofia turned the gift over in her hand. Her eyes were moist with gratitude. "Papa, why are you—" she began, but he cut her off.

"Ssshhhh, it's yours now. I want you to have it." He turned to me and held out his hands to ask for forgiveness.

"Do you mind, Ti?" he asked. "I'd understand it if you did."

I searched my feelings, unwilling to lie to him. "It's a surprise, and I always wanted it, but..." Here I looked at my sister, who was examining the ring with eager eyes. "If it changes the way things are, then it's better for Sofia to have it."

"Thank you, son."

Papa had no dearer possession from his parents than that gold band. It had been handed down in our family from my great-grandfather Berekiah, who had been given it by his closest friend, Farid. Our father clearly wanted to show Sofia the depth of his caring for her. While she tested it on different fingers, he said he'd talk to Uncle Isaac and Aunt Maria on his next trip to Goa and that he'd ask them to agree to a wedding date in September, four months hence.

I'd forgotten about my aunt in all my worry, but I could guess easily enough that she wouldn't want her son to marry a Jewish girl and suffer the same stigma she had on being wed to Isaac. Maybe

Sofia, fearing that new source of resistance, made a reply she never intended. Or maybe she had to tell Papa what she wanted one last time; sometimes we must let a last drop of acid fall against a loved one's heart before we're ready to start over.

Whatever the reason, Sofia looked down for a moment, measuring her words against the solemnity of the moment. She hadn't yet put on the ring. She held it in her fist again.

"I don't think I should have to wait, Papa," she said.

She didn't speak harshly. Her words had the tone of an apology, and I remember thinking that she was finally ready for a compromise. Unfortunately, our father hadn't expected anything but her thanks. His face went pale and he stood up. As soon as he walked out, he locked himself inside his room and would not reply when Sofia and I begged him to let us in. We went around the house to his windows, but the shutters were already closed tight, and though I kept knocking, he wouldn't open them. I remember Sofia holding a big red hibiscus flower in her hands while we waited. Nupi had told her to give it to Papa. She was now wearing his ring as well.

My sister knew she'd made a fatal error that evening, and she sobbed in Nupi's arms.

Papa told her in the morning that he'd never permit her to go to Goa again.

*   *   *

Sofia remained in her room most of the next week, and her unhappiness haunted everything Papa, Nupi, and I said to each other. The air around us seemed damp with worry, and my mind was pursued by shadows climbing up every wall. Even the unstoppable Indian sun seemed to hesitate over our rooftop—to be unsure of itself for the first time.

My letters from this time to Tejal were so joyless that it seemed they might turn to powder in my hands. I hated Sofia for putting us through this and told her so with my frigid looks each time she came to watch me working at my illuminations. I didn't mind her disliking me now; she and Wadi were no longer in any position to hurt me, and I wanted nothing to do with them.

Papa had to put off Torah lessons with Tejal and asked me to apologize to her in my letters. I resented being kept apart from her and for a few weeks was beset by worry that our plans wouldn't work out as we wished, but after I expressed my concerns to Tejal she found the courage to ask her father what he would say if I were to ask for her hand in marriage, and he had replied favorably.

"My mother told me it will be a fine marriage for our family," she wrote me, and I could see the happiness in her swirling handwriting.

I told Papa the good news, and he made every effort to show me a genuine smile, but his heart was in pieces.

At this time it often seemed to me that if Sofia couldn't get his approval for her to wed, then she would do everything to keep us in a state of constant desperation, though maybe she was as confused as we were as to how we had fallen so quickly into this abyss. Could she really have known what she was doing?

*   *   *

One morning, while Papa and I were studying Torah, Sofia knocked softly on the library door and asked for permission to go to the market in Ponda with Nupi. My sister gazed down at the floor as though afraid to hope for his approval. These were the first words we'd heard from her in days.

"Be back by sundown," Papa told her without lifting his Torah pointer from the page. When the door had closed behind her, I asked him what he thought she wanted in town.

He broke off reading for only a moment to say he didn't care. Anyone who didn't know him might have thought he meant it, but his clenched jaw and stiff shoulders told me he would spend the rest of the day thinking of nothing else.

Sofia and Nupi came back in the late afternoon. I cornered our old cook in the courtyard right away, and she answered my question without my having to ask. "She cried some on the way to town, but she was all right once we were there. She sat at a food stall by herself. I didn't even see her talk to anyone."

"Did she tell you why she wanted to go to Ponda?"

Nupi sucked on her rickety teeth. "No, she just asked to be alone. I left her sitting there, poor thing. I think she needed to be somewhere to think without being interrupted all the time." She clamped her hands over her ears. "It's always so very loud here."

"Loud? My father and I have hardly spoken to her in weeks."

"Ti, there's very little that's louder than this family's silence."

*   *   *

Sofia now began to accompany Nupi on all her errands. One Sunday, she returned from Ponda with a high fever and chills. Nupi said she'd vomited twice on the way home, after eating okra that must have been spoiled, but Papa was certain it was all the silent warfare in our home that had made her ill. We pulled her bed next to the hearth and covered her with blankets. Nupi darted into the kitchen to make her guava-leaf tea.

Papa sat with my sister as she took tiny sips from a steaming earthenware bowl, his hand propped behind her head, his eyes rimmed with dark worry—they'd hardly talked for a month and here she was, as sick as our mother had been before death.

"No more tea," Sofia finally said with a moan. "Just let me sleep." She grimaced as she lay back down.

"Sofia, where does it hurt?" I asked, but she didn't answer.

Papa caressed her hair. "Forget your problems," he whispered, "and when you wake up, everything will be as it was before we started arguing."

She twisted on her side and held his hand. After a few minutes, when she began to breathe more easily, she tucked her hands up by her chin and her legs to her belly like a little girl making herself as small as possible. Papa fetched the gold ring he'd given her from her room and put it on her finger.

"It'll protect her with all our family's history," he told me.

After fetching his *tallith,* his holy shawl, he draped it over his shoulders and began praying for her. His eyes soon fluttered closed, but he continued to pray for her all the rest of the day, not even pausing for food.

Sofia faded further into illness despite Papa's appeals. By the next morning, her chest was rising and falling so weakly that we were sure she was fading from us. Whenever she awakened, she spoke as if already distant from the world. Her eyes had become a dull gray—as though she were looking at us through a mist—and her face became so pale that we thought blood must have been seeping from a deep cut, but she had no wound anywhere. She ached all over. Nupi applied hot poultices to her chest.

"I've used pepper and basil," she whispered dramatically to me when I sniffed at them, making it clear with her tone that this was a life-and-death battle—that she needed the power of the holiest of plants to save her beloved goddaughter.

Papa and I prayed all that second day by her bedside. Nupi kept us going with rice broth and darkly brewed tea, making offerings of flowers and fruit to Sitala Devi—the local goddess of last appeal—in her room. Word spread fast about our misfortune. Villagers from Ramnath came at all hours to pay condolence calls, barefoot and glum-faced, their fear of death making them unsure where to put their hands and feet. I assumed responsibility for escorting them in and out of the sickroom as quickly as possible, since my father didn't want his attention from his daughter averted for even an instant.

"A blink of the eyes is enough time for the Angel of Death to toss a bitter drop into a child's mouth and poison her," he told me.

Nupi's women friends came from Ramnath and Ponda, bringing sweet limes, cheese, mangoes, and whatever else they thought we might need, conversing with her in the courtyard, speaking in hushed tones about all the inevitable sadnesses of motherhood. I remember their hands clasped together at their chests while they sat in a circle listening to each other, as if they were all part of an unnamed society whose job it was to stand vigil at the deathbed of their children. Their eyes haunt me even today—confronting me like secret thoughts that can never be spoken, staring at me through a small window of the heart that I know I'll never be able to completely close, no matter how many years and miles may separate my sister and me.

On departing, the old women would press a hand to my chest as though to make sure I was solid and tell me how sorry they were, which I only resented, since it seemed they had already given up on Sofia.

Your poor mother, and now this, I could hear them thinking.

A knot of ragged, marble-eyed beggars with yellowing skin, stinking like rotting meat, appeared one morning, calling from the garden. They'd heard they could get food in exchange for their prayers for my sister's health, but Nupi was in no mood for them. She hurled two small sacks of rice out the door and shooed them away while shaking a large chopping knife at them, muttering as they fled, "Sometimes I think it will be the greatest joy in my life when I *never* have to speak to another living soul."

That evening at dusk we heard cackling from the garden. Thinking the beggars had come back, I rushed to the door, anger rising in my chest, but I found Jaidev—the holy man from the village marketplace—standing at the foot of the verandah stairs, powdered with dry soil, a garland of frangipani and marigold flowers around his neck, and a great Indian hornbill shrieking on his shoulder as if trying to wake all of India. The magnificent bird was three feet tall, black, with pure white wingtips. It glared at me, accusatory, as if I were the reincarnation of an old enemy.

I stepped outside but kept my distance.

The *sadhu* laughed. "Have no fear, Ti, Sujay prefers more tender fruit than you."

"Just the same, I think I'll shake his hand some other time."

Jaidev's eyes narrowed with worry. His white hair, shiny with coconut oil, fell in a tangle all the way to his waist.

"I have heard that our Sofia is in trouble," he said.

"Yes, she's been gravely ill."

He kneeled so that Sujay could hop down on the verandah. The bird's right wing drooped down painfully as he stepped around.

"Is it broken?" I asked.

Jaidev nodded. "I'm feeding him, and hoping he'll recover." The holy man came to me, and when he gently caressed my cheek, my worries over Sofia's health washed over me. In his arms, I cried over many things, but most of all, over how I'd failed to protect my sister.

Jaidev and I sat together, his bony arm around my waist. He smelled like warm dry clay, as though he were becoming, in his old age, part of the earth itself. I told him how everything had gone wrong. As I spoke, he tossed the hornbill loquats he took from a cloth pouch around his waist. A light flickered inside me as I watched the generous complicity between the two of them. It was as if their simple and unlikely relationship meant something about hope—and not just for me, but for all the world.

When I'd finished telling Jaidev about Sofia's troubles, he pointed at Sujay. "His wing was broken by some hunters, I think. I hated to see him dragging it along while begging for food. So now we're together."

We left Sujay in our courtyard, where the bird could make little trouble, and went to Papa, who'd fallen asleep in his room. He was so moved by Jaidev's appearance that he kissed his hands, which I'd never seen him do before with any man. The *sadhu* sat next to my sister, his dark fingers fanning out over her head, and entered a trance. He was gone to the world for nearly an hour, as motionless as a statue. Papa and I prayed. When Jaidev shook himself awake, he said that Vishnu had called to him from out of the waters of the Ganges.

"He said that it is not yet time for Sofia," Jaidev told us. His smile was one of shining relief, but he, too, wiped away tears.

"What's wrong?" Papa asked him.

"I see much suffering on my journeys."

We sent the holy man on his way with ripe papayas from one of our trees.

"Imagine bringing that filthy bird here," Nupi told me with her nose in the air when he had gone, pausing as she swept up Sujay's droppings. "Sometimes I think that *sadhu* has the brain of a grasshopper."

Renewed by Jaidev's certainty, Papa and I went back to praying over my sister. With each word I knew I was fighting not just for her but for everything in my life—even my love for Tejal. Yet Sofia was no better that afternoon or evening, and that night I sat on the verandah, listening to the sounds of the forest as though all of India itself were awaiting the news of her death.

*   *   *

The next morning, I awoke to find Sofia missing from her bed, along with a blanket of red wool that had been my mother's. Her pillow still had a hollow crease where her head had been, but it was cold to the touch. Papa was asleep in his bed, the ends of his prayer shawl gripped in both his hands, as if he were pulling bell-ropes in a dream and sounding a warning.

I ran out of the house and found my sister sitting beneath a palm at the fringe of our garden, her blanket draped over her shoulders. She gave a little wave, then reached up to grab the half-moon— chalky-white in the hazy light of morning—and pretended to fold it into her mouth.

*   *   *

Papa watched Sofia that morning as though she'd just been born, unwilling to take his grateful eyes from her as she ate solid food for the first time in days. She laughed freely when he stole pieces of her chapatti. Even Nupi sat with us when I grabbed the old woman and led her to the table.

I was young enough to let myself believe that the world had spun around to the exact position it had been in before our problems, but Papa soon called me away and confessed that he'd received a letter from his brother during Sofia's illness that was filling him with dread. Uncle Isaac had written that he'd seen Wadi strolling with Sarah along the river—and that it probably wasn't the first time. My cousin vigorously denied to his father that he'd taken up with Sarah again, but Isaac was of the opinion that we had best proceed cautiously. We might even, he suggested, start preparing my sister for the worst.

"Wadi wants us to know that he can behave any way he likes," I told Papa. "He knows Sofia is devoted to him. He's enjoying his power over us—and her."

Papa took what seemed the only sensible next step: he wrote to his brother saying that we would come to Goa as soon as we were certain that Sofia was well, so that we could talk things out calmly. We'd either reach an agreement on a date for their marriage or—if Wadi had indeed fallen out of love—insist on a definitive break between the two of them.

My father and I dared not mention anything to my sister about Wadi's duplicity. Nor did we tell Nupi, who was such a poor actress that she'd have undoubtedly revealed something.

In my next letter to Tejal I wrote her of our plans and added that Papa had promised he would begin Torah lessons with her once we were in Goa. I sent along a flattened and dried cat's whisker as well.

I didn't think Sofia had guessed that anything might still be wrong, but a few days later she tiptoed to me before bed and said, "Tell me honestly, Ti: Papa still doesn't want me to marry Wadi, does he?"

"He'd prefer that you wait a while, that's all."

"You're sure?"

"Of course."

I could see she didn't believe me. "Sofia," I said reassuringly, "you're going to marry Wadi one way or another, sooner or later. So stop worrying." I tugged on her hand and honked like an elephant to cheer her up, but she didn't smile. "You'll have what you want," I said forcefully. "And if we all can stay calm for another few weeks, then Papa will have what he wants, too."

I wasn't sure I believed my words, but they sounded right to us both, and sometimes that is all one needs to keep going.

*   *   *

Sofia and I had been badly scared by her illness, and her recovery left us both a bit wild and giddy. There were whole afternoons when we could hardly stop laughing, no matter how Nupi scowled at us or chased us screaming out of her kitchen. Looking back, I know we were given a second chance at a golden age, and I'm grateful. We'd reverted to little children, but we didn't think there was any harm in it.

One evening, Papa stained his hands pink preparing wild duck in pomegranate sauce for us—the only dish he knew how to cook. Sofia wore the coral necklace he'd given her and told him how wonderful the food was, though in truth we chipped at that poor bird as though it had died of thirst in the Arabian desert.

Nupi decided the next day that we had to air out our house and clean everything to remove the last vestiges of the evil presence that had made Sofia ill. Papa scoffed at that, and though the stubborn old mongoose agreed not to touch anything, she started dragging out chairs and rugs the next morning, making such an unholy racket that we all woke up and began to help while mumbling our complaints.

Once we had everything out of the house—with Mama's statue of Shiva standing guard on top of our verandah steps—Sofia asked Papa if we might paint her room. He danced her around the garden on hearing that, since—as he later told me—he interpreted it to mean that she wouldn't be leaving us anytime soon to live with Wadi in Goa.

I was not so sure.

While Nupi flicked her feather duster back and forth over every-thing, and while Sofia and I beat clouds of dust from our rugs, Papa left for Ponda with our donkey cart. Two hours later he came back with two giant bags of lime for whitewash and sacks of pigments for our colors. We painted Sofia's room saffron yellow, as though bathed in sunlight; mine we made olive green with a rose ceiling, the colors of a parrot I'd loved as a young boy. When we got to Nupi's room, she asked that Sofia and I paint portraits of Sujay and Jaidev against a background of deep blue.

"We must give them their due," the cook told me.

"But you thought Jaidev was mad for bringing along that filthy bird, as you called it."

"The bird and he are both a mess, but whatever they did worked. What preserves life is good and is worth our thanks. The rest is just leaves already fallen to the ground."

*   *   *

Tejal surprised us all by arriving later that week in a cart driven by Igbal Aziz, a curd maker from Ponda who had given her a ride all the way from Goa. She was wearing her school dress but carried a flour sack with a change of clothes.

"I couldn't stay away any longer," she told me with an embar-rassed smile as I raced out of the house to greet her. "I told my teach-ers I had to go back to Benali for a wedding."

"You're wicked," I replied with admiration.

Tejal blushed, but I could see in her confident eyes that she was well aware of the power she'd gained over her own destiny now that we were to be wed. She told me we'd have three days together before she had to return.

I'd never discussed with Sofia my worry that she wouldn't want to be friends with Tejal, but my sister must have sensed it; running out to us, giggling with complicity at Tejal's audacity, Sofia took her hand and rushed her away to her room to help her wash off the dust and grime, and change into a sari. Papa brought tea to her there, and Nupi began brushing her hair, which had gotten mussed on the long ride.

Once we were all together on the verandah, Sofia hushed all of Papa's friendly plans for Tejal. In the little-girl voice that melted his resistance, she said, "Please, Papa, let Ti and Tejal go for a walk together first. They haven't seen each other in weeks."

He realized instantly the mistake he'd made and pushed us off.

Strolling to Ramnath, we passed red poppies growing wild along our pathway and dozens of yellow-footed egrets walking in their hesitant way through the rice fields. A woman cradling a baby goat in her arms smiled warmly at us. Her curious little boy, with eyes like black marbles, clung to the fringe of her sari. He asked us where we were going and if we had any children. We knew we'd remember them forever because they'd seen our love.

Tejal had her first Torah lesson with my father that afternoon, and that evening she and Nupi prepared a banquet of fresh prawns and pomfret in a coconut and tamarind sauce, the way they always made it in their village. I remained in the kitchen with them, hardly saying a word, glad to be able to sit quietly in their presence. Such a burden it was to always need to say things to other people!

I loved their quick sure movements, the tingling smell of the spices, and the hissing of the coals. But most of all, I admired the seriousness of their eyes. It was as though they believed that making a meal was the most important thing in the world.

Tejal let me taste the successive stages of her sauce from her wooden spoon, though when Nupi's opinion differed from mine, they simply disregarded what I had to say, which made me laugh. I was keenly aware that I came from the world of men and that they were women, and I valued the difference more and more.

*   *   *

That night, Sofia pleaded successfully with Papa for Tejal to be able to sleep in her room rather than with Nupi. Sometime after midnight I awoke to see my sister holding a candle, leaning over my bed with a finger to her lips. "Sssshhhh. Go into my room as quietly as a mouse."

I understood immediately why she'd fought to have Tejal with her. "You would do this for me?" I asked.

She smacked my head playfully. "Not for you—for Tejal!"

Or for herself? I hadn't entirely forgotten Sofia's betrayals, and I did wonder—for a panicked instant—if helping me now might somehow fit into her plans, but if it did, I didn't care; I'd discovered my own potential for deception.

Tejal was fast asleep when I crawled under the blanket and nestled behind her. Caressing my hand lightly over her behind and hip, which was very cool to my touch, I snuck my hand around to the warm firmness of her breasts. I kissed her neck, which I already knew smelled more like her than any other place on her body, and though I was very nervous I told myself that I was only doing what God had intended men and women to do. She moaned gently and made a soft protest from out of her deep sleep. I didn't move, allowing my heat to overwhelm her, and when I found the courage to press my growing need into the cleft between her buttocks, she pulled me into the moist warmth hidden there as though she could wait no longer to find our future.

Afterward, I clung to Tejal as if we both had been in danger of falling from a death-defying height. We fell asleep together for the first time, my leg over her belly, her arm circling my waist, trying to make a knot out of our bodies that could never be undone.

Once during her stay, we united with such urgency while standing waist deep in Indra's Millstream that when we came apart it was as though we had broken something. It was frightening. And yet, as far as I was concerned, we were married that very moment. What better witnesses could we have had than the waters and sky, and a flock of chattering parakeets in a teak tree behind us?

*   *   *

I was glum as could be after Tejal departed, since she seemed to take all that was best in me with her, but Sofia worked hard to cheer me up until Papa told us we'd be going to Goa in ten days. After that, my sister was so nervous that she even veiled her hair in front of her face when Nupi's friends came to our house to see for themselves that she'd recovered. Papa and I put off asking her what was wrong for a few days, but when her mood didn't break, I came to her while she was sitting in her bed, sharpening her reed pen.

"Something is obviously bothering you," I said. "I haven't asked until now, but maybe we should talk."

Without looking up, she replied, "I think that maybe I'm leading us somewhere where we shouldn't go."

I sat next to her. Her magnifying glass was on her pillow, and I held it right up to her face to make her eyes look like a camel's. She stuck out her tongue playfully at me.

"Papa has to talk things over with Uncle Isaac and Aunt Maria," I said. "There's simply no other way."

"I know, but . . . but . . ."

I thought I knew what she was too frightened to say: "What if Aunt Maria doesn't want you to marry him? That's it, isn't it?"

I know now I ought to have given her more time to tell me what she was thinking; she might have saved several lives if she'd had the courage to say the right words at that moment.

"Sometimes I think that she doesn't like me at all," Sofia agreed, shame in her voice. "Sometimes I don't know what she wants. Or if I should trust her."

"She never liked anyone!" I exclaimed. "But Uncle Isaac and Papa will overcome her objections. Have faith in Papa. He loves you more than anything."

She raked her hands back through her hair. "Remember when I told you that I wanted to crawl out of my skin?" she asked. "That's how I feel now. Only I'm already grown up and there's nothing more I can become."

I wanted to say, *If you love Wadi and he loves you, then nothing bad can happen,* but I was so unsure of our cousin's motives that I didn't dare. "I promise to help in any way I can," was all I could say. "We've all learned our lesson from your illness."

I thought that would reassure her; instead, she burst into tears, trembling inside my embrace as if she were too terrified to hope for a happy ending.

*   *   *

Nupi sent us to the city with a lunch of *samosas* and fruit, and a pouch of cardamom cakes colored with saffron for Uncle Isaac. We reached Goa near sundown. At supper, Aunt Maria doted on everyone, twittering around in a red silk gown like a finch in its favorite fountain. Wadi, very likely following her lead, was as charming as he could be, and gallant with Sofia. I didn't believe any of it.

Once, I caught my aunt's reflection in the gilded mirror above the mantelpiece, and for an instant I could plainly hear her saying to me: *I cannot be anything but the woman you see. That is good enough for me, so do not expect anything more.*

I caught Papa's reflection when I went to his side of the table to fetch the honey-pot, and in his eyes I saw him telling me: *Those who always wear a mask believe everyone does, so they fear what might be beneath yours more than you can ever know.*

It was a meal in which we broached nothing of what ought to have been said. I didn't mind, however; the usefulness of subterfuge in matters of the heart was becoming ever more obvious to me.

After dessert, Sofia went to her room and changed into an elegant blue dress with a ruffled black collar, a recent gift from Aunt Maria. She and Wadi then said they were going for a stroll. Papa had misgivings about their spending time together before he'd had a chance to talk with his brother, but he kept to diplomatic silence. In my room upstairs, I hid behind my lace curtains and watched the couple whispering just outside the front door, which might have been only natural for lovers who hadn't seen each other in months, yet Wadi was plainly agitated. It occurred to me that he might be bullying Sofia into getting married.

He was carrying a leather satchel over his shoulder, and I'd learned from Papa just before bed that it contained a Latin schoolbook—commentaries on Cicero's *Stoic Paradoxes*—that he'd borrowed from a friend and needed to return that evening, but I presumed it was an excuse for staying away with Sofia longer than we might consider appropriate.

While I drifted to sleep, my father stayed talking with Uncle Isaac, and in the morning he told me they'd decided that Wadi and Sofia would meet with them separately that very evening. Each would have ample opportunity to say if marriage was truly what he or she wanted.

It was a Sunday, so Aunt Maria, Wadi, and Uncle Isaac left for Mass early that morning. My aunt rushed away in a brocade palanquin carried by four Indians. Once we were alone in the house, the shadows seemed to crowd in on us. Papa and Sofia could hardly say a word to each other, they were so nervous. A drenching rainstorm only made us feel our isolation more acutely, so when the sun returned I suggested that we get a look at the caravels just in from Lisbon. Isaac had told us that an African king as big as Goliath had been taken captive in Angola and was aboard one of the ships. Sofia answered that she preferred to stay home, adding that Africans ought to be permitted to remain in their own continent, which might have been a veiled criticism of our father having come to India, but—happily—he didn't take it that way. He didn't want to leave her alone, but he feared making her feel watched. In the end, he agreed to accompany me.

Seagulls wheeled overhead as we made our way toward the river. We had paused to watch a ragged Indian drover trying to repair the axle of his cart when three soldiers came up to us.

"Are you Berekiah Zarco?" the shortest of the men asked my father.

"Yes."

"Then you're under arrest."

"For what?"

"Take him," the soldier ordered his companions.

"I won't struggle against you," Papa told them as they gripped his arms to lead him away. "It's three against two, and you've got swords..." He seemed amused. "Ti, go find your uncle and tell him what's happened."

"But you've done nothing wrong."

"Just do as I say," he instructed calmly. Seeing how upset I was, he winked. "Don't worry, Isaac knows the governor. He'll have me out of prison in an hour. It's just an error. They must have me confused with another Berekiah Zarco."

At the time I believed he was joking. Now, I'm not so certain that he didn't know what was about to happen and pretended amusement only to keep me from quarreling with the soldiers. Likely he feared I'd be taken away with him—or beaten—unless he kept me in the dark.

*   *   *

I'd never been in a church before and was made even more frantic by the packed crowd and sickly smell of rain-soaked clothing. The sound of chanted Latin echoed harshly off the stone walls. As I pushed my way to the front, I could feel time pulsing around me: every second of delay, I feared, might cost Papa a month of freedom. When I spotted my uncle, I called to him and waved frantically. He jumped up and made his way to me without a word to Aunt Maria or Wadi.

"It's Papa," I told him once he'd reached me. "He's been arrested."

Isaac gasped and went pale. Wadi and Aunt Maria followed us outside.

"Go home," my uncle told the three of us. "I'll go to the jailhouse."

"I'm coming," I said.

"No. Sofia will need you. And it's better if I go alone." Looking around to check that we weren't being overheard, Isaac whispered, "You're a Jew, too, Ti, and would only make things worse."

With that, he was striding off. My aunt spoke to me in a sooth-ing voice on the way home, but I haven't any idea what she said; sharp thoughts of death clung greedily to me, as though searching for my weakest spot. When we reached our street, Wadi didn't wait for me to tell Sofia what had happened but rushed ahead to inform her himself, something which I found hard to forgive. Yet if he *was* in love with her, what could've been more natural—even laudable— than his wanting to be with her alone at this terrible moment?

*   *   *

Sofia was in trance of heavy desolation when Aunt Maria and I reached her. She was seated on her bed, ashen-faced, shivering as though she were soaked. Wadi had enveloped her in his black cape and was kneeling next to her, afraid to touch her.

"Ti, what's going to happen to Papa?" she asked me in a frail voice when I spoke her name.

"Uncle Isaac says he'll be home soon. Don't worry. It's just a mis-take. You must lie down and rest."

"I don't think I can. . . ."

"Please try, dear," Aunt Maria said gently.

I asked Wadi to leave so I could undress Sofia and get her under the covers. I don't believe I spoke harshly. I know I was trying to stay calm for my sister's sake.

"Don't talk to me like that!" he snapped, as if he intended to start a fight. "This is my house, not yours!"

"I'll thank you to keep your voice down," Aunt Maria told him. "There will be no quarrels in this house while Uncle Berekiah re-mains in prison. Do you boys hear that?"

"Francisco Xavier," I said, careful to use his Christian name in front of his mother, "I thought you loved my sister and wanted what's best for her."

"You obviously don't believe I do."

"All I believe at the moment is that you have to leave us alone. Or do you want to watch me help her get undressed? Maybe you want to do it for me. Is that it?"

He gave me a long, contemptuous look, which gratified me a great deal, then did as I asked, although he left the door open, forcing Aunt Maria to close it. When Sofia finally stopped shaking and closed her eyes, my aunt left us alone, but nothing I said could get my sister to speak to me.

*   *   *

Isaac returned that afternoon to tell us that he'd failed to win my father's release; he'd have to spend the night in the municipal prison.

"What crime is he to be charged with?" I questioned.

"They wouldn't tell me."

I asked him then what he meant about my being Jewish worsening our situation.

"Ti, the Inquisition regards you as a heretic."

"But I've done nothing!"

"Tiago," Aunt Maria said, giving me a punishing look, "you seem to be unaware what a danger you and your father are to the Church, and that it must defend itself against you."

"You sound as if you're in favor of what's happened!"

"No, I merely understand it."

"But the Holy Office has no power over us," I told Isaac. "Papa told me it can only punish Jews who have already converted to Christianity."

"That's what I thought, too, but there may be some complication that we don't understand."

His tone was so dark that I realized for the first time that my uncle was in fear for his own life. Maybe that was the real reason he didn't want a Jew with him at the jailhouse. Worse, I now understood that he might not be able to intercede forcefully on Papa's behalf, or ask for an audience with the Governor, since the more he did for his Jewish brother, the more likely it was that Isaac himself would be accused of betraying his Christian faith.

I was fairly certain that my father hadn't had time to think of any of these complications or he'd never have spoken so casually of his arrest. *How quickly a whole family can be put in a position of check,* I thought.

CHAPTER 15

I'd underestimated Isaac's courage. The next day, he rushed off at first light to begin his campaign to win Papa's freedom. He returned toward midday, his eyes bloodshot and his cape stinking like a dung heap. He flung it into the back garden right away with a muttered curse.

"Have it burned!" he commanded Aunt Maria.

While scrubbing his hands, he told us that Papa hadn't been taken to the Municipal Jailhouse, as we'd expected, but instead to the Aljouvar, the prison of the Archbishop of Goa. Tears sprouted in Isaac's eyes when he said that.

"Church officials must believe he's uttered some terrible blasphemy," my uncle said, shaking his head in despair.

My aunt brought him a glass of brandy and he gulped it down greedily. He told us he'd been allowed to see my father only briefly. Papa was being held in a cavernous cell with several dozen other prisoners. "At least he has the comfort of conversation, thank God," my uncle told us. "A French merchant is with him, and an Indian

Brahmin." He shuddered. "The prisoners make do with a pit dug in the floor for their necessities. It has long ago filled up and now the muck and vermin have spread everywhere."

"Isaac, I'll thank you to omit certain details!" Aunt Maria scolded.

"No!" I told her, stung. "You should have to hear how your beloved Church treats good men."

"Those *good men* must nearly all be murderers and thieves," she retorted with disdain.

"And which is my father?" I demanded.

Isaac held up his hand to stop our quarrel. "None of this makes any difference," he said. Calling Sofia and me over to him, he delivered the worst possible news: "Your father is being transferred this afternoon to the Palace of the Inquisition."

*   *   *

Once Wadi had helped Sofia back to bed, I had a chance to question Uncle Isaac about the Inquisition. Aunt Maria listened closely to his explanations as well, but she absolutely refused to believe that Papa was likely to be tortured, dismissing our fears as "mere morbid fantasy," but her husband—for the first time in memory—burst out in anger at her insistence.

"Maria," he said murderously, "your ignorance of the Church's methods is tantamount to approval. I will not allow you to repeat your doubts in this house again! No one in this city wants to know what goes on—or what they sanction with their silence."

Badly shaken, she clapped her hand over her heart and fled to the kitchen with an excuse about needing to supervise supper preparations. When she returned, she had on the long ruby earrings she normally wore only for formal occasions. She informed us she was going to pay a call on Father António, her confessor, and ask the priest to intercede. Just as I was about to thank her for her generosity, she insisted that Sofia and I accompany her.

"And it would be a good thing if you were to get on your knees and beg for mercy," she added, righteousness in her voice, as though she'd been waiting years to say this to me. "Go put on your best clothing as quickly as you can."

It occurred to me only later that she was trying to transfer her humiliation to Sofia and me. At the time, I could only stutter a refusal, protesting that Papa would be furious if my sister and I were to visit a priest with her. With naive bravado, I swore I'd never fall to my knees in front of a Christian.

"Don't you see that we're all in terrible danger?" Maria raged. "We must show everyone that you may be Jews but that you respect our traditions. If the Church believes you are troublemakers, we might all end up with your father."

"She's right," Isaac said solemnly, and I could read his apology to me in his downturned eyes, a gesture so reminiscent of my father that I felt helpless to continue my protest.

I needed time to talk over our options with Sofia, and asked to be excused so that I might speak with her alone.

"Don't take too long," my aunt warned. She was making the most of this opportunity for vengeance against me.

*   *   *

Wadi answered my knocks. He was sitting at Sofia's bedside, and from the way he was leaning toward her, his hand on her shoulder, I saw they'd been embracing. She was breathing in hesitant gasps. I feared she'd make herself ill again. Wadi's glum expression made me want to reach out to him, but I didn't want to risk being close to him ever again.

"May I have a few minutes alone with my sister?" I asked him.

"Please, Tiger, I have to stay with her," he said gently.

He hadn't used my nickname for many months. I felt as if we were both stepping across broken glass.

"It will be easier on us all if you wait outside," I told him. "Then you won't be put in the difficult position of having to either lie to your mother or tell her a truth I'd rather you not reveal to her."

"He's right," Sofia whispered.

Wadi kissed her brow and went to the door.

"Call me when you're done," he told her.

He loves her in his own way, I realized. *And maybe I don't have the right to ask for more from him.*

"We've fallen very far in only a day," I told my sister when he'd left the room. "I need you to summon all the strength I know is inside you. Papa is going to need it, and so am I. Maybe for months. We might have a long battle ahead of us."

"I'll do whatever I have to," she agreed. As she wiped her face with the sleeve of her nightdress, I told her what Aunt Maria was proposing and asked for her opinion.

"I don't mind going to church if it will help Papa," she said.

"But you know he'd forbid it."

"Oh, Ti, I'll do anything—anything at all!"

"Will you be angry at me if I don't go?"

"No, but maybe you'll be putting us all at risk."

"I don't think so. Uncle Isaac told me that someone must have made an accusation against Papa of blasphemy. That's the way the Inquisition works. They need an accusation to start proceedings. It must have been something Papa said or did on one of our previous stays in Goa. I don't think they're concerned about me right now." In a whisper, I added, "It may even be one of them."

"Who? I don't understand."

"Perhaps Aunt Maria accused Papa of some crime against the Church."

My sister gazed at me, puzzled. "You mean . . . you mean, this could have happened because of something she said?"

"Or did."

Sofia moaned.

"Although perhaps not on purpose," I hastened to add. "Maybe she said something while making confession, thinking it was innocent enough."

My sister looked at the door as if she might run downstairs at that very moment to confront our aunt. Her face was flushed. I dared not add that Wadi might have been the one who'd betrayed our father. Our cousin might very well have decided to use the Inquisition to remove Papa from our lives and make his opposition to their marriage of no consequence.

"Sofia, listen, if you go with Aunt Maria now, you must not say a word about Papa to any priest, or to anyone else, even if you think it will help him. Don't even speak to Wadi about him. He loves you, but he might reveal something that could make things worse."

"I understand, Ti."

"And there is one other thing you must never do . . . Papa was always afraid that Aunt Maria would convince you to convert, but if you allow yourself to be baptized, even to try to make things better, the Inquisition will have complete power over you. If you become a Christian, they will own your love for Wadi, Papa, and me. You will be their slave. Do you understand what I'm saying?"

Sofia nodded thoughtfully. "I won't say anything, and I'll get him out of prison if it's the last thing I ever do," she declared, a dark radiance in her eyes, as though she were staking her very life on winning this battle.

*   *   *

Over the next month, Sofia went with our aunt and uncle to church every day, but they weren't even able to learn what the charges were against Papa. My sister told me one evening that she had begun to say Christian prayers to the Virgin.

"I know it's wrong, Ti, but I'll do anything I have to," she whispered guiltily.

She added that she intoned the Jewish ones in her head, too, but that she sometimes feared that Aunt Maria could read her thoughts.

My sister was separating into two people, one deeply hidden under Christian piety.

"I'm glad," she announced indignantly when I pointed that out. "Why should people be allowed to see anything that's inside me?"

*   *   *

My own place of worship became the square outside the Palace of the Inquisition, a broad three-story fortress of barred windows. According to a Jesuit from Porto who approached me on my second day of vigil to ask for directions, the three great wooden doors in front opened only to let out prisoners who were true Christians.

"And false ones?" I asked, falling into his trap.

"Once they go inside, heretics remain there until they find Christ"—and here the priest crossed himself—"or die trying."

Facing the Palace as though it were the Mount of Olives, I learned how its shadows crept down the walls of the salmon-colored mansion behind me in the morning and crawled slowly across the cobblestones in the afternoon. Sometimes I would stand there in the rain, listening to the deafening sound of the heavens opening, letting all that insistent water soak into my hope, fighting the urge to flee, testing my will.

Once, an elderly Indian merchant in a tattered black cloak, his face as gnarled as a walnut, took pity on me and gave me a bunch of frangipani and gardenia. Scent and memory must meet in the heart, and that sweetly decaying smell in my hands soon became no different from a thousand memories of my father.

Watching the gulls landing on the palace's roof at dusk, calling toward the western ocean from which my father had come, I sensed that my own home—some ten miles to the southeast—had receded far from me already, pulled away by a tide that no god had created, and which therefore would not respond to my prayers.

In my dreams, I saw Papa blinded with a poker drawn red from a fire, and I heard his screams as though they tore apart my chest.

Every night in bed I saw his eyes put out, and upon waking I would think: *None of this waiting is getting me anywhere at all, but I have no choice. I must watch and listen closely. And everything has to be observed with Sofia's micrographic detail, or I might miss something important—something that no one else knows and that could free my father.*

*   *   *

I often thought of writing to Tejal. I knew she must have been wondering about my silence, but the nuns believed she had converted to Christianity and I could not risk her being arrested by the Inquisition. I never ventured near her convent; nor, for that matter, did I wander more than a few blocks from the Palace of the Inquisition. Whenever I'd look at the horizon in the distance, I felt as though I were swimming in an open ocean, bobbing over an immensity of dark water seeking to pull me under. I sent a letter to Nupi five days after Papa was taken prisoner. "We are all doing very well, but we will be staying for several more weeks," I lied, like a thief already safe in another country.

Nupi had never learned to read despite my father's attempts to teach her, so I sent my letter to a Hindu priest in Ponda with the request that he read it to her.

*   *   *

In the evenings, upon returning home from my vigil, I would go straight to my room and sit on my bed, inside a magic square I made from blue silk cushions, the wooden candlestick on my night table, and a Portuguese marionette. Sofia often came in to read to me from the Torah. I did not ask how she and Wadi were doing or if they'd made any plans for their future together. I told her only that I was grateful for her relieving me of the need to go to church—of doing what was tactically wise.

I suspected I'd have to pay someday for my different behavior toward my aunt, uncle, and cousin, but for now it was the way things were and it wouldn't change until Papa was free, and I made no apologies to anyone.

*   *   *

Eleven days after my father's arrest, Aunt Maria knocked on my bedroom door, waking me from a fitful sleep. It was surely near midnight.

"Nupi is outside asking after you," she said angrily, clutching the folds of her nightdress together, the pouches of skin around her eyes accented by the harsh candlelight, so that I was reminded of how old she'd become. "That cook of yours says she won't come in. Don't talk with her long—we're probably being watched."

She saw from the surprise in my face that such a possibility hadn't occurred to me.

"Well, why wouldn't they watch us?" she said irritably. "I have two Jews staying with me and a *converso* husband. It doesn't get much worse than that."

The lateness of the hour must have loosened her tongue, and her speaking of the three of us as though we were obstacles made my cheeks burn. For once in my life, I found the right reply.

"And don't forget your Arab son," I said with mocking sweetness.

She gasped at my effrontery, her lips twisted into an ugly frown. At that very moment, I think she began to fear what I could say and do. I was extremely glad.

*   *   *

Nupi stood on the street, her shoulders hunched under a dark shawl, the moonlight casting a gauze of shadow between us.

"I was so worried," she moaned. She stepped back and raised her hand as though to strike me for creating mischief. "You will now describe to me the exact nature of what's kept you here."

"Come inside," I said, reaching for her arm.

"I won't set foot in that woman's house," she snapped, folding her hands behind her back. "I'm certain as the sun at dawn that she's behind whatever evil has kept you here."

"How can you be sure without even knowing what's happened?"

"Ashoka interpreted the fall of petals in my shrine. No mistake has been made."

Ashoka was the Hindu priest to whom I'd sent my message for her.

"Whatever the case, we can't talk out here," I told her.

She agreed to follow me into the foyer. "But no further!" she warned with a wagging finger.

The house was completely dark; Aunt Maria must have gone to bed. Or was she hiding, listening to our conversation?

I lit the taper fastened to the wall above the mirror in the entranceway, then fetched a chair and made Nupi sit. She placed her hands in her lap. They gripped a cloth pouch swollen with something that made metallic noises.

I explained about Papa's arrest, purposely avoiding any conjectures about who had betrayed him in the event that my aunt was eavesdropping. The old cook's face grew hard.

"I thought it might be something like that," she told me, handing me her pouch, motioning for me to open it. She'd brought all her bangles—seven in silver and two in gold. Except for her saris, they represented her entire earthly wealth. There were also two letters from Tejal.

"What are your bangles for?"

"To ransom your father."

"Nupi, I can't take these from you."

"You must. I could not live with myself if I held anything back." She stood up. "You are to let me know the moment he is free. In the meantime, I will take care of the house. Are you eating well?"

I smiled. "Not like at home," I told her.

"No, I didn't think so," she said, as though I'd given the correct answer. I could see she was desperate to kiss me, but she also didn't wish to begin weeping, and neither did I. There is something about crying in a sleeping house that cannot easily be forgotten. We both knew that from past experience.

At length, I said, "You can't go. It's too late."

"I will leave now and be home by sunrise," she declared. "I send my love to Sofia and Uncle Isaac. When you see your father, tell him I am waiting for him."

"It's too dangerous to make your way home at night—"

She flapped her hands at me. "No one will bother an old woman."

I offered to fetch her some biscuits and a jug of water.

"No, I shall go home with nothing," she said. "As it should be."

And then, slowly but unstoppably, she walked away from me.

CHAPTER 16

Tejal mostly sent news of her studies in her letters, although
her second one expressed worry over why she hadn't heard
from me.

I still didn't dare write her about our troubles. Two terrible weeks
passed; we couldn't even confirm that Papa was still alive.

Another letter arrived then from Tejal, care of my uncle.

"Why have you sent no word?" she wrote. "Is Sofia ill again and
have you gone to Goa to see a Portuguese physician? Please write to
me in Benali. I will be going there soon."

I rushed out the next morning in the chilly dark before dawn,
hoping to make certain I wasn't being followed by taking a route
that took me to the southern gates of the city and back. I prayed I
was doing the right thing. A tiny, olive-complexioned nun answered
my knocks at the convent door. When I explained that Tejal was my
sister, she smiled, crinkling the skin around her eyes in an endearing way.

"What a lovely girl she is!" she told me, her hands clasped together in delight.

She steered me into a tiny chapel with a fresco of a winged angel and a young woman on the ceiling, then darted off. A few minutes later, Tejal appeared in the doorway, her hair pulled tightly back by a ribbon. Her face—lit by surprise—seemed narrower and more adult than I'd remembered it. From the way she clung to me, I thought she'd learned about my father, but as soon as the nun separated us, Tejal said, "Ti, whatever I did wrong, I am sorry. Forgive me or my life is ruined." She spoke in Konkani so that we wouldn't be understood.

Her use of the word *ruined* made me understand for the first time how I'd compromised her entire future by sleeping with her.

"You didn't do anything wrong. It's my fault—all mine. Papa's been imprisoned by the Inquisition. I didn't know what to say to you that wouldn't worry you and put you in danger."

"But what's he done?"

"We don't know. Uncle Isaac thinks someone must have accused him of blasphemy."

"Have you been allowed to see him in the Orlem Gor? Is he all right?"

Orlem Gor meant "manor house," and was what the local people called the Palace of the Inquisition. The nun must have understood the term, because she came to Tejal and slapped her arm so hard that she yelped.

"I don't want you speaking that heathen language anymore!" she warned.

For a moment, stunned, I just stared at her. Then I said in a tone of warning, "I'd appreciate it if you'd mind your own business." When she frowned defiantly, I added, "And don't hit my sister again."

The nun rushed out of the room, doubtless to get help.

"Papa was fine when Uncle Isaac saw him," I hurried to add now, knowing Tejal and I wouldn't have much time, "but we haven't had word of him in weeks. Listen closely . . . I may have created problems for you by coming here, because I'm probably being watched. I didn't see anyone, but Aunt Maria thinks we must be. I'm sorry."

"Don't be—I'm glad you came. I feared my . . . my giving myself to you made you hate me."

She reached toward my face as though to caress my cheek, then thought better of showing her feelings inside the chapel. I kissed her palm, desperate to reassure her.

"After I go, you must tell the nuns not to let me in again," I said. "They have to think you dislike me. Tell them you don't trust me. That's very important, Tejal."

"It won't matter. I'm going to leave here very soon."

"You said you were going to Benali. Has something happened?"

"I'm pregnant."

I looked at her belly but could see no difference.

She tweaked my nose playfully. "The baby has not yet shown himself, but I've missed my cycle of the moon twice."

As we embraced, I thought, *Tejal and our baby will be waiting for me at the end of this long, slow road.* I was terrified for us all, however, and deeply wished that we'd waited to make a new life between us.

A burly nun with a pinched face strode into the room and began yelling at me.

"I'm going," I told her, holding up my hands. To Tejal, I said, "Write to me at my uncle's house as soon as you reach home. And if you see Nupi, be careful what you say to her. She knows about Papa, but I don't want her worrying too much."

Her eyes filled with tears.

"We'll get married as soon as we're again together," I promised her, knowing now her greatest fear.

She could only nod.

As soon as I was out the door I realized I ought to have put something into her hands to seal my pledge, even a copper coin she could have worn around her neck, but by then the nuns had firmly locked and bolted the door behind me.

*   *   *

Later that morning, as I stood vigil in front of the Palace of the Inquisition, I learned just how easy it was to fall victim to the fanatical hatred that prevailed in Goa.

Just after the ringing of the cathedral bells for sext, I spotted Senhor Saraiva, the ancient New Christian chandler from whom we bought candles, hobbling across the square as though on a vital mission. I called to him loudly and, although he must have heard me, he didn't turn or wave, which was uncharacteristic of him. Even odder, he continued across the square and knocked at the doors of the Palace, where a priest welcomed him inside.

Curiosity got the better of me, and I headed to his tiny shop, which, like many in Goa, was open at the front. His gnarled wife was standing behind her wooden desk, wrapping beeswax tapers for the only customer there, a heavyset, round-faced young woman wearing a simple brown dress. The two women were conversing in a friendly way. Not wishing to interrupt, I called a quick greeting to Senhora Saraiva, then started back for the square.

Two bailiffs with unsheathed swords suddenly came around the corner, heading straight toward me. Behind them marched a small, wiry priest carrying a crucifix. A few paces further back was Senhor Saraiva, doing his best to keep up despite his limp.

My heart began to pound; I believed they were coming for me. Instead, as I held my breath, they continued past me directly to the chandler's shop.

Relief swept through me, and I ridiculed my own terror with a little laugh. Yet as soon as the bailiffs entered the shop, I heard the woman customer begin to plead.

"No, I've done nothing wrong! I don't understand. Please don't do this to me."

The bailiffs made me fearful for my own safety, but I hurried back down the street toward the shop and positioned myself so that I could watch from a safe distance. The young woman was on her knees. Lifting her hands in supplication toward the senior bailiff, she began to speak, but her voice was so frail that I only caught a few tentative words: "I was only purchasing candles. There's . . . there's nothing wrong with that, is there?"

"Stand up, Senhora Barbosa!" the man commanded, but the poor woman hung her head and began to pray.

The old chandler, who must have gone off to the Palace of the Inquisition as soon as Senhora Barbosa had entered his shop, pointed down at her, plainly enraged. To my great frustration, I could hear almost nothing of what he said. I crept closer, to the side of the shop. I could no longer see inside, but I could hear every word that was uttered.

"You won't get the better of me," Senhor Saraiva was saying to her angrily, in summation of what I must have missed.

"I . . . I don't understand," Senhora Barbosa stammered, echoing my own confusion.

"We won't risk being accused of selling candles to filthy Jews for their celebrations," Senhora Saraiva spat, saying the word "Jews" as if it had a foul taste.

"Keep quiet, woman!" the senior bailiff ordered her.

I didn't understand why he was rude to her until later, when my uncle told me that by mentioning candles, the chandler's wife had given Senhora Barbosa a clue as to why she was being arrested—information that the Inquisitors would have preferred to keep for themselves.

"I light our candles at sundown every night," Senhora Barbosa said in a terrified voice. "Who doesn't? Who can live without light?"

"But you've bought them on three straight Fridays," Senhora Saraiva informed her.

"Don't say another word!" her husband ordered, and I heard a slap.

"I don't keep track of the days on which I buy candles. Why would I? I do my marketing on Fridays, because that's when my sister is free to watch my daughter. Summon my sister if you don't believe me. Or send for my husband. He'll tell you I'm speaking the truth. I've always been a good Christian."

I heard a moan from Senhora Barbosa and the sound of a brief scuffle. I believe one of the two bailiffs must have tugged her to her feet, then shaken her.

"Don't make this more difficult than it already is, my child," the priest advised her.

"Please, Father," the young woman implored, "send for my husband. He works at the port—not five minutes from here."

"Your husband cannot help you now," the senior bailiff told her.

"But we've been married for nearly ten years. He knows me better than anyone and can tell you—" She gasped, realizing in an instant of terror what her captor was implying. "You've . . . you've arrested him, too?"

"He's being escorted to our Palace at this very moment," the priest answered.

"And our daughter?" the mortified woman asked frantically. "What's to become of her?"

"That depends entirely on you confessing your crimes, my child."

"Let's go," the senior bailiff growled.

Hearing footsteps from inside the shop, I hurried off down the street to be less conspicuous. When I dared turn around, Senhora Barbosa was being helped along by the priest. All the color had vanished from her face and she was stumbling across the cobblestones.

To my great shame, I averted my gaze as she passed. The chandler stood in his doorway watching the men escort her away. He was eating a handful of dried figs. A small crowd of neighbors had gathered.

Confusion and anger prompted me to approach him.

"Senhor Saraiva," I began, "what did that poor woman do wrong?"

"Tiago, take my advice and stay out of this," he replied.

"Please, my father is a prisoner. And I am ignorant of the ways of the Inquisition."

The chandler stared hard at me while he considered what to do, then tugged me to the back of his shop.

"Senhora Barbosa bought candles on three straight Fridays," he told me.

"But that's no proof she's celebrating the Jewish Sabbath."

"I'm sorry, Tiago, but that's proof enough for me," he declared. "And I can't discuss these things with you. You should go now."

"But have you ever been to her home? Have you ever heard her utter a Jewish prayer?"

"No."

"Then you don't know anything!"

"I know that it's up to the priests to say whether she's telling the truth or not!" he snapped. In a conciliatory tone, he added, "The Inquisitors have been building a case against her for weeks. They told me—"

"For weeks?" I questioned.

"The priests told me to begin watching her closely at least two months ago. Apparently, other people have already testified against her."

"Who?"

"Only the Inquisitors know that."

"Will they ever tell her who her accusers are?"

"No, she'll have to deduce their names." He frowned. "Although now she knows that we are among them. I asked the bailiffs to take her into custody later, but they told me they had been waiting for just one more incident of heresy to arrest her." Seeing my look of outrage, he added, "Tiago, I merely told them what she did. No one can say I did anything wrong. I did my duty."

"But she'll be put in a prison cell now—maybe for years. She might even be tortured. How could you do that to her without any real proof?"

"Don't you understand anything, Tiago? If I'd waited to tell the priests about her, they might have accused me of conspiring with her. I might have been arrested. I could be in prison *myself* now."

"But for that to happen, someone would have to report you to the Inquisition. Who would ever notice on what days you sell candles to Senhora Barbosa?"

"Another customer, a neighbor...Everyone watches things closely in Goa. Everyone is a spy. And everyone has enemies."

"Enemies?"

"Imagine a customer who doesn't want to pay his debts to me. He might lie about my being a lapsed Christian myself. He might hand some of his friends a few copper coins to swear they heard me speaking Hebrew at my mother's graveside. I assure you it happens all the time." He drew his fingertip across his neck. I noticed a faint line of scar tissue. "One clever lie and the next thing you know you are at the mercy of the priests."

"So you were imprisoned by the—"

"It was many years ago, and I'm not permitted to talk about it."

"But you admit that all the charges against Senhora Barbosa might be lies."

"Lies or total nonsense. But that's not for me to decide. Or you." The chandler peered past me, where neighbors were still gathered. Giving me a worried look, he led me to the front of the shop. "People are watching—you'll have to go," he whispered.

"But if you know what they are capable of doing, then—"

He pushed me away roughly. In a furious voice, so that those outside would hear, he said, "Go away, Tiago! You and your family don't belong in Goa."

His words chilled me as I walked back toward the Palace of the Inquisition, for they seemed a kind of curse. But it was Senhora Barbosa's cry of despair over her daughter's safety that woke me that night from sleep—after all, how certain was I that the child growing inside Tejal would not one day suffer a similar fate?

*   *   *

Two days later, Isaac burst in the front door near dusk. "Everyone get down here!" he shouted. "I've got wonderful news from the warden!"

I bounded down the stairs.

"I am to be allowed to see your father again tomorrow morning," he told me.

Hearing the commotion, Sofia and Wadi came racing in from the back garden. When my sister heard our good fortune, she gave thanks, her lips sculpting the words silently in Hebrew. She came to me and we hugged.

"I think this means Berekiah will be released soon," Isaac added. "They must know the case against him is weak. Maybe they'll want a small gift in exchange for his freedom. I'll give them whatever they want."

Wadi gripped my arm. "All will be well now, Tiger," he said, smiling at me as he used to.

Even so, I sensed a part of me standing back from him, as though peering over a fence.

My aunt came downstairs now, her expression hard. Isaac began to explain to her in an excited voice how things stood, but she shushed him up as though he were a child.

"You never see the snares ahead, do you?" she snapped. "After you leave your brother tomorrow, they'll arrest *you*. They'll say your visiting him is proof that you're a secret Jew. Ti must go instead of you, Isaac. He has nothing to lose."

"But Berekiah is *my* brother." As that declaration merely made his wife sneer, Isaac added in a hard voice, "No matter what religion he is."

"Don't ever repeat such a thing outside this house," my aunt ordered, glaring at him. She dabbed at her neck and brow; she always sweated a great deal when she was angry.

My uncle looked at me for support, but I could see in his desperate, yearning expression that he knew she'd reached a reasonable conclusion.

"Aunt Maria is right," I told him, relieving him of the need to say so. "I'll go tomorrow to see Papa."

"I'll accompany you to the prison," my uncle replied defiantly.

"So will I," Wadi declared.

"Francisco Xavier, you will stay right here with Sofia!" Aunt Maria was obviously not about to permit any debate on the subject. "As for you, Isaac, you may accompany Tiago, but you mustn't enter the Holy Office. You must promise me that."

He nodded, but she insisted on hearing the words spoken aloud.

"I swear! Is that enough for you?" he shouted at her. He looked at her with contempt.

We were all silent after that, as if my aunt and uncle had shattered something that could never be repaired.

*　　*　　*

Their confessor, Father António, came to our door the next morning. A painfully thin man with a childlike, fleeting smile, he greeted everyone in the family warmly, holding my sister's shoulders as he kissed her cheeks. His hands and face were bone-white. He looked as though he lived in forced isolation.

"How are you, Sofia?" he asked with what sounded to me like false sincerity, but my dislike for priests was no doubt filtering my observations of him.

"Well, Father," she replied, her tone constricted. I wondered how many sermons about converting to Christianity she'd had to suffer in silence over the past weeks.

When it was my turn, Father António shook my hand for far longer than would be considered appropriate by most men.

"You've been hiding from me, Tiago Zarco," he said, a twinkle of mischievousness in his eye.

"He's very shy," my aunt hastened to reply, fearing I might tell him what I thought of the work of the Church in India.

"Really?" he said doubtfully. "You look like a very assured young man to me."

"Not at all," I replied. "I'd probably never leave the house if my aunt didn't keep prodding me to go." Smiling to soften my next words, I added, "It sometimes seems to me that she's particularly insistent whenever guests appear."

Aunt Maria shot me a dirty look, which gratified me, but Sofia looked at me crossly. *Don't put Papa in further jeopardy,* I could hear her warn, and I signaled my agreement to her with an upraised hand, which made her put her index finger to her ear as we did as children, so I knew she understood me.

"Come with me into the garden for a moment, Father António," my uncle said. "I need to discuss something with you before we go."

Sitting under the tamarind tree, Isaac explained to the priest about the delicate position we were in and the need for me to substitute for him as a visitor to Papa's cell. As I was later to learn, he also gave his guest four gold rings, one for himself and three others to bribe the people of his choosing at the right moment. Maybe for that reason Father António was in a bright mood when he came back inside, and he even gave me a hearty pat on the back. "Well, young man, we had best be off!" he said eagerly, as though we had a trip to the flower market in mind.

Before leaving, I fetched from the kitchen a small pot of chicken stew made by my aunt and uncle's cook, since I was sure that Papa must have been eating miserably.

Sofia watched me with worried eyes as we left. She looked like a girl who couldn't go any further with her life without some guiding words, but—feeling useless and desolate—I knew I didn't have any.

"Tell Papa I love him more than anything," she called. She held up her hand to wave to me, then, seeing the priest watching her closely, quickly brushed a lock of hair back over her ear instead.

*   *   *

"That chicken smells heavenly," Father António said as we got on our way. "But I prefer to eat only eggs in the morning. I boil them with salt, of course, since only the Hindus add the salt afterward, which is forbidden by the Holy Office. Although I don't suppose you know that, living outside Goa as you do."

"No, I had no idea," I replied distantly. "I'm sorry I'm so ignorant about the ways of the Church."

He waved away my apology and smiled. Maybe he was simply looking for a way to start a conversation with me.

"Where exactly do you live?" he asked.

"Near the village of Ramnath—not far from Ponda."

As we walked, he asked me a great many questions about our lives. At first, each seemed innocent enough, but I began to suspect he wanted potentially damaging information when he asked if my father had close friends living near our farm and what work we'd done of late for the Sultan. I made vague replies, although sometimes I answered with an outright lie; I could not risk supplying him with evidence against us.

When we reached our destination, we were met by another priest, Father Crispiano, a tall, dark-complexioned Castilian.

"I know I have asked too many questions," Father António told me before taking his leave. "But your family is of great interest to me, and I've only been in India for a few years, so everything here is still new to me. I only hope we can meet again under more pleasant circumstances."

"When my father is freed, I'll visit you and thank you more fully."

"I look forward to that."

He crossed himself, then did the same over my forehead. I bowed my head and wished him a good day.

When I stepped into the dominion of the Inquisition beside Father Crispiano, no cold shadow fell over me. The walls of the palace seemed no more barren or heartless than stone anywhere, and the constellation of flames in the sinuous Venetian-glass candelabrum hanging from the ceiling seemed very much the same as lights anywhere.

Perhaps the worst was over; perhaps we were beginning the journey back to the way things had always been.

The guards soon confiscated Papa's chicken stew. They took a small pocketknife from me as well, though I was promised its return when I left. Everyone was formal with me but quite polite.

I confess that I can't recall a single thing that Father Crispiano said to me once we'd started up the staircase toward the long gallery of cells above; I was conversing with my father in my head, searching for the voice that would defray both his fear and my own. I imagined myself telling him it was only a matter of days before we were all together again. Surely that might be true. . . .

Soon we were facing his cell. I was dizzy, and everything seemed dim, as though we were underground.

The first iron door clanged open to reveal a second, inner door. With a grinding of metal, Papa appeared in front of me—seated on his cot, bare-chested, in rough gray trousers, his hair cropped too closely. Dark bruises ringed his eyes, which were puffy and nearly closed. Blood crusted at the corners of his mouth. Around his neck was a line of torn skin. A noose must have been tightened around it.

"Papa!"

We embraced for a long time. He spoke endearments to me as the priest left us and the inner door banged closed.

"Let me get a good look at you," Papa said.

He showed me a sweet smile, and I kissed him on the lips. His eyes looked like slits of cloudy glass.

Seeing the physical suffering of a parent reaches deeply into the recesses of the mind; I felt a sudden terror that he'd never again look like himself and that he would die in agony.

"I'd like to kill them all for what they've done to you," I began. "Tell me who has—"

He held up his hand to keep me from saying more.

"You were such a beautiful baby," he said eagerly. "So fragile. I worried you'd never make it to adulthood, but here you are a handsome young man with all the world ahead of you." He gripped my hands. "Ti, I want you to know I'm very proud of you."

The way he spoke—as if for posterity—turned the words in my throat to sand. He gave me his earthenware jug to drink from.

"How's Sofia? She hasn't fallen ill again, has she?" he asked.

"No. She's sad and worried, like all of us, but she's well."

"I'm guessing that you have been staying with Uncle Isaac."

"Yes."

I touched my fingertip to the line of inflamed skin across his neck. He winced.

"Are you . . . are you in much pain?"

My fearful and hesitant voice was not the one I'd wanted, and I was angry at myself for not being able to control my emotions.

"Don't worry about me. What have you told Nupi?"

"She knows the truth. She came one night to Goa, and I could not lie to her."

"She must be worrying terribly," he said, and when he grimaced, one of the tiny scabs at the corners of his mouth broke open; blood trickled over his chin. I wiped it away with my finger.

He took that opportunity to press his lips to my hand, which made me so upset that I couldn't talk again for some time.

At length, he said, "You must be very strong, Ti."

He made me smile by imitating the way Nupi raised her hand to threaten Sofia and me.

"I hope Aunt Maria isn't being too critical of you," he said. "And that you've been patient with her."

"We fight sometimes, but mostly I stay to myself."

"Ti, I've been thinking a great deal about you of late. From now on promise me you'll do what you need to do to find your own way. Don't worry so much about Sofia or Wadi, or anyone else. Make your life with Tejal."

"I'll do anything you say, Papa."

"Good. And how is Tejal? Have you seen her lately?"

"She is well." I didn't say anything yet about our child. I needed more time to talk about what he'd been through—and to hear his plans for how we were going to free him.

"And Isaac?" he asked.

"Papa, everyone is fine," I said impatiently. "But we can think of nothing but you. Are you all right?"

"Of course. The only difficult part is the boredom. Four walls and mosquitoes—it isn't much. My mind sometimes...it doesn't seem to work properly. And the food. Mostly I live on rice broth." He tapped his forehead. "You know, I hadn't realized how much was stored in my memory. It's what saved me from going mad. I'm very grateful for the past."

"I tried to bring you chicken stew, but they took it from me."

His face seemed to drain of blood, and a moan escaped from his mouth. Knowing he'd made an error by revealing his despair, he hugged me again for a long time. "It doesn't matter," he kept whispering, as though casting a spell over us both. In a voice of grand triumph, he added, "You and I are together, and that's more than I ever could have hoped for."

I could feel his heartbeat surrounding me. I didn't want to ever leave him.

"Isaac says my being allowed to visit you must mean their case against you is very weak." In a whisper, I added, "He thinks they are waiting for a bribe."

"No. They are...they are hoping you'll convince me to give them what they want."

Papa had switched to Konkani, which made his speech awkward, and later on I wondered if he might not have given me other options if we'd spoken in Portuguese. This marked then the beginning of my helpless descent into a what-if world, the landscape of useless speculations where I have lived ever since.

"What do your jailors want?" I asked him.

"Names."

"I don't understand, Papa."

"They want the names of secret Jews living in Goa. Only then will they accept my confession of having uttered a blasphemy against the Church. They think that my seeing you will weaken my resistance." He smiled fleetingly. "They're right, of course. Seeing your face is like standing before God—an extremely dangerous thing for a man like me. They think you will defeat me where they have failed." He winked cagily. "But I remember Masada, and how the hundreds of courageous Jews corralled on that mountaintop refused to surrender to the Romans. I won't let my ancestors die in vain."

"These secret Jews—who are they?" I asked.

"Men and women who have converted to Christianity to please the Inquisition but who practice our religion in secret. There are a few dozen in Goa. I know many of them. But the Church will never have their names. You will see to that."

"Me?"

He put his arm over my shoulder.

"Papa, the way you talk, and how you're behaving—it frightens me."

"I'm sorry, but I just can't see any other way. It's like this, Ti. A week ago, when they tied me down with ropes and hurt me, I felt my soul leaving me. I could feel it flowing right through the top of my head—it was an odd sensation. I knew then that I wouldn't last much longer, that I would give them the names of the Jews they wanted."

"What did they do to you?"

"It's better you don't know. At some point, I lost consciousness. I woke up back here in my cell, but next time I may not be so fortunate." He gazed away for a moment, his brow wrinkled, considering, I knew, how to tell me what he must have preferred to keep secret. "Ti, torture changes you. It's as if I no longer know who I am when I'm lying in the dark. Something has become dislodged in me—my soul, perhaps." He pressed his hand against my chest, then drew it back quickly. "My spark of God wants to return home. It wants to go to the sun that lights the Torah. That's why I know I won't be able to trust myself. And they know it, too. They're not stupid men— they're evil, and ignorant of their own true motives, but they're clever. They will torture me until they get what they want—or until they murder me."

"Papa, we must try to bribe—"

"No, listen to me! Even the Sultan's emeralds would buy us only a few weeks. And my soul will leave me the next time I'm tortured. It will seek to flee the pain and return home. I'll end up giving them the names they want. And when I do, many good men and women will end where I am now. I couldn't live with that. I need your help, Ti. Will you help me even if it means doing something you hate?"

"Yes."

"Good." He gripped my arm. "I'm sorry to be talking like this and worrying you. It's because I'm nervous, and also because I'm about to injure the one person I never believed I could. Now, do you remember that expression of Nupi's about the Guardian of the Dawn? Remember how she sometimes used it to mean that we must protect one another—no matter what the risk?

"Of course."

"Ti, you're going to be my Guardian."

When he grinned, I caught a glimpse of a madness in him that I'd never seen before.

He's not who he was, I realized. *That man has been taken from me. . . .*

"How?" I asked.

Papa's tone became conspiratorial. "I need you to go to see a *pandito* who lives near that teahouse you and Wadi used to go to— the rickety one in the Hindu neighborhood. His name is . . ."

A *pandito* was an Indian physician. Papa spoke the man's name in a whisper and said I was to ask for him at a tannery where we sometimes bought vellum, adding in a tone of warning that I was never, under any circumstances, to reveal this *pandito*'s identity to anyone. He spoke very deliberately, using his hands for emphasis, as an adult does to focus the mind of a distracted child. I imagine my face must have been showing all my confusion.

"When you tell him where I am," he continued, "he will give you a small glass vial with a powder inside. You must not let it out of your possession."

"A powder?"

"A very powerful poison."

"And what am I to do with it?"

"You are to bring it to me."

"Do you intend to kill your guard? Do you think you can escape?" My heart was racing; stupidly, I had mistaken our last steps across a collapsing bridge for the way home.

"No, no, I'll use it to end my life. You will save me from all the misery I might cause."

"No!"

Seeing my terror, he tried to hug me, but I pushed him away.

"Ti, this isn't easy for me," he said. "Please understand, dying is the last thing I want to do. I'd like to have a long life with you and Sofia—to see you two grow up. But that's not going to happen now." He kneeled before me. "Son, we may not have that much time. I cannot ask anyone else. You're my only hope. Do not be so sad. I've had a very good and full life—you and Sofia are more than any man could ever have hoped for. And I had such good fortune to meet your mother. It still amazes me that she fell in love with me."

"Papa, Tejal is pregnant," I announced.

I see now that I said it as a bribe. Surely with a grandchild on the way he wouldn't choose death. . . .

He gasped. Tears seeped from his bruised eyes. He took my head in his hands and pressed his lips to both my cheeks, then my lips. "Oh, my boy, you have made me very happy—you and Tejal. Tell her thank you for me."

"You have to live so you can see the baby, Papa. It won't be any good if you're not with us."

He stood up, wincing from the pain and wiping away his tears. "Listen closely, Ti. You'll be allowed to see me one more time. I've arranged that."

"How?"

"I have some friends who know their way around these corridors. And as I've said, the Inquisitors hope you will weaken my resolve and make me confess."

"But if you have friends who can help, then why can't—"

Again he held up his hand to halt my question. "I am too far gone, Ti. They'll be able to do nothing more for me after your second visit. Now, before you come again to see me, you must conceal the vial where no one will find it. It's no bigger than a fingernail, and they won't search inside you." He tapped his bottom so that I understood what he meant. "I apologize for the indignity I am inflicting on you, son, but it is the only way to be sure."

"Papa, I won't be able to poison you. I won't be able to do it!"

He sat down beside me again. "You won't have to. I'll take the poison a few days after your visit, so that they don't suspect you. You must never tell them what you've done, of course, or you will end up here."

"I won't even be able to bring it to you—"

"You'll have to. Only you can be my Guardian. You understand? You're the only one who can make sure that dawn continues to come for all the Jews I know. Ti, the Torah says that in saving one person, you save an entire universe. Imagine being able to protect all the good people I might name under torture. Imagine saving twenty or thirty of them! Your name will be written by the Angel Metatron in the Book of the Righteous."

"But there has to be another way to save you and to—"

"I've searched my mind and found nothing," he interrupted. "And we are running out of time. Ti, you'll be allowed back to visit me exactly two days from now. You can't discuss this with anyone. If you tell Sofia or Uncle Isaac, they—and you—will be in great danger. As will all the secret Jews."

"Maybe if we make the person who denounced you recant, we can—"

"Once a charge has been made, it can't be taken back. And the Holy Office must have managed to convince more than one witness to testify against me—that is the way the process works."

"Do you know who denounced you?"

"No."

"Could it have been someone we know?"

"I suppose. Though it could just as well have been someone in the street."

"Aunt Maria—could it have been her?"

He shook his head. "I can't believe your aunt would be capable of this. She certainly wouldn't be able to hide what she'd done from Isaac for long."

I thought of the fight they'd had. Could my uncle have suspected her, too?

"Papa, you're not a lapsed Christian, you're a Jew. So how is it that they can hold you?"

"No one has told me that, and maybe they never will. I suspect that the same person responsible for my being here must have sworn I'd been baptized at some time or other."

"But you haven't!"

"No, but if he swears it . . . Ti, please, there's no time for these explanations—the guard may return at any moment. Just do as I say."

"But what if I can't find him?" I asked, and here I named the physician who would give me the poison.

"Just go to the tannery as soon as you leave here. It's my only hope." He stood and drew me to my feet. "I want to embrace you as a man," he said, and when we were in each other's arms, he whispered in my ear, "May God and you both forgive me for what I've asked you to do."

I tasted the blood on his lips as he kissed me again. I closed my eyes, wishing to make time come to a halt. I don't know how long we hugged each other without speaking. Too soon I heard a key turning in the lock. Papa held me away, and our last gaze became too intimate. Sobbing, he turned his face to the wall.

"Don't look at me, Ti," he said. "And don't say anything more."

Covering his eyes with his hands, Papa began praying in Hebrew, swaying, his head bent toward the ground.

CHAPTER 17

I trudged to the Hindu neighborhood, wandering around the rickety wooden stalls and crowded streets, the air thick with the rotting sweetness of spices and coconut oil. The sky was now so heavy with dark-edged clouds billowing in from the west that it might have been smoke from a burning city. When the rain came a few minutes later it pounded down in swirling sheets, and steam rose up from the baking ground in ghostlike wisps. I stood shivering under the wooden awning of a stone-carver's hut, picturing the drowning of flowers and grasses across all of India. On the ground beside me was a row of stone gods, each statuette no bigger than my hand—like a set of chess pieces waiting patiently for a game to begin. A soapstone likeness of Sarasvati, the goddess of music, art, and literature, caught my attention. She was riding a fan-tailed peacock and carrying a book, two lotus flowers, and a *vati*—a long-necked Indian lute—in her four arms.

What would I have to give her in exchange for her knowledge of how to remake the past? I wondered.

Hoping to find solace in another person's voice, I peered through the low doorway behind me and found the carver sitting on his haunches, cooking two finger-sized silver fish on a handful of red-hot coals clumped on the floor. A slender white cat with matted fur squatted next to him, regarding me with mad, suspicious eyes. Something about the creature seemed human—the reincarnation of a child who died frightened and now could never be anything else, through endless cycles of rebirth.

I've seen that cat in many dreams since that day and it's always shrinking away from me, as if my face had become something monstrous—or, more to the point, as if it suspected what I was about to do to my own father....

"Do you want to buy something?" the carver asked me hopefully.

"No. I'm just waiting out the rain."

His interest in me vanished. Chomping on a piece of rice bread, he went back to his cooking.

I stood to the side of the door, where the carver couldn't see me, and nudged the likeness of Sarasvati closer to me with my foot. I was prickly with panic. It was as though a creature of talons and spines lived inside me, preying on my doubt.

I grabbed Sarasvati and ran, tossed like a stone at the ocean's edge by my own lunatic swiftness, but the humid air—so heavy with my past—made me tire quickly. Panting for breath, doubled over, I felt as though my throat had been scraped by a rusty knife.

Carrying Sarasvati like a spoil of war, craving her solidity for the contrast it made with my own weightlessness of spirit, I walked to the tannery. As I entered the compound, the stink of dung in the stone vats brought me back to my body. The old Tamil proprietor welcomed me with his toothless smile.

He asked where I'd gotten my statuette and I told him a friend had sculpted it.

"Making music has given her a very sweet face," he commented.

I insisted he take it as a small gift, and he accepted it with a happy laugh.

"Now, what can I do for you today?" he asked.

When I spoke of the *pandito,* he raised his eyebrows and cupped his hand around his ear as if he'd heard me wrong. In a low voice, he asked if my father had been taken by the Holy Office.

"Yes, and he's being tortured," I replied bluntly.

"Then come," the tanner said, his eyes grave, wanting me to see in them what he dared not say about the Portuguese rulers of his city. After exchanging some words with his foreman, he led me through a tiny back door on which beautiful florid lettering said in Portuguese: *Many are the roads leading to the Lord, but how fortunate are we that there is only one path beyond.*

"What does that mean?" I asked him.

He shook his head. "I didn't write it—your father did."

"My father? When?"

"Years ago. He came here one day and asked my permission to write on the door. It's a kind of prayer, I think. My Portuguese is not very good. A friend of his was about to be arrested by the Inquisition and needed the *pandito*'s help. Your father wanted his friend to be able to see those words before the man purchased poison and ended his own life."

We soon came to a small valley of scattered dwellings on the outskirts of the city. Elephant-eared plants skirted our pathway, and rainwater trapped in their folds was glinting in the moist sunlight breaking through the clouds. After watching a hawk wheeling in the sky as though it were an impossible-to-decipher omen, my guide pointed me toward a one-story house with a wooden balcony all the way around. "All life is suffering, so pray for a good death," he recited as he bid me goodbye. I guessed he said that to everyone who passed through his hands into the underworld.

*　　　*　　　*

The physician's front door was painted deep blue, with a small hibiscus flower in pink and white at its center, like a mandala just forming. I rang a brass bell hanging from a fraying string.

The bearded, turbaned servant who answered the door gazed at me skeptically and refused to let me inside the house until I'd dried myself. He handed me a rough towel scented with rosewater.

The expert in poisons greeted me just inside the door. He had a crest of silky white hair, obsidian-black intelligent eyes, and smooth cinnamon-colored skin. His bearing was confident and exquisitely stylized, as though he'd been raised as a dancer. From that, I knew he was a Brahmin; he looked at the world—and even at the drenched young man in front of him—from the crown of his prestigious family tree, one that no doubt stretched back four thousand years or more.

It calmed me to be in the presence of so much history, and I can see now that I handed a part of myself into his care the moment our eyes met.

As soon as I identified myself, he smiled. "Call me Vaasuki," he told me in Konkani, "though that, like the name your father gave you, is not my real name. For my safety and yours, I will never tell you that."

There was avuncular goodwill in the way he invited me to sit, his hand indicating a cane chair by a low bamboo table. He sat down opposite me, his posture erect. It did not seem to me that this man was capable of a false word or gesture, but I probably only wanted that to be true—who would wish to hand his whole future to a man hiding his motives?

While his servant brought us tea, Vaasuki made it clear with his bearing that we were to partake of this small ritual before we could speak about more pressing matters.

We were sitting in a large room amongst a forest of delicate palms and fleshy bushes in brightly painted ceramic vases. In a far corner was an altar to Lord Shiva, who was painted blue up to his neck. A banana tree dangled heart-shaped, blood-red flowers before the god, as if they would become offerings when they fell at his feet. A door at the back was open, and two tiny yellow finches had flown inside. The birds hopped across the branches of the small, willowy tree beside me, picking off seeds.

"The Pakló erect big stone walls wherever they go," Vaasuki said, using that local expression to refer to the Portuguese. *Pakló* meant feather-wearers, since the first colonizers to come to Goa were renowned for the plumes in their hats. He sipped his tea and encouraged me to do the same. "They don't mind killing birds so that they can make use of their colors, but they are frightened of having them in their homes. They need to keep outside and inside clearly separated."

The finches hopped to the ground and began foraging there. Warm air was coming in waves through the doorway. It made my skin tingle.

"I know this must be difficult for you," he said. "Maybe I should start by telling you a little about myself." He made a motion of blessing over me. "Don't worry. Although you are beginning to understand that this place is not a part of your world, I promise to send you safely home."

The servant refilled my teacup. Vaasuki told me he had been born near Panaji, a few miles west of the city of Goa, where the Mandavi River opened into a wide bay as it met the coast. By his own admission, he'd been a selfish young man. He'd spent all his free time gambling. He'd studied Ayurvedic medicine with a master from Delhi only because his father had ordered him to do so—and because Brahmins had lost the right to become Hindu priests inside Portuguese territory. He'd complained constantly about his destiny until the end of his apprenticeship, when he discovered that the Portuguese and other Europeans in Goa treated him with a respect not given other Indians. They even permitted him to be carried around in a palanquin.

"Have you always…always helped people like me to get poisons?" I asked in a whisper.

"No, but about a dozen years ago, a man came to me and asked me to visit a friend of his who was dying. When I reached the address in question, I found my father, pale and withered, sitting on a mat. I hadn't seen him in years. I'd resented him for many things, including—but not only—my choice of profession. My father had tricked me into coming to him because he knew I wouldn't have gone voluntarily to his home. We sat together and he told me he was trying to hide how ill he was, because if the Church found out, they'd make sure a priest visited him to give him the last rites. I realized I could either let him die as a false Christian or give him the death as a Hindu he desired. So you see, I do understand a little of what you are feeling. After I helped my father to die the way he wanted," he added with a smile, "riding three feet above the ground in a palanquin no longer seemed so important to me."

"But helping someone commit suicide is forbidden in Hinduism." My words came out as a criticism, so I quickly added, "At least, that is what I've been told."

"Imagine that you are in the desert, and you come upon a woman dying of thirst. Perhaps she is your sister or mother. Would it be a sin to give this woman water? Would it not be your duty even to give her your very blood?"

"But in that case, you would be enabling her to live."

"And that, Tiago, is *precisely* what my father told me after he'd taken the poison from me. 'My son, now I can continue in peace toward my end. You have saved my life.'"

*   *   *

As Vaasuki continued to tell me of his past, I grew exceedingly drowsy. I'd guess—given my host's profession—that his servant had poured a powder of valerian or henbane, or any one of a dozen other calming agents, into my teacup. Very likely he'd decided my agitation was putting us both at risk.

I woke to discover Vaasuki's hands in mine; he was helping me to stand up. I was startled but I felt much lighter than I'd been.

"Welcome back," he said, bowing his head in a friendly way.

"How long have I been asleep?"

"Just long enough." He laughed, patting my cheek gently.

He gave me water, then had me kneel down in front of Shiva. He spoke a prayer for us both and placed a tiny vial of ruby-colored glass in my palm.

"For now, you can keep it in your shoe," he told me. "But has your father explained where you must keep this when you visit him in prison?"

"Yes."

"Good. Ti, you'll be carrying your own death inside you, so be very careful."

At the door, the *pandito* apologized for having to help me in this way. "Your father will be missed," he said. "But I'm certain that his reincarnation will be a good one."

I held out all the silver coins I had for him and promised to get more, but he folded my fist around them and placed his hand on top of mine. "There's no need," he said.

"Thank you. . . . Vaasuki, on the tanner's door, my father wrote something about a path that leads beyond the Lord."

"Yes, I've seen it, of course."

"Do you know what that path is? Is it death?"

"That's what everyone thinks," he replied, smiling cagily.

"But it's not?"

"Where are we before we are born?"

"In our mother's womb."

"Yes, that's true enough." He nodded, amused, as though I'd given a child's answer. "But before that?"

I shrugged. "I don't know if we're anywhere."

He tapped his head, then mine. "Where does the *I* inside our mind come from? And why are you inside your head and not someone else's?"

"I don't know."

He patted my shoulder. "When you know the answer, you'll also learn where the path out of the Lord leads. But it's not important for now—that sign was not meant for a young man like you. Tiago, remember what my father told me. Hold tight to his words. And wish your father a good journey from me. Give him my blessings and thanks."

"I'm grateful to you," I said.

His eyes turned grave. "I wouldn't like to see you or any of your family back here. Take my advice: Leave Goa as soon as this is finished, and do not return."

*   *   *

When I reached home, Sofia and my family rushed to me.

"Papa is healthy and in good spirits, and he sends everyone his greetings," I told them, doing my best to sound cheerful.

"Thank God!" my sister said.

While my aunt had fresh clothes brought to me, I invented a story for them all—the one I, too, would have preferred: Papa was strong and well, and hadn't been tortured; he agreed with Isaac that a bribe was what the Inquisitors wanted, and he was certain that once they had it, he'd be released.

"Was he angry at me for not coming?" Isaac asked fearfully.

"No, of course, not. He thanks you for all your help."

"Were you able to give him the chicken?" Wadi asked.

"It was confiscated from me by guards. But he isn't eating badly."
I apologized to my aunt for forgetting her pot. I promised I would retrieve it the next day.

She brushed my arm sweetly. Apparently, even she could see what I'd been through. "It isn't important," she said.

After I'd answered all their questions, I confessed my exhaustion and asked if I might be excused. Sofia pushed me playfully up the stairs and helped me put on my nightshirt. She wouldn't leave me, so I had to keep the poison hidden in my shoe.

Lifting my covers away, she ordered me into bed. I saw the resemblance to my father in her lips, which seemed so thoughtful, and in the way she rubbed her temples with her thumb and fore-finger.

"Ti," she said in a timid voice, sitting down next to me, "the others may not have noticed, but I could see you were lying."

"I wasn't," I insisted.

She frowned, expecting greater loyalty from me. "Tell me the truth—you must."

I'd foreseen this possibility and had decided to admit a small lie so that she would believe the big one. "You mustn't tell anyone else—not even Wadi."

"I promise."

"It's just that Papa hasn't been eating well. He lives mostly on rice broth. His stomach has been aching, and he has become terribly thin. He was upset that I couldn't give him the chicken. He moaned when I told him it had been confiscated."

"Oh, Ti," she said, "I'm sure we can get some proper food to him if we keep trying! I'll ask Aunt Maria to talk to Father António first thing in the morning. I'm sure he'll help us. I'll make chapatti with dal. That will be easy on Papa's stomach."

"And I'll bring him mangoes." I smiled, wanting to bury myself deeper in this lie so that I would not be tempted to reveal greater truths to her.

The joy of being useful again made her jump to her feet.

"Yes, Papa will love that. You rest," she said eagerly, already look-ing off into her plans, "and I'll take care of everything."

*   *   *

The next day Father António assured my aunt and uncle that one of their gold rings had already been given to a man near the top of the Inquisitional hierarchy. The priest explained that he couldn't guar-antee anything in terms of concessions, but their gift had been ap-preciated—though they were, naturally enough, never to mention it to a soul. He also assured them that he'd requested that Papa be given fresh fish and fruit to eat, and never pork or squid, though he dared not mention that this was for religious reasons having to do with our kosher laws.

Wadi, Sofia, and I went to the Holy Office at midday, the three of us walking side by side, with my sister in the middle, as we had done when we were children. Since neither knew the truth about Papa, unspoken relief quickened all that they said to me that morning. It was as though we'd pieced together what had been broken between us. Wadi carried a wooden tray on which Sofia had put her pot of dal, a cup of rice pudding, and two mangoes.

A priest with dull gray eyes and sallow skin the color of ancient wax answered our knocks at the door of the Holy Office. He repulsed me, which made it easier to beg, as though it was only right that the last vestiges of my pride be trampled. A thin, fraying tone entered my voice as soon as I requested that he have our food brought to Papa. After his initial refusal, which was rude and harsh, I tried to reach the core of solidarity that must, I was still sure, be present in all men to differing degrees—after all, we can see through each other's eyes easily enough, anytime we want. I told him of our worry for our father's health, but, seeing his distant expression, I began to speak like a boy forced to play cards with an experienced gambler—fumbling his words, knowing he is about to lose everything.

My humiliation soon infected Sofia and prompted her to kneel. "Father, I know that Christ is compassion, and because of all He suffered I believe that God will permit you to help us," she told the man, her voice so clear and sure that I realized she'd practiced this speech. "I have been told that His compassion extends to those who do not even deserve it. And I think we must imitate Him in all we do so that ... so that His sacrifice can be made good. Or what does any of what He said and did really mean?"

If this world were one of justice and magic, her eloquence would have shattered every lock in every cell and given all the miserable prisoners wings to fly home. But the world is what it is and the rusted metal remained where it was—listening unperturbed to our pleas.

Faith is useless ornamentation and has no place in here, I could hear the barren stone of the walls saying to us.

The priest might have heard something similar spoken by the ground on which he stood; he gazed at my sister down the length of his nose as if she were a mad little urchin, then signaled with a flick of his wrist for one of the guards to usher us out.

He was already walking away when Wadi set his tray down on the floor. "Your Excellency, come back," he called. "Please, you must help us. . . ."

But the priest never looked back.

*   *   *

On the way home, Sofia and I spoke in hushed tones about needing to wait for Uncle Isaac's bribe to have its effect, trying to encourage each other. Wadi said nothing, his jaw clenched angrily. Suddenly the tray he carried crashed to the ground and he reached out a straining hand to me.

"Tiger, the air is burning!" he shouted.

"Hold on," I told him. "Sofia, grab his arms while I get behind him."

Before she could reach him, his eyes rolled back in his head and his knees buckled. I managed to break his fall, but he landed hard on his left hip, with his wrist pinned behind his back.

He writhed as though he were being flayed. I held his head, and Sofia tried to secure his feet, but he kicked her on the shoulder so hard that she toppled backward.

"Try again!" I ordered, and this time her movements were quick and strong.

By now, a gawking crowd had gathered, and I overheard several Portuguese women say that he'd been bewitched. If Aunt Maria found out about him having a fit in public, she'd make us all pay.

"What's wrong with him?" a donkey-faced merchant in a long red cape asked me in horror. I did not reply.

Wadi was tossed around in his own violent world for minutes. After he'd calmed, Sofia caressed his sweat-soaked hair, then dashed off for some water. He winced when I touched his left wrist; it was already swelling up.

"I'm sorry," he murmured mournfully. "This was the last thing we needed."

"You didn't do it on purpose. Just rest."

"I'm sorry . . . so sorry . . ."

"It's the least of our worries."

Sitting with Wadi's head in my lap, waiting for my sister to return, I let myself fall gratefully into the gravity of long-gone memories. The closer I got to the present time, however, the more my life began to seem unreal, as though the river we'd all been riding on did not lead to the sea, as all waters should, but to a high mountain that could never be scaled—to my father's death and all that would never come to pass because of it. I had to keep my distance from Wadi—that was the message of my memories. Perhaps he was the one responsible for Papa's imprisonment.

"Take me somewhere I can't be seen, Tiger," my cousin implored me. "I don't want to be seen like this. I don't think I could bear one of my mother's lectures today."

"As soon as Sofia gets back, we'll go."

"I wish we could return in time to when you last came to Goa. I'd tell your father to go back home and never come back here. I'd do anything to undo what's happened."

"I know you would," I lied.

Did he so deeply regret having denounced my father that he needed to make up for it now?

Sofia returned and lifted an earthenware jar of water to Wadi's lips. He gulped at it like a wolf, then let us lift him to his feet.

"I'm sorry, Sofia," he said.

"Ssshhhh. We need to get you home," she told him.

We lumbered through the crowd. Not a single person asked after

Wadi's well-being. *I can understand why Papa wants to leave this monstrous world behind,* I told myself, and yet a deeper truth revealed itself right away:

Even a tortured prisoner knows that the world is beautiful, and he longs to choose his moment of death precisely so he can give that beauty the end it deserves. To him, as to all of us, it makes no difference whether the sun and sea and stars—or men and women—are able to ease our pain. We are fragile beings, and life is good, and we suffer endlessly, just as the Buddha said. That was the saddest and most obvious thing in the world to me as we made our way home.

*   *   *

I sat up in bed through most of that night, thoughts of my father hidden away in my chest, where only my heartbeat would know of their existence. Exhaustion slowly spread through me until I felt the calm of being forsaken. *I can rely only on myself now,* I thought, and I was glad of it because I was now free of illusions.

I awoke before dawn. Uncle Isaac was feeling guilty about leaving home to supervise work at his warehouses, but I assured him that he had no choice but to check on shipments leaving that afternoon for Lisbon—that it was what his brother would want. In his eyes, I saw he was eager to get away from Aunt Maria, with whom he was plainly still quarreling.

"We cannot give in to despair while we wait for Papa," I told him.

He looked at me hard. "You've become a man these past weeks," he said, but his tone was somber.

Sofia made two huge plates of potato bhaji—one for Papa and the other for the mean-spirited priest who'd refused us the day before.

"I won't give up," she declared to all of us.

Wadi carried the steaming plates for her to the Holy Office. I didn't accompany them, and instead sat in my room by the open window, feeling the moist breeze playing over my hair as if it were the caress of my coming crime. I knew I was to be called today to visit my father and began juggling strategies for how to convince him to refrain from employing the poison. When Sofia returned near noon, she and Wadi told me excitedly that a different priest—one showing a benevolent smile—had allowed them to leave their food with him, promising to get it to my father.

Later that day, a barefoot boy came to the door with a letter from Tejal. Sofia, Wadi, and Aunt Maria were at the marketplace, and my uncle was still at work. The little courier—Tejal's cousin Jai—had walked all the way from Benali, though he was only eleven years old.

I pray that your father is home now, Tejal wrote to me. *I am with my parents, and our baby is growing safely inside me. I beg you to join me as soon as you can. Bring books you can read to me and, if possible, have your father choose them. Send word with Jai. Love, Tejal.*

I gave Jai a brief note for her and a book of Samuel Ha-Levi's poetry. I also sent him off with a small sack of coconut biscuits, which made him dash off down the street, elbows flying, as though to get them to a secret hiding place before anyone asked him to share them.

At the end of the afternoon, Sofia raced up the stairs and threw open my door.

"You're being summoned to the Holy Office!" she announced. "Maybe they're going to send Papa home with you."

I acted surprised, and even did my best to smile, but she instantly noticed something in my face.

"You think it's bad news, don't you?" she asked hesitantly, her voice breaking, as though she feared I was about to tell her that our father was already dead.

"I just don't trust them," I answered. "Though I'm sure the bribe has worked. It's only a matter of time now."

Her face brightened again. I was astonished by how easy it was to lift her spirits. Maybe she had invested too much in a happy ending to believe that anything else might happen.

*　　*　　*

I found my father in much worse physical shape, his right eye swollen shut and the rope marks on his neck red with infection, as if worms had burrowed under his skin. His hands were shaking, and he smelled like a rotting animal.

When I stepped into his cell, he clung to me, the heat of fever radiating from him.

Behind us, the iron door banged closed.

"Have you brought it?" he whispered into my ear.

I nodded. I felt light-headed, as though I might faint.

"Bless you, Ti."

He knelt to peer through the grill in the door to make sure we weren't being watched. When he stood again, he held out his hand, his fingers straining, his eyes on fire, as though this was the most important moment he'd ever lived.

He snatched the vial from me like a thief and began to cry silently.

"Oh, Papa," I moaned.

"Everything is all right now," he kept repeating, brushing my hair, kissing my cheeks. His strength came back to him, and when he held me it was with sure hands. "You and I have foiled their plans," he whispered, coughing from his excitement.

He dropped his trousers and wiggled like a duck shaking water from its tail, trying to make me smile. Then he put the vial where no one would find it and turned in a circle, his arms out, doing a slow dance of triumph. "Don't worry," he told me, "I'm not mad. I'm just happy—so happy to have you here with me at this moment. Ti, you've saved so many lives. God bless you always."

"Then you haven't given them any names...."

"No, and now I never will."

We sat together on his cot.

"You know what I'd like now?" he asked, tapping the top of my head playfully.

"No, what?"

"Nupi's tamarind custard." He licked his lips and pretended to swoon.

"Did you get the food we left you?"

He shook his head.

"Sofia made you potato bhaji."

"Thank her for me. Tell me, has Wadi been good to her?"

"Yes, I think he regrets his betrayals now. I think they'll be happy together."

I didn't know if that was true, but I couldn't let Papa worry about her.

"Wonderful. Give them both my blessings. That's important. Will you do that for me?"

He held my hand to his cheek as I agreed.

"Papa, you're burning with fever," I said.

"It makes no difference now. Ti, I will take the poison two days from now. No one will suspect it was you." He made a throwing motion toward the window. "I will get rid of the vial, and you must never admit you brought it to me. Not while anyone in our family lives within reach of the Inquisition. Do you understand me?"

"I'll never tell a soul."

"Good boy."

"Papa . . . Are you sure you have to do this?"

"They almost broke me this last time. With the funnel in my mouth and a rope around my neck, I might say anything. Believe me, there is no other way. Now let's not waste any more time over this. Tell me about Tejal and my grandchild."

"But Papa, we have to talk more about—"

He held a finger to his lips. "How is Tejal?"

"I've received word that she's returned to her village. She wants me to visit her there."

"As soon as you leave here, go to her, son. And stay there. Don't come back to Goa even when you hear . . . you hear what's happened. Stay with her. And when you go back to our farm—"

"But…but afterward, after you…the…" I could not bring myself to say the word.

"There will be no funeral. I'll be buried here without a ceremony."

"But this is not holy ground. I can't leave you here."

"They bury all dead prisoners here, but my body is of no importance." He wiped my tears with his thumbs. "You know that."

"But your soul may wander the Lower Realms forever if we don't—"

"That's superstitious nonsense. My soul will be back with God by the time the Inquisitors find my body." He made his hands into flapping wings. "They won't be able to catch me. Ti, sometimes I think we ought to simply do what the Zoroastrians do and leave the body on a tower and let the vultures pick it clean—much more sensible."

"Papa, don't talk like that! I can't bear—"

"I'm sorry, I'm sorry to talk so stupidly. Ssshhhhhh."

He rocked me in his arms and began to talk of when I was a baby. Far too soon, the door opened and a guard stepped inside. A priest stood behind him.

"We haven't had enough time," Papa said angrily.

"Your son has to go," the guard told him.

"I won't!" I shouted.

"Regret nothing that has ever come to pass between us, Ti," Papa said in Konkani, then kissed my lips. "I'll always be with you. And I love you more than anything."

It was as though my heart were exploding. I vowed not to stand up. I would stay with Papa and die with him.

The guard gripped my arm. "Get up!" he shouted, tugging me to my feet.

"Ti, look at me!" Papa exclaimed. "Go to the Sultan with Sofia," he told me. "The Sultan will take care of you. Years ago, he promised me he would do that, and he is not a man to go back on his word."

"Papa," I replied, "I won't leave you."

"You must. I'm expecting you to take care of yourself now. You must make a good life for that grandchild of mine!"

I berated the guard and the priest as they dragged me out of the cell. I didn't stop shouting even when I was out on the street and gazing at the closed doors through which no prisoner ever left without accepting Christ as his savior.

*　　　*　　　*

For two days I told myself that Papa would not take the poison. But late on the third morning, Father António came to our home and informed us glumly that Papa was dead. It was the fourth of November 1591. In the quiet of my heart, so far down that even my sister's wailing came from a distant place, I thought: *We will not be able to go on with our lives....*

If there were any justice, my screams would have ripped up the cobbles from all the streets in Goa, and sent the houses crashing to the ground. What right had the world to be so indifferent to our fate?

Wadi was very gentle with both me and Sofia, but Aunt Maria, kneeling before my sister, soon said something that made me believe that even if she wasn't responsible for Papa's death she didn't regret it.

"You'll forget this terrible moment someday. I'll help you forget. We'll all help."

"Shut up!" I shouted, all of me on fire. "*I* won't help. Why would we want to forget the moment we learned of our father's death? You can only speak this way because you despised him for living openly as a Jew!"

*　　　*　　　*

Wadi and Uncle Isaac went to the Holy Office to try to recover my father's body. Papa had told me that this would not be possible, and he was proved right, so the time had come for me to carry out his last wishes. I went upstairs to speak to Sofia, asking Aunt Maria if I could be alone with her. My sister had not spoken or eaten since we'd learned of Papa's death. Her eyes were open but were staring at nothing; she'd fled deep inside herself.

Once my aunt was gone, I sat by Sofia's side and gripped her hand. "I'm going to go now, Sofia. I'm going to stay in Tejal's village for a few days. Can you hear me?" She blinked once. "I need to see Tejal or I won't survive this. I'll be back within a week. Will you be all right without me?"

She closed her eyes, which I took as silent condemnation.

"Sofia, I wish you wouldn't leave me all alone like this. I need you. Do you understand what I'm saying? Do you want to come with me? We'll leave together. We don't ever have to come back."

She wouldn't look at me. I felt abandoned and miserable. "I'm going," I said. "When I return, we'll have a long talk, but I won't stay another night in Goa. I'll take you home and then we'll go visit the Sultan. Unless...unless you decide to stay with Wadi and marry him right away. You know you had Papa's blessing before he died, though I think you ought to come back home for a few days—if for nothing else, then to reassure Nupi that you are..." I was about to say *well*, but it would be many years before we could say that. "To re-assure her that you are going to recover," I ended.

I almost sat down to try to coax her to look at me, but I knew that if I did so I'd be tempted to remain with her. Remembering how Papa had urged me to take care of myself and my future, I closed the door gently on the way out.

*   *   *

The dog was big and shaggy, its eyes black beads inside a wooly mass of chestnut-brown fur. I had just turned a corner to make my way toward the southern gates of the city when I nearly fell over him. A little boy wearing a wide-brimmed hat made of rushes called him away.

"*Vem, Carlito!*" he shouted. "Come here, Carlito!"

As I straightened my pouch over my shoulder, a man identifying himself as a city bailiff came to me and asked for my name. When I told him, he informed me that I was under arrest. He'd been waiting hours for me, he said. He'd decided not to arrest me at the house so as not to embarrass my uncle.

Maybe I was held back from running by my sense of being trapped by the world itself. Or by my need to see Sofia again.

Or had my desire to confront my father's persecutors already blinded me to the peril I faced?

Perhaps it was a mixture of all of those reasons, but I sometimes think that a vengeful part of me—a thief of souls I didn't yet know anything about—was already standing behind a door in my mind, waiting and plotting for a chance to finish what a traitor against my family had begun.

CHAPTER 18

On the afternoon of January 17, 1594, more than two years after my arrest and a little over a month after the Act of Faith at which Phanishwar was turned to smoke, rusty irons weighted with the lives of dozens of men broken before me were fastened to my ankles, and I was led to the sailing ship that would take me to prison in Lisbon. I had turned twenty-one only three days before.

Once we were on deck, Captain Martins, a cruelly handsome silver-haired man with sun-wrinkled skin, was obliged by a priest to swear on a Missal that he would faithfully deliver me to the Inquisition. In his sneering voice, it was easy to hear that the Captain didn't like being given orders by a man with no dirt under his fingernails.

A barefoot crewman who spoke only rudimentary Portuguese put me in a storeroom with four man-sized barrels of wine. He handed me a bowl of water, two crusts of bread, and a knot of smelly old cheese. When he locked the door, I feared I'd spend the whole voyage trapped in that airless dark, but early the next morning, as we made our way downriver, the Captain had me brought on deck. Once we were out of sight of the city, he had my chains removed. Tears seeped into my eyes when the last links thudded onto the deck, but my gratitude only incensed Martins.

"If I find you making a nuisance of yourself, I'll have you whipped till your New Christian hide is running with blood!" he told me.

Clinging to the rail that first day, with the salt wind blowing against my face and the endless sea lifting the ship up toward the sky, even his contempt could not harm me. I felt that if I could see the sun, I'd be able to resist my destiny. Yet with the descent of dusk, a dread lodged deep within me. The darkening horizon reminded me of the finality of my departure from India and seemed to call me toward inevitable ruin. I wouldn't have the strength to last six years in another prison cell. Not with Papa dead.

After supper, a young member of the crew showed me my cot. He gave me an orange from his personal stash before leaving me. With the deck guarding me from above, peeling the fruit with my chipped and dirty fingernails, I felt more secure. After nearly two years in an eight-by-ten-foot room, I clearly needed to have walls and a ceiling around me.

Over those first few days, whenever I tried to recall the sequence of events in my life, I realized that incarceration had badly damaged my mind; it took me days to remember the names of villagers I'd known since I was a boy, and some of the key moments in my life—even my mother's death—seemed to have been lived by a distant ancestor. If I were to look in a mirror, I was sure I'd see a man I wouldn't recognize—too thin even to have a real shadow, too hesitant and fragile, with scars on his wrists where his soul had tried to flee.

At first I feared to be heading so far from home, as though I might simply vanish, but after a week at sea I began to believe I'd been given a unique opportunity. I'd soon be on another continent, far from anyone who had expectations of me. I didn't have to reveal the truth about myself or my life to anyone.

I could remake myself as someone new.

*   *   *

Taking meals with the crew, I couldn't avoid saying a few words on occasion, if only about the slack winds or flying fish, or the exuberant dolphins that played sometimes alongside the ship, and I soon befriended a seventeen-year-old deckhand from a small town called Tavira named José, who had been enchanted by India and who was eager to hear my stories of a childhood spent in the countryside. I spoke of frogs in slippers and a hornbill named Sujay, but I never once broached the subject of my father's death, or my own imprisonment, and José never asked me why I was being sent to Lisbon. Our friendship skated across the surface of things—as seemed right, for I knew I couldn't risk anything more than that.

If I'd told him that I was still alive only so that I could find who'd betrayed my father and end that person's life, would he have even believed me?

I learned from José that he and most of the other sailors were born to destitute parents, or had no family at all, and that they signed up for service to the Crown when they were just boys. Aside from the Captain and myself, he was the only one aboard who could read and write; he'd had the luck of being taught at his orphanage by a Franciscan monk who'd taken a vow to educate the poor.

José, God keep him safe wherever he is now, lent me two of his prized books without even my asking: the *Lusíadas* by Luís de Camões and the New Testament, both presents from his beloved teacher.

Placing my cheek up against those pages and sniffing the musty scent of fish glue and paper was like falling into my father's embrace. I liked to read in my cot by the light of a single candle while the others were on deck, hearing their footsteps above me as though they were gods in heaven. Over the coming weeks, I memorized all I could of the Gospels, testing myself by reciting when alone on deck. "There are many dwelling-places in my Father's house," John wrote in his Gospel, and I built many rooms in my mind for keeping my quotations safe for later use.

Aboard the *Santa Cecilia,* I often thought of Papa and of Phanishwar, of course, and always with a sense of having failed them both, but the ghosts who haunted me every morning and night were Sofia and Tejal. It tormented me that I hadn't caught even a glimpse of them at the Act of Faith.

In my daydreams, I saw Aunt Maria and Wadi standing over my father's unmarked grave. One of them must have been overjoyed by the news that I would be gone for at least six years, but which? Or were both of them responsible for all that had befallen my family?

*   *   *

After traveling south for six weeks and circling Africa at the Cape of Good Hope, we sailed northwest and arrived at São Salvador, the capital of Brazil, four months later, on the twelfth of May. I was locked up in a public prison. In the yard below my barred window, cragged-faced vultures picked night and day at discarded refuse as though scavaging for lost treasure. I gave them affectionate names like Comilão and Barrigudo—Overeater and Big Belly—since watching their squabbles over scraps eased my boredom.

I asked for a pen and ink right away, so that I might write to my family and to Tejal, but my guard said it was against the rules. So, too, were books.

Women, apparently, were not, and my guard told me that for a silver *tostão* he would bring me an African or mulatta—or even a native Brazilian with red paint around her eyes and on her breasts. He spoke of what marvels such exotic women could do for me in a way sure to arouse my interest, but even if I'd wanted their company, I hadn't a single copper coin to my name.

*   *   *

One morning, about three weeks after my arrival in Brazil, a young man with a yellowish complexion and thick black hair like a horse's mane conducted me high up into the verdant hills above the city, to a coral-colored mansion belonging to a gnarled old man with a gentle face named Afonso Gil Pereira da Silva, who told me over a glass of wine that I'd be working for him until my ship left for Portugal. As for when that might be, da Silva wasn't sure, but it could take months, he explained.

Dom Afonso, as he liked to be called, was the owner of twenty thousand hectares of sugar-cane plantations, and he needed an assistant to read his correspondence and write his replies, as his eyesight was failing miserably. I was to be given my own desk in an upstairs office and to be paid a small weekly wage, but I'd still have to sleep nights in my cell. I'd have Sundays off to roam about the city without even a guard.

"And you can have all the sugar you can eat!" the old man told me, as though it were a prize fit for a king.

Which maybe it was, for what won me to my new benefactor right away were the coconut cakes his personal slave brought to us. That first day with Dom Afonso, I ate until my belly was sore, which made him laugh affectionately. The plantation owner seemed inordinately pleased to have contracted me, though I didn't yet suspect why.

The wealthy residents of São Salvador never traveled about in palanquins, as they did in Goa, or even on horseback, but in hammocks tied to poles and carried by African slaves. Dom Afonso went everywhere in a ruby-red one fringed with hundreds of glittering amethysts embroidered into the fabric, and he dressed me in an emerald-green brocade doublet and puffy crimson trousers, so that I must have looked to his foremen and slaves like a parrot. He had me walk alongside him as he inspected his properties; armed with my paper and pen, I took down page after page of his flowery Portuguese. A taciturn slave of fourteen named Melaço—Portuguese for "molasses"—held my inkstand, cupping it in his hands as though it contained a magic potion.

On occasion, Dom Afonso even took me to dinner parties, where I was made to taste all his food, since he feared poisoning, and carry out his every whim. I overheard two gentlemen joking that I even held his member when he peed, which they found extremely amusing.

The countryside around São Salvador was lush and hilly, full of palms and fruit trees, and the white-sand beaches were as resplendent as those of India. Brazil was a wondrous and beautiful land, but it reminded me too much of home, and I grew to hate it.

*   *   *

As soon as I was shown my desk, I spent hours composing letters to my family and Nupi. It was hard to find the right tone to adopt with my sister, and to know how to refer to the treachery that had cost our father his life, since Aunt Maria, Wadi, or maybe even Uncle Isaac had testified against both him and me and given my great-grandfather Berekiah Zarco's manuscript to our enemies. I thought I might be putting Sofia at risk if I were to write of my suspicions: I had little doubt she'd show my letter to Wadi, even if I begged her not to. Bitterness and grief cramped my first few attempts, and then anger. When Dom Afonso left me alone, I locked myself in my office and ripped to shreds the clothing I'd worn on the trip from India, wanting to destroy the boy I'd been, screaming to heaven that I'd kill whoever had denounced Papa to the Inquisition.

I finally realized that the most important thing was to convince Sofia to make the best life she could and to forget about me until I returned. After describing to her my new employment, and asking her to offer help to Tejal, I ended my first letter by mentioning our unfortunate destiny only briefly:

> I'm sure you're unable to sleep at times wondering how Papa could've ended up in prison, and maybe you even blame yourself for not shielding him from harm, but you are to put all that behind you until I return. Make a good life with Wadi. Don't

think about me too often. What took place must remain a mystery for now. It will be hard to be patient, but it's our only option. Later, when I'm closer to serving out my sentence, I'll ask Uncle Isaac to work toward having my banishment order lifted so that I can return to you. When we're together again, we'll do our best to start over.

To end, I quoted Luke, thinking of my own need to be patient: "He gives orders to the unclean spirits with authority and power, and they must depart."

In my first letter to Tejal, I asked that she wait for me and pledged my devotion to her. I begged her to send news of our child. I ended by suggesting she go to my uncle if she needed any assistance, but only when my aunt was sure to be away. I sent a dried wildflower along, as I had so many times in India.

I wrote to Tejal and to my family twice a month from that point on, sending descriptions of the city and of my small adventures with Dom Afonso, since there seemed no point in bringing up more unpleasant matters. I did not expect to receive any replies, since we were months by ship from Goa. When none arrived, however, I couldn't help feeling a disappointment that made me sluggish and mean-spirited. I'd asked for Sofia and Tejal to write to me at the Galé Prison in Lisbon, and I hoped I'd find their letters waiting for me there in a few months.

*   *   *

Just before my departure from Brazil in August, I overheard Dom Afonso explaining my circumstances to a merchant dealing in exotic furs who'd recently come from Lisbon. Among other things, the plantation owner claimed that I was the eldest son of a rich nobleman who collected port duties in Goa for the king. Everything made sense then: Captain Martins must have told Dom Afonso I was from an important family, and the old man believed employing me was a way to increase his standing in the city. All the time we had been together he'd been showing me off as a trophy!

I also discovered in the same conversation that the Captain was keeping all of my salary, and that he was being paid only half the going rate—proof, I suppose, that things are hardly ever what they seem in this earthly life. And that most people prefer it that way.

*   *   *

We arrived in Lisbon on November 11, 1594, after another three months at sea and a brief stopover on the island of Terceira in the mid-Atlantic. Of those first days in Portugal, I mostly remember the cold rains and winds. I felt as though my bones were made of frozen glass.

After one night in a cell at the Inquisitorial Palace on Lisbon's main square, I was brought to the Galé Prison, on the banks of the Tagus River about a mile from the port. A barber shaved my face and head, and I was chained to the leg of an elderly New Christian from Santarém by the name of Manuel Lopes. He had sickly skin—the color of ash—and a deep stoop from having been recently tortured. He refused to look at me or say anything at all. Later, another prisoner told me that while being strung up by his wrists Manuel had named his wife and children as secret Jews. In that way, he'd saved himself from being burned to death, but his family was now rotting in the bowels of an Inquisitional dungeon.

I've met many miserable men, but Manuel was the only one whose spirit had been utterly extinguished. Even today, I don't know how he continued to live.

I asked immediately for my letters but was told that none had arrived. I suspected they were being held back from me, but I elicited only threats when I begged the guards. "Even Jesus was given the scroll of Isaiah," I told them, but they obviously didn't care much about their own savior and gave me a beating.

Along with about two hundred other prisoners, Manuel and I

were marched to the shipyards that first day of my new life and set to work as stevedores, which was to be my lot for the duration of my sentence. From sunup to sundown we unloaded dried fruit, sugar, cotton cloth, spices, wood, and whatever else could be sent for a profit from the colonies, and were also given menial tasks, such as collecting stones for ballast, repairing netting, and cleaning gorse for rope-making. A score of African slaves being punished for trying to escape from their masters were kept apart from us. At the slightest whimper, these pitiful wretches were flogged with a knotted cord. Also working separately were half a dozen Moors who'd been captured in a naval battle off the coast of Morocco. During my third month of labor, I saw a Moslem stabbed with a dagger in his right cheek by a guard for refusing to jump into the Tagus River to recover a basket that had fallen overboard. In a thick Arabic accent, the poor man swore he couldn't swim, but that was apparently not considered a valid excuse.

We slept on pallets in a dank dormitory—common criminals and men transferred from the Inquisition together—and were each given a loose-fitting blue shirt and cap, as well as an overcoat of thick gray wool, which doubled as a blanket at night. We could eat as much as we liked of a kind of black biscuit that was so hard that the men called it *tijolo esmagado,* crushed brick. Salt meat and fava beans were given us sparingly. I fantasized about mangoes, and sometimes smelled Nupi's vindaloo in my sleep.

On Sundays, we went to Mass at the prison chapel. I quoted the Evangelists so well by now that I was thought of by one and all as a pious convert. The elderly priest, Father Pedro, had me assist him in services, and it became my duty to light all the tapers, since he could no longer climb a ladder. He was a wonderful man who often tried to make me laugh, but his clowning only reminded me of my father.

I was ill most of that winter, and often had shivering fevers from the miserably cold weather, but by March, when the sun began to linger longer over the city, I felt my strength returning. Subtracting the time I'd spent at sea and in São Salvador with Dom Afonso, I now had a little less than five years to go on my sentence.

*   *   *

I'm sure Papa would have wanted me to ennoble myself through labor over the coming years, to make the most of my contact with the
other prisoners, but instead, I hoarded my bitterness and rage like a
youthful Midas, lying on my back on my cot and holding them up
to the light so that I could see their shape and luster, polishing them
when alone, always impressed by their purposeful radiance.

I soon came to understand that whoever had betrayed my father
to the Inquisition must have been plotting against him for months;
to be sure of success, this traitor would have considered it essential to
note down all the instances of Papa's heresy, no matter how small the
infraction. Furthermore, he or she would have had to plan extremely
carefully in order to steal my great-grandfather's manuscript at just
the right moment and smuggle it off our farm without being caught.

The Inquisitors who received that valuable old text would have
had to mount a thorough investigation of my father in order to
build a solid case against him. Even if Papa's secret enemy supplied
these priests with the names of possible witnesses—and even if he or
she offered bribes to these witnesses to induce them to testify against
my father—the process of accumulating testimonies would have
taken several weeks at the very least.

I came to believe as well, that Wadi and Aunt Maria were the
only people I knew who were devious enough to instigate such a
conspiracy—and the only ones who might have disliked my father
enough to scheme against him for months.

It was this willful premeditation that made their crime seem so
evil to me and which, in the end, turned my fantasies to the cruelest
forms of murder.

Over and over, I locked my aunt and cousin in a dungeon and
starved them until they both confessed to having stolen my great-
grandfather's manuscript in order to destroy Papa. As for Father
Carlos Miguel Fonseca, whom I despised with almost equal passion,
I lured him into the torture chamber in my mind with deception,

just as he had tricked Phanishwar out of his life. Then I broke him with ropes and pulleys.

All the tens of thousands of crates I lifted and carts of merchandise I dragged came to be infused with my murderous fantasies against Wadi, Aunt Maria, and the Inquisitors, and these fantasies, in turn, strengthened my muscles and my will. Would it be an exaggeration to say they refashioned me as something new and better?

Giving free rein to my hatred gave me back a purpose in life, and yet, over my first few months in Lisbon I sometimes struggled against my darker emotions—like an opium addict spurning the soothing scent of his pipe. Sometimes I let my frustration get the best of me and wound up in fights with other men. Once, feeling the urgent need to make an error that could never be taken back, I seized a plank of wood and drove it straight into the face of a robber from Coimbra who tried to steal my cape, breaking his cheekbone. As for the scar on my right ear in the shape of a C, it was made by the thumbnail of a murderer from Bragança who didn't appreciate my telling him not to spit near me. He jumped on me while I was unloading salt cod, but I succeeded in throwing him off and into the river before he could leave more scars on my face.

Once I accepted my exile from India and my destiny, I began to understand the utility of forming alliances in prison, and I befriended some of the men. Even the more swaggering and brutish among them grew to understand I'd never give up in a fight and tended to stay away from me.

One of the prisoners I befriended was an Oxford-educated minister of the Anglican Church named Benedict Gray, who was to later write so eloquently about his prison experiences in a volume published in London in 1602 and entitled, *A Brief Narrative of the Lisbon Inquisition*. I'm told the book has sold very well and can now be found in many a library in Britain.

I came to study English with Benedict Gray every evening, since I now believed that knowing another European language could prove useful, and that having a friend in a country free of Catholicism could also one day be a great advantage to me.

In discussing his views on Christianity, Benedict told me that King Henry VIII had forbidden Papists, as the Anglicans called Roman Catholics, from worshiping in England. The minister even believed that the Pope was an anti-Christ whose aim was to lure men and women away from the Messiah's true message of compassion.

I told him and the others that I was the adopted son of an exporter of fabrics. I had no siblings. I'd excelled at Latin and archery at my Jesuit school in Goa.

Did they believe me? I didn't care; it made me feel safe to steal another man's past, and next to that their opinions of me were less important even than the dust from Portugal's colonies in India, Africa, and Brazil that I shook off my tattered clothes every evening. My need to hunt down my father's murderer crouched behind all the pious words and friendly lies I uttered in public.

*   *   *

No letters from Sofia, Tejal, or my aunt and uncle reached me. I began to write to them on the last Sunday of each month, since on our day of rest a sweet-faced old nun named Maria Madalena would come to the prison with a pen and paper, taking down in her very precise script what each man wished to say to his family. Sister Maria Madalena soon learned that I could write for myself and, pushing a reed pen into my hand, insisted that I never give up hope of a response.

When still no news arrived from home, however, I stopped taking advantage of her visits, thinking the situation hopeless. I guessed that any letters I did receive were still being confiscated.

Late in my third year in Lisbon, a New Christian merchant named Marcos Severino Pereira started distributing alms to prisoners. On giving me a thick woolen blanket, his chestnut-brown eyes showed such compassion that I impulsively asked him if I might tell my family to write to me care of him. At first, fidgeting with the key chain attached to his doublet, he stammered an excuse about having to be away from Lisbon for several months. He clearly feared—despite my reputation—that I was still a heretic, but when I assured him that I was only desperate to get news of my sister, he agreed, reserving the right to read my correspondence.

A first letter arrived at his home from my uncle several months later, nearly four years after my arrival in Lisbon. On seeing Isaac's looping handwriting, so like my father's, I grew dizzy and my hands began to tremble. All the time I'd spent away from India was reduced to nothing. As I read his letter, I floated beyond myself, to a place where his words were whispered endearments.

It was very clever of you to ask Senhor Pereira for help, he wrote. *I have every hope that these words of mine will finally reach you. I send you all my fondness and all my love.* He then gave me the news I craved most: *Your banishment order has been lifted. So you are free to return to us as soon as you have served out your term. I will have ample funds transferred to you care of Senhor Pereira, so that you may make the voyage back without having to labor further.*

My uncle also wrote that Wadi had taken over much of his work in Goa. Isaac himself was spending the greater part of his time in Damão and Diu, small Portuguese colonies in India, where he was hoping to establish greater trade links. In between the lines, I read that his marriage to my aunt was all but finished.

About my sister and my future bride, he only wrote one line: *Sofia misses you terribly, and I have had news recently from Tejal that she is doing well.*

Maybe he said no more than that because they intended to write to me separately, but nothing they sent ever reached me. Given so little information, my mind soon rushed off into fantasies of misfortunes they might have suffered and which my uncle was keeping from me. I asked him in subsequent letters to tell me all about them, and to beg them to write to me directly, but he never told me more than that they were doing fine.

He said nothing at all about my child, even though I'd written to him about Tejal being pregnant at the time of my arrest. Had the baby been stillborn? That became my biggest fear, and I worried that if our child was dead, Tejal might have been obliged by her parents to marry someone else. I began to understand that a world I wouldn't recognize awaited me in India. I tried to ready myself for the worst, but I had learned only too well that preparations are of little use in matters of the heart.

*   *   *

Benedict Gray was released shortly after I began receiving letters from my uncle. Just before our final farewell, while we were carrying ballast stones onto a ship bound for Brazil, the Englishman handed me a piece of paper on which he'd written his address. After reading it quickly, I tossed the scrap into the river.

"Why'd you do that?" he asked with a shocked expression.

"I don't want any evidence my enemies can find. Don't worry, I won't forget where you live." I then asked if he would receive letters for me in Oxford and post them to Senhor Pereira.

"But why? It'll take many extra weeks for them to reach you from Oxford."

"It's better you don't know," I answered.

He smiled cagily at that. " 'Be on your guard against the leaven of the Pharisees and Sadducees,' " he quoted from Matthew 16.

Was he warning me against falling into the hands of the Inquisition again? Or of living out my own secret wishes? I never dared ask.

"If you do this for me," I warned him instead, "you can never return to Portugal, since what I write and receive may put you in danger."

His eyes shone with the fire of his contempt for Papists.

"I'll do whatever you ask," he assured me.

"The name on the letters for me will be James Matthews," I told him. "You must never admit to anyone where you send them or Senhor Pereira will be in danger."

"I shall be silence itself," Benedict swore, extending his hand, which I held tightly in both of mine, knowing we would never meet again.

*   *   *

Letters came only infrequently from Isaac over my last years in prison. In little hints my uncle dropped, I began to understand that he was not in good health, and only upon my insistence did he write me that Tejal had given birth to a boy named Kama. The name made me smile, since Kama was the mischief-making Hindu god of love—the equivalent of Cupid. Both my son and his mother were living in Benali, and both were in good health. I asked why Tejal didn't write to me, but Isaac never answered that question. Life had probably been a struggle for her since my departure. By now, she might have felt nothing but resentment for me, and my uncle wished to spare me that knowledge.

Kama . . . I pictured him as a blue-eyed little boy with Tejal's dark hair, shooting arrows of passion into the villagers. I allowed myself to believe that if he was well, then I would be, too.

Uncle Isaac wrote that he knew nothing of Nupi's whereabouts. He feared she blamed herself for what had happened and was begging in some far-off city as penance.

I spent much of my time alone brooding about how to approach Tejal after I returned. Silly how the mind grabs on to a solution that later seems absurd; I came to fantasize that I'd rescue Nupi from her state of self-reproaching desolation, just as my parents had, and that she would convince the girl to return to me. How desperately I must have needed to invent intricate fantasies of redemption.

A letter arrived from my aunt one autumn day. She asked after me only briefly but wrote of her dinner parties in excruciating detail—two and a half pages of ornamented description. Wadi added five words to the bottom: *Tigre, Espero que estejas bem*—Tiger, I hope you are well.

I suppose I ought to have been gratified that my cousin took time off from his busy schedule to express so much of his old feelings for me.

*   *   *

With a year remaining on my sentence, I began to feel the end of my time in prison quickening my pulse. Having earned the warden's confidence with my frequent quotations from the New Testament, I was soon able to visit Senhor Pereira and his family on a Sunday without the usual presence of a guard, and there, after our midday meal, I sat at a small desk in his study and wrote the following letter, making several spelling errors in Portuguese that would lend veracity to my story:

> *Dearest Father Carlos Miguel Fonseca,*
>
> *Please excuse my writing to Your Excellency without benefit of an introduction. My name is James Matthews, and I belong to a race much persecuted in Britain and with which you will, perhaps, sympathize—the English Catholic. I've had to go into hiding once again because of my beliefs and because of this I'm asking you to send your reply care of a trusted friend.*
>
> *From an English acquaintance of mine who had the good fortune to stay in Goa for a few weeks, I've recently learned of your valuable work in codifying the practices of many of the heathen sects that plague India at present. Through your work, no doubt, a great many Indian infidels have already been baptized and ushered through the gate of our Lord's compassion.*
>
> *I'm particularly interested in those primitives that go by the name of Jain. I've been told this sect is most peculiar, and that its adherents even believe that animals have souls! (My friends laugh at such beliefs, but I've assured them that heresy of so simple-minded a sort is no matter for mirth in India and other dark countries!)*
>
> *For my own ongoing studies, which center upon the possi-*

bility of Judaism being the hidden and unsuspected origin of a great range of heresies, including that of the Jain, I would be most grateful if you could write me of the beliefs of these horrid beggars with regard to the soul. I'd be only too pleased to pay for this service and thank you in advance for your valuable help.

If you one day come to Europe, I'd be most pleased to converse about such matters with you, and you may, of course, stay with me in my home, though my circumstances are quite modest. I hope to be able to send you a permanent address at a later date, but for now, please write to me care of my friend.

"From east and west people will come, from north and south, for the feast in the kingdom of God"—Luke 13.

Yours,
James Matthews

As a postscript, I added in English:

You will please excuse any grammatical errors I may have made in this letter. Though I have lived in many countries, my knowledge of languages is not so great as that of the Jesuits.

I decided against delivering the letter directly to the Holy Office. Instead, I addressed it in care of Senhor Jácome Morais, the man who had escorted me through my Act of Faith. He would undoubtedly wonder why he was being used as an intermediary, but his confusion would only serve my interests in the end.

When Senhor Pereira asked why I was addressing a letter in care of the Captain of the King's fleet in Goa, I explained that an important priest I wasn't at liberty to identify had begged me to keep him informed of my spiritual progress as a newly converted Christian, but that he didn't think it convenient for our names to be associated together, so he'd asked me to write to him through a close acquaintance.

Senhor Pereira was pleased to learn of my diligent fulfillment of a priest's request and because of the letter's supposedly intimate nature waived his right to read what I'd written. He gave it to an acquaintance of his sailing to Malacca by way of Goa. As I didn't wish to put anyone else at risk, I instructed him to tell this man to deliver my letter by courier. "In order to protect the priest," I explained, adding from Luke 11, " 'When a strong and fully armed man guards his castle, his possessions are safe.' "

*   *   *

Two months went by, which was hardly enough time for my letter to reach Goa and summon a reply, but nervousness impelled me to write again to Father Carlos. I repeated my original request and this time sent along a silver ring recently given to me as a birthday present by Senhor Pereira, which I'd etched with a tiny menorah using a knife I'd taken from his kitchen. I asked the priest to please accept the small gift as advance payment on the service he was doing me and explained that it had been given to me by a Jesuit friend, who'd taken it off a Jew burnt for heresy in Seville. *I suspect the menorah may be a talisman of some sort,* I wrote, *and therefore of great interest to you in your research. The ring itself may also be very ancient, judging from the poor quality of the etching, but with your knowledge of the Hebrew race, you'll undoubtedly be able to shed more light on this matter.*

I sent my letter to Goa in the hands of a courier recommended to me by Senhor Pereira. The ring left a circular impression in the sealed paper, which made it nearly certain that Captain Morais would open it before passing it on. Picturing him holding my little trinket up to the light for closer inspection filled me with a vibrant sense of accomplishment—my first since my arrest, more than five years earlier.

*   *   *

Three more months passed, and then a letter from Benedict Gray arrived. My flattering words had piqued Father Carlos' interest: he'd sent a long letter to me care of my old English friend, in which he expounded on what he called the "Jain heresy." The priest's descriptions of ritual and belief were erudite and even poetic but of no interest to me. His handwriting was what I was after. It was neat and square, except on words beginning new paragraphs, which were ornamented with grand flourishes. His signature was florid and large. The many hours I'd spent at manuscript illumination came in very handy now, and after several weeks of practice I was able to imitate his writing without glancing at his original letter, at which point I felt confident enough to write to him again:

To His Excellency Father Carlos Miguel Fonseca,

Having been entrusted by Your Excellency to find a suitable boat or ship for taking you from Lisbon to the Holy Land after you come to Europe from Goa, I have taken the liberty of contacting a fellow Englishman possessing the most subtle knowledge of such matters. He goes by the name of Charles Benjamin, and he had the great pleasure of meeting you in Goa several years ago. Indeed, he has never forgotten your many kindnesses. He has assured me that he will write to you as soon as he has worked out suitable plans, since you may have to travel to a Mediterranean port to catch a ship to the Holy Land. In his letter, he vows to make all the relevant details explicit to you and help you find a suitably modest house to stay in. I do hope that this meets with your approval.

"The honest man comes to the light so that it may be clearly seen that God is in all he does"—John 3.

Yours truly,
James Matthews

The casual reader of this letter would assume that Father Carlos had employed me to help make his travel plans to the Holy Land, but I took care to add expressions of local New Christian code that I had picked up from other prisoners:

"The most subtle knowledge" meant the Torah; "modest house" meant synagogue.

A third expression was less known: *porto* literally meant port, but in my letter it referred to the mezuzah, the small prayer case that was affixed to the doorpost of a Jewish home and which was believed to offer protection.

The words "for taking you from Lisbon to the Holy Land" would reinforce this coded significance and also make reference to the spiritual journey that the mezuzah would help the Jesuit make.

To anyone familiar with these expressions—to the Inquisitors, for instance—I'd just informed Father Carlos that an English Jew named Charles Benjamin would be supplying him with a mezuzah. Furthermore, it was to be for his own spiritual needs, and the Englishman would be in touch with him shortly.

I sent my letter care of Jácome Morais once again, but this time wrote *urgente e pessoal*—urgent and personal—beneath the seal. Given the curiosity my previous letter surely must have aroused in the Captain, and given the seething climate of suspicion created and nurtured by the Inquisition, this would ensure that he would read its contents.

*   *   *

Now, with seven months to go on my sentence, my uncle succeeded in transferring funds to me care of Senhor Pereira. Walking unaccompanied to his home one Sunday afternoon, I purchased a slender silver jewelry box at a ragged marketplace for secondhand merchandise and stolen goods pitched near the river. Before heading back to my dormitory that evening, I was able to sneak away for a few minutes and lock myself inside my host's study. On the cover of the silver box I etched "Hear, O Israel," which were the first words of the Hebrew prayer kept in a mezuzah. Below this inscription, I designed a tiny menorah. The following Sunday, I wrote out the prayer itself on a ribbon of paper, scrolled it up tightly, and tucked it inside.

In my accompanying note, I wrote: *This case to be opened only by Father Carlos Miguel Fonseca.* I signed it as Charles Benjamin.

As a postscript, I added that I'd be happy to fulfill the priest's request to arrange similar travel for the prison guard named António Ribeiro whom he'd mentioned, along with the other friends indicated on his list. António Ribeiro was the Illiterate's real name; I had never forgotten—or forgiven—his slapping the face of the elderly flower seller who'd offered me a hibiscus blossom as I was being dragged to my baptism.

That evening, I sent the mezuzah off with a courier.

*   *   *

Six weeks later, on what had by now become my regular Sunday visit, Senhor Pereira handed me a letter from Benedict Gray that had just arrived. It contained a short message from Father Carlos. The point of the Jesuit's plume had slipped in two places, causing deep ink stains, and he had nearly pushed through the paper when he'd signed his name. He wrote:

> *I do not know who you are, sir, nor who you think I am, but I order you to stop sending me any correspondence or any more rings, or any other so-called gifts. You plainly have me confused with some heretic of a debased nature. I do not think you are a believing Catholic at all. You may consider our correspondence ended.*

I tore up his note and threw it in the river while walking back to prison. I was jittery and excited. I felt as though I were crossing a bridge made of my own forbidden desires.

Several days later, I wrote again, saying I'd heard nothing from the good Father about his travel plans.

I'm so very disappointed not to have any word at all, especially as your trip was so carefully planned by Mr. Benjamin. I was sure you would appreciate all he had worked out for you, and though I trust that your silence is due only to the unreliability of communications between Goa and Lisbon, I cannot help but wonder if something has happened. I pray you are not ill or angry with me for some reason. Please be kind enough to write to your humble servant.

Over the next fortnight, I drew a detailed portrait of Father Carlos from memory, with the Holy Office of Goa in the background. I then sent two more letters to him. The first one said:

How good it was to finally get news of you, Your Excellency. Thank you for your gifts. My wife greatly appreciated the beautiful silk scarf. Such glorious embroidery must have been done by the most agile-fingered Indian girls. As for my tortoiseshell hairbrush, I only wish I had more hair to comb!

All your friends of the most subtle knowledge thank you for your good wishes.

I must add that it was not necessary for you to send me any such gifts, as it was a great honor for me to be able to help you with your plans. I hope that the Holy Land will always live inside you now.

I've been in touch with Charles Benjamin and he assures me that Senhor António Ribeiro's wishes have also been recently satisfied.

Yours truly,
James Matthews

P.S. I've given your payment to Charles Benjamin, who is extremely grateful for the generous gratuity you added.

"A good man produces good from the store of good within himself"—Matthew 12.

My second letter included my sketched portrait of Father Carlos. It was prompted by the priest's assertion that my alter ego, James Matthews, had mistaken him for another man. I wrote across the top of the drawing in English:

> *To His Reverence, Father Carlos Miguel Fonseca:*
>
> *I made this drawing while I was in Goa, as you can see. I trust you haven't changed so much over the last three years and will recognize yourself despite my humble talents!*
> *It was a pleasure to conduct business with you and Mr. Matthews.*
>
> *Best wishes,*
> *Charles Benjamin*

Anyone who opened my letter and saw my drawing would know immediately, of course, that no mistake of identity had been made.

*   *   *

I received no more communications from Benedict Gray over the next weeks and concluded that Father Carlos had decided upon silence as his safest recourse.

That autumn a letter did arrive, however, from someone I hadn't seen in many years—Sarah, the girl Wadi had cast aside for my sister. She wrote that she'd been given Mr. Pereira's address by my uncle. After expressing her hopes that I was in good health, she told me that she'd promised Uncle Isaac that she wouldn't mention certain particularly delicate matters to me. "And yet I feel compelled to, at the very least, say the following," she wrote, adding:

> *Your aunt and uncle are very likely to hide from you some of the things that have taken place over these past years. I feel obliged to write to you about this because what they tell you will*

*probably contradict what your sister told me. Therefore, when
you return to Goa, I beg you to visit me. Please, Tiago—do not
form too many definite opinions about what happened between
Wadi and your sister until you have spoken with me!*

With dread, I wondered what she could have been referring to,
but more than that I wondered if it was possible that Sarah knew
who had betrayed my father and me. Unfortunately, no more letters
arrived to explain her cryptic words.

*   *   *

On December 19, 1599, having completed my six-year debt to the
Holy Office, I walked out the front door of the Galé Prison into the
unforgiving wind and rain that I've always associated with the Lisbon
winter. I crossed myself right away and mumbled Christian
prayers as I walked to the center of the city.

Over those first days outside my dormitory, I felt abandoned. It
seemed impossible that no one was watching me and that I was free
of shackles. In my disorientation, I imagined that many of the people
I passed in the streets were spies hired to follow me. I looked over
my shoulder constantly when I walked.

Using my uncle's funds, I got myself a garret room at a crumbling
inn behind the Church of São Miguel, in the Alfama neighborhood.
I hid there over the next days, huddled under my woolen blanket, eating
cheese and bread and drinking only water. My sleep was feverish.
The silence at night hid monsters with Kali's bloody teeth. I hadn't
dreamt of these murderous creatures since my mother's death.

When I dared to go out for more than a few minutes, I had myself
deloused by a barber and my fingernails clipped short. I bought
warm clothing, including a fine pair of fawn-colored trousers, along
the Rua Nova, where many converted Jews had their shops. I almost
purchased a New Testament as well, to refresh my memory, but inside
the small bookshop the smell of leather and paper was too reminiscent
of my father's library, and I turned and fled. I bathed a few

miles upriver, near some washerwomen pounding laundry against stones. One of them gave me a sliver of coarse black soap. It was the first time I'd been clean since arriving in Lisbon. I felt I'd been given my body back. On my walk home, my fear of being watched began to ease: it was as though the cool river water had convinced me that I was a free man at last.

Over the next few days I discovered much in Lisbon I hadn't seen before. For hours I'd sit on top of Graça hill and watch the people in the streets hundreds of feet below, all of them with their own stories to tell. Although I desperately craved the comfort of their friendship, I thought, *When this is over, I'll go off by myself for many years. . . .*

I began each day by purchasing bread and fruit on the Rua de São Pedro, where my father's grandparents had lived. The shopkeepers had never heard of mangoes or papayas, so I bought small red apples and green pears instead, but the fruit of Europe has always been too hard for me and I made little headway. I did manage to find grapes and dried figs—and finally, some dried coconut. I mixed the flakes with honey and spread the paste on *broa,* the coarse peasant bread they made in Portugal, though I soon also began to simply eat it with a spoon. The taste brought me back to India. Sometimes, when the sun entered my room, I closed my eyes and imagined Mama's statue of Shiva guarding me from the doorway.

*   *   *

At the end of my first week of freedom, I sat on my floor with an inkstand and carefully scripted two letters in Father Carlos' handwriting, dating them before my last letter to him. I hadn't dared to work on these before leaving prison because I'd have had to keep them somewhere in Senhor Pereira's home, which would have put him at serious risk.

In each of them, I made coded references to his desire to have proper religious implements for the practice of Judaism, as these were impossible to find in Goa. Fearing that subtlety would not accomplish all I wanted, I made explicit reference to our need for secrecy. *You must never tell a soul of our transactions or the Holy Office will imprison me,* I wrote in the first, *and you must always take pains to write to me in care of my valued friend, Jácome Morais, who is a man who will not identify me—or you—even under torture.*

I gave an even friendlier tone to the second letter. I allowed the Jesuit to ask Mr. Matthews personal questions about his family and to express his gratitude. *You are a true friend, and I am eternally grateful for the care you have taken in keeping my travel plans to the Holy Land hidden from those with bad intentions.*

I closed both letters with a reference from Exodus 15 of the Torah: *"Thy Right hand, O Lord, will shatter the enemy."* That added just the right tone of devilish Jewish defiance, I thought.

And then I signed Father Carlos' name with a great flourish.

I kept these forged letters under my mattress for the time being; I would use them only when I was ready to leave for Goa.

*   *   *

By now, Father Carlos and Captain Morais had probably met several times to discuss my strange correspondence and unwanted gifts. Very likely the Illiterate had been called before them and questioned. The prison guard and the priest had undoubtedly denied any knowledge of a James Matthews or Charles Benjamin, but Morais had probably not believed them. The Captain would suspect that he was being used by secret Jews who refused to reveal why he was being compromised in this way.

"Why have you chosen me?" he must have shouted over and over.

"But I haven't!" the Jesuit had probably cried. "I know nothing of these matters—absolutely nothing!"

Morais might very well have believed the priest at first, but all too soon he would understand that his connection to my letters and gifts could land him in prison. Unless he acted first and betrayed Father Carlos . . . and the Illiterate, too . . .

I'd have wagered that Morais had kept my drawing of Father Carlos for himself, saving it for later use against him.

The priest had probably written a stern letter to my friend Benedict Gray, to try to unravel this mystery, but my old prison cohort would never have replied.

Each man I'd implicated would deny any knowledge of my letters in any Inquisitorial process started against them, but their captors would think it only natural and proper for secret Jews like them to lie—at least until they were tortured.

The best part was that their confusion would only make them seem more suspect. That gratified me immensely. I took pride in my forged claim that Jácome Morais would not utter Father Carlos' name even under torture. That would surely seem a wonderful challenge to the Inquisitors.

With his feet roasted over coals, the Illiterate would quickly confess to being part of a Jewish conspiracy. And as I had learned in prison that unbreakable men do not exist, Jácome Morais would eventually agree with him. Father Carlos, too.

The Holy Office would be delighted to find three men of such different backgrounds agreeing so readily with one another! It was really only a question of which man betrayed the others first, hoping to save his own skin.

*   *   *

I booked passage on a ship leaving for Goa in a month, the earliest departure I could find. I then wrote to Benedict Gray to beg for more news.

Nineteen days later, I received the following:

Dearest Mr. Matthews—

What a happy coincidence; I was about to write to you when your correspondence arrived. I am overjoyed to hear you are free. May you one day join me in England!
I was about to write because a most curious man visited me just two days ago. He was Portuguese and tiny as a sparrow. We

communicated in Latin, as I claimed to know nothing of his language. His particular cadence in that ancient tongue led me to believe that he was a priest, but he was dressed like a Continental gentleman and vehemently denied any connection to the Papist hierarchy. He claimed to be a trade representative of the Portuguese Crown based in Goa. Early on in our conversation he made reference to the letter I had received from Father Carlos Fonseca. He was obviously extremely curious as to its content. I did not deny having received such a missive, but I told him nothing of what it contained, of course. This was quite easy, as I had not read it. I did not tell him to whom I had sent it, or indeed if I had sent it to anyone, though he begged me to give him all the information I could, whereupon I simply showed him the deep scars on my feet and asked him to leave my house. On my doorstep, he reached into his pocket and took out a small silver box etched with Hebrew lettering and what I think you people call a menorah—a seven-armed candelabrum, in any case. "Have you ever seen this?" he asked me.

I replied in the negative, of course.

Mr. Matthews, I suspect you know the meaning of this little box, and I ask that you tell me since my curiosity has gotten the better of me. (If it will not compromise either of us too greatly, I ask you to write sooner rather than later!)

After I read this, I might have felt the exultation of the victorious, since this meant that Father Carlos was probably in prison and most certainly being questioned severely, but after a short, luminous spell of ecstasy, I became dispirited. I can see now that exhaustion from all my years of labor and incarceration had caught up with me. I think, too, that I was incapable of feeling any true happiness, as I still faced a long sea journey before I'd be able to see my sister and Tejal.

I wrote a quick note of explanation to Benedict Gray, then did my best to celebrate with a bottle of wine in the dark of my room, feeling weak of mind and body—as though crushed by loneliness. I slept for most of the next three days. When I finally went outside again into the December damp, I slunk along like a beggar. Everywhere I turned, I faced guilt at having poisoned my father. I lifted my head over the rim of my melancholy only several days later, when I bought a knife I could conceal in my boots, thinking in a paraphrase of Jesus, *Anyone can walk in daylight without stumbling, but in the nightfall of where I am going, I may need something to justify my words.* John 11.

I still had one more brick to put in place in order to seal Father Carlos in hell, so I let my beard grow over the next week. On my final day in Lisbon, wearing my ragged prison shirt, I hired a chimney sweep to take a pouch bearing my two forged letters—the highly incriminating ones the Jesuit had supposedly written to Mr. Matthews—to the Inquisitional Palace. I followed the sweep in secret to make certain he carried out my wishes, which he did faithfully.

I'd inserted a brief note from an unidentified innkeeper to the Grand Inquisitor of Lisbon.

I am but a poor innkeeper, I wrote, *and until this morning I had no idea that I'd rented a room to an English heretic until I discovered these two letters hidden under his mattress. Forgive me.*

I cried once my pouch was safely delivered—as I had not sobbed in six years.

CHAPTER 19

As soon as my ship docked in Goa in early May of 1600, the moist tropical air against my face and hair and the stench of rotting mimosa flowers on the storm-drenched streets filled me with a heavy homesickness so disorienting that I had to sit abruptly on the stones of the wharf after I disembarked. Fate itself seemed to have knocked me over.

Then I ran to my aunt and uncle's home, tugged all the way by my years of absence. Aunt Maria answered my knocks. My hair was long and scruffy, my skin sun-baked. I'd worn the same shirt and trousers for weeks. I was panting. I must have had the odor and look of a wild animal.

She gasped, then reached out to me with straining hands. Even as we hugged, a small part of me shrank away from her, as it always had in my childhood. I don't think I'd ever noticed her slightly decaying scent before, as though her elaborate clothes had been too long in a chest.

When I held her away, her eyes were open wide in fear; she was more nervous than I was. Under better circumstances, I might have laughed.

"Your uncle is in Diu," she told me. "He's going to be overjoyed to see you."

She had aged well. Her eyes were clear and sharp, and her soft hair, gray in front, made her look as though she had become a graceful matron. She wore an elegant crimson dress and a necklace of tourmaline beads—she must've been about to go out.

"Is Sofia here?" I asked.

"No. Come inside and I'll explain."

A servant I didn't recognize took my bag. My aunt coaxed me into an armchair, but I jumped up right away. I was frantic with the need to hold my sister.

"Are you thirsty?" she asked, and before I could answer she ordered her servant to fetch us some cashew punch.

"Is Sofia with Wadi?"

"No, *Francisco Xavier* is at work—at the warehouses," she replied, emphasizing my gaffe with a look down her nose.

You may have been six years in prison, but I won't let you get away with insinuations about my son's origins, she was telling me.

"Then where is she? At our farm?"

"Sit," she said.

"No, please just tell me," I begged.

"Tiago, there are some things we dared not write about in our letters. Sofia . . . there was an accident near your farm. Isaac thought it best—"

"What kind of accident?"

"She fell . . . she fell down a steep ravine not long after you . . . after you were ordered to leave Goa. She was killed. We had the funeral shortly—"

"It's not possible," I interrupted.

"I'm afraid it is. She was buried not a year after you left. If you want . . ."

My aunt continued speaking, but I heard none of it. Yet as I stared at her cold, hard eyes, I could see she was telling the truth. After a time, I realized, too, that she was enraged at me. *This should be your uncle's work, telling you of Sofia's death,* I knew she was thinking.

My disbelief became desperation. And then I began to shake. Afterward, I remember feeling as though my heart had stopped and that time had vanished from the world. My aunt was squatting next to me. She forced a glass of wine into my hand.

"Drink," she commanded gently.

"Where is Sofia?" I asked again.

"Tiago, haven't you understood a word of what I've said?"

*   *   *

The wine numbed my desire to flee. My aunt stood over me, fingering her beads nervously, and told me that Sofia had been walking on the mountain near our farm that we called Hanuman's Head. She was found at the bottom of the steep cliff on its western side.

"It wasn't a total surprise," she said.

"I don't understand."

"Sofia was...she was distracted after you left—detached. Her mind seized things only incompletely. She was miserable much of the time, as you can imagine. Francisco Xavier did what he could to cheer her up, and we did, too, but it wasn't much use."

As my aunt spoke, I remembered that Wadi had taken my sister up to the top of Hanuman's Head just after they'd fallen in love and that she'd been deathly afraid there. I couldn't believe she'd have climbed to the summit again. Not voluntarily. And certainly not alone.

"Who found her?" I asked.

"Francisco Xavier and Isaac."

"Together?"

She nodded, tugging at her necklace now, the tendons in her hand so taut that I thought she might break the cord and send the beads scurrying, as I'd once done with the rosary of a priest.

"Do you know if she wrote to me before she died?"

"She must have. We all did—though from your letters we understood you weren't getting ours."

"Where is she buried?"

"Here, in the municipal cemetery."

"Not on our farm?"

"No, we thought it best that—"

"Is Nupi at the farm now?"

"No, we've hired a caretaker. We've had no word from Nupi since Sofia died."

"And Tejal?"

My aunt stood up and took my glass. She moved to the mantelpiece and poured more wine. Handing me my drink, she said, "I'm afraid I'll have to give you more unpleasant news now."

"If you tell me Tejal is dead, I won't believe you! Uncle Isaac told me she was well."

"No, the girl is alive and living in her village. But shortly after your child was born, he grew ill. Tiago, your son didn't live long."

"That's not what your husband wrote me. Why are you lying?"

"*Isaac* was lying. He didn't believe you'd survive hearing the truth."

I must have betrayed my skepticism, because she gave me a haughty look and added, "You can despise me if you like, but this is the way things are. Everything went wrong after your father died. *Everything!* And if you don't hear the truth from me now, how will you be able to go on with your life?"

I downed my drink in two gulps, spitting on her advice in my mind, and then fetched my bag from the foyer.

"Where are you going?" she demanded.

I didn't answer.

At the door, she grabbed my arm. "Why don't you speak?" she asked.

"'How blessed are those who have suffered persecution for the cause of right?'" I said, quoting from scripture, but making Christ's statement into a question. As I spoke I realized I'd been waiting since I first read the Gospels to ask this of her.

"I don't understand...."

"Am I blessed for having been betrayed?" I demanded. "Was my father? If so, then what does such a blessing mean? And does the person who betrayed us to the Church believe he was doing good for me and my family? Can you tell me that?"

"I—I don't know what you mean," she stammered, obviously caught off guard.

"No, you wouldn't, would you?"

She glanced down, ashamed and uncomfortable. I could see she wished I'd stayed in Lisbon. I was bringing up memories and emotions she didn't want—including, perhaps, her guilt at having testified against us to the Inquisition.

"Don't you even know the Sermon on the Mount?" I asked spitefully. "That's what I was quoting."

"I know it, but how do you?"

"Only in Christ was I able to find solace. And I'll need Him now if I'm to endure this."

She leaned toward me. "Are you telling me the truth?" she whispered anxiously.

"Why would I lie after all that's happened?"

"I don't know, but we must be careful. This is still Goa and the Holy Office is still—"

"I have nothing to fear from the Holy Office now. Christ will protect me."

When I crossed myself, she looked shocked. Our eyes met; I didn't flinch.

"If... if you are truly a Christian, Ti, then everything will be all right. It changes everything."

I pulled my arm from her grasp.

"You must stay here until Fransisco Xavier comes home," she said sharply. "I'll send for him. He'll help you."

"I don't need his help."

"Don't you understand how badly Tejal suffered after you left? She was disgraced—with nothing to show for it. If the infant had lived, maybe then... maybe..."

I opened the door.

"What's done is done!" my aunt shouted after me. "Tejal has returned to her Hindu ways, Ti. Leave things the way they are!"

*   *   *

I don't know how my feet kept walking the miles I traveled over the next two days. When I asked directions in the rice fields, my own voice amazed me, as though it were coming from a hollow being. I wouldn't have been surprised to have been visited by the Lord and told that these were my last minutes of life. Did I eat and drink? Did anyone I spoke to notice my despair and offer words of solace?

One does what one has to, especially if death is walking nearby. Perhaps that is the greatest rule of life. Or its most astonishing mystery.

I fled deep inside my thoughts of disbelief. My body was a shell around them. My hands were ice.

Take care of your sister.... That's what my mother had come across a bridge from the underworld to tell me. Yet I had no power to change anything. The Lord did what He wanted with all of us.

Slowly, as though succumbing to a river's current, I let myself be tugged along by my fantasies as I walked toward Benali. I began to believe that my aunt and uncle were keeping my sister from me. They'd thought I was putting her at risk. Maybe she'd been told I'd died in Lisbon.

Aunt Maria had said my Christianity changed everything. Did she mean they could now tell me where Sofia was?

What would Wadi have gained from killing her? Did he believe I'd never come home and that with Sofia's death he'd get ownership of our farm? After all, the Church must not have been able to appropriate it, since it was outside Portuguese territory. Maybe he simply wanted his freedom—to rid himself of a wife he no longer loved.

*   *   *

The sun was shimmering gold and pink over the ocean's horizon when I reached Benali. The village huts looked sadder than I remembered them, huddled like sleeping orphans under the tamarisks and peepul trees. Teenage boys were playing on the strand, laughing and shouting to provoke one another. One of them had bangs and great brown eyes.

"Arjuna?" I called.

Another young man, slightly older than the first—perhaps they were brothers—turned as if pierced by an arrow.

"How do you know my name?" he demanded, standing erect, like a warrior.

"If you're the boy I knew, then we played Ganesha together many years ago." To his puzzled look, I added, "My sister and I visited with Nupi one year, and Madesh knocked me over the head with a sword."

He grinned. "I remember you now! You're Tiago."

He and the others ran to me. I told them I'd been studying in Lisbon and that Sofia was well. They shook their heads when I asked if Tejal still lived with her parents.

"No, she lives over there now." Arjuna pointed to one of the farthest huts.

He told me he'd run ahead to tell her I was in Benali, but I said it wasn't necessary; I let optimism for my future convince me that surprising Tejal would be more exciting for us both.

Tejal was kneeling on the dung-polished porch that faced the ocean when I saw her, watering basil plants in earthenware pots. Her profile was older, and her curves were fuller and softer than I remembered. She was a woman now. When she turned to me, her black eyes were so filled with emotional depth that I imagined they contained all my hopes as well as her own.

The need to touch her made me moan as our eyes met. I wasn't sure I'd be able to assemble a voice from all the broken things inside me. Instead, I waved. It was a silly gesture, but there was a storm of emotion inside me that couldn't be expressed yet.

She started, dropping her pitcher, which cracked in half.

I smiled, as some of us do when we can see how life has tossed us around. I held up my hands in a position of apology.

"I've come back to you," I said.

She stood up, but instead of running to me or even calling a greeting, she turned away.

"Tejal, I'm home for good and we can start over," I vowed.

She hugged her arms around her chest as though suddenly chilled.

"Please . . . Please just face me," I begged.

But she never did; she rushed back inside and eased the door closed.

I hung my head, cursing myself for surprising her. She needed time to prepare for our reunion. I ought to have let Arjuna tell her I was here. He knew the ways of an Indian village far better than I did. After all, a young Hindu woman couldn't be expected to welcome her lost love with immediate kisses.

When I called out to her again, my voice sounded frail. In the terrible silence afterward I realized the village was alive with muffled sounds—Tejal's neighbors were hiding from me and whispering amongst themselves.

They're waiting to see what I will do, I thought.

I considered calling out again but felt I might summon the sky to fall on us if I did. I wanted to howl with frustration.

I'll wait for her, I thought. *It's the only thing I know how to do.*

I sat down in the warm sand, preparing to remain there for as long as it took for her to come out to me, but Ajira, Nupi's sister, suddenly came rushing toward me, ahead of a group of women, clutching the folds in her sari. Dusk had now turned the whole world to shadow. Ajira cupped an oil lamp in her hand, making her gray hair shimmer like silver.

I stood up to greet her, but she backed away.

"Tejal's husband will be home very soon. He must not find you here."

"So Tejal is married?"

Before Ajira could reply, Darpak, one of the elders who'd chosen Sofia and me to play Ganesha, joined us. His white hair had thinned, and a large wooden cross hung around his neck. Little children jostled behind him, peeking around his legs for a glimpse of me.

"You must go," he told me.

"But what of Kama, my son?"

"The goddess Kali took him away from us," the old man said. "She made him ill after he was born."

"So my son is dead?" I asked Ajira.

She bit her lip and glanced away fearfully. Her refusal to look at me convinced me that village rules were preventing her from telling me the truth—that Kama was still alive.

Darpak gripped my shoulder. "Ajira may not speak to you. You must leave."

"Who are you to decide whether she can speak to me?" I demanded.

"You've done great damage to Tejal. You will do no more. She has a husband now—Durio. And a son and daughter by him. There is no room for you in our village. It is too late—much too late. Go now, before Tejal's father and Durio learn you are here, or we will have trouble—so much trouble."

I was silent, considering my options. I knew I must speak to Tejal herself.

"Come," Arjuna said, and he reached for my hand. "I'll walk with you out of the village."

If he hadn't smiled compassionately at me, would I have gone?

I left in order to give myself time to think about how to win her back. We walked inland out of the village so that our movements would be concealed from Durio and the other men in boats, then headed north toward Goa. Lanterns lit the fishermen's faces in moth shapes of dark and light. Arjuna and I did not speak until we were far out of sight, concealed by a grove of palms.

"I'll leave you here," he said.

"What is Durio like?" I asked.

"He's a fisherman," the boy replied, as if there was nothing more to say.

"How old is he?"

He shrugged. "He already has a grown son older than me—from his first wife."

"Is he good to Tejal?"

"I don't know that either."

"And Kama, he's alive, isn't he? That's the name of Tejal's little boy."

Arjuna nodded.

"How old is he?"

"Six or seven."

"He's not really Durio's, is he?"

"How can I know that? You ask too many questions."

He frowned and started to depart.

"Just one more . . . Why does Darpak wear a cross?"

"Portuguese soldiers came two years ago. They destroyed all the Hindu gods we had left to us. The elders wear crosses now in case the soldiers return."

"Did the Ganesha heads we wore survive?"

He shook his head. "The Portuguese burned them. Everything is gone."

As Arjuna disappeared down the strand, I slumped in the sandy soil and gazed up at the Milky Way, which soon became all the seas I'd crossed. How many more would I have to journey over to reach home? Everything had been turned upside down. If my sister was dead and Tejal no longer loved me, I was alone in the world.

Was this the way God wanted it?

I see what You have in store for me, I thought, with that exaggerated sense of self one feels when addressing the Lord in anger.

I crept back toward Benali, not wanting to be detected. When I was able to make out the faces of the villagers, I dropped down behind some bushes and began watching Tejal's hut for any sign of movement. I took out my knife, feeling like a beggar outside a palace, wondering what I would do for a chance to get inside and change places with the king.

*   *   *

Ajira shook me awake at dawn, carrying a ripe yellow papaya and three warm chapatti.

My knife had dropped from my hand in the middle of the night. Ajira looked at it fearfully, then led me away from the village. She sat close to me as I ate, unhappy, sprinkling sand on her feet as though she were counting the time before her obligations to me would be over. Sucking on her rickety front teeth the way Nupi used to, she said in a crusty voice that it was better if we didn't talk about Tejal or Kama. In her furtive glances I could see she wished to unburden herself of some secret misery. I didn't yet know that her need to find her sister was playing havoc with her emotions.

When I finally asked after Nupi, Ajira burst into tears, sobbing that her sister had not returned to the village in five years. "So worried I am, so very worried," she moaned. "Please, if you know anything, you must tell me. You must tell me now."

"You only brought me breakfast to find out if I knew anything about her," I said resentfully.

"I brought you food because you are her godson!" she replied, anger flashing in her eyes. "And because you have suffered. Like all of us."

Speaking and thinking in Konkani—which I hadn't done in years—made me feel fragile. All my words seemed so much more graceful and meaningful than they did in Portuguese.

"I know nothing about Nupi," I said, instantly sorry for my cruelty to her. "But I feel certain I can find her, and when I do, I'll send word to you. I promise to search for her. Now, I need something from you. I have to know what happened to Tejal."

"I cannot tell you," she said. "It is forbidden."

"Nupi would want you to tell me everything."

"Perhaps." Ajira's shoulders slumped. "You did a very bad thing all those years ago," she said, her voice deepening with resentment.

She needs to punish me before giving me the gift of her knowledge, I thought.

"What did I do? I fell in love with Tejal. Is that so terrible?"

"You . . . you shared a bed with her."

"I intended to marry her. Her father had already agreed, as had mine."

"But you didn't marry her, did you?" she snapped.

"I was arrested by the Inquisition! I was sent to a prison in Lisbon."

"Keep your voice down! The reason doesn't matter. What do we know of Lisbon here? When Tejal came back to the village, she was with child and there was no father. That's all we knew. Shame . . . a girl can be crushed by it. You men never understand that." She clasped her hands together and rocked back and forth with grief. When tears slid down her cheeks, she wiped them away roughly. "Nupi and I and all the other women gave what we could to her dowry, in secret, but still the only one who would take her in that condition was Durio."

"Is he a bad man?"

"No, he is a very good man, but he is old. He could be her grandfather."

"And the child. Is he mine or his?"

"He's Durio's!" she declared, too vehemently for me to believe her. "Tell me, if you really loved Tejal, why didn't you wait to lie with her?" Ajira glared at me.

I had no answer to that. For the first time, I could see clearly how I'd ruined Tejal's life through my selfishness—and my fear of Wadi and Sofia's charges against me. I'd been a coward.

"Does she hate me?" I asked.

"She does not think of you at all!" Ajira snapped spitefully, but then she reached out to me, regretting her words.

I brought her hand to my lips, then let it fall. I did not say that she was lying, since we both knew it plainly enough.

"I don't believe Kama is Durio's," I said instead. "And I can't go without seeing him. You have to find a way to bring him outside. I'll stay hidden. He won't see me."

"No, I will not help you anymore. You have to go."

She waved me off just as Nupi used to. It made me desperate and anxious.

"I just want to look at him. Please . . . If I have to beg I will."

"It's impossible! Tejal will not let me have him."

"Tell her that you have a gift for him outside. Give him this," I said, reaching into my bag. I'd brought him a present from Lisbon—a red and yellow dragon whose wings flapped when its wheels were rolled along the ground.

Ajira's eyes opened wide. It was a beautiful toy—finely carved and painted in the most vibrant colors.

"I can't. Everyone will know it's from you."

"Say it was Sofia's as a child. That it's from my sister. I brought it with me and have left. Say that Sofia told me in a letter that she wanted Tejal to have it for our son."

I held the little dragon out to Ajira. Scowling, fighting her better judgment, she took it.

"If you had the courage to come out here to me, then you can do this," I told her.

I helped her to her feet. In her yearning eyes, I could see she wanted to tell me more, but she shook her head as if it would be of no use and started away.

An hour later, when she led a lithe young boy out of Tejal's door by the hand, I saw that his hair was honey-colored, the exact shade of Sofia's when she was his age.

CHAPTER 20

I ought to have turned away from Kama the moment I knew he was mine. Like a Jain under a vow of *ahimsa,* of nonviolence, I could have folded myself into the landscape of sea and sand, into that chance for a quiet redemption, or simply walked into the depth of the jungle a few miles inland and made wherever I emerged my sanctuary. Indeed, I was gripped by the certainty that if I turned away now, everything could end without blood—my own included. I could have mastered the slow walk of resignation. I could have kept my eyes closed. I didn't have to ask any more questions of Wadi, or even see Uncle Isaac. What were they to me now? I didn't need to know if Father Carlos was a prisoner of the Holy Office or if the Illiterate had been executed. I might have made a new life somehow. People do—even Job struggled on after God betrayed him. And I was only twenty-eight years old, after all; the sun of adulthood had barely risen into my sky.

I stayed two days in the countryside surrounding Benali, living on coarse black rice and scraps of fish I begged at villages along the coast. Every evening at dusk, I snuck up within shouting distance of

Tejal's hut, like a leper who dares not show his diseased face during the day. I sat in the sand, burrowing down and waiting. Here, I could even pretend that Sofia was still alive, hidden from me.

On the third day, I woke before dawn. In my half-sleep, I remembered a long-ago conversation I'd had with Phanishwar. His voice was like a hand leading me off to a safer place, and when he described his son Rama, he spoke with such a depth of love that I was left sobbing. I sat up, imagining the boy before me, his eyes full of terror for what was about to happen to his father.

These memories of Phanishwar reduced all my sense of righteousness to ashes.

Moments later, I caught a glimpse of Kama being led out the door of his hut by Durio. They were heading toward the ocean, maybe to bathe. Watching the gray-haired old fisherman lifting the sleep-heavy boy into his arms, I knew I had to settle things with my aunt and cousin before I could separate father and son. I had to be fully damned by God before I could steal the boy from those who loved him.

Without waiting any longer, I picked up a white pebble smoothed by the sea and threw it onto Tejal's rooftop. It was like the stone we Jews leave behind on a gravestone. *I remember,* its very presence said. *And I will be back.*

Only when I was far away did I turn to face Benali. I hoped old Durio would die of illness—or drown at sea—before I next returned. It would make what I had to do much easier.

*   *   *

I lingered just outside the city of Goa for another day, taking a room at a ramshackle inn nestled into the curve of a lazy stream. It was only a thatched hut made of dried mud, but I discovered that a grinning Ganesha holding an emerald parrot in his trunk was painted on the inside of my wooden doorway. Somehow, the Hindu god had escaped the inspections of the Portuguese. When the innkeeper told me that the bird was an incarnation of Lord Shiva, I sat down before the image and prayed that he and Ganesha would protect me from all that was Portuguese, even the language....

My room had window shutters made of polished oyster shells and a dung-hardened floor. That afternoon, a thunderstorm sent small, ring-tailed monkeys swinging for cover in a nearby grove of nutmeg trees. Afterward, with drops of water falling onto my face from the dangling yellow fruit, I walked upriver and bathed with oxen swatting away flies with their tails and an infinitely patient blue-gray heron that speared wriggling fish with its long beak. Is there magic in grief? While drying myself on the bank, a small crimson butterfly descended onto my hand. There is no red more beautiful than one that is fluttering with exuberance, and no blue as transparent as the blue that opens over India after the rain, and looking toward the sun, I knew again that the earth was beautiful and that this was the only country I wished to die in. It gave me courage. After all, death was the worst that would happen now, since I wouldn't let them capture me alive.

In my bare feet, my toes curling around the luxurious mud of the riverbank, I picked cat's whiskers, avoiding two brown-nosed vipers licking the air with their tongues as though hoping to make me their supper. I whispered endearments to the snakes just as Phanishwar might have and started back to the inn. With Kama in my thoughts, I gave my flowers to the proprietor's seven-year-old son. His mother wove them in his thick black hair as a violet-colored crown. He'd just learned some arithmetic, and he led me out to the garden and challenged me to stump him with numbers he could multiply in his head.

I sat with him, tossing him numbers, and his exuberance reminded me of Wadi. I thought of my cousin now as one does a skillful opponent at chess; he lived in a secret world as large as my own, and I'd have to always be on my guard.

"Two more," yelled the boy, arriving fast at his latest calculation.

"Seven times nine."

"That's too easy!" he moaned. "It's sixty-three."

"Twenty-six times . . . times five."

I chose those numbers because the value of YHWH—the name of the Lord of the Old Testament—was twenty-six in Hebrew, a language in which letters also had numerical values. My father had always told me to meditate on an image of five sets of the holy name whenever I wanted to see the way ahead.

As the boy scratched his calculations in the soil between us, I did as Papa had instructed me, but all I could see was what I already knew: that I'd have to rely on the New Testament to divert Wadi's attention whenever I felt my mask slipping.

"Who do men say I am?" asked Jesus of his disciples outside the villages of Caesarea Philippi.

"Some say John the Baptist, others Elijah, others one of the prophets," they answered.

Like a lesser form of Christ, I'd have to be one man to myself and quite another to Wadi and everyone else. Or was that precisely what Jesus had not been able to do, why he'd failed to save himself?

"One hundred and thirty!" the innkeeper's son shouted in triumph.

*   *   *

And so I made my way back to my aunt and uncle's house, fully aware that I ought to choose a different path if I valued my life. It was Wadi who answered my knocks. Are there people who grow stronger on the suffering of others? He was broader and taller than I remembered him, and more dominating, and his skin was sun-darkened and smooth, except on his cheeks and chin, which were bristling with stubble.

That is for my benefit, I thought—*so I can see he was too troubled by my return to go to a barber.*

The power and confidence in him was obvious, even in his glistening skullcap of black hair. His eyes opened wide with radiance. I'd never realized there was so much light in them—as though he'd been born of the sun.

"Tiago!" he exclaimed, throwing his arms around me.

I hugged him back, watching both of us from a safe distance.

He took my bag and led me inside. I stepped through the house as though the velvet sofas and gilded mirrors were spies. The plush softness of everything—even the way my feet eased into the Persian rugs—repulsed me. Meeting his gaze, I was terrified of giving myself away; all my years of planning could have been ruined in an instant.

"My mother's upstairs. Let me get her," he said.

So you don't want to be alone with me. I was relieved that he was as uncomfortable as I.

"No, please," I said hesitantly. "First . . . first tell me some things while we're alone."

"Anything. What do you want to know?"

"Sofia. Start with her."

"Sit, sit . . . ," he said, beckoning me to an armchair. "I can't believe you're finally here. Wait just a minute." He summoned a kitchen servant and ordered her to bring us some tea. "Is that all right with you?" he rushed to ask me afterward, grimacing and adding, "Or would you prefer a cold drink? I ought to have asked you first."

"Tea is fine," I replied. "Thank you. I'm very thirsty from my walk."

"Where were you?"

"Benali."

"Did you see Tejal?" he asked urgently.

I thought I heard genuine hope for me in his voice, but I couldn't be sure. Did I want him to care about my future and my feelings?

"Just once, and we can talk about it later, but please tell me about Sofia now."

"It was terrible," he said, running his hand roughly through his hair. "A nightmare."

He pulled a chair up to mine and leaned close, hunching his shoulders and squeezing his hands together between his legs, like a boy who feared punishment. It was charming in so powerful a man. I could see how women must have found him endearing, and I wondered whom he'd chosen after Sofia. Whoever she was, she must have thought, *He may look fearsome, but he's really just a lamb. . . .* My knowledge of the secret desires he might have once had for me was beating a code of warning in my heart. I knew we could never even broach that subject or there'd be violence between us.

"We were married two months after you . . . after you were . . . after you disappeared," he began.

"Please Wadi, I didn't *disappear.* I was arrested. After exile and prison, and my father's death, I don't think we should mince words about what happened."

"I'm sorry," he said, shaking his head. "This is awkward."

I was a fool to let my resentment show. I patted his leg to make up for my mistake in tactics, then leaned back and sighed, as though it were bodily exhaustion and not irritation that made me shrink away from him. "I shouldn't have spoken like that," I told him. "It's the years I've spent alone. I'm afraid I'm not very good at conversation any longer." As I spoke, I saw that the way forward was to show sympathy for him—to pretend he was the one who'd suffered most. Happy with myself for discovering this in time, I added, "I know this must be very hard for you."

Wadi grew at ease on hearing my conciliatory words. I suspect they were the sign he'd been waiting for. He told me how he'd found Sofia at the base of Hanuman's Head, her body broken and twisted—and so cold. He spoke carefully, and in his voice was the small quaver I remembered from our childhood—placed there on purpose, I'd have wagered, to assure me that for him nothing could be more serious or terrible than discussing my sister's death. On that, I agreed with him, of course, but I vowed not to show him anything but the surface of my emotions—I would not descend inside myself to the place where all my memories of her lay buried until I was alone again.

Tea had been served by now, and I drank mine to the bottom in a single gulp. "It must have been horrible," I said, wiping my mouth. "I can't imagine what you suffered."

Did I sound as false to him as I did to myself? He didn't seem to notice.

"It was hard to bear—hard for all of us," he replied, pouring me another cup. "My father in particular—he was so fond of Sofia."

"Did she and you live on our farm after you were married?"

"No, but we'd go there for a week or two every few months. I thought it would help her—after you were arrested, her hope just seemed to wither and die. But going to the farm only made her worse, I think, though at the time I didn't realize it. She kept to herself when we were there. Ti, every time I thought she was getting over all that suffering, she'd have a relapse. There were days when she didn't get out of bed at all."

"Poor Sofia." I looked away to pretend I was considering his words. "Tell me, did she often go on walks alone?"

"Sometimes—and mostly down to Indra's Millstream, to where we caught the frogs. Remember?" he asked hopefully.

"Of course."

He smiled, and I did, too.

If I'm a faithful mirror, he won't know what's in my head, I was thinking.

His face darkened. "You want to know how she came to be walking on Hanuman's Head?" he asked solemnly.

"Yes."

"I don't know." He took two quick sips of tea to steady himself. "I only know that the day she died, she insisted on going out early. It's my fault, in a way. I mean, I let her go. I could have stopped her, but I saw it as a good sign, her wanting to take a long walk. Around noon, when she didn't come back, I started to get worried. Nupi was still with us. She and I searched around the house, and then I went out looking for her. I remembered Sofia saying it was an unusually clear day and that she intended to climb a hill for the view toward the ocean. Later, my father joined us. When we found her, she'd been dead for several hours. She fell very far—she must have died right away." He reached out to grip my shoulder. "Ti, I want you to know she didn't suffer."

You don't think she suffered? I longed to shout. *Are you an idiot? Have you learned nothing in all these years?*

I asked him to tell me everything about that day: what she'd had for breakfast (chapatti with palm sugar, a habit she'd picked up from me), what she had worn (a lavender silk dress Aunt Maria had bought her), and even how she'd done her hair (she'd let it fall loosely down her back).

When I asked what the weather was like, he said it had been misty and warm.

"But she'd said it was an unusually clear day," I reminded him.

"I know. It was an odd thing for her to say." He shrugged. "Maybe she meant it would be clear from the top of Hanuman's Head. She was so distracted and upset at the time, I didn't want to correct her."

I quizzed him further, but the only other unusual thing he could recall was that Sofia, upon waking that morning, had told him that she wanted to give the large statue of Shiva that guarded our doorway to Nupi.

"Did she say why?"

"Just that Nupi would make better use of it than we would. It made sense, since we'd be living most of the time in Goa. I told her it was fine with me—which it was. You know, Ti, all these years I've wished I'd gone with her on that walk." His eyes became glassy and he shook his head remorsefully. "I could have," he added in a trembling whisper. "I had nothing important to do that day. But I didn't—I didn't...."

The last thing I wanted was for him to see that I suspected him of having murdered her; I saw now I had to reassure him.

"Don't blame yourself," I urged him. "I'm sure you did everything you could for her. I know she loved you very much. And I want to thank you for telling me everything so carefully." I made myself gaze down, as though into wistful memory, but it was to pre-pare an important lie. "Sofia told me once that she loved the time you brought her to the top of Hanuman's Head, just after you two fell in love."

"She did?" he exclaimed. "She seemed angry at the time. She even yelled at me."

"She was just being coy. You know how girls can be."

He smiled knowingly. I hated him for that—for not understand-ing my sister at all. I smiled back, however, as though we two were men who had learned through experience that women were a differ-ent—and more deceptive—form of life.

"Wadi, did you bring her body back here to Goa?"

"Yes, we buried her in the municipal cemetery."

"As a Christian?"

"We had to. She'd...she'd converted."

"Good. At least that's a comfort."

"It is? You're not angry?"

"On the contrary, it consoles me."

"Ti, you're really full of surprises today."

"Didn't your mother tell you? Christ was my solace in prison."

"She did, but I thought you'd been...been..."

"Teasing her? I might still have my problems with your mother, but at least we agree about Christ now. 'Fear no more, daughter of Zion; see, your king is coming.'"

He was silent for a time, considering how to react. As I sipped my tea, he stood and walked to the window, bracing his hands on the sill, gazing out, no doubt wishing he were far away. When he came to me, he kneeled by my chair and reached for my hand as though he were thanking me for caring for him after one of his fits. "I'm sorry for all that happened to you and your family," he said. "I know I didn't write to you, but after Sofia died I had nothing to say to anyone. Also, I couldn't lie to you, and I knew...I knew that if I told you what had happened, you might not have the strength to go on. You'd never survive prison. You'd never come back to us. I'm sorry, so sorry..."

Tears seeped from his eyes. I was quite moved. We hugged for a time without saying a word, feeling each other's grief. Despite all my contempt for him and six years of knotted suspicions, I felt myself opening to him. I didn't cry, however. At least I managed that.

After we separated, he glanced fearfully toward his mother's room, hoping she hadn't seen or heard us.

"Don't worry about your mother on my account," I said. "Prison was worse than I thought it would be—I won't lie about that—but in Christ I discovered forgiveness for us all. 'Anyone who nurses anger must be brought to judgment,' our Savior told us. I'm no heretic now, and we don't need to keep any bad feelings or coolness between us. Not for ourselves and not for your mother. In fact, as she told me recently, what's done is done."

*   *   *

After successfully convincing Wadi of my honest conversion and of my fondness for him, I soon settled into a comfortable routine in his home, living in the guest bedroom I'd always had, eating supper with Aunt Maria and him every evening, and occasionally even helping the cook to prepare breakfast. My first Saturday as their guest, I insisted on going to the marketplace and buying our fruits and vegetables, since the sight of all those ripe papayas and mangoes—and those luxurious red quilts of thousands of drying chili pods—was, to me, like knowing that generosity could still exist in our world. Over that first week, I ate like a crocodile. Just a whiff of simmering curry from a food stall was enough to make me take out my coin purse.

I attended Mass at the cathedral with my new family on Sunday, of course. I was reserved but friendly with everyone, and quick to express my gratitude to my aunt and cousin in front of their friends, as seemed appropriate for a young man who'd lost everything due to his own recklessness and heresy. Whenever I was alone, however, I found errands for their servants to do outside the house and searched for evidence of Aunt Maria or Wadi having plotted against my father, rifling through chests, wardrobes, cupboards, and cabinets, searching under mattresses and rugs, intimately learning the quick-pulsed joys and frustrations of having a clandestine purpose. I was looking for a note from the Inquisitors to my cousin or aunt, or maybe a scribbled list of charges against my father—anything that might be a link back to Papa. To my great disappointment, I turned up nothing except evidence of my uncle's infidelity; hidden underneath my aunt's lacquer perfume box was a florid love letter from a woman named Antónia that she must have stolen.

Twice I was nearly caught by Wadi, who, unlike my aunt, walked the streets unaccompanied by a slave and had the habit of slipping into the house without warning.

Not a thing remained of my sister's clothes and belongings—not a single hairpin, ribbon, or scripted prayer. In my naiveté, that confirmed to me that Wadi must have come to despise and resent her, since I was too inexperienced to know that the scent of her still inside her saris—even the sight of her jewelry or handwriting—might have been too much for a young widower to bear.

We'd sent letters to Isaac upon my return, but they would take at least a week to ten days to reach him. In truth, I preferred him to stay away, since my uncle would want me to reveal myself to him so that he might have the opportunity to comfort me. I hoped that he was so deeply in love that he wouldn't want to leave Antónia even for a day. At least that way some good might have come out of my father's arrest and death.

What did my hosts really think of me? I didn't care, as long as neither realized that I was playing a part. They asked me precious little of what I'd endured in Lisbon, so it was quite easy to remain in a dark corner of my invented personality.

They may look and look, but see nothing; they may hear and hear, but understand nothing—Mark 4.

*   *   *

I sought out Father António, my aunt and uncle's confessor, after Mass on my second Sunday. Aunt Maria had raced off to plan an upcoming supper party with several friends, and Wadi had gone home for an early siesta, so I was able to snatch a minute alone with the priest. He was as slight as ever, and ivory-pale, as though he'd been drained recently by leeches. After greeting him on the cathedral steps and reminding him who I was, I turned the subject to Father Carlos Miguel Fonseca.

"Why do you ask after him, my son?" Father António whispered, shocked.

"He asked me to give word to him when I'd returned. He was very interested in my spiritual growth. Please tell him I'm back in Goa if you see him."

He patted the air between us to keep me from saying more. "Keep your voice down." Leaning toward me, he confided, "He's been imprisoned by the Holy Office."

I felt a swell of joy lifting me up, but I managed to produce tears by thinking, *It's not enough, Phanishwar, but it is all I can now give to you. . . .*

"I pray he won't be there long," I lied.

Father António shook his head as if the Jesuit's case was already lost. He took my arm and led me away from some worshipers who'd gathered near us.

"Let me give you some advice," he said. "Don't ever speak of him, and don't ever tell anyone you knew him."

"But why not? He's got to be innocent."

"They say he was head of a plot developed by secret Jews to wrest control of the Holy Office itself."

"Secret Jews? Impossible!"

"No, some of the guards—and even the Captain of the fleet—were members of this group. I've learned that the English Protestants may have been supporting them, too. In London, they hate the Pope."

This was the best present I could have imagined: nefarious Jews and Protestants everywhere—and threatening the very power of the Inquisition itself!

"I suppose it may take some time for the prosecutors to find out how far his plot leads," I said. "'Cast the net out wide and you will make a catch,'" I added, quoting from the Gospel of Saint John.

"You must not tell anyone we spoke of this," the priest said, gazing around to check that we were not being overheard. When he looked up to heaven and mumbled an Ave Maria, I saw that he was afraid for himself, which made me feel as though I were seated on a throne made of darkness.

*   *   *

I needed something to occupy my days while I looked for clues to who'd betrayed Papa and me. Since I could hardly illuminate Korans and prayer books for the Sultan while in Portuguese territory, Wadi suggested I train as an assistant to the manager of his main warehouse, a lazy but sweet-natured man who'd worked for Uncle Isaac for many years. This manager always shuffled along in crimson silk slippers with pointed toes, which had earned him the nickname Chinelos, meaning "slippers." It soon became my duty to log all the merchandise we received from our Indian suppliers and shipped out to Lisbon. Old Chinelos was very patient with me, and I found this work to my liking, especially as it frequently gave me a chance to observe Wadi without having to talk to him. The Indian laborers all spoke respectfully to my cousin's face, but I soon noticed that when his back was turned, more than a few of them gave their employer sidelong, contemptuous glances. Chinelos told me my cousin once let his temper get the best of him and had given a brutal palming to an Indian elder for dropping and shattering a richly decorated porcelain serving tray that Wadi was giving as a gift to the Duke of

Lerma, a powerful Castilian nobleman whom he'd been courting—unsuccessfully, as it turned out—as a possible business partner.

"The man's hands ran with blood that day," the warehouse manager told me sadly. "The workers have never forgotten."

*   *   *

I often sat at Sofia's graveside after work, late in the afternoons, offering her frangipani and marigold flowers I'd bought at the marketplace and whispering in Konkani about the things I'd seen and done over the last few years. Afterward, at sundown, I'd slip away to one or another of the Indian neighborhoods, in part because I wanted anyone who might be following me to see there was nothing suspicious in my spending time there, but also because I craved time free of the Portuguese. Alone with the people of my homeland, I'd gorge on coconut sweets and sip bitter tea, sometimes letting myself cry silently over all that I'd lost, especially my son. The memory of lying next to Tejal sat in my chest like stones. On these occasions, I didn't even bother to cover my eyes, exhibiting my misery like a beggar.

I don't want to exaggerate my unhappiness. It came to me in waves, and for whole days at a time I was free of gloom. Even when morose thoughts threatened to drown me, I regarded them as unimportant, a nuisance that would not deter me from the voyage I had to make. Besides, concealment made my actions meaningful in a way they'd never been before. I'd been able to ruin a respected and learned priest from four thousand miles away, to seal him in a prison cell no different from the one I'd been in for two years. I had power, and I was beginning to believe that I'd been a very dim-witted young man for not understanding that the God of the Old Testament respected such power more than anything else. He—and any other gods who might be observing our world—might condemn me when I was done, but they'd admire me as well.

Although Wadi and I had a few long conversations over my first two weeks with him, we found ourselves encumbered by a mutual fear of giving offense. All that began to ease when I took to teasing him—about his bristly hair, for instance, or the expensive velvet doublets with gold embroidery that he now wore on formal occasions. All this he took as a sign of my renewed affection, just as I'd hoped—an indication, too, of my subservient position, since I worked hard at finding new jibes for his amusement, as though I were his younger brother. He began to laugh spontaneously, and to be less careful of his manners at the supper table, and even to roll his eyes when his mother said something self-aggrandizing or vain. The two of us soon formed a united front against her, as when we were boys, finding our way back toward friendship through a common enemy. It must have made him feel safe that we could re-create a bit of the magic of our youth. It probably made Aunt Maria feel sure of herself, as well—that nothing of import had changed.

I soon felt secure enough to ask about Berekiah Zarco's manuscript. When I told them I'd no idea if it was still on our farm, Wadi said that it must have been safe in its hiding place, and that he'd given orders to the caretaker he'd hired to be especially vigilant of our furniture. Aunt Maria said in a matter-of-fact voice that she'd completely forgotten the manuscript's existence.

Neither suggested we go back to the farm anytime soon to make sure it was still there. Likely, they'd agreed what to say if they were ever questioned by me about it, but just maybe they were telling the truth.

And yet I saw now it didn't matter. They were the only people who knew of the manuscript's existence, so one or both of them was guilty and I no longer cared which. *Let them work that out between them when the time comes,* I thought.

Once, while we were conversing about work in the back garden, Wadi reached out for me. "The air is burning!" he shouted.

I caught him as he began to writhe. I'd forgotten the violence of his convulsions and the terror they could rouse in me. When the seizure was finished, he leaned heavily on me as I walked him to his bed. I sat with him until he fell asleep, trying not to feel what I felt for him.

*   *   *

The time had come for me to talk to Sarah. Looking back, I think I'd been waiting to visit her until I was certain that whatever she'd tell me would not undo my resolve.

I was about to pay a call on her at her home, in fact, when I discovered Wadi slipping out of the house for the second night in a row without telling me or his mother where he was going, doused with enough sandalwood perfume for a small army.

Believing I was on to something exciting, and possibly incriminating, I tracked him that night to a tiny wooden house on a scruffy alleyway on the outskirts of the city, about two hundred paces east of the Governor's residence. Wadi entered with a key taken from his waistcoat pocket. Upstairs, a candlestick was soon lit and two shadows passed by the curtains, the second much smaller than the first— a woman. I crept closer but couldn't hear a thing. Nearly an hour later, Wadi hastened back home.

That night he left his bedroom door open. With my knife in my fist, I watched him sleep. He stirred when I leaned over him.

"Tiger, is that you?" he asked, sitting up.

I hid my blade behind my back. "It's me. I'm sorry if I disturbed you."

"What are you doing here?"

I was just seeing if I could murder you without you having time to scream, I thought, gratified that he was now at my mercy.

"I heard you calling out and came to see if you were all right," I answered. "You had better go back to sleep or you'll be tired all day at work."

I followed him again the very next evening, but this time I remained behind after he left the scene, hiding around the corner from the house he'd entered. His lover emerged a few minutes after his departure. She was a slight girl, probably no more than sixteen or seventeen, but it was impossible to see her face clearly in the darkness, especially as she wore a wide-brimmed black hat topped by a long feather. She walked as though tugged by a rope, running at times, looking back over her shoulder, obviously anxious to get home and clearly terrified of being caught. I sensed her heartbeat drumming almost as fast as mine. It made me feel that I was right where I ought to be.

Carrying neither candle nor oil lamp, she entered the side gate of a turreted mansion between the cathedral and the river, then tiptoed along the side garden to the back of the house. She must have had a way of coming and going through a rear door that let her slip away without being missed.

This was a very secret liaison that we three were engaged in.

CHAPTER 21

I went to see Sarah the next evening, wishing not only to learn what she had to tell me about Sofia, but also to persuade her to help me learn the identity of Wadi's lover. When she opened her door, she showed me such a relieved expression that I was stunned. It was an evening of misty rain, and Sarah led me into her sitting room to dry off, tugging me ahead in a girlish way. A small coal fire glowed in the hearth. I held out my hands to feel its warmth.

"Did you get my letter?" she asked, watching my face as though the world depended on my answer.

"Yes."

"Thank God. Then you haven't believed all your aunt has told you."

"Sarah, I'm not sure what you mean."

"Wait," she said. She asked for my sandals, which were soaked, and hung them over her fireplace guard. She then fetched a towel and stood back with an expression of maternal pleasure as I dried my hair and face. Her deep-set green eyes were intelligent and bright.

Her black hair was coiled elegantly on top of her head, and though she had put on some weight, her rounder contours suited her. She looked as if she was happy with herself.

"What is it?" I asked when she continued smiling at me.

"It's just that you've become a man. And you've grown strong. Those Inquisitors didn't break you. Thank God for that."

"I've become a Christian," I told her.

"Please, Tiago," she said with an amused twist to her lips. "I believe in the goodness of the Lord with all my heart, but we both know that even the most devout Christian can't really be a Christian in Goa."

"What's that mean?"

"It means they'd arrest Christ if he dared show his face in this wretched city!"

She spoke so openly that I gaped at her.

"Don't worry," she hurried to assure me. "I have no servants in the evening. I can't bear having them waiting on me all the time. I don't understand how people do it."

"And your father?"

"He died a few years after you left—some horrible disease that took many people that year."

"I'm sorry."

"One gets used to anything after a while." She gazed around, smiling at her surroundings. "It was hard at first, but now I like living alone."

"Are you married?"

She shook her head vigorously and laughed. "I've had good luck—no husband would have me. Now tell me everything. I want to know how you've been. And then I'll tell you what I know. I've had other friends imprisoned by the Holy Office, so I'm only too aware of your need to protect yourself. You must feel free to lie to me whenever you sense yourself in peril." She gave me a cagey look, intent on mischief. "Just let me know when you are about to make something up by scratching your nose."

Again I gaped.

"I'm sorry. It's my nerves," Sarah said. "I try to be amusing because we have much more serious matters to talk about. And I want to make a good first impression on you. It's been so long. Forgive me, Ti."

She motioned me to sit on her sofa.

"There were times when I was sure you wouldn't make it home to us," she said with a soft sigh, sitting next to me.

"I almost didn't," I replied, holding up one of my wrists and saying, "I did a bad job of it," to discount the importance of my suicide attempt.

She caressed a fingertip across my scars, which was disquieting, as though she were trying to trap me with her caring for me. She must have sensed my discomfort. Leaning back, she put a pillow over her lap, which made me think of Tejal and her shyness.

"You know, Ti, I think the entire Portuguese empire ought to be destroyed. Don't you think so?"

"I'm not sure," I said.

"You forgot to scratch your nose," she teased. "Now, if I remember right, your father died shortly after his imprisonment. And almost immediately after, you were arrested."

"You really want to hear all this?"

"Does that surprise you?"

"It's just that Wadi and my aunt aren't particularly interested."

"They're afraid they might hear something heretical."

"And you're not afraid?"

"I haven't any children, parents, or servants, so who could testify against me? The walls? They're free of any obligation to spy, not being good Christians themselves. Only my bedroom mirror occasionally looks as if it would like to tell on me." When I didn't laugh, she patted my arm encouragingly. "You know," she added, "I've heard it said there's safety in numbers, but it's quite the opposite in Goa."

On her continued insistence, I spoke of my father's demise, not mentioning his having poisoned himself, of course, then talked for a time about Phanishwar. I spoke with some of the desperate emotion I'd then felt, but I omitted any mention of my suspicions of Wadi and his mother. For Sarah's safety and my own, I made up a tale of having a revelation about Christ's divinity after a night of particular torment, when I imagined the Archangel Gabriel coming into my prison cell and reciting the Sermon on the Mount to me. Though Sarah must have doubted this absurd story, she nodded as though she believed me. I was glad she would lie for the sake of my safety—and sit with me without interrupting. There is something akin to redemption in the eyes of a friend willing to listen to everything we say.

I then started to describe the *auto-da-fé* where Phanishwar had been burnt.

"I called out to you that morning!" Sarah exclaimed.

"You were there?" I was stunned.

"I could never have stayed away. Scenes of barbarity like that must have witnesses."

I liked this woman more and more, but that only made me reticent to speak further about my past, since I didn't wish to create trouble for her. So I brought my monologue to a quick end by saying that days and nights in Lisbon had been tedious, and that I had used them as an opportunity to build up my physical strength and resilience.

"And now I'm back," I concluded with a shrug, as if it had all been over in just a few days.

"I heard a week ago that you'd returned. I don't mean to pry, but may I ask why you didn't come to see me sooner?"

"I couldn't. I needed to go to Benali. The girl I was going to marry lives there. Though maybe . . . maybe I've also stayed away because I've been afraid of what you might say about my sister's marriage to Wadi. I had to . . . prepare myself."

"I don't want to hurt you, but your instincts were right—I'm going to have to talk about some things you won't like and can't hear from anyone else. But I need to speak about them . . . for Sofia's sake."

She held out her right hand. On her index finger was a gold

band. I hadn't noticed it, and I didn't recognize it until she slipped it off and held it out to me.

"Your sister asked me to give this to you," she said, laying it in my palm. "She said it rightfully belonged to you."

I looked inside to read the Hebrew inscription from my great-grandfather's best friend: *For Berekiah, we shall face Jerusalem together, Farid.*

My guilt at still being alive clung tight to my breathing. *I should be dead instead of Sofia,* I thought.

As I slipped the ring on, Sarah noticed my effort to control my grief and went off for a carafe of brandy. When she returned, she pulled up her chair close to mine and forced me to drink a very large glass.

"I'm becoming a drunkard," I told her, laughing at myself to keep from descending into despair over the unfairness of my sister's death.

She took my right hand, the one with the ring, and kissed it. "Sofia knew I was her friend, even though we hadn't spoken in years. That's why she came to me. I won't betray either of you. She said I had to give the ring to you as soon as you returned. And now I've done my duty. I can tell you, Ti, I feel very relieved. A vow to the dead . . . it sits so heavy on one's shoulders. There's no weight quite like it."

"When did she give it to you?"

"After you were exiled to Lisbon. She came here one evening, looking desperately sad. It was a shock to see how frail she'd become. I hadn't seen her in years. I don't believe she had anyone else she could talk to."

"What did she say?"

"That her marriage had come to an end. That Wadi had tried to help her and had been kind, but he'd lost interest in her. That he'd been her only hope of salvation, and now he was almost a stranger to her. But it was her own fault, she said, for being so morose all the time."

I gazed down, thinking, *If only I'd been here, she'd still be alive.*

"Ti, don't think too harshly of Wadi," Sarah continued. "He has limited patience for sorrows. He'd prefer not to think about them, or to have responsibilities, so he rushes off to something—or someone—new when things get difficult. I learned that many years ago." She shrugged as if there were nothing to be done about it. "So it's not that he didn't love Sofia. He must have. All I can say is, when she came to see me, she was not angry at Wadi. I believe she forgave him his distance. She seemed angry only at herself."

"For marrying him?"

"No. For being unable to recover from your father's death and your imprisonment—or be the girl she once was. Does that make sense?"

"It might. Sarah, did she seem frightened of Wadi?"

"No, merely...disappointed." She looked away, considering the truth of what she'd just said. "Yes, disappointed—that's right. Ti," she continued, sitting up straight, as though to gain renewed resolve. "Sofia gave me more than just the ring. She brought me some bangles and a sari. If you want them, they're yours. I asked why she was giving them to me, of course, and she said it was because she wanted to make up a little for having betrayed me. I told her that I'd never held her responsible for Wadi leaving me, which was true, but she was insistent that I keep her gifts. Then something odd happened. When she said goodbye, I felt overwhelmed by the conviction that it was the last time I would ever see her. It was like...like I could see into the future, and this was going to be my only chance to keep her from going. I thought she might have been planning to leave for Portugal or some other place in Europe. Why else would she give me your father's ring and not wait to give it to you yourself? I asked her about that when she was standing right there." She pointed toward the front door. "I can still see her as if it were yesterday. She said the ring reminded her of too many things that she wished to forget. We kissed goodbye. I wanted to tell her not to go, but I didn't. I should have. I owed it to her, but I was afraid—afraid of making things worse, of begging her to stay in Goa when she wanted only to get away. As soon as I closed the door, I burst into tears. The feeling of her departing forever was *that* strong." She shook her head with self-reproach. "Three weeks later, I heard she was dead."

"Do you . . . do you believe she was murdered?"

"Murdered?" She drew back, shocked, then stood up and took a calming breath. "No, Ti. I'm afraid I'm fairly sure she took her own life. The gifts she gave me—it was her way of saying farewell, of leaving this life with less to weigh her down. Do you see what I mean?"

I tried to reply, but silence seemed the only way to meet her revelation. I knew that what she said made sense, especially since Wadi had told me Sofia had wanted to give away our mother's statue of Shiva, but it was still murder as far as I was concerned: her husband had killed her by abandoning her.

"Did you ever talk to Wadi about your feeling that Sofia took her own life?" I asked.

"No, never." She walked to the window and drew the curtains closed with a hard tug, seemingly angry with herself. Turning back to me, she said, "After your sister's funeral, I didn't think I'd ever speak to him again. I didn't want to. I guess I couldn't help blaming him. But about six months later he came to visit me here." She sat down again, her hands clasped together in her lap. "I didn't tell him about my conversation with Sofia. He came because he was lonely. He was grieving and had lost a great deal of weight. I couldn't help feeling sorry for him. But Wadi . . . he's always been ruled by certain physical urgencies, if I can put it that way, and he was desperate for . . . companionship." She smiled fleetingly. "He even wanted me to attend to him, but I was no longer quite as stupid as I once was. I did introduce him to several young women friends over the next two weeks. I made dinner parties. Then I never saw him again. I'd served my purpose."

"So this is the first time you've spoken to anyone about your suspicion that Sofia took her own life?"

"Yes. It didn't seem wise to tell anyone else."

"Good, then let's keep all this just between us. Tell me, do you know who Wadi has been seeing?"

"Ti, do you know something I don't?"

"I spotted him meeting in secret with a girl. She was very young, I think, but I didn't get a good look at her." I described the mansion I'd seen her enter.

"I know that house!" Sarah exclaimed, grinning as if something glorious had happened. "What a scandal!"

"Why? Who is she?"

"Ana . . . Ana Pontes Dias. I introduced Wadi to a cousin of Ana's at one of those parties I mentioned. That's how he must have met her. Ana just happens to be the only daughter . . . the *much beloved* only daughter of Rafael Dias, the wealthy spice merchant."

"The one with the glass eye?" I asked, remembering having seen him riding in a palanquin years before, children racing after him and pointing.

"That's him, and I happen to know that our Ana has been betrothed to Gonçalo Bruges for more than a year. And *that* young man," she said in triumph, enjoying this part of the scandal the most, "is the eldest son of Francisco Bruges, the miserable old miser who collects duties on the ferries going in and out of Goa. I know the boy well. He's very nice, and he's mad about Ana. Ti, do you understand? Wadi is threatening to break up one of those marriages meant to bring two empires together. If the fathers knew . . ." She shook her hands in the Portuguese way meant to indicate disaster.

"Would they really care so much? Uncle Isaac's business is going very well now, and if Ana is really in love with Wadi, then—"

"But he's no match for Gonçalo Bruges!" she interrupted. "Ana's father would never permit any marriage to your cousin, and a broken engagement would destroy everything the old merchant has been planning. There's also the little matter of Wadi's having been adopted—the Little Moor and all that. And his convulsions. This is a very small city—and people don't forget such things."

"I need to be sure that the girl I saw is really Ana."

"Why?"

"Sarah, I am not what I am, and this is where I have to start lying to you." I scratched my nose, just as she'd asked me to do.

She grinned. "Just tell me if your verifying this girl's identity will help Ana in some way. Or at least Gonçalo."

"It depends what you mean by *help*."

She leaned toward me with an eager face. "Will it protect either of these two young people from Wadi? I assure you, he's only leading Ana into a dead end. And poor Gonçalo—I'd rather not see the boy hurt."

"What I'm planning should help them—though I have to confess it's not my main purpose. And . . . and that's all I can tell you."

"Then show me the house this girl returned to after meeting Wadi—show it to me now." She stood up, rubbing her hands together, eager to embark on an adventure.

"Sarah, if it is her, I'll need you to do me one more favor. I don't think it will put you at any risk, but I can't be absolutely sure."

I then explained those parts of my plan that she needed to know.

*   *   *

Certain that I'd never be able to fully control the events I was about to set in motion, I headed the next afternoon to the tannery where Papa and I used to purchase vellum, making sure I wasn't being followed. The Tamil proprietor met me at the door. He'd aged badly and was stooped over a wooden cane, unable to lift his head high enough to meet my gaze.

"It's been a long time," he said, sighing the way some Hindus do, meaning, *There's no need to tell me why, since we all know that life pulls us inevitably away from each other . . .*

"I need to visit the expert in poisons again," I told him. "I want Garuda to carry me away if they catch me."

"Then come," the Tamil said, gesturing for me to follow him.

He hobbled ahead of me to the back entrance. My father's writing on the door, though faded, was still visible. *Many are the roads leading to the Lord, but how fortunate are we that there is only one path beyond.*

Reading the words now, I took them to mean that we would not have to be reborn into this world, though perhaps that was not what my father had intended at all.

*   *   *

Vaasuki's door was still painted deep blue, with a pink and white hibiscus flower at its center. At my knock he opened the door himself and raised an eyebrow in puzzlement. He'd let his white hair grow long and it fell to his bare shoulders.

"Do you remember me?" I asked.

"Yes, and I advised you not to return to Goa," he answered angrily.

"I'm sorry. It could not be helped. And now I need something to protect my life in case the worst happens."

"Do you expect the worst to happen?"

"Yes."

It was the first time I'd admitted to myself that I would not live long. I realized then what I should have earlier—that it was a good thing that Tejal had spurned me. She had set me free to do what was necessary. Maybe she even understood that somehow.

"Come in, then," Vaasuki said, his voice now friendly.

Taking me by the arm, he led me into his conservatory. With feather-leafed palms arching over his head, he knelt in front of his statue of Shiva and prayed. Likely he was thinking of the need to help another man take his own life. Maybe he was asking the gods to forgive him. Or me.

His supplications finished, he asked me to sit with him and tell him what had happened to me. We spoke for two hours, and he questioned me urgently, as though I could offer him armaments that might win a war. We spoke in detail about my captors, even their names, and after a time, I realized he was very carefully cataloguing all I could tell him about the workings of the Inquisition in Goa and the Galé Prison in Lisbon. When I was done, he blessed me, and I asked him why he needed to know so much.

"I can assure you, it's always good to know one's enemy as well as one can," he said with a knowing nod.

It was the first time I realized that saving individual victims was not enough for him. "You'd like to chase all the Portuguese from India, wouldn't you?" I asked.

"Wouldn't you?" he shot back, shocked that I might think otherwise.

I, too, was surprised that it had taken me so long to understand that the Empire—that great machinery of death—had to be utterly destroyed. Sarah had been the first to imply that to me, but I hadn't understood. With my vision clouded by sorrow and rage, I'd mistaken my battle for the whole cause.

Vaasuki left me for a few minutes. When he returned, he asked me to bow down, then slipped a silver cross around my neck.

"I don't want this," I said vehemently, and I started to take it off.

"No, wait," he said, stilling my hand. Lifting the cross and holding it horizontally, he flicked a latch and opened a compartment with an amber-colored glass ampoule inside.

"Just put it in your mouth and bite down," he told me. "There will be a little blood, but it will not matter. After a few seconds, you will feel some pain in your belly and chest, but it will be over in two or three minutes. Now practice opening the cross. If they come for you, you may not have much time."

After a few repetitions, I could undo the latch and spill the ampoule into my palm in only a second. I was pleased with myself.

"Yes, it's easy now," Vaasuki said sternly, "but when the time comes, your hand may not be so sure."

"If it isn't, then pray that I find another way to die," I replied.

*   *   *

Three days later, Uncle Isaac arrived. He'd wanted to come sooner but had been gravely ill and was still suffering with some unknown malady, although he waved away my concern. His eyes protruded alarmingly, and his skin was a waxen yellow. His long hair was gray now, and badly tangled from the sea journey. Even so, the warm scent of him was just as it had always been, and his comic smile as wildly infectious, and they instantly undid me.

He ran to me the moment he saw me, his eyes so flooded that he grew angry he couldn't see me. I'd been sketching in the garden, and he kept his arm around my shoulder as we talked under the tamarind tree I'd planted years earlier.

For a few minutes I let myself surrender to his love, a little boy adored by his uncle.

He didn't want us to go back inside and join the others, though Wadi had appeared twice to ask us if we wanted something to eat or drink.

"You're all I've left now of my beloved brother and niece," Isaac told me, kissing my brow. "It's selfish, but I don't want to share you with anyone."

That hit me hard, especially because it implied a responsibility to him that I could no longer accept.

He and my aunt were barely civil that first day, and I could tell from her sharp glances that she despised him with all her being and was barely containing a tirade of rage. Nights, he slept in his study, although I offered him my room. With his son, he was friendly, but there was a distance between the two that seemed completely new. I had the feeling that Wadi must have sided with his mother in his parents' quarrels and that my uncle feared his accusations of betrayal. I almost asked after Antónia but decided his replies would only link me to him more intimately. I couldn't afford for our bond to be strengthened and deepened. Or, more importantly, I didn't think he couldn't afford it.

Fearing Isaac's judgment, I was unable to spout a single quote from the New Testament in his presence, though when Aunt Maria asked me to say grace over our first supper together, I did find the courage to tell him I'd found solace in Christ. In his look of sadness, I saw that he guessed my duplicity—and understood only too well my need for it. Twice over the next days I caught him staring at me from my doorway in the early morning before I got up, and I was sure he was looking for the boy he used to know. At those times, he resembled my father so much that I could have begged him to take me away with him.

On one of these occasions, he brought me fresh bread with fig jam to have breakfast in bed, and as we sat together I was certain that he wanted me to open my heart to him, but I simply couldn't, for fear of losing all I'd become.

One evening when we were alone I asked if he'd seen Berekiah Zarco's manuscript lately.

"No, I thought it best to leave it on your farm," he replied. "In Goa, if anyone found out about it, we'd be in trouble again."

"Did you ever learn...who might have testified against my father?" I asked.

He shook his head. "I tried, but Father António said they'd already started investigating me, so I had to give up."

Isaac only stayed four days, explaining he had to get back to Diu for business. He asked Wadi to join him there as soon as possible; he had contracts pending that would involve delicate coordination between the warehouses there and in Goa. He made me promise to join him as well, and I agreed I would, but after my uncle was safely aboard his ship, I felt a great wind of relief blowing through me as I waved farewell, and I knew I'd never go.

*　　*　　*

Sarah had been able to verify that Ana was the young lady I'd seen by following her on several occasions as she left her father's mansion. Not only did Ana meet Wadi in secret twice again, but she also wore a wide-brimmed black hat that matched perfectly the one I'd described earlier.

The day after Isaac left for Diu, Gonçalo Bruges, Ana's fiancé, came to Sarah's house in the late evening. We'd asked him to come at exactly the time Ana always left to meet Wadi.

Gonçalo was tiny, barely five feet tall, and very youthful, with milky skin and only a dusting of beard on his chin and cheeks. Ringlets of brown hair fell loosely over his brow and ears, and he had sharp green eyes, like a kitten. He was seventeen, a year older than Ana. They were to be married in seven months, just after his eighteenth birthday.

I was standing in the parlor when he stepped inside the house. I enjoyed his light laughter when Sarah teased him about the small fortune in pearls sewn onto the lapels of his crimson coat and collar of his olive-green doublet.

"So what's this mystery you invited me for?" he asked cheerfully. He must have believed this was some game she'd concocted for his enjoyment.

Asking him to be patient, Sarah hooked her arm in his and walked him to the sitting room, where she introduced us. I liked the vigorous way the young man shook my hand, clearly pleased to meet any friend of Sarah's. After we were seated, she explained to Gonçalo that she'd invited me to her home since what she had to tell him was not pleasant and she'd felt the need to have an old and trusted friend with her when she did so.

"I assure you that Tiago will not breathe a word of this to anyone," she said gravely, turning to me at just the right moment, as we'd practiced.

"You have my word," I confirmed, putting my hand over my heart. I remembered how much the Portuguese in Goa appreciated dramatic gestures.

In the years since, I've wondered why Sarah agreed to lie for me. I know she wanted to save young Ana from heartbreak, and if that meant creating some trouble for Wadi, so much the better, yet I sometimes think she already knew how far into the shadows I was willing to descend. I wonder if she wanted revenge. And whether she knew if it was for Sofia or for herself.

"Sarah, I hope it's not something bad I've done." Gonçalo grimaced boyishly, hoping his charm could win him a reprieve if he'd somehow offended her.

He was sitting on the sofa, hunched, but trying not to look too anxious. I was seated next to him and Sarah had taken an armchair directly in front of us.

"I'm not mad at you at all," Sarah hastened to reassure him. "But it'll take me a minute to explain." She stood and began to pour brandy into three tiny glasses of red crystal that she'd placed on a wooden tray. "Gonçalo, one evening I was walking at the eastern edge of the city and I saw something I shouldn't have. I'd really just been wandering around, thinking hard about some things that were bothering me."

She handed us our drinks and sat down. I led a toast to Gonçalo's health.

"Then I saw my old friend Francisco Xavier down the street," Sarah continued, her tone firmer now, as if she'd become sure of her purpose. "How odd, I thought. Now, maybe you don't know it, Gonçalo, but at one time, Francisco Xavier and I were very close. You'd have been just a toddler. Well, I almost called out to him, but he was walking so fast and looked so determined . . . He was gazing around all the time, as if he was afraid of being followed. Naturally, I didn't want to disturb him if he was on a delicate mission of some sort. I had no intention of spying on him, although I admit I was curious, but from where I was standing I couldn't help seeing him go into a small, two-story house. He had a key. I found that odd, too, and I stood there for a minute or so after he went in, just wondering what he could be up to. Maybe it had something to do with some secret merchandise, I thought."

Sarah wiped her brow with her handkerchief. "Gonçalo," she said softly, "I fear you are going to hate me very soon."

"I promise I won't," he replied immediately. "Just tell me, please!"

"As I stood there," she began again, "I saw a girl rushing down the street. She wore a fancy black hat that cast a shadow over her face, but I recognized who it was." She gazed down with a troubled expression. "She, too, had a key for the house. She went inside. Gonçalo, the girl was Ana Dias. Now, I know what you are thinking," she rushed to add, holding out her hand to stop him from speaking. "I'm sure there is a perfectly good explanation. There must be. I'd guess you can tell me what it is, which is why . . . which is why, in fact, I asked you here."

She smiled benevolently at him.

Gonçalo had gone very pale by now, and his jaw was clenched. "Are you sure it was Ana?" he asked hesitantly.

Sarah bit her lip, turning to me with a pleading look.

"Several nights after Sarah saw these things," I said, "she asked me to follow the girl as she came out of the house. I felt bad about it, but Sarah was so upset. . . . And I knew she had your best interests at heart." I reached out for her hand and gave it a quick squeeze. Her embarrassed smile seemed perfect to me. "I saw the girl return to a very large mansion," I added, and I went on to describe it to him in detail. After I mentioned a fire-colored bougainvillea cascading across the façade, however, he leapt to his feet.

"How long was she with Francisco Xavier?" he demanded.

"An hour or so on the night I followed her," I replied evenly.

Sarah said, "I feel certain there must be—"

Before she could get out another word, Gonçalo rushed out of the room. Sarah gave me a frightened look, because we hadn't expected this. I caught him just as he reached the door.

"Where are you going?" I asked.

"To my father. He'll get to the bottom of this."

"Please don't," I told him. "The conclusions you've drawn may be mistaken. There could be some very innocent reason why she went there. That's why I wasn't sure Sarah should tell you. In fact, I counseled her against it."

Sarah had joined us now. She took Gonçalo's arm.

"I know you are angry, but you have to think of what's best for Ana. If you go to your father, the scandal will taint her forever. You must see her father instead. Please, Gonçalo, you must not compromise her. Senhor Dias will do anything to prevent his daughter from becoming involved in a scandal. He'll speak to Ana with no one present but you. You'll have the truth either way—but this way will guarantee a measure of . . . of honor for all concerned."

"Honor?" the boy snapped. "There's no honor in what she's done!"

"You must do what Sarah says," I interposed, "and though it may compromise me as a spy, I'll go with you. After all, before confronting his daughter, he'll want to know exactly what we saw. Only I can tell him, especially as I don't wish to see Sarah become more involved. As a single woman, you understand, she needs to be careful. A scandal might cause complications for her."

"You would do that for me?" Gonçalo asked, gratitude already in his voice, since he hadn't the vaguest idea of what I had in store for him.

CHAPTER 22

An Indian servant holding a lighted taper answered our knocks at the Dias mansion. The great hall behind him seemed cavernous in the darkness.

"Master Gonçalo!" he exclaimed in a shocked whisper.

"Tell Senhor Dias I'm here," the young man commanded.

"But he's sound asleep! You know he goes to bed early."

"Then wake him!"

"He doesn't like to be disturbed after—"

Gonçalo pushed past him into the foyer. He was carrying a porcelain lantern, and the flickering light on his features emphasized his anger, haloing him with violence.

"Very well, but you will please wait here," the servant told him, scorn in his voice. He took his time walking up a curving staircase to the gallery.

"I'll have your head if you don't move that Indian behind of yours!" Gonçalo snarled at him.

The man continued his leisurely journey without looking down at us, disappearing into a corridor to the side of the gallery.

A series of marble statues of the Virgin Mary and the Evangelists separated the foyer from the hall beyond. In the back wall was a ruby-red and blue rosette of stained glass, glowing faintly in the moonlight. When my eyes had better adjusted, I could make out the gilded frames of religious paintings on the walls, and a stone crucifix on a large table—perhaps an altar. The room might have served as the family's chapel.

"This house must be worth a fortune," I remarked, having decided there was no need to be subtle in making reference to what he'd lose if his engagement to Ana were broken.

Gonçalo gave me a despairing look. "My father will kill me," he moaned.

I hadn't suspected this added fear of his until now; I'd thought his father would blame only Ana.

"I can't imagine living without her," Gonçalo continued morosely. "She's my whole future. I thought she loved me, too."

"Don't blame yourself," I said, genuinely sorry for him, but also wanting to fan the coals of his rage. "There was nothing you could do. A girl's heart is not so resistant as we might like. And Francisco Xavier can be very seductive when he wants to be."

Tears of humiliation stung his eyes, and he stepped hastily into the hall's darkness, blowing out his lamp and turning himself into a shadow. Only on hearing voices upstairs did he return to me. And even then, his eyes were moist.

"Be strong," I told him, "and she may still be yours."

I held his lantern while he set his flint to the candle inside.

"Thank you for your kindness," he whispered to me, emphasizing the depth of feeling behind his words by squeezing my hand, which moved me.

Together, we stood at the base of the staircase, gazing up to the gallery. The Indian servant reappeared, carrying a sinuous candelabrum before his master, who took tiny, unsure steps, leaning on a silver cane with his left hand and clinging to the banister with his right. Senhor Dias wore a dark dressing gown with pearls sewn onto the ruffled collar, which I understood by now to be a kind of family emblem, and the reason why Sarah had teased Gonçalo; the boy's doublet and coat must have been a gift from Ana's father.

Senhor Dias' thinning hair was wet and stood out in a comical way; he'd probably splashed himself with water to awaken. He had not had time to put in his glass eye, and he wore a black patch instead. His one good eye was crinkled with weariness. In his free hand, wound around his knuckles, dangled a rosary.

"I apologize for waking you, Senhor Dias," Gonçalo said meekly, possibly having second thoughts, "but this . . . this couldn't wait."

The two men shook hands, and Gonçalo introduced me.

"Young people believe everything is an emergency," our host said in a tone of a lament, more to himself than to either of us. He gave a heavy sigh and asked his servant for a chair.

Gonçalo waited until he was comfortably seated, then said, "I'm afraid you've been robbed, Senhor Dias."

"What are you talking about?"

"Ana is gone. You won't find her at home."

"Have you lost your wits? Where would Ana go?"

"Young girls can be surprisingly resourceful in the service of their desires," I told the old man. Allowing myself a small jibe, I added, "I'd guess she's gone to visit a Moorish kingdom."

"What are you talking about—this is Goa!"

"Then send for her," Gonçalo challenged.

Our host waved an angry hand at his Indian servant. "Go find my daughter, and for God's sake, don't dawdle!" Then he turned to Gonçalo. "If this is some sort of joke," Dias threatened, "I promise that your father will take a whip to you. And so will I!"

"You can save the punishments for your daughter," the young man replied, "though if I am wrong, you may let loose the justice of all of Portugal against me." Proud of his heroic retort, which I thought a sure sign of his youth, he turned to me with a righteous expression. "Tell him, Tiago."

In a troubled voice, I recounted my tale of having seen Ana and

Wadi together, referring to Sarah only as a friend who'd asked for my help. I also confessed my shame at having followed his daughter in secret and my discomfort at being involved, since Wadi was my oldest and *dearest* friend, as well as my cousin. "He's almost a brother to me," I added, "and I don't feel comfortable at all condemning him too quickly. Though I must tell you he tends to . . . to grow bored of his women rather easily. Also, he was taken as a child from an Arab ship, and so—"

"He's a Moor? Is that what you meant before?"

"He was born to Moslem parents, but he was adopted by my aunt and uncle when he was very young. He's been a pious Christian ever since, so I hope you won't jump to any conclusions about any sort of savageness that might still remain in his character."

I could see I'd set the poor man's heart thundering. He jerked his head away, horrified, his mind chasing nightmares. When we heard running on the upstairs gallery, he jumped up as he probably hadn't in years. Nothing like a daughter's ruin to put some youth into an old codger's legs!

"She's gone, Senhor Dias!" the servant called down, leaning over the banister. He came to us panting. "Her bed has not been slept in," he added.

"Did you check in every room upstairs?"

"I did, Senhor Dias."

"Damn her! Senhor Zarco, would you take me to the house where you saw her?" he asked hopefully.

"I would, but I think you had best wait here for her to return. The damage on this night is already done, and by the time we reach their meeting place, they'll already be gone. You've no choice but to count your minutes of anguish here." I made a small bow of apology. "I cannot stay with you, however. I must go home so that I can be there when Wadi returns. After so many years of friendship, I want to warn him that his world is about to come crashing down. You may not agree with my loyalty to him, but I hope you will respect it. I think it only fair that I be there for him."

"We wait without you, then," Dias said, holding out his fist and giving it a sharp twist, a gesture I didn't then understand, but which I'd now guess was him locking his determination inside his head with a kind of mental key. He closed his eyes, and I thought he was calm, but without warning he swung his cane around viciously. It slammed into the banister with a wild crack, splintering the wood. "Goddamn a daughter's treason!" he yelled, so loud that I heard its echo in my ears as a condemnation that would never be forgiven.

*   *   *

I waited for Wadi outside his house, unwilling to go inside and have to converse with Aunt Maria. My heart was drumming excitedly, and the night sky had never looked so alive with stars. I felt drunk on their distant light.

I had been there for only a few minutes when Wadi came sauntering up in his brown velvet cape, smiling with the afterglow of his secret conquest.

"Are you going out?" he asked with a roguish smile, undoubtedly hoping that I, too, had an evening of debauchery in mind.

On his breath I smelled *feni*. "We need to talk," I said in a serious tone.

"Then let's go inside," he replied, taking my shoulder. "I'm bone tired."

"No, I don't want your mother to hear us."

"What's wrong?"

"Listen, you remember I went to visit Sarah a while back? She told me some things that I've tried to keep quiet, but I've failed." I shook my head as though I were deeply disappointed with myself.

"What did she tell you?"

"She saw you with a girl . . . a girl named Ana."

"That bitch!" He stamped the ground like a taunted bull. "What did she tell you?"

"That she'd seen you together. And she insisted I go to see the house where you've been meeting this girl. I needed to see how bad things stood for us, so I went. Unfortunately, Sarah didn't listen to my advice after I returned. She told Gonçalo Bruges everything she saw, and he has just now gone to see her father."

"Damn her! She's always wanted to get back at me. I ought to strangle her, the lying bitch!"

"Wadi, Sarah is no longer the problem—Senhor Dias is. He might even come to see you tonight with Ana."

"How do you know that?" he asked suspiciously.

In the way he stared at me, I could see it had only just occurred to him that I might be against him. My awareness that he was drunk and might attack me amplified my senses. I could feel the dangerous tautness of his anger, but I wanted him to lunge at me, for I could then hold it against him.

"I went with Gonçalo to see Senhor Dias," I said, to provoke him further.

"It's you!" he growled.

He gave me no warning, charging into me so hard that I was knocked back against the wall of his house.

"You son of a bitch!" he shouted at me.

The breath was taken from me. I fell to my knees, struggling for air.

"What have you done?" he demanded, reaching under his cape for a knife, standing over me as though about to plunge it into my back.

I thrust up my hand. "It's not me," I said, gasping. "I only went with Gonçalo to hear what he told Ana's father. I pretended to befriend him in order to spy for you! I did it all for you!"

Wadi gave me a puzzled look.

"Yes, I've compromised myself to help you!" I said bitterly.

The hand gripping the knife fell to his side.

"Why must you always misunderstand me?" I said, shaking my head despairingly.

"So what did Gonçalo say?" he asked with a sneer, whether for Gonçalo or me I couldn't tell. Perhaps for us both. I hoped he despised my weakness, since it was sure to make him overconfident.

I brushed dirt off my shoulders. "Put that knife away. Don't let all you've drunk ruin your chances to save yourself." After he sheathed it, I got back to my feet. "If it weren't for me," I said, "Gonçalo would have gone to his own father, who might just have had you killed without waiting for any evidence. I was the one who convinced the boy to go to Senhor Dias instead. He won't want a scandal for his family, so I've saved your skin. If you don't believe me, then ask Gonçalo. Or ask Sarah."

"I thought that you . . . that you might have kept a grudge." The "truth" of my brave efforts on his behalf made him stumble over his words. "I should have known it was Sarah and not you. I'm sorry." He kicked the ground between us dejectedly. "Will you forgive me?" he asked.

I took his hand when he reached out. Holding it was like saying goodbye. Or like closing a book we had opened together when we were only eight.

"I've always forgiven you," I answered, "but what's important now is to figure out what we're going to do."

The *we* I regarded as a very nice touch.

"We don't need to do anything," Wadi said.

"Why not?"

He smiled as though pleased with himself. "Ana and I were wed in a secret ceremony a few months ago."

"You're married?"

"Yes."

"Why didn't you tell her father?"

"Ana wouldn't let me. She hates him. We've been thinking of moving together to Diu to get away from him—to disappear without warning. My father has been setting things up for us."

When I turned away to consider how Wadi's secret union might affect my strategy, I saw immediately that I could use it to my own advantage. I felt blessed to have such a rash enemy. "Uncle Isaac *knows* you're married?" I asked.

"Yes."

"But your mother doesn't?"

He snorted. "If I told her, the whole world would have found out long ago. Though I'll have to tell her now, I suppose." He looked up at the sky and put both hands atop his head, as though to feel the weight of his mother's ambitions pressing down on him. Gazing at me sadly, he added, "It's strange, Tiger, but more than any condemnation, I dread my mother praising me for having made an important marriage."

*   *   *

An hour later, after Wadi and Aunt Maria had discussed his marriage behind the closed door to her bedroom, I heard footsteps outside our front door. I eased it open just as Senhor Dias and his daughter were being helped out of their palanquins by their footmen. The merchant shook my hand with both of his, as if I were an old friend, trying to smile, but his misery returned when he looked back for his daughter. Ana was cowering in his wake, her hands clasped together in front of her chest as though she had taken a vow of silence. I decided it would be awkward to kiss her cheeks and instead simply said I was glad to make her acquaintance, to which she gave me an almost imperceptible nod. She was a slight girl, with dark blond hair falling down her back, and eyes that looked bruised. There was an angry red scrape on her cheek. Maybe her father had beaten her. Her hands trembled when he helped her straighten the black mantle across her shoulders.

As I showed them into the parlor, Aunt Maria greeted them warmly, offering Senhor Dias a glass of our best Portuguese wine, but he pushed it away with impatience. She then tried praising his clothing, particularly his ruby-red waistcoat, which was sewn with pink pearls around the buttonholes.

"Please keep quiet, woman!" he snapped. He was wearing his glass eye now, which gave him an otherworldly, intimidating gaze.

My aunt's face froze with horror. She knew now that her delight in the news of Wadi's marriage to a wealthy bride had been premature.

Without waiting for permission, Senhor Dias and his daughter sat together on our sofa, his hand clasped firmly around hers; he wasn't going to give up ownership of the girl easily.

Wadi and I took chairs a safe distance away, next to each other, in front of the fireplace; he'd made me promise to sit beside him when they arrived. My aunt remained standing, wiping streams of perspiration from her cheeks. How that woman could sweat!

Wadi's treachery lay like a decaying corpse between us. Senhor Dias let the silence accumulate to make its stench even worse. We dared not speak before he did so.

"Your son has stolen my daughter and corrupted her," he told my aunt. "And I intend to begin legal proceedings."

"But—but tonight—tonight is the first time I've heard of these matters," she stammered, leaving Wadi on his own. Whether she did this intentionally or out of nervousness I can only speculate, but her son shot her a murderous look.

"I stole nothing," Wadi said defiantly, first to her, then again to Senhor Dias.

"It must be some devilish trickery," the old man countered. Disdain made him spit his words. "I refuse to believe my daughter would give herself freely to the likes of you. I want to know through what means you weakened her will. And how you intend to give us her honor back."

"I don't owe you a thing. We were married four months ago. There was no magic. Your daughter is everything to me. I'm not ashamed to say so in front of any judge you choose. I love her as I loved only once before."

Wadi glanced over at me to acknowledge that he meant Sofia, and I smiled as gratefully as I knew how. He was speaking well for himself. Were it not for me, he might yet survive this shipwreck.

"Why she fell in love with me is a mystery, but I'll always be thankful for it," he continued. He smiled tenderly at Ana. It seemed to me for just that one moment that he risked revealing the most fragile part of himself. "This is my friend Tiago," he told his wife, holding my arm. "When we met I told you about all his troubles and how bad I felt. I believe your heart . . . that it was then you opened it to me for the first time."

Ana gazed down, afraid to speak, but we all knew that Wadi had spoken the truth.

I was grinning to myself at the irony; he had won this girl through my suffering!

"If you saw no shame in what you've been doing," Senhor Dias demanded, "why in God's name did you keep it a secret?"

"Tell him, Ana," Wadi said encouragingly. "Now is your chance—our chance. I will stand by you no matter what he says or does."

"Speak up!" her father thundered.

"I could not face your anger," she whispered, shrinking away from him, plainly afraid he'd rear back and wallop her.

"Then you *are* wed to this man? What he says is true?"

"Yes."

"Have I been so terrible a father that you defy me in this way— and fear me?"

Ana began to cry silently, her head in her hands. She was little more than a child. She must have been wondering how she'd fallen so far in a few short months. And all because she wished to live her own life.

"This matter will not end here," her father declared to Wadi. Turning to his daughter, he added, "I'm taking you home now."

"You don't have to go with him ever again," Wadi told her.

She stared with gratitude at her husband, an expression of courage creeping slowly over her face, her breathing deepening. "You have always been my lord and master," she told her father, wiping her eyes, "but I'm married now. And just as my mother's first duty was to you, so is mine to Francisco Xavier."

Senhor Dias lifted her hand to his lips tenderly, then dropped it into her lap.

"You are dead to me, my daughter," he said with terrible calm.

It was as though a leaden bell had sounded the end of a battle. The cruelty of his words rings inside me even today.

Senhor Dias struggled to his feet, refusing his daughter's assistance. "Remember this," he said to Wadi, his hands held high over his head, as though he were invoking the Lord of the Old Testament. "She deceived her father—and she may yet deceive her husband!"

He spoke as if it were a curse, but I understood it as the old man's profoundest hope. And as my way forward...

*   *   *

Ana shared Wadi's bedroom for the first time that night, and he must have spent most of it reassuring her that her father would reconsider. I heard sobbing until long after midnight. "I've lost everything!" she shrieked once in the early hours.

Was Ana worried that her father would find a legal way to remove her from his will?

I pictured Aunt Maria shaken awake by that unholy cry, pacing her room and cursing her son for sparking a scandal. I saw her peering into her mirror by the light of a single candle, comparing her face with her new daughter-in-law's and regretting that she had not the magic to steal away the girl's youth.

Ana didn't come downstairs in the morning. Wadi's eyes drooped and his body sagged. Aunt Maria was cold to us both.

"You must help me with Ana," my cousin begged me after his mother left the breakfast table to dress. "We've gotten off to a bad start."

I agreed I would, but when I went upstairs his bride wouldn't let me inside their room. She wouldn't even speak to me through the door.

Wadi went in to sit with her for a time and came to work late, as glum as could be. "She won't even eat a crust of bread," he said, and in a pleading voice added, "Tiger, you have to do something. I'm no good at this. It's got to be you."

I jumped at the chance to encourage him and left early for home that afternoon to see what I could do. This time, I managed to get her to speak to me as I stood outside her locked door.

"Please, I don't need anything," she protested in a frail voice.

"I'll leave some rice and chicken at the door, and a carafe of water," I said patiently. "I'll go away and then you can come out and take it."

"No, please don't."

I fetched the food from the kitchen, knocked quietly, and stood back. When Ana appeared, she was still in her robe. She blushed at seeing me.

"I'll help you," I said, trying to win her over with the gentleness in my voice.

"There's nothing you can do," she stated gloomily.

"I know what suffering is, Ana. Even orphans like us have a future. Look at me—I'm the proof of it."

I managed to squeeze some tears out, which spread yearning compassion across her young face. Wadi may have been her husband, but when she stepped out to me now, I knew I would become her confidant.

She dressed quickly and came downstairs when I told her that Aunt Maria had gone to visit a friend. It was a lovely day, with a cool breeze coming from the ocean. I suggested we take a walk by the river.

"I want to prove to you that despite what's happened, you can still be the same person you've always been," I told the girl, which made her smile for the first time since I'd met her.

She leaned on me hard as people passed us, believing that they somehow knew of her banishment from her father's home, and I thought she might faint.

"They all despise me," she said more than once, and I occasionally had to tug her forward, which only made her more fondly dependent on me, since she sensed a strength in me that would be hers whenever she wanted it.

Walking beside Ana, I often remembered Sofia telling me she longed to shed her skin. It seemed I'd been given a second chance to help a shy and confused young girl make her way in the world.

I told her that she couldn't capitulate to her father. "It's clear to anyone who looks at his face how much he loves you," I said, "and after a time, he'll have no choice but to abide by your decision."

She might have questioned where I'd picked up such wisdom in prison, but since I was only telling her what she wanted to hear she asked nothing of me except that I not let go of her arm for even an instant.

*   *   *

Over the next week I played royal clown and advisor to Ana and Wadi, though I found that my first assessment of the girl had been partially wrong; though she was timid, there was a glowing fire at her center that could also make her astonishingly excitable and willful. She loved to watch boat races in the river and even cheer at cockfights, and if she didn't get her way, she barricaded herself behind a frigid expression of contempt worthy of her aristocratic upbringing. She swiftly gained confidence enough to become Wadi's equal in a quarrel, making up in stubbornness what she lacked in strategizing.

She was also ambitious—eager to travel, in particular—and possessed all the pent-up desire for new experiences of a girl whose talents and curiosity have been stunted for years. Superficially at least, there was much about Ana that reminded me of Sofia, and I began to understand that it was no accident that Wadi had fallen in love with her. Perhaps he'd even sought her out to maintain the illusion that my sister was still alive in some way.

One evening when we were alone, Ana confessed—just as I'd suspected—that she didn't care so much about her father's rage but was in a state of constant worry about possibly losing her inheritance.

"Not so much for myself, but for Wadi," she informed me.

The Indian practice of dowry giving had deeply infiltrated her way of thinking, as it had with many Portuguese girls. She spoke of herself as unworthy of the marriage if it was not sealed with riches from her father. Although she didn't say it in so many words, she was also upset that her new and less luxurious life might not offer her the adventures she'd long hoped for. A provincial existence in a port city four months' journey by ship from the capitals of Europe must have seemed to her a truly miserable fate.

I assured her that although Wadi might have preferred a wealthy bride, his love for her would see him through any doubts and disappointments, and that if he knew of her desire to travel, he'd surely save the funds necessary to visit Lisbon every few years and stay for several months. I insisted she discuss this with him, promising her that her complete honesty would gratify him and confirm to him her unswerving loyalty.

I believed quite the opposite, of course—that by bringing up her feelings of distress and unworthiness, she would give Wadi the impression she was having second thoughts about their marriage. He'd also begin to worry that he'd never be able to provide her with what she most wanted.

In this effort to undermine their affection, my greatest ally was their own ignorance of each other; like most young couples, they'd never seriously discussed what they expected from their union.

A few days later, my cousin shuffled up to me one day at work with a troubled face. "I think she'll never get over losing her father's love," he said, not wanting to reveal to me what she'd really told him.

"Ana's lost a great deal that would be hard for anyone to give up," I told him. "Give her time. Though maybe..." I shook my head dramatically. "No. It's a bad idea."

"What?" he asked.

"I shouldn't say anything more. It's not my place."

"Tiger, please, I'm counting on you."

"It's just that Ana's father . . . If only he could hear you speak of your love for her again. I feel certain you could win him over, though I suppose he may try to humiliate you again, and that's too great a risk. With that single eye targeted on you, he's like a cyclops, and I—"

"I'm not afraid of him!" Wadi declared.

"I know you're not," I assured him, eagerly nudging him toward disaster. "I only meant that his contempt is hard to bear. It will be difficult for you to face him. I know it would be for me."

"Life isn't always easy, you know."

I genuinely adored these moments of wisdom from Wadi. They were so unintentionally comical.

"In that case, I think you should go see him," I said encouragingly.

"Would you come with me?"

Senhor Dias would surely think Wadi a coward if I accompanied him. "Me? I spied on his daughter, and I made no secret of telling him that I was your best friend. I don't think he's apt to like me very much."

"You have to come! I'm not very good with words, and I may need you to speak up for me." Whispering, he added, "And if I sense a detour coming on, I'll need you to get me out of there as quickly as you can."

*   *   *

The next evening, just before dinner, we went to the Dias' mansion. Senhor Dias gave his personal servant instructions to make us wait outside and admit us only when he was already in the foyer. He was seated in an armchair, a tiny wooly dog with a crimson ribbon around its neck on his lap, and two lighted golden candlesticks on the table next to him—a small reminder of the riches Wadi would never get, most likely. On the floor before him was a tattered jute rug smelling of manure, undoubtedly taken from his stables. The servant told us it was Senhor Dias' wish that we stand on it so as not to soil his marble floor.

Wadi was vibrating with fury. I really thought he might go for the old man's throat. I hoped he had his knife with him.

Dias' one real eye looked my cousin up and down slowly while the other, of glass, remained staring ahead at nothing. The merchant made no attempt to hide his repulsion.

"Say what you have to," he told Wadi, meaning, *Let's get this over with.*

My cousin contained his rage admirably and began to describe his love for Ana as having rescued him from despair. Though he relied on florid metaphors better saved for troubadour poetry, I was moved by how desperately my old friend wanted to be understood by an enemy. Wadi had wagered his future on being wed to her and was now trying to explain the ineffable workings of the heart to someone who was hardly even listening. One could not fault him for his effort or his feelings. But Senhor Dias had been turned to iron by his daughter's corruption. He petted his dog languidly while Wadi pleaded.

In the end, seeing that he'd been unable to dent our host's armor of disdain, my cousin turned to me. "Please," he whispered desperately.

"There must be some gesture that Francisco Xavier could make that would prove to you his complete devotion to your daughter," I began. "Something that could reunite you with Ana at the same time, since that is his greatest wish. I remind you, as a pious Christian, that there is nothing impossible, not even life everlasting, for those who believe in the Son of God."

"I'm afraid the only way for such a man to prove his devotion," Dias replied, speaking to me with amused spite, "would be for him to petition a judge to annul his ruinous marriage." He pointed at Wadi as though consigning him to hell. "Only if you do that will I believe that your love for my daughter is true and that you want what's best for her. And only then will she be allowed into my home again and be given my blessings for her marriage to Gonçalo." He pushed his little dog roughly to the floor and got to his feet. Speaking to me as though Wadi had already left the room, he said, "Although I have to tell you, Senhor Zarco, I have grave doubts that Gonçalo or any other Christian man will have her in the debauched state your Moorish friend has left her in."

It was checkmate, and Wadi and I both knew it. We trudged home in silence. Later that evening, he exploded at Ana over supper, sending her soup bowl crashing to the floor with a murderous swipe when she commented that it needed to be heated further.

"If what we have in my house isn't good enough for you, then you won't have anything at all!" he raged.

She ran to their room, holding her sopping dress away from her skin and sobbing. Wadi gripped his head in his hands while Aunt Maria directed a kitchen servant to mop the floor. I suffered with them for the required few minutes, then started eagerly on the duck with plums, which tasted heavenly. For dessert, I had a double portion of coconut pudding. I was so happy that I might even have considered easing up on Ana and Wadi for a few days, but the next morning my cousin's bride came downstairs for Sunday Mass wearing my sister's moonstone head scarf.

CHAPTER 23

When I think back to Ana's sweet round face framed protectively by Sofia's silken scarf, I can feel myself recoiling even now, curling into a closed space of shadows and murmurs.

Wadi must have gone through Sofia's possessions after he found her body and given Ana what he hoped she'd like, I thought. *Or maybe the fool really was trying to turn her into my sister.*

I managed to eat that morning, but I sat as silent as a dead man. I can't recall the order of events that day or even the next.

Could it be that the most important feelings exist so far below the surface of daily life that they're not affected by time? After all, we can love someone with the same fervor after twenty years of absence. And hate them, too.

That timeless realm was where I now lived, and in that dark place, everything was confused: inside and outside, past and present, even good and evil. Though I'm willing to admit that I may only be offering an easy excuse for the blood that was about to cover my hands....

*   *   *

It was probably right after Mass that I approached Father António, though it might have been later that afternoon. Over the previous weeks, I hadn't wanted to risk setting off alarm bells in the priest's mind by asking too many questions, but now even being caught seemed worth the risk. He'd always acted as Aunt Maria's closest confidant inside the Church, and if anyone could act as an unintentional witness against her or Wadi, then it was he.

I managed to corner him just inside the entrance to the cathedral. That I *do* remember. I can see the harsh light from the open doors slicing across his legs. And the ornate shine of the silver ciborium—the chalice that held the Blessed Sacrament—in his hands. I asked him to step into the darkness of a side chapel with me.

"Excuse me, Father," I began, "but I've been very worried about something. My aunt says that in order to try to help my father find Christ when he was a prisoner of the Holy Office, she gave you a manuscript written by my great-grandfather. Can you remember it?"

"I remember a hand-scripted manuscript given me by Francisco Xavier. Is that what you're thinking of?"

"It might be. What did my cousin tell you about it?"

"He said the text included a record of your great-grandfather's conversion to Christianity."

"Yes, that's the one," I said, smiling. To make my incorrect guess about my aunt seem consistent, I added, "Aunt Maria must have sent it through him."

I waited several seconds for the priest to disagree with my statement, but he simply nodded and said, "What do you want to know about it, Tiago?"

He was so sure that what the three of them had done was a good thing that he didn't even suspect that he had just testified against his co-conspirators.

"It's a very dangerous manuscript," I replied, "because it says horrible things about the Christians in Portugal and what they did to the converted Jews. I'm worried because if it fell into the hands of someone young and gullible, like the boy I was...You see what I mean, don't you? I can't get it out of my head at night."

"The Inquisitors must have burned it long ago," he told me, patting my arm as though I mustn't worry about it. "It's what they do with heretical books."

He turned to take his leave.

"Just one more thing, Father. Please don't tell anyone I asked about the manuscript. Not even my aunt. I wouldn't want her to know that I'd been thinking of it. It might worry her, and she has enough on her mind at the moment."

"Of course, Tiago. Now if you'll excuse me, I must be off."

*   *   *

The rest of that day is lost to me. I may have gone to one of the Indian neighborhoods; I remember speaking Konkani, since Portuguese only made the throbbing in my head much worse. More likely I wandered aimlessly. I remember nothing more until a sunset of fire began to wash across the western sky. When I saw the sun about to sink below the horizon, I checked for the poison in my cross. I slipped the ampoule in my mouth and kept it there as I walked back home. The feeling of death on my tongue was a great relief; it gave me the freedom to keep going to the end.

*   *   *

I went to see Gonçalo the next day after work. I told him that I was worried about Ana, since she was very unhappy with Wadi. I suggested he might be able to win her back if he did exactly as I said. At one point, he surprised me by asking if I hated my old friend. Very likely the boy simply needed a reason he could understand for my trying to undo my cousin's marriage, so I told him that after all our years of friendship Wadi had forced me to work like a slave for the incompetent old fool who ran his warehouse. I'd overheard, too, that I was not to receive the promotion I'd counted on. Gonçalo accepted these as solid reasons for my behavior, and when I told him my plan, he readily agreed to it.

*   *   *

The next few days were all storms between Wadi and Ana, in part because my cousin got drunk on *feni* every evening after supper. She cried out sometimes in the middle of the night, begging help from God, so that I knew he was thrashing her. I'd guess that he was beginning to understand that this marriage would be no happier than his one to Sofia. Or maybe it had just occurred to him that Ana was not my sister and would never be.

One night, the young bride snuck into my bedroom to ask me to protect her. She told me that Wadi was in the garden drinking.

"Is he beating you?" I asked urgently, feigning fear for her safety.

She kneeled beside me, showing me bruises on her arms. "Yes, but it's not that. It's that he wants to have a child so badly that he pushes himself on me. And when I resist . . ."

Her confession surprised me. "I . . . I don't know what to say," I stammered. "He's obviously very troubled. It's not like him."

"He thinks if I get pregnant, our marriage could never be annulled. So every night he forces me. . . ." Tears rolled down her cheeks. "I know it's my duty, Ti. I know I should want it. But I can't . . . I can't seem to think or feel what I ought to."

"Ana, I may have a solution—a way to appease both Wadi and your father."

"I'll do anything!" she said fervently. "I can't go on much longer. I didn't expect marriage to . . . to be like this. Sometimes he seems no different from my father."

She began to sob. I held her until she could smile when I wiped her eyes with my thumbs.

"I've spoken to Gonçalo and he is willing to ask your father to forgive you," I told her gently. "If the boy is successful in this effort, then everything is sure to improve between you and Wadi. When your father accepts the marriage, your husband won't feel as urgent a need to produce a child. Relations will calm between you."

Ana's pretty face brightened. "I've never met anyone like you. You're everything Wadi told me you were."

"There's only one small problem. . . . Gonçalo wants you to talk to him—in secret, of course. You must tell no one. Certainly not Wadi, or all will be lost. You can't tell him anything, even if he beats you. Ana, can you be that strong?"

Her eyes flashed. "Yes, I can do it."

"In the meantime, I'll also have a word with Wadi to calm him down."

"I don't know how I'll ever repay you! You've been so wonderful to me."

"Thank you, but listen, Ana—Gonçalo wants you to apologize to him and to ask him yourself for this favor. And I have to say, I think he's right to make this demand."

"I understand. When does he want to see me?"

"Give me a few days to set things up. And another thing—I have to warn you that Gonçalo still loves you. But he doesn't want to see you hurt, even if it means giving you up."

"He was always a good friend." She kissed my cheek. "Just like you, Tiger."

*   *   *

I got dressed and went down to Wadi. "You'd best be careful with Ana," I told him. "I ran into her father, and he told me that she'd visited him the other day. She begged him to ask Gonçalo to forgive her. Senhor Dias chased her out of his house. He was very hard on her. So she must be really suffering right now."

"She asked her father to give a message to Gonçalo?"

"Only to say she bitterly regrets betraying him. At least, that was what her father told me, though I don't trust him, of course. Come to think of it, maybe she didn't even go to him. Maybe he's lying. Still, treating her too roughly may drive her away. Suffering makes young girls fickle, Wadi. They are not like men—not like you and me."

Wadi grew pensive, and that night, I heard neither shouting nor sobbing coming from their bedroom.

*   *   *

I stole Ana's moonstone head scarf from her chest the next morning and confirmed it had been my sister's—the micrographic lotus flower was faded but still visible. I went immediately to Sarah's house and gave it to her, elucidating a bit more of my plan when she questioned me. She passed it on to Gonçalo that evening, explaining that Ana wished him to keep it as a token of her regret for having hurt him so deeply. Sarah told the boy that he was to wear the scarf as a cravat at the next Mass, as a signal that he had not wavered in his desire to speak with Ana. Gonçalo understood from me that his meeting with the girl was to discuss their possible reconciliation.

On Sunday, I told Ana not to come to the cathedral with us, but to wait at home and feign a slight fever. I explained that I'd yet to work out one detail with Gonçalo; in truth, I didn't wish to risk a scene in public that might have put the final stage of my plan in jeopardy.

It was all too simple to point Gonçalo out to my aunt before Mass and to suggest that I'd seen his cravat somewhere before. She took care of the rest.

"I'll kill him!" Wadi snarled to me after his mother had taken him aside. He turned furiously toward Gonçalo, but I stepped in front of him.

"Don't jump to conclusions," I whispered. "It's a common fabric. Even my sister had a scarf that was similar, though it had a black fringe, as I recall."

I said that, of course, to give Wadi an alibi.

"I think I remember it," he said, his acting capable.

I looked away quickly to hide my revulsion. It astonishes me to this day that my cousin was not embarrassed at having given something that Sofia loved to Ana. Maybe, like many men, he discounted the importance of such keepsakes.

Whatever the case, Wadi raced right home. I followed close behind him. He took the stairs two at a time to his bedroom and threw open the door. Ana sat sewing the hem of one of her dresses.

"Where is it?" he demanded.

"Where's what?"

I reached the doorway at that moment. Ana was holding her hands up in front of her face, no doubt fearing he would strike her.

"The head scarf I gave you as a gift. The white one."

"I seem to have lost it."

His laughter was contemptuous. "Lost it where?"

"If I knew that, Francisco Xavier, I would have found it by now."

"Whore!" He lunged to slap her face, but she ducked in time and his hand struck her shoulder. She tumbled off her chair and banged her head hard against the wall.

"Enough!" I shouted, grabbing Wadi.

"I've been faithful to you, Francisco," Ana moaned from the floor.

"You lying whore!"

I tugged on his arm. "Shut up!" I said. "Can't you see this must all be just some misunderstanding?"

"Get away from me!" he shouted, throwing me off.

He stood over Ana, who was sobbing, and unsheathed his knife. Squatting next to her, he put it to her throat. She held her breath, trembling. I was afraid to move.

Ana closed her eyes, praying for life.

This is it—this is the gift I give my sister, I thought.

Seconds later, Wadi surprised me. He threw his blade to the floor. He stood up and hung his head, then looked back at me helplessly. He must have smelled the air catching on fire around him; soon he was on his back, writhing and foaming.

*   *   *

Wadi was too weak to confront his wife again that day, and before bed I convinced him to do nothing more. "Let me investigate how Gonçalo got the scarf," I urged him. "If you let your jealousy feed upon itself, if you act rashly now, your marriage will end before it's even begun," I added.

"Be quick about it," he snapped back, his anger beginning to seethe again.

Exhausted from his fit, he fell asleep early. I went to see Sarah, to make certain she'd be home the next day to receive Ana. Back at Wadi's house, I took the girl into our garden, where Aunt Maria couldn't hear us. I asked if she still had the key to the house where she used to meet Wadi.

Ana nodded, too afraid to voice an answer.

"Good. Then tomorrow afternoon, you are to go there. Gonçalo will be waiting for you nearby. He will knock at the door twice, then once more."

"At what time?"

"First you must go to my friend Sarah's house around midday. She's invited you to eat with her. I don't want you here if Wadi comes home to take siesta. He's very observant: he may see your secret in your eyes. At the tolling of nones you must be all the way across the city, at the rendezvous house, so set out early. You'll have an hour to speak to Gonçalo. I'll make sure Wadi goes back to work if he does come home. Rush back here after your meeting. Tell no one where you were or who you saw."

Ana clasped my hands and brought them to her lips.

"If Wadi sees you, we're both going to have problems," I warned her. "I'm not sure he trusts even me anymore."

*   *   *

Late that night, after drawing a map for Gonçalo, I snuck out of the house and, using the key to his gate that the young man had given me, I entered the grounds of his estate. His bedroom was upstairs, at the back of the manor house, and by throwing pebbles at the shutters I was able to rouse him from sleep. He dashed down to me in his bare feet.

"Ana will come to you tomorrow afternoon at the stroke of nones, at the house where Francisco Xavier always met her." I handed him the map I'd drawn, with the location circled. "Be there then. You'll have an hour to speak with her. After that, she must get back home so that Wadi doesn't suspect anything. You must make sure that—"

"But what if she's not there?"

"She'll be there. Just go to the door and knock twice, then once more."

"If this works, I'll owe you everything," he said, gripping my hand.

"If this works, you'll owe me nothing." I bowed graciously. "The gift is always in the deed itself." For good measure, I added from Luke 38: "'Give and gifts will be given you.'"

*   *   *

I caught only glimpses of sleep that night. All that had happened in my life kept tumbling through my mind. I didn't think once of Gonçalo's safety, or even Ana's.

I dreamt of an ocean that had turned to glass—and of a blazing sun reflected in its surface. In the morning, I left for work before the others were up. I didn't want to have to talk to anyone.

As soon as we arrived home for siesta, I handed Wadi a large glass of *feni*.

"To help you nap," I told him.

An hour later, when I roused him from sleep, he was still a little drunk. I helped him wash his face and told him that I had just spoken to a friend of Gonçalo's.

"When?"

"While you slept. Gonçalo wants you to meet him at the house where you were intimate with Ana."

"Today?"

"Yes, a few minutes after nones. You mustn't go there any earlier."

"What's he want?"

"I'm not sure. It seems he interpreted Ana's gift of her head scarf as encouragement, though I don't think she meant it that way. He'll only tell you what he wants when you see him. But listen—he'll have people watching you, and if you leave earlier, he won't meet you there. And you have to come alone," I added dramatically, "which is why . . . why I'm worried this may be a trap."

"A trap?"

"I don't trust him. Bring your knife. He may do something crazy to try to avenge Ana's honor. He may think that if he kills you, he won't be punished. After all, his father is rich and powerful. So if you see any men with him, anyone at all, get out of there quickly. I'll be waiting nearby to help you. I won't let myself be seen. Wadi, listen . . ." I took his shoulder and gripped it tightly. "Even if he's alone, he may try to attack you when you least expect it, so be careful— though I'm certain you'll come out of any fair fight the winner."

*   *   *

As we waited for the tolling of nones, Wadi paced. He refused more *feni,* but I didn't think it necessary; he was already like a hawk ready to swoop down on its prey.

When the bells of the cathedral struck, we were off. Having reminded my cousin that he was going to be watched and that I'd need to remain hidden if I was to do him any good, I insisted that I take a different route across the city. I hid a drawstring bag with Nupi's bangles and a few keepsakes under my cape, knowing I'd be unable to remain in Goa after this, whatever the outcome. I ran all the way there as though I were flying. I felt like a god, far above everything around me.

When I reached the house, all was quiet. Ana and Gonçalo must have already been inside. Likely they were arguing in hushed voices, Ana declaring she had absolutely no intention of having her marriage annulled, Gonçalo denying what I'd promised her—that he'd agreed to ask her father to forgive her. Though maybe the two saw that there could be some benefit in forming a secret alliance and were cautiously discussing how best to proceed. It was even possible, I suppose, that the girl realized she was no longer in love with Wadi. It was one thing to meet a man surreptitiously for lovemaking, quite another to share his life and be disowned for it.

Did they see my handwriting in their destiny? From my hiding place, I could hear Ana saying disappointedly, "And yet Tiago seemed such a friend to me..."

Wadi came rushing up as though not to be fooled with. He pounded at the door twice, then several more times. It eased open. From my position, I couldn't see who stood in the entranceway, but when he reached out to grab an arm, I glimpsed Ana's profile for just an instant. I feared he might pull her outside, but he thrust his way in instead.

Did Gonçalo call down to ask who it was? Did Wadi see the boy's face—lit with fear perhaps—at the top of the stairs?

When I crept to the door I could already hear shouting. Then a scream from Ana. Then silence.

My mind seemed to float outside my body. I've no idea how long I stood there, fighting my dizziness. I knocked on the door feebly, then called Wadi's name once, then again, louder. I heard footsteps, slow and heavy, coming toward me.

When he met me at the door he was carrying his knife in one hand and my sister's scarf in the other. He was drenched with blood, as though he'd bathed in it. There was a streak even across his lips. His eyes were glazed. He looked like a blind man.

"I've killed her," he said numbly.

"Don't move!" I told him.

I pushed inside and closed the door behind us. Upstairs, miraculously, Gonçalo was still alive. The boy was crawling on his belly toward the window. I crouched next to him. His throat had been cut from ear to ear. What gave him life was spilling dark and hot onto the wooden floor. He couldn't speak, although there must have been much he wanted to say about a life that would never now be lived. A horrid choking sound was all that came out. I believed he was trying to speak my name.

As Wadi had said, Ana was dead. She lay on her back, one arm pinned behind her, her dress soaked with all that had seeped from the vicious wounds in her neck and chest, her head bent at an impossible angle, her eyes gazing at nothing. A boot was gripped in her hands. She must have held on to Wadi's leg with all her strength, desperately trying to tug him away from Gonçalo.

"I'll get help," I told the boy, though I knew it was too late.

Wadi was still standing at the bottom of the stairs. I saw now that his right foot was bare. He gazed up at me, puzzled, as if he didn't even understand how he'd gotten here.

"Ana still has your boot," I told him. "Come up and take it from her."

Upstairs, he found he hadn't the courage to pry it from the dead girl's hands.

"Why did she have to betray me?" he moaned, his head in his hands. "I loved her."

He fell against me, but I pushed him off.

"It's me," I said, shaking him by the shoulders.

"What do you mean?"

"Ana wasn't betraying you, I was. I stole her head scarf because it was my sister's. And I gave it to Gonçalo. Ana came here only to try to convince him to ask her father for forgiveness—to accept you as her husband. She loved you. As did Sofia. As even I did—once, long ago. Now do you see what you've done? And what you've always done?"

He gazed at me in anguish. "But . . . but I had to protect my honor."

"So you think there's honor in murder?" I sneered.

I didn't wait for his answer, and I didn't offer him any further explanation; he was intelligent enough to figure out the precise shape and scope of my plot against him. Pushing him aside, I rushed from the house, wiping the blood from my hands on the packed dirt of the street. An Indian chimney sweep was standing nearby, his face black with coal dust.

"Get help!" I called to him. "Ana Dias has been murdered by Francisco Xavier Zarco. And the boy she was meant to marry is dying."

CHAPTER 24

I considered heading to Benali to steal my son, but the village was inside Portuguese territory and it would be safer for me—at least for now—to cross the border into lands controlled by the Sultan of Bijapur. Later, when I had a plan, I could come back for Kama—and plead with Tejal to leave with us.

I walked south past the College of São Paulo and out the city gates. My escape was free of doubt and worry. My crime glowed in my mind, radiant as a myth or a dream, and as I walked, the moist sunlight and blue of the sky seemed to enter into me. If a person can fall—as well as rise—into a state of ecstasy, then I'd achieved it.

*   *   *

I found our farm in a state of complete disrepair. In the sitting room, clumps of bamboo and weeds as tall as a man grew out of mud swept inside by monsoon rains. Of the caretaker my uncle and aunt had employed, there was no sign.

The roof had given way over my bedroom, which seemed to be inhabited by at least one bearded monkey; the little creature raised its head as though I were a long-waited enemy, its ageless eyes gleaming with wary anticipation, then dashed shrieking through the broken window when I stepped inside. In Papa's room, I found that the drawing he'd hung on the wall behind his bed—of my mother shining like the sun inside a cavern of dark cloud—had been stolen. So, too, the sketches of her he'd always kept in his desk. His books were covered with mold. Sofia's bed was gone, along with our statue of Shiva.

This is the way it should be, I thought. Our house should not be intact, not with my family all dead.

When I crossed the overgrown patio into the kitchen, I found a warm pot of dal resting on Nupi's wooden table. Garlic bulbs were braided together on a cord hanging from the ceiling. A dozen sweet limes and two nutmeg kernels nestled in a reed basket. I dropped down on a stool and waited. She would throw her arms around me. We'd fix up the house. It would take months, and I'd never leave home again.

When I grew weary, I moved my stool near the door and slept with my back against the wall. A woman I'd never seen before woke me at sunset. She had long gray hair and a wispy mustache, and her faded yellow sari was badly soiled. I didn't ask where she'd come from. It didn't matter.

"Have you seen Nupi, the woman who used to live here?" I asked her.

"They say she begs in front of the temple in Ponda."

It was too late to walk there. I decided to head to the closest village, Ramnath. The barber, Kahi, let me sleep on his floor. People I'd known as a boy came to see me in the morning, bringing me fruit and vegetables. I'd torn a band on my sandals while walking from Goa, and a leatherworker I'd never met before fixed it for me. No one had seen Jaidev, the holy man, in years. One day, he'd simply walked out of the village, saying he was off to die in the waters of the Ganges.

I found Nupi sitting outside the temple in Ponda, wearing little more than rags. She was scooping rice from a wooden bowl and folding it into her toothless mouth. When she saw me, she struggled to her feet. She was bent and twisted, as though her bones had been broken many times, but her face was bright with love for me.

I ran to her and hugged her into me while she wailed. We sat down together so that we could look into each other's eyes. I don't know what she saw in mine, but in hers I found Sofia and my father, and sunsets watched from our verandah—even my mother as she lay on her deathbed.

She touched her hands all over my face as though sculpting me into her memory, no doubt comparing me with the way I'd looked. I gave her back her bangles.

Neither of us spoke. I kissed her gnarled hands and buried my head in her thick white hair, which smelled like my childhood. After a time, she asked me to help her stand again, and she smoothed the front of her tattered sari with great care.

"I couldn't stay on our farm after Sofia died. I tried, but..." She shook her head guiltily. "I wandered for years. I only returned a year ago. I'm sorry, Ti."

"It doesn't matter. You did your best. Nupi, your sister is very worried about you. You must go see her."

"You were in Benali?"

"Yes, I went there to see Tejal. She married someone else. She couldn't wait for me."

The old cook showed me a wistful smile. "Kali has hurled all her weapons at us, hasn't she?"

"Yes."

"But we can still be together. That must mean something."

"Perhaps."

She pressed her hand into my chest to make certain that I was real, and it was then that I felt my first twinge of guilt for what I'd done, like the quick beating of a drum. Then it was gone.

*   *   *

We went home. Sofia's room was not in such bad shape, and villagers gave us jute pads to sleep on. Nupi retrieved a coconut fallen to the ground and walked it around me twice to keep me from being haunted, as was the custom around here. The mosquitoes were terrible that night, and the moon so bright that I could hardly sleep. I was thinking of many things, but mostly of being glad to be alive. I believed I could start over.

We let the old woman who'd moved into our kitchen stay with us. Her name was Charu, the widow of a well digger, who'd left her village for reasons we didn't ask. In the morning, Charu made us chapatti, but Nupi didn't think them good enough for me and made me two with her own hands. I ate them with a ripe papaya from the garden. Nupi watched me, smiling toothlessly. I'm sure she thought the worst was behind us.

After breakfast, the old cook told me she had a secret reason for wanting to come to our farm right away, and she fetched a drawing that she'd hidden behind my father's bookshelves. We sat together on the verandah to look at it. It was a micrographic sketch of a delicate hand, its contours made with Hebrew letters. When I covered it with my own palm and fingers, I realized from its shape and size that it was my sister's. Her words were still readable. Each finger of the drawing read:

Turn your eyes away from me, leave me to weep in misery. Do not thrust consolation on me for the ruin of my own people.

It was a quote from Isaiah. I didn't understand why Sofia had left it to me as her final gift, but when I translated it for Nupi, the old woman hung her head and said, "Sofia tried to wait for you, but she just couldn't go on."

"I don't understand."

"I see that Wadi didn't tell you."

"Tell me what?"

"I do not think we should speak of these things now that you are home. No, no—we must try to fix the house. Then you will visit the Sultan and find out. . . ."

She struggled to stand up, but I tugged her back down to me.

"Nupi, tell me everything you know."

"Some stones look polished only when they are in the river. When we take them out and look more closely—"

"Please, no riddles or sayings! Tell me clearly."

"Your sister told me that when she converted to Christianity, she—"

"She converted?"

"Yes."

"But why?"

"To marry Wadi. She said it was necessary."

"When?"

"I'm not sure, but it must have been ... it would have to have been before your father was arrested."

"Go on."

"She was told by Aunt Maria that she would have to bring an offering to a priest in Goa in order to be allowed to convert."

"What kind of offering?"

Nupi shrugged. "Ti, I do not know a thing about Christianity. Sofia told me only that she had to bring the priest something that would prove she did not pray to the Jewish God any longer, that would show that your father no longer controlled her beliefs. So she—"

As Nupi spoke, it was as though the past reassembled itself into an order previously hidden from me. I now knew why the Inquisitor hadn't questioned me at length about my sister.

"She gave them my great-grandfather's manuscript," I interrupted.

"Yes. She carried it with her on one of your trips to Goa— secretly. She had Wadi deliver it to a priest—the one your aunt knew so well. I do not know his name."

"Father António."

I had looked down from my window one evening to see Wadi and Sofia talking just outside the front door of my uncle's house, carrying what they said was a schoolbook in a leather satchel.... My sister had even worn an elegant new dress for the occasion.

"Aunt Maria tricked her!" I said hotly. "And Wadi, too. They did this to her!"

"Oh, Ti, there is still so much you do not understand about your sister. Bringing the manuscript was Sofia's idea. Your aunt didn't even want it in her house, but Sofia was insistent. She was so angry at your father for his refusing to bless her marriage to Wadi—so angry, so angry... And at you, for having Tejal. And for other things. She wanted—"

"What other things?" I interrupted.

"She wanted a dowry. Your father hadn't given that any thought. At least, she didn't think he had. He gave the wet nurse, Kiran, two of your mother's saris. You remember?"

"Yes."

"That gave your sister the idea that your father had completely forgotten her marriage needs. Oh, so worried that little girl was. She thought she looked strange, too. Such a timid little sprite. You remember? She believed her dowry would have to be impressive. That's why she stole the two silver bangles from my sister when we were in Benali."

"I didn't realize she'd taken them."

"Sofia told me just before she married, when she handed them back to me. Maybe she took other things, too—I have no way of knowing. I brought the bangles back to Ajira and told her I'd accidentally put them with my things when we left her home all those years before and that I had only just discovered them. Ti, you remember how Sofia saved beads and shells, even that horrible frangipani necklace that Wadi won and let you keep?"

"You knew about that?"

Nupi rolled her eyes. "How could I not know? In Sofia's young mind, she was saving for her marriage."

"Papa would have given her everything!"

"Fear is like the monsoon." The old woman waved her hands

before her eyes as though a thick rain were preventing her from see-ing. "It made her wish to hurt your father even more, in ways that would make deep wounds."

"Even so, I don't believe she'd betray us."

"Ti, she *had* to be married. Don't you understand? It was no dif-ferent from you and Tejal. Youth makes the same mistakes all the time. Nothing ever changes. Do you really think she was so different from you?"

"She was with child?"

Nupi nodded shamefully.

"And you helped her . . . helped her take care of it when Papa wouldn't relent."

"Yes, we went to Ponda, and I gave her a tea made of hibiscus blossoms. It made her lose what was growing inside her but it was dangerous. That was why she got so ill." She grimaced. "I almost killed the poor child."

I remembered how Sofia had arranged for me to sleep with Tejal in her room. She was trying to get me to make the same mistake she had. Fool that I was, she'd succeeded—although, of course, the fault was all mine.

Nupi gave a deep sigh. "I am certain she did not mean to cause your father's death, but she *did* mean to make trouble. Ti, your sister believed she was listening to Hanuman, but it was Kali who whis-pered into her ear at night. When your father died, she understood that, and she could never forgive herself for listening. There was so much sorrow in that girl. A sorrow with no bottom. Then you were arrested. . . ." Nupi put her hands together as though about to pray. "It was over for her then. She tried to wait for you, Ti, but she could not. She told me to ask your forgiveness." Nupi leaned down to kiss my feet, but I wouldn't allow it and lifted her up. "Please," she said, giving way to tears, "I promised her I would beg you to forgive her, and now I must."

*   *   *

That very afternoon I left Nupi at the farm, stealing away into the paddies while she was sweeping out my father's study. I told Charu to tell her that if she spoke to my aunt or uncle, she would learn why I couldn't remain with her. "And tell her that she must not wait for me, because I'll never return," I added. "And that I forgive my sister."

I understood now how Sofia could've wanted to crawl out of her skin; I'd have done anything to exchange my life for that of the lowest Untouchable.

I made my way to Bijapur, begging rice and fruit along the way. My skin grew dark and hard, my beard and hair wild. After two weeks, an old peasant who gave me shelter from the rain said my blue eyes looked like turquoise embedded in coal. I wore only a loincloth and drank from streams beside oxen. I often kept my poison ampoule in my mouth. My only peace came while walking.

After sundown, darkness seemed to rise out of the ground and pool around me like dank water. Gonçalo and Ana would come to sit with me as I prepared for bed, full of accusatory questions for which I no longer had answers. Sometimes behind them I could hear Nupi singing quietly to herself and scraping coconut. I hoped there was a special place in hell for those who murdered young people in love. If not, what did life mean?

When I reached Bijapur, I told the Sultan that my father, before his death, had instructed me to come to him. The old monarch had me bathed and barbered, and set me to work. For sixteen years, I've remained in his service, creating prayer books and Korans for his courtiers and wives.

Each day was made of shadows the color of dry ink—of all that had come to pass and that could never be undone. When I asked after Kiran, Sofia's wet nurse, I was told that she had died of the plague two years before my arrival. I stayed in Bijapur because the Sultan was India's best hope of smashing the Portuguese hold on Goa, and I seized every opportunity to encourage him to form a united front with the other principalities. It has been my one true hope all these years, although I no longer believe anything will come of it; I've dis-covered that the Indian princes and kings—both Hindu and Moslem—regard themselves as so superior to Europeans that the presence of the Portuguese on their subcontinent upsets only their sense of perfection and vanity. They regard these upstarts merely as an unsightly growth.

It took me many years to see with any clarity the distorted shape of all I'd done, but by then my understanding seemed of no use to anyone. When not at work in my small home, I'd go for long walks in the countryside. I kept to myself, wanting to do as little damage as possible in the years remaining to me. Most people thought I'd taken a vow of silence.

A year into my service, I learned that Wadi had been executed, his head stuck on a post at the wharf. It was like being told the moon would never rise again in the evening. I fainted for the first time in my life.

Later, I found out that Father Carlos had been murdered by a cellmate at the Galé Prison in Lisbon. The news troubled me only briefly, since I knew he'd have killed many more Jains and Hindus if he could have. The Illiterate and Jácome Morais, the other two men I'd implicated in my letters, survived several years of incarceration and were living again in Goa.

After her beloved son's terrible death, Aunt Maria had fled her sorrows for Lisbon. Uncle Isaac was living with Antónia in Diu, where he had relocated most of his business interests.

The Sultan had spies in Portuguese territory who passed such in-formation on to him regularly.

I wrote to Sarah to apologize for involving her in my plans but never heard from her. I thought of my son often and always with gratitude to Tejal for keeping him away from me. I clung to that one small bit of good I'd done in my life: I had not stolen him from her. It was the only thing I could think of that gave me the right to be alive.

It turns out there was one more reason why I'd never bitten down on my ampoule of poison, but I didn't know it yet....

When I was forty-four, an old acquaintance of my Anglican minister friend Benedict Gray visited Bijapur. I'd written Gray once since fleeing Goa, to beg his forgiveness for using him, so he knew where to find me. The man, by the name of Nicholas Gonzaga Wood, was English by birth and the owner of a small theater in Madrid, where his mother was from. He was touring India, which had always been his dream. We met for a midday meal at the palace. He was short and stocky, with his mother's dark skin, and he brought back many memories of Lisbon to me because of his scent of olive oil. After dessert, Wood asked me how I'd ended up in Bijapur, and I began to tell him a brief version of my life. Slowly, he drew me out with his questions. I held nothing back of my treachery. I even mentioned the soapstone statuette of Sarasvati I'd stolen from a Hindu shop after being asked by my father to poison him; it sometimes seemed to me now that it was with that act, and at that instant, that I left the path I'd always been on—and never found my way back.

When I was done, he said that quite apart from its tragic dimension, it was a good story, but that it would need to be changed if it was ever to reach the stage.

"Art is different from life," he explained. "In this case, we'd have to cut your childhood with Wadi and his betrayals, and move the action closer to Spain."

"In any case, it's just a story—it's not for any audience," I said dismissively. "Besides, if my childhood were removed, then no one could possibly understand how everything in my life came to pass—and how my family ended in utter ruin."

"But we've only got two hours on the stage! We'd have to come up with something simpler to explain your contempt for Wadi. You weren't happy with the work he gave you, for instance. That's what you told Gonçalo. Anyway, I can assure you that understanding intricacies isn't the important thing for a gravedigger who wants his money's worth at the theater. Now, what *is* important," he added, wagging his finger at me, "is that *you'd* have to be the villain."

"That, Senhor Wood, is exactly what I've been saying."

"From the very beginning, I mean."

"But why?"

"Because you're the Jew."

*   *   *

Senhor Wood wearied me. I gave him a quick tour of the palace, then left him in the hands of an escort who'd show him around the city.

"Look, Senhor Zarco, why don't you write a memoir?" he suggested to me upon taking leave of me, sensing he'd upset me. "At least then you can tell everything the way you want to."

It seemed an absurd idea, but a few days after he departed, I got out my calamus and my ink. Working in this way produced an odd feeling of rightness in me. Later, I understood that I'd been waiting to give voice to my story since the Grand Inquisitor first told me his riddle about how a book can continue speaking to readers long after they've finished it. After all, putting my story down on paper was the only way I could speak of all that had happened from out of my grave. And it was something—maybe the only thing—I could give back to the world for all the evil I'd created.

The head of the Inquisition in Goa would never have guessed that he could help me in this way. That seemed fitting, as well.

Over the last months, sitting at my desk and writing of Sofia, Wadi, Tejal, Papa, and Phanishwar, I've been able to see beyond myself into the dungeons of Goa, Lisbon, and a hundred other cities in Asia, Europe, and America. I've seen the men and women languishing there in the name of Christ, Mohammed, and Krishna. I wish I could offer them more than this, but this is all I have.

Soon you will close the cover of this manuscript, seal me inside, and go on your way, as you should, but maybe you'll think of these prisoners—and me—from time to time. As I take out my sister's last drawing and look at it by the light of a single candle, maybe you can even feel the warm breeze coming in my window in Bijapur, trailing the scent of tamarind blossoms. Can you see me putting my hand over the outline of fingers that Sofia drew so long ago? I'll pray you can, and for many other things:

That Ana, Gonçalo, Papa, Sofia, Wadi, and all the dead may rest in peace.

That Phanishwar has had a good rebirth.

That Nupi has forgiven her godson.

That my son never learned of me and that Tejal has been happy.

Then I'll fetch my silver cross and go out to my verandah to watch the sunset. I'll try to find some of Papa's courage, but please don't think too badly of me if you see me tremble. After all, you know already I'm not a very brave man, and in any case, it's not an easy thing to end a story, even one in which I have played the villain.

Tiago Zarco
Bijapur, May 14, 1616

ABOUT THE AUTHOR

RICHARD ZIMLER was born in Roslyn Heights, New York. He currently resides in Portugal, where he is an associate professor of journalism at the University of Porto. He is the author of *Hunting Midnight, The Last Kabbalist of Lisbon, The Angelic Darkness,* and *Unholy Ghosts.* He also writes for the *San Francisco Chronicle* and *Livros* (Lisbon).